ISSUE 2 : MAY 2013

CONTENTS

THE EDITOR'S WORD by Mike Resnick	3
ALIENS ATE MY PICKUP by Mercedes Lackey	5
EFFECT AND CAUSE by Ken Liu	8
WHEN WE WENT TO SEE THE END OF THE WORLD by Robert Silverberg	10
FROM THE HEART'S BASEMENT by Barry Malzberg	14
TODAY I AM NOBODY by Tina Gower	16
HAPPILY EVER AFTER by C. L. Moore	19
THE FLAMINGO GIRL by Brad R. Torgersen	21
REX by David Gerrold	32
GHOST IN THE MACHINE by Ralph Roberts	40
ECHEA by Kristine Kathryn Rusch	48
SPARKLER by Gio Clairval	68
CHILD OF THE GODS by Bruce McAllister	70
THE FEYNMAN SALTATION by Charles Sheffield	72
BOOK REVIEWS by Paul Cook	82
THE REAL FUTURE OF SPACE by Gregory Benford	87
PHOENIX PICK PRESENTS	94
SERIALIZATION: *DARK UNIVERSE* by Daniel F. Galouye	118
CHAPTER SIX	119
CHAPTER SEVEN	124
CHAPTER EIGHT	129
CHAPTER NINE	134

Mike Resnick, Editor
Shahid Mahmud, Publisher

Published by Arc Manor/Phoenix Pick
P.O. Box 10339
Rockville, MD 20849-0339

Galaxy's Edge is published every two months: March, May, July, September, November & January

www.GalaxysEdge.com

Galaxy's Edge is an invitation-only magazine. We do not accept unsolicited manuscripts. Unsolicited manuscripts will be disposed of or mailed back to the sender (unopened) at our discretion.

All material is either copyright © by Arc Manor LLC, Rockville, MD, or copyright © by the respective authors as indicated within the magazine.

This magazine (or any portion of it) may not be copied or reproduced, in whole or in part, by any means, electronic, mechanical or otherwise, without written permission from the publisher, except by a reviewer who may quote brief passages in a review.

Each issue of *Galaxy's Edge* is issued as a stand-alone "book" with a separate ISBN and may be purchased at wholesale venues dedicated to book sales (e.g., Ingram) or directly from the publisher's website.

ISBN (Amazon Only): 9781976874284
Advertising in the magazine is available. Quarter page (half column), $95 per issue. Half page (full column, vertical or two half columns, horizontal) $165 per issue. Full page (two full columns) $295 per issue. Back Cover (full color) $495 per issue. All interior advertising is in black and white.

Please write to advert@GalaxysEdge.com.

"The most fun I ever had in my life was the two months that I sat at the typewriter working on *Adventures*. I've done books of more lasting import, and I've created characters of far more depth and complexity, but during that period I fell, hopelessly and eternally, in love with Lucifer Jones."
—*Mike Resnick,
Introduction to* Adventures

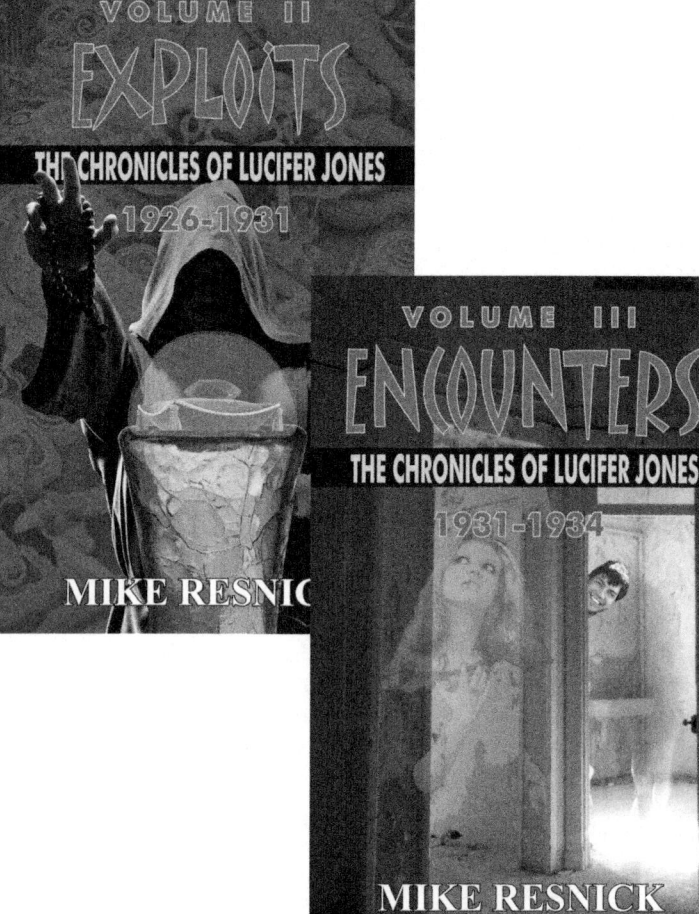

THE EDITOR'S WORD

by Mike Resnick

Welcome to the second issue of *Galaxy's Edge*. Like the first, and all future issues, this one is a mixture of new stories and reprints, reviews and columns. The reprints are stories you may have missed by very-well-known authors, and the new stories are by authors who we expect to join the ranks of the well-known somewhere up the road.

And while I'm on the subject of well-known authors…

We have quite a coup this issue. The magnificent C. L. Moore has been one of my two or three favorite authors for the past half century, and I assure you I'm not alone in this regard. She broke into print in her early twenties, and her very first story, "Shambleau," which appeared in a 1933 issue of *Weird Tales*, is an acknowledged classic.

Well, "Shambleau" was her first *professional* story, but it turns out that her very first *published* story was "Happily Ever After," which appeared in the November 1930 issue of *The Vagabond*, a student magazine published by Indiana University. It's quite short, but it shows that she had the right stuff even then. And with this issue, *Galaxy's Edge* is thrilled to be able to present—for the first time in 83 years—C. L. Moore's very first story. Thanks to Catherine for writing it, and to Andrew Liptak for unearthing it.

And why (I hear you ask) was she "C. L." rather than "Catherine"? The general assumption is that she was hiding her gender in what was an almost all-male field. Logical, but wrong. She was hiding her *name* from her employer, a bank president who viewed the pulps with total loathing.

An interesting historical tidbit?

Yes, it is—and it's just one of many.

So many people are so interested in the giants of our field—many, alas, no longer with us—that I thought I'd share some memories of them with you before they're all forgotten by me and others.

✧

The late Robert Sheckley was my good friend, and even my collaborator the year before his death.

Bob occasionally suffered from Writer's Block, but he had an infallible way of beating it. He set himself an absolute minimum production of 5,000 words a day. If he couldn't think of anything else, he told me, he'd write his name 2,500 times. And on those days he *was* blocked, he'd sit down and force himself to start typing. And to quote him: "By the time I'd typed 'Robert Sheckley' 800 or 900 times, a little subconscious editor would kick in and say 'Fuck it, as long as you're stuck here for another 3,300 words, you might as well write a story.'"

According to Bob, it never failed.

✧

E. E. "Doc" Smith was the first pro I ever met at a con, back in 1963. Sweet man, very fond of fandom, very accessible to anyone. I always thought his greatest invention (other than the Lens and the Lensmen) was the seasonal Ploorians. Doc's daughter, Verna Trestrail, became a good friend, and I used to see her every year at Midwestcon and Rivercon. She once remarked that she helped her dad from time to time. So I asked how, and she replied that, among other things, she had invented the Ploorians.

(Verna also created the planet where Clarissa had to function in the nude. She told me that Doc bought a gorgeous painting of it—and Mrs. Doc took one look at it and consigned it to the attic for the next 25 years.)

✧

I met Robert A. Heinlein only a couple of times, at the 1976 and 1977 Worldcons, so I have no personal anecdotes to tell you about him—but Theodore Sturgeon had one. There was a point in the mid-1940s where Sturgeon was played out. He couldn't come up with any saleable stories, his creditors were after him, and he was terminally depressed…and he mentioned it to Heinlein in a letter. A week later he got a letter from Heinlein with 26 story ideas and a $100 bill to tide him over until he started selling again. And, according to Sturgeon, before the decade was over he had written and sold all 26 stories.

✧

I never met Fredric Brown. I know he grew up in Cincinnati, where I have lived the past 37 years, but no one here remembers meeting him. And I know he spent a lot of time working in Chicago, where I spent my first 33 years, and I never met anyone there who knew him either. But I do know he had a habit, especially when writing his mysteries (which far outnumbered his science fiction) of getting on a Greyhound bus and riding it for hundreds, sometimes thousands, of miles, until he had his plot worked out to the last detail. Then he'd come home, sit down, and quickly type the book he'd already written in his head while touring the countryside.

✧

Phil Klass (who wrote as "William Tenn") told this one on a panel I moderated at Noreascon IV, the 2004 Worldcon where he was the Guest of Honor.

He was dating a new girl, and he mentioned it to Ted Sturgeon when they were both living in New York. Sturgeon urged Phil to bring the girl to his apartment for dinner. He and his wife would lay out an impressive spread, and Ted would regale the girl with tales of how talented and important Phil was. Phil happily agreed.

What he didn't know was that Ted and his then-wife were nudists. So Phil and the girl walk up to the door of Ted's apartment, Phil knocks, the door opens, and there are Ted and his wife, totally naked. They greet them and start leading them to the dining room.

Phil's girl turns to him and whispers: "You didn't tell me we had to dress for dinner!"

✧

Speaking of dinners…

At our first Worldcon, Discon I in 1963—I was 21, my still-beautiful child-bride Carol was 20—Randall Garrett invited a bunch of new writers and their spouses out for dinner—his treat. Then, during dessert, he excused himself to say something of vital importance to his agent, who was walking past the restaurant. He left the table—and we never saw him again. The rest of us got stuck with the tab (it was an expensive restaurant, we were broke kids, and Randy himself had the most expensive dish and wine on the menu).

Move the clock ahead three years. Randy spots Carol and me at Tricon (the 1966 Worldcon in Cleveland) and offers to buy us dinner. We say sure. During dessert Carol excuses herself to go powder her nose, and I remember a phone call I have to make. We meet and walk out, leaving Randy with the tab he had promised to pay (but, according to Bob Bloch, Bob Tucker, and others I'd spoken to before going out with him, had no intention of paying).

Move the clock ahead one more year, and we're at NYcon III, the 1967 Worldcon in New York. On opening night Randy spots me across the room, turns red in the face, and yells: "Resnick, I'm never eating dinner with you again!"

I got an ovation from every pro and fan he'd ever stuck with a dinner check.

✧

And let me end with one about a living giant, just to be different—my friend, Nebula Grand Master, Worldcon Guest of Honor, and contributor to this issue, Robert Silverberg.

When Bob started submitting to *Astounding*, John Campbell turned down his first few stories, and Bob's sometime collaborator Randy Garrett (they wrote as "Robert Randall") suggested that Campbell disliked Jewish names, so Bob submitted one under the name of "Calvin M. Knox," and Campbell bought it.

Over the years he sold to Campbell as both "Knox" and Silverberg. Some years later John Campbell asked him why he'd used the Knox name. Bob gave him an honest answer. Campbell's reply: "Did you ever hear of Isaac Asimov?"

Then, as the conversation was drawing to a close and Bob was about to leave, Campbell asked him why of all the pseudonyms in the world he chose Calvin M. Knox. Bob replied that it was the most Protestant-sounding name he could think of.

Finally, as he's going out the door, Campbell asks him what the "M" stands for.

Bob's answer: "Moses."

✧

How can you not love this field?

Mercedes Lackey, author of the wildly popular Valdemar universe, has written a seemingly endless series of bestsellers, and has also collaborated with Andre Norton, Anne McCaffrey, and Marion Zimmer Bradley.

I don't do humor very often. Funny scenes in books sometimes, but comedy is hard… But about the time I was asked to write a humorous story I heard a filk song called "Stray Dog Man" by Bill Sutton, and that gave me the idea. Now both of us start with the notion that an alien pet gets dumped (in my case, lost) and taken in by a very folksy type. And the "pooch" will eat about anything. But that is where our two stories part company; living as I do in rural Oklahoma I have powerful respect for the shrewdness of my neighbors. They like to fool outsiders, but—

Well, see for yourself.

ALIENS ATE MY PICKUP

by Mercedes Lackey

Yes'm, I'm serious. Aliens ate my pickup. Only it weren't really aliens, jest one, even though it was my Chevy four-ton, and he was a little bitty feller, not like some Japanese giant thing…an' he didn't really eat it, he just kinda chewed it up a little, look, you can see the teeth-marks on the bumper here an'…

Oh, start at the beginnin'? Well, all right, I guess.

My name? It's Jed, Jed Pryor. I was born an' raised on this farm outsid'a Claremore, been here all my life. Well, 'cept for when I went t'OU.

What? Well, heck fire, sure I graduated!

What? Well, what makes you thank Okies tawk funny?

Degree? You bet I gotta degree! I gotta Batchler in Land Management right there on the wall of m'livingroom and—

Oh, the alien. Yeah, well, it was dark of the moon, middle of this June, when I was out doin' some night-fishin' on m'pond. Stocked it about five years ago with black an' stripy bass, just let 'em be, started fishin' it this year. I'm tellin' you, I got a five pounder on m'third cast this spring an'—

Right, the alien. Well, I was out there drownin' a coupla lures about midnight, makin' the fish laugh, when *wham!* all of a sudden the sky lights up like Riverparks on Fourth of July. I mean t'tell you, I haven't seen nothin' like that in all my born days! I 'bout thought them scifi writers lives over on the next farm had gone an' bought out one'a them fireworks factories in Tennessee again, like they did just before New Years. Boy howdy, that was a night! I swan, it looked like the sky over ol' Baghdad, let me tell you! Good thing they warned us they was gonna set off some doozies, or—

Right, the night'a them aliens. Well, anyway, the sky lit up, but it was all over in less'n a minute, so I figgered it couldn't be them writers. Now, we get us some weird stuff ev'ry now an' again, y'know, what with MacDac—that's MacDonald-Douglas t'you—bein' right over the county line an' all, well I just figgered they was testin' somethin' that I wasn't supposed t'know about an' I went back t'drownin' worms.

What? Why didn' I thank it was a UFO? Ma'am, what makes you thank Okies got hayseeds in their haids? I got a satylite dish on m'front lawn, I watch NASA channel an' PBS an' science shows all the time, an' I got me a subscription t'Skeptical Inquirer, an' I ain't never seen nothin' t'make me thank there was such a thang as UFOs. Nope, I purely don't believe in 'em. Or I didn't, anyway.

So, like I was sayin' I went back t'murderin' worms an' makin' the bass laugh, an' finally got tired'a bein' the main course fer the skeeters an' chiggers an' headed back home. I fell inta bed an' didn' thank nothin' about it till I walked out next mornin'.

An' dang if there ain't a big ol' mess in the middle'a my best hayfield! What? Oh heckfire, ma'am, it was one'a them crop circle things, like on the cover'a that Led Zeppelin record. Purely ruint m'hay. You cain't let hay get flattened down like that, spoils it right quick 'round here if they's been any dew, an' it was plenty damp that mornin'.

How'd I feel? Ma'am, I was hot. I figgered it was them scifi writers, foolin' with me; them city folk, they dunno you cain't do that t'hay. But they didn' have no cause t'fool with me like that, we bin pretty good neighbors so far, I even bought their books an' liked 'em pretty much too, 'cept for the stuff 'bout the horses. Ev'body knows a white horse's deaf as a post, like as not, less'n' it's one'a them Lippyzaners. Ain't no horse gonna go read yer mind, or go ridin' through fire an' all like that an'—

Oh, yeah. Well, I got on th' phone, gonna give 'em what for, an' turns out they're gone! One'a them scifi conventions. So it cain't be them.

Well, shoot, now I dunno what t'thank. That's when I heerd it, under th' porch. Somethin' whimperin', like.

Now y'know what happens when you live out in the country. People dump their dang-blasted strays all th' time, thankin' some farmer'll take care of 'em. Then like as not they hook up with one'a the dog packs an' go wild an' start runnin' stock. Well, I guess I gotta soft heart t'match my soft haid, I take 'em in, most times. Get 'em fixed, let 'em run th' rabbits outa my garden. Coyotes get 'em sooner or later, but I figger while they're with me, they at least got t'eat and gotta place t'sleep. So I figgered it was 'nother dang stray, an' I better get 'im out from under th' porch 'fore he messes under there an' it starts t'smell.

So I got down on m'hands an' knees like a pure durn fool, an' I whistled an' coaxed, an' carried on like some kinda dim bulb, an' finally that stray come out. But ma'am, what come outa that porch weren't no dog.

It was about the ugliest thing on six legs I ever seen in my life. Ma'am, that critter looked like somebody done beat out a fire on its face with a ugly stick. Looked like five miles 'a bad road. Like the reason first cousins hadn't ought t'get married. Two liddle, squinchy eyes that wuz all pupil, nose like a burnt pancake, jaws like a bear-trap. Hide all mangy and patchy, part scales and part fur, an' all of it putrid green. No ears that I could see. Six legs, like I said, an' three tails, two of 'em whippy and ratty, an' one sorta like a club. It drooled, an' its nose ran. I'd a been afraid of it, 'cept it crawled outa there with its three tails 'tween its legs, whimperin' an' wheezin' an' lookin' up at me like it was 'fraid I was gonna beat it. I figgered, hell, poor critter's scarder of me than I am of it—an' if it looks ugly t'me, reckon I must look just's ugly right back.

So I petted it, an' it rolled over on its back an' stuck all six legs in th' air, an' just acted about like any other pup. I went off t'the barn an' got Thang—I ended up callin' it Thang fer's long as I had it—I got Thang a big ol' bowl'a dog food, didn' know what else t'give it. Well, he looked pretty pleased, an' he ate it right up—but then he sicked it right back up too. I shoulda figgered, I guess, he bein' from someplace else an' all, but it was worth a try.

But 'fore I could try somethin' else, he started off fer m'bushes. I figgered he was gonna use 'em fer the usual—

But heckfire if he didn't munch down m'junipers, an' then sick them up! Boy howdy, was that a mess! Look, you can see the place right there—

Yes'm, I know. I got th' stuff tested later, after it was all over. Chemist said th' closest thang he'd ever seen to't was somethin' he called Aquia Reqa or somethin' like—kind've a mix a' all kinda acids together, real nasty stuff, etches glass an' everthang.

Anyhow, I reckon gettin' fed an' then sickin' it all back up agin jest made the poor critter 'bout half crazy bein' hungry. But next I know, Thang's took off like a shot, a headin' fer one'a my chickens!

Well, he caught it, an he ate it down, beak an' feathers, an' he sicked it right back up agin' 'fore I could stop 'im.

That made me hot all over agin'. Some dang idjut makes a mess'a my hayfield, then this Thang makes messes all over m'yard, an' then it eats one'a my chickens. Now I'm a soft man, but there's one thing I don't stand for, an' that's critters messin' with the stock. I won't have no dog that runs cows, sucks eggs, or kills chickens. So I just grabbed me the first thang that I could and I went after that Thang t'lay inta him good. Happens it was a shovel, an' I whanged him a good one right upside th' haid 'fore he'd even finished bein' sick. Well, it seemed t'hurt him 'bout as much as a rolled-up paper'll hurt a pup, so I kept whangin' him an' he kept cowerin' an' whimperin' an' then he grabbed the shovel, the metal end.

An' he ate it.

He didn't sick that up, neither.

Well, we looked at each other, an' he kinda wagged his tails, an' I kinda forgave 'im, an' we went lookin' fer some more stuff he could eat.

I tell you, I was a pretty happy man 'fore the day was over. I reckoned I had me th' answer to one of m'bills. See, I c'n compost 'bout ev'thang organic, an' I can turn them aluminum cans in, but the rest of th' trash I gotta pay for pickup, an' on a farm, they's a lot of it what they call hazardous, an' that's extra. What? Oh, you know, barrels what had chemicals in 'em, bug-killer, weed-killer, fertilizer. That an' there's just junk that kinda accumulates. An' people are always dumpin' their dang old cars out here, like they dump their dang dogs. Lotsa trash that I cain't get rid of an' gotta pay someone t'haul.

But ol' Thang, he just ate it right up. Plastic an' metal, yes'm, that was what he et. Didn' matter how nasty, neither. Fed 'im them chemical barrels, fed 'im ol' spray-paint cans, fed 'im th' cans from chargin' the air-conditioner, he just kept waggin' his tails an' lookin' fer more. That's how he come t'chew on my Chevy; I was lookin' fer somethin' else t'feed him, an' he started chawin' on the bumpers. Look, see them teethmarks? Yes'm, he had him one good set of choppers all right. Naw, I never took thought t'be afraid of him, he was just a big puppy.

Well, like I said, by sundown I was one happy man. I figgered I not only had my trash problem licked, I could purt-near take care of the whole dang county. You know how much them fellers get t'take care'a hazardous waste? Heckfire, all I had t'do was feed it t'ol' Thang, an' what came out t'other end looked pretty much like ash. I had me a goldmine, that's how I figgered.

Yeah, I tied ol' Thang up with what was left of a couch t'chew on an' a happy grin on his ugly face, an' I went t'sleep with m'accountin' program dancin' magic numbers an m'haid.

An' I woke up with a big, bright light in m'eyes, an' not able t'move. I kinda passed out, an' when I came to, Thang was gone, an' all that was left was the leash an' collar. All I can figger is that whoever messed up m'hayfield was havin' a picnic or somethin' an' left their doggie by accident. But I reckon they figger I took pretty good care of 'im, since I 'spect he weighed 'bout forty, fifty pounds more when they got 'im back.

But I s'pose it ain't all bad. I gotta friend got a plane, an' he's been chargin' a hunnert bucks t'take people over th' field, an' splittin' it with me after he pays fer the gas. And folks that comes by here, well, I tell 'em, the story, they get kinda excited an....

What ma'am? Pictures? Samples? Well sure. It'll cost you fifty bucks fer a sample'a where Thang got sick, an' seventy-five fer a picture of the bumper of my Chevy.

Why ma'am, what made you thank Okies was dumb?

Copyright © 1998 by Mercedes Lackey

ON SALE NOW

Paper, ePub, MOBI
www.PhoenixPick.com
www.Amazon.com
www.BN.com

COMING SOON
(by popular demand)
REBOOTS II

Ken Liu, a relative newcomer to the field, was nominated for two Hugos in 2012 (and won one); for two Nebulas (and won one); and he also won a 2012 World Fantasy Award. As this issue goes to press, he has been nominated for three 2013 Nebulas and a 2013 Hugo. Ken also does translations from the Chinese, and is working on his first novel.

EFFECT AND CAUSE

by Ken Liu

.ssengnihton, neht dnA

✧

Flash white blinding a.

✧

"Brace for impact," says the computer.

The superheated air cools. Out of the white light, things emerge: the instrument panels; myself in the chair, clutching the handholds; the jagged edges of the cockpit wall knit themselves into a pristine whole.

"T minus one. Shields breached."

Through the porthole, I see a silvery fishlike shape depart. Already, it's kilometers away.

"T minus ten."

The silver light winks out at the edge of visibility like a dying star.

✧

Dashing about the cockpit, I frantically punch lit up buttons to make them go dim. The anxiety subsides.

I run backwards out of the cockpit until I end up in the galley.

The klaxon goes off.

"Incoming: theta six-one, phi one-four-eight, distance six-five-five, velocity one-oh-seven."

Ignoring this, I sit down at the table and pick up a cup to spit scalding hot coffee into it. Then I proceed to vomit food onto my plate so I can sculpt it with a knife and fork into peas, carrots, an omelette.

✧

A shiver, and my thoughts flow forward again.

"What…happened?" I ask.

"Unknown." The computer pauses. "System clock is out of sync with sidereal observations."

"It's like someone just took his finger off the RE-WIND button." I set down the cup of coffee that had just come out of me, nauseated. "We were dead."

"Affirmative." The computer hesitates. "And impossible."

"An Azazin ship," I say.

✧

We know almost nothing about the Azazin save that they've made repeated incursions into this region of Union space. My one-man sentry ship is our first line of defense.

"They seem to believe in preemptive attacks," I say.

"Hypothesis: we hit a temporal anomaly that briefly reversed the flow of time," the computer says.

"I'm going to return fire."

"But if time has been reversed, our attack now would be unprovoked."

I shrug. "The military lawyers can sort out causality later."

From the trajectory of the projectile that hit me, it's easy to calculate the location of the stealth Azazin ship.

"Subphotonic missile ready."

The *click* from the big red button is satisfying.

I press up against the porthole. Watching flickering numbers on a screen is never as good as the actual explosion.

"T minus ten."

The passing seconds seem to slow down.

"T minus zero."

But there is no dazzling flare, no new star in the sky.

".orez sunim T"

The arrow of time.

…The missile reverses its course, now flying backwards, retracing its arc back to the launch tube…

…I rush around the cockpit, frantically pushing buttons…

✧

The galley. Spitting coffee. Someone takes his finger off the REWIND button.

We've been through it dozens of times. Sometimes I shoot at them; sometimes they shoot at me. But always, we end up back here, fifteen minutes earlier.

"They can temporarily reverse the local flow of time in a bubble for up to fifteen minutes," the computer says. "Perhaps it's even triggered automatically when their ship is destroyed."

"I think the time-reverser is designed to allow those in its field, including the Azazin, to keep their thoughts and experiences," I say, finally understanding. "They're repeating the experiment to gather intel on our tactical responses, like running rats through a maze."

Ignoring the computer's vociferous objections, I engage the manual override targeting system.

I press the big red button; the *click* is satisfying.

The faint trail of the missile approaches the spot in space where I know the Azazin ship is hiding.

"T minus ten."

So close—

My heart is in my throat.

—nothing.

"A miss. Closest approach to target: fifty meters." There's a faint trace of *I-told-you-so* in the computer's voice.

Time continues to flow forward. The Azazin were able to tell that I was going to miss, and they didn't bother to reverse time for my useless attack.

No choice now. "Set a collision course. Full speed ahead."

"They will simply rever—"

"DO IT!"

We dive towards the invisible target, the oldest, most desperate tactic known to man. But, perhaps, they cannot believe that I will actually go through with it.

✧

.ssengnihton, neht dnA

✧

Flash white blinding a.

✧

The ship zooms backwards, in front of me a dark, looming bulk that quickly fades against the stars.

And then the finger is off the REWIND button. It's fifteen minutes earlier.

"A miss—"

Before the computer can finish, I punch a small black button: my jury-rigged secret. It sends a signal that shuts off the antimatter containment field in the subphotonic missile's warhead.

A dazzling flare, and then the most beautiful sight in the universe: the spinning, glowing vortex of a matter-antimatter annihilation explosion.

"Well done," says the computer.

I gambled that the Azazin time reverser could not be triggered twice in quick succession. The missile was meant to come close, but miss. My suicide collision course was calculated to take exactly fifteen minutes. When the Azazin reversed time's arrow, they brought the missile back to its point of closest approach. Effect became cause.

"Thinking backwards hurts," I say, as we continue to watch the spinning vortex.

Original (First) Publication
Copyright © 2013 by Ken Liu

Robert Silverberg is one of the true giants of science fiction. He is a multiple Hugo and Nebula winner, a Nebula Grand Master, and a Worldcon Guest of Honor, the author of numerous acknowledged classics in the field. This story was both a Hugo and a Nebula nominee in 1973.

WHEN WE WENT TO SEE THE END OF THE WORLD

by Robert Silverberg

Nick and Jane were glad that they had gone to see the end of the world, because it gave them something special to talk about at Mike and Ruby's party. One always likes to come to a party armed with a little conversation. Mike and Ruby give marvelous parties.

Their home is superb, one of the finest in the neighborhood. It is truly a home for all seasons, all moods. Their very special corner of the world. With more space indoors and out…more wide-open freedom. The living room with its exposed ceiling beams is a natural focal point for entertaining. Custom-finished, with a conversation pit and fireplace. There's also a family room with beamed ceiling and wood paneling…plus a study. And a magnificent master suite with twelve-foot dressing room and private bath. Solidly impressive exterior design. Sheltered courtyard. Beautifully wooded ⅓-acre grounds. Their parties are highlights of any month. Nick and Jane waited until they thought enough people had arrived. Then Jane nudged Nick and Nick said gaily, "You know what we did last week? Hey, we went to see the end of the world!"

"The end of the world?" Henry asked.

"You went to see it?" said Henry's wife Cynthia.

"How did you manage that?" Paula wanted to know.

"It's been available since March," Stan told her. "I think a division of American Express runs it."

Nick was put out to discover that Stan already knew. Quickly, before Stan could say anything more, Nick said, "Yes, it's just started. Our travel agent found out for us. What they do is they put you in this machine, it looks like a tiny teeny submarine, you know, with dials and levers up front behind a plastic wall to keep you from touching anything, and they send you into the future. You can charge it with any of the regular credit cards."

"It must be very expensive," Marcia said.

"They're bringing the costs down rapidly," Jane said. "Last year only millionaires could afford it. Really, haven't you heard about it before?"

"What did you see?" Henry asked.

"For a while, just greyness outside the porthole," said Nick. "And a kind of flickering effect." Everybody was looking at him. He enjoyed the attention. Jane wore a rapt, loving expression. "Then the haze cleared and a voice said over a loudspeaker that we had now reached the very end of time, when life had become impossible on Earth. Of course, we were sealed into the submarine thing. Only looking out. On this beach, this empty beach. The water a funny grey color with a pink sheen. And then the sun came up. It was red like it sometimes is at sunrise, only it stayed red as it got to the middle of the sky, and it looked lumpy and saggy at the edges. Like a few of us, hah hah. Lumpy and sagging at the edges. A cold wind blowing across the beach."

"If you were sealed in the submarine, how did you know there was a cold wind?" Cynthia asked.

Jane glared at her. Nick said, "We could see the sand blowing around. And it looked cold. The grey ocean. Like winter."

"Tell them about the crab," said Jane.

"Yes, the crab. The last life-form on Earth. It wasn't really a crab, of course, it was something about two feet wide and a foot high, with thick shiny green armor and maybe a dozen legs and some curving horns coming up, and it moved slowly from right to left in front of us. It took all day to cross the beach. And toward nightfall it died. Its horns went limp and it stopped moving. The tide came in and carried it away. The sun went down. There wasn't any moon. The stars didn't seem to be in the right places. The loudspeaker told us we had just seen the death of Earth's last living thing."

"How eerie!" cried Paula.

"Were you gone very long?" Ruby asked.

"Three hours," Jane said. "You can spend weeks or days at the end of the world, if you want to pay extra, but they always bring you back to a point three hours after you went. To hold down the babysitter expenses."

Mike offered Nick some pot. "That's really something," he said. "To have gone to the end of the world. Hey, Ruby, maybe we'll talk to the travel agent about it."

Nick took a deep drag and passed the joint to Jane. He felt pleased with himself about the way he had told the story. They had all been very impressed. That swollen red sun, that scuttling crab. The trip had cost more than a month in Japan, but it had been a good investment. He and Jane were the first in the neighborhood who had gone. That was important. Paula was staring at him in awe. Nick knew that she regarded him in a completely different light now. Possibly she would meet him at a motel on Tuesday at lunchtime. Last month she had turned him down but now he had an extra attractiveness for her. Nick winked at her. Cynthia was holding hands with Stan. Henry and Mike both were crouched at Jane's feet. Mike and Ruby's twelve-year-old son came into the room and stood at the edge of the conversation pit. He said, "There just was a bulletin on the news. Mutated amoebas escaped from a government research station and got into Lake Michigan. They're carrying a tissue-dissolving virus and everybody in seven states is supposed to boil their water until further notice." Mike scowled at the boy and said, "It's after your bedtime, Timmy." The boy went out. The doorbell rang. Ruby answered it and returned with Eddie and Fran.

Paula said, "Nick and Jane went to see the end of the world. They've just been telling us about it."

"Gee," said Eddie, "We did that too, on Wednesday night."

Nick was crestfallen. Jane bit her lip and asked Cynthia quietly why Fran always wore such flashy dresses. Ruby said, "You saw the whole works, eh? The crab and everything?"

"The crab?" Eddie said. "What crab? We didn't see the crab."

"It must have died the time before," Paula said. "When Nick and Jane were there."

Mike said, "A fresh shipment of Cuernavaca Lightning is in. Here, have a toke."

"How long ago did you do it?" Eddie said to Nick. "Sunday afternoon. I guess we were about the first."

"Great trip, isn't it?" Eddie said. "A little somber, though. When the last hill crumbles into the sea."

"That's not what we saw," said Jane. "And you didn't see the crab? Maybe we were on different trips."

Mike said, "What was it like for you, Eddie?"

Eddie put his arms around Cynthia from behind. He said, "They put us into this little capsule, with a porthole, you know, and a lot of instruments and—"

"We heard that part," said Paula. "What did you see?"

"The end of the world," Eddie said. "When water covers everything. The sun and the moon were in the sky at the same time—"

"We didn't see the moon at all," Jane remarked. "It just wasn't there."

"It was on one side and the sun was on the other," Eddie went on. "The moon was closer than it should have been. And a funny color, almost like bronze. And the ocean creeping up. We went halfway around the world and all we saw was ocean. Except in one place, there was this chunk of land sticking up, this hill, and the guide told us it was the top of Mount Everest." He waved to Fran. "That was groovy, huh, floating in our tin boat next to the top of Mount Everest. Maybe ten feet of it sticking up. And the water rising all the time. Up, up, up. Up and over the top. Glub. No land left. I have to admit it was a little disappointing, except of course the idea of the thing. That human ingenuity can design a machine that can send people billions of years forward in time and bring them back, wow! But there was just this ocean."

"How strange," said Jane. "We saw the ocean too, but there was a beach, a kind of nasty beach, and the crab-thing walking along it, and the sun—it was all red, was the sun red when you saw it?"

"A kind of pale green," Fran said.

"Are you people talking about the end of the world?" Tom asked. He and Harriet were standing by the door taking off their coats. Mike's son must have let them in. Tom gave his coat to Ruby and said, "Man, what a spectacle!"

"So you did it, too?" Jane asked, a little hollowly.

"Two weeks ago," said Tom. "The travel agent called and said, Guess what we're offering now, the end of the goddamned world! With all the extras it didn't really cost so much. So we went right down there to the office, Saturday, I think—was it a Friday?—the day of the big riot, anyway, when they burned St Louis—"

"That was a Saturday," Cynthia said. "I remember I was coming back from the shopping center when the radio said they were using nuclears—"

"Saturday, yes," Tom said. "And we told them we were ready to go, and off they sent us."

"Did you see a beach with crabs," Stan demanded, "or was it a world full of water?"

"Neither one. It was like a big ice age. Glaciers covered everything. No oceans showing, no mountains. We flew clear around the world and it was all a huge snowball. They had floodlights on the vehicle because the sun had gone out."

"I was sure I could see the sun still hanging up there," Harriet put in. "Like a ball of cinders in the sky. But the guide said no, nobody could see it."

"How come everybody gets to visit a different kind of end of the world?" Henry asked. "You'd think there'd be only one kind of end of the world. I mean, it ends, and this is how it ends, and there can't be more than one way."

"Could it be fake?" Stan asked. Everybody turned around and looked at him. Nick's face got very red. Fran looked so mean that Eddie let go of Cynthia and started to rub Fran's shoulders. Stan shrugged. "I'm not suggesting it is," he said defensively. "I was just wondering."

"Seemed pretty real to me," said Tom. "The sun burned out. A big ball of ice. The atmosphere, you know, frozen. The end of the goddamned world."

The telephone rang. Ruby went to answer it. Nick asked Paula about lunch on Tuesday. She said yes. "Let's meet at the motel," he said, and she grinned. Eddie was making out with Cynthia again. Henry looked very stoned and was having trouble staying awake. Phil and Isabel arrived. They heard Tom and Fran talking about their trips to the end of the world and Isabel said she and Phil had gone only the day before yesterday. "Goddamn," Tom said, "everybody's doing it! What was your trip like?"

Ruby came back into the room. "That was my sister calling from Fresno to say she's safe. Fresno wasn't hit by the earthquake at all."

"Earthquake?" Paula asked.

"In California," Mike told her. "This afternoon. You didn't know? Wiped out most of Los Angeles and ran right up the coast practically to Monterey. They think it was on account of the underground bomb test in the Mohave Desert."

"California's always having such awful disasters," Marcia said.

"Good thing those amoebas got loose back east," said Nick. "Imagine how complicated it would be if they had them in LA now too."

"They will," Tom said. "Two to one they reproduce by airborne spores."

"Like the typhoid germs last November," Jane said.

"That was typhus," Nick corrected.

"Anyway," Phil said, "I was telling Tom and Fran about what we saw at the end of the world. It was the sun going nova. They showed it very cleverly, too. I mean, you can't actually sit around and experience it, on account of the heat and the hard radiation and all. But they give it to you in a peripheral way, very elegant in the McLuhanesque sense of the word. First they take you to a point about two hours before the blowup, right? It's I don't know how many jillion years from now, but a long way, anyhow, because the trees are all different, they've got blue scales and ropy branches, and the animals are like things with one leg that jump on pogo sticks—"

"Oh, I don't believe that," Cynthia drawled.

Phil ignored her gracefully. "And we didn't see any sign of human beings, not a house, not a telephone pole, nothing, so I suppose we must have been extinct a long time before. Anyway, they let us look at that for a while. Not getting out of our time machine, naturally, because they said the atmosphere was wrong. Gradually the sun started to puff up. We were nervous—weren't we, Iz?—I mean, suppose they miscalculated things? This whole trip is a very new concept and things might go wrong. The sun was getting bigger and bigger, and then this thing like an arm seemed to pop out of its left side, a big fiery arm reaching out across space, getting closer and closer. We saw it through smoked glass, like you do an eclipse. They gave us about two minutes of the explosion, and we could feel it getting hot already. Then we jumped a couple of years forward in time. The sun was back to its regular shape, only it was smaller, sort of like a little white sun instead of a big yellow one. And on Earth everything was ashes."

"Ashes," Isabel said, with emphasis.

"It looked like Detroit after the union nuked Ford," Phil said. "Only much, much worse. Whole mountains were melted. The oceans were dried up. Everything was ashes." He shuddered and took a joint from Mike. "Isabel was crying."

"The things with one leg," Isabel said. "I mean, they must have all been wiped out." She began to sob. Stan comforted her. "I wonder why it's a different way for everyone who goes," he said. "Freezing. Or the oceans. Or the sun blowing up. Or the thing Nick and Jane saw."

"I'm convinced that each of us had a genuine experience in the far future," said Nick. He felt he had to regain control of the group somehow. It had been so good when he was telling his story, before those others had come. "That is to say, the world suffers a variety of natural calamities, it doesn't just have one end of the world, and they keep mixing things up and sending people to different catastrophes. But never for a moment did I doubt that I was seeing an authentic event."

"We have to do it," Ruby said to Mike. "It's only three hours. What about calling them first thing Monday and making an appointment for Thursday night?"

"Monday's the President's funeral," Tom pointed out. "The travel agency will be closed."

"Have they caught the assassin yet?" Fran asked.

"They didn't mention it on the four o'clock news," said Stan. "I guess he'll get away like the last one."

"Beats me why anybody wants to be President," Phil said.

Mike put on some music. Nick danced with Paula. Eddie danced with Cynthia. Henry was asleep. Dave, Paula's husband, was on crutches because of his mugging, and he asked Isabel to sit and talk with him. Tom danced with Harriet even though he was married to her. She hadn't been out of the hospital more than a few months since the transplant and he treated her extremely tenderly. Mike danced with Fran. Phil danced with Jane. Stan danced with Marcia. Ruby cut in on Eddie and Cynthia. Afterward Tom danced with Jane and Phil danced with Paula. Mike and Ruby's little girl woke up and came out to say hello. Mike sent her back to bed. Far away there was the sound of an explosion. Nick danced with Paula again, but he didn't want her to get bored with him before Tuesday, so he excused himself and went to talk with Dave. Dave handled most of Nick's investments. Ruby said to Mike, "The day after the funeral, will you call the travel agent?" Mike said he would, but Tom said somebody would probably shoot the new President too and there'd be another funeral. These funerals were demolishing the gross national product, Stan observed, on account of how everything had to close all the time. Nick saw Cynthia wake Henry up and ask him sharply if he would take her on the end-of-the-world trip. Henry looked embarrassed. His factory had been blown up at Christmas in a peace demonstration and everybody knew he was in bad shape financially. "You can charge it," Cynthia said, her fierce voice carrying above the chitchat. "And it's so beautiful, Henry. The ice. Or the sun exploding. I want to go."

"Lou and Janet were going to be here tonight, too," Ruby said to Paula. "But their younger boy came back from Texas with that new kind of cholera and they had to cancel."

Phil said, "I understand that one couple saw the moon come apart. It got too close to the Earth and split into chunks and the chunks fell like meteors. Smashing everything up, you know. One big piece nearly hit their time machine."

"I wouldn't have liked that at all," Marcia said.

"Our trip was very lovely," said Jane. "No violent things at all. Just the big red sun and the tide and that crab creeping along the beach. We were both deeply moved."

"It's amazing what science can accomplish nowadays," Fran said.

Mike and Ruby agreed they would try to arrange a trip to the end of the world as soon as the funeral was over. Cynthia drank too much and got sick. Phil, Tom, and Dave discussed the stock market. Harriet told Nick about her operation. Isabel flirted with Mike, tugging her neckline lower. At midnight someone turned on the news. They had some shots of the earthquake and a warning about boiling your water if you lived in the affected states. The President's widow was shown visiting the last President's widow to get some pointers for the funeral. Then there was an interview with an executive of the time-trip company. "Business is phenomenal," he said. "Time-tripping will be the nation's number one growth industry next year." The reporter asked him if his company would soon be offering something besides the end-of-the-world trip. "Later on, we hope to," the executive said. "We plan to apply for Congressional approval soon. But meanwhile the demand for our present offering is running very high. You can't imagine. Of course, you have to expect apocalyptic stuff to attain immense popularity in times like these." The reporter said, "What do you mean, times like these?" but as the time-trip man started to reply, he was interrupted by the commercial. Mike shut off the set. Nick discovered that he was extremely depressed. He decided that it was because so many of his friends had made the journey, and he had thought he and Jane were the only ones who had. He found himself standing next to Marcia and tried to describe the way the crab had moved, but Marcia only shrugged. No one was talking about time-trips now. The party had moved beyond that point. Nick and Jane left quite early and went right to sleep, without making love. The next morning the Sunday paper wasn't delivered because of the Bridge Authority strike, and the radio said that the mutant amoebas were proving harder to eradicate than originally anticipated. They were spreading into Lake Superior and everyone in the region would have to boil all their drinking water. Nick and Jane discussed where they would go for their next vacation. "What about going to see the end of the world all over again?" Jane suggested, and Nick laughed quite a good deal.

Copyright © 1972 by Agberg, Inc.

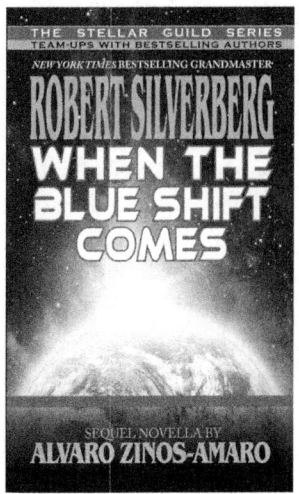

Views expressed by guest or resident columnists are entirely their own.

FROM THE HEART'S BASEMENT

by Barry Malzberg

Barry N. Malzberg won the very first Campbell Memorial Award, and is a multiple Hugo and Nebula nominee. He is the author or co-author of more than 90 books.

The Sine Curve

I gave a brief eulogy at Robert Sheckley's funeral (12/12/05); and concluded, after a quick precis of that anguished, thoughtful, scattered, thoughtless life and its wreckage: "But this can be said: he was the best-loved writer of the best-loved magazine through the run of science fiction's best-loved decade. That isn't bad." Of course his four children (from three marriages) might have had something to say on the question of "best-loved."

But that is another essay in another time. There is much to be written on Old Sheck, who was also, probably, best-loved and imitated by plagiarists, influences and derivatives to a degree which would have infuriated him if he were not, ultimately, so detached and emotionally repressed. The "another essay in another time" of which I am thinking is *The Fifties*, a summary of that decade I wrote in 1978 for the *Analog Yearbook* and which has probably gotten around more than any other segment of my short nonfiction. I was perhaps the first to argue that our field's most visionary, inventive, signatory period was that decade, that in the 1950s science fiction had become at its peak and in the collective work at its strongest an instrument of beauty and precision, the flame that cuts, knife that burns. The magazine editors were shaping science fiction then, the book market was almost entirely derivative and Gold, Boucher, McComas, Shaw, Mines, and Merwin knew in their various ways what they were doing and what they wanted. Campbell had gone half-mad in the wake of Dianetics but was still the editor who essentially discovered Walter M. Miller,

Jr., and who published Godwin's "The Cold Equations," Boucher knew that science fiction was integrally literature and used Matheson, Oliver, Margaret St. Clair, Shirley Jackson and fifty others to prove it. Horace Gold, that madman and stupefying genius, was a flaming transgressive masquerading as Ben Hibbs. ("I want *Galaxy* to read as if it were *The Saturday Evening Post* fiction of the 22nd century.") Bester, Wyman Guinn, Phil Klass, Damon Knight, Pohl & Kornbluth, to say nothing of Sheckley (as serious as Voltaire), burned the page. Fred Pohl wrote of that decade, "The only venue in which you could find the truth of mid-century America was in the science fiction magazines.

The stereotype, the received wisdom, the canonic teaching at the time I published that essay, was that the visionary '40s of Campbell, and the rebellious '60s of Moorcock and Ballard, Ellison and Brunner were the more crucial decades, but in my essay I presented a different view. Coming on to 40 years later, I believe that it is my case which has edged close to the canon of received wisdom and as these dreadful post-Tolkien, post-*Star Wars*, post-*Avatar* and post-*Blade Runner* consequences shape our latter destiny, I am surer that if there are any miserable graduate students writing theses on the true and terrible history of science fiction, those unhappy scholars will be ever more reliant upon my argument and ever more dedicated to its substantiation.

Meanwhile, the ever fewer who remain dedicated to what James Blish more than 60 years ago deemed "The True Quill" find ourselves on Malcolm Arnold's vast and darkling plane, surrounded by elves and wizards who clash by night and soar the paved spaceways in the more eternal dark.

The True Quill, science fiction as seen through James Blish's lens, has become a subsidiary, perhaps a minor appendage to fantasy or corrupted versions of the corrupted science fiction of the post-*Star Wars* period. (I would like to affix responsibility equally to *Star Trek*, which has ten years of seniority and in the past did so but have repented; there is no fair comparison of the two properties. *Star Trek*, an earnest, sentimental '30s Civilize-The-Galaxy procedure, was a failed television series which carried its influence largely to the already-convinced and it recycled a lot of familiar plots as it gave employment to recyclable science fiction writers like Sturgeon, Ellison or Spinrad. *Star Wars* had its corporate and engineering fix on the widest possible audience from the outset and it blew up the Foundation Series and the Lensmen into gaudy, gas-filled dirigibles that soared over the cities the way that our current travelers soar those old paved, blackened, decomposing spaceways.) "Science fiction has become a small special interest at science fiction Conventions", Spinrad said thirty years ago (I have quoted him to distraction), and science fiction Conventions have, with few exceptions, become fantasy Conventions with just enough rocketry on the panels and in the dealer rooms to put a bit of sheen on decomposition.

Decadent. That is what has happened to the True Quill to the degree that the TQ survives in *Asimov's, Analog*, and the suburban reaches of Tor Books. "Arcane" might serve just as well in the way it describes the inaccessibility of an output which seems—to those not wholly familiar with the field—to be written in a kind of code. Horace Gold had Ben Hibbs (and for all we know the Tractor series and Mr. Moto) as a kind of aspiration. Maybe not everyone liked that stuff but at least a third of Hibbs' readership of ten million would read it. Meanwhile, who reads Stross and McAuley or Stephen Baxter? Who reads the non-collaborative Bruce Sterling? Making no judgment of the considerable skills and fierce intelligence of these worthies, exactly who is their audience? And, stipulating that such an audience exists, what are its dimensions? Can it sustain careers beyond the enthusiasm and commitment of the few editors still defending and propitiating science fiction? (Everyone in the business knows that even for the small and specialty presses, science fiction is a charitable enterprise. The routine fantasy novel by a little-known or unknown writer will outsell an equivalent science fiction novel by at least fifty percent. "Why should I publish science fiction?" the revered Judy-Lynn del Rey asked me almost thirty years ago. "It's like short story collections. I only publish it to lose money." (Which in fact, she did. Publish me. Lose money. Judy-Lynn could not completely sequester her tender and vulnerable heart.)

We are in trouble, folks. We have been in trouble for a long time. The science fiction that the aged among us loved, which shaped and darkened and exploited and framed us, that science fiction has become a decadent and marginal form of human activity. In *The Engines of the Night* I self-quoted a phrase which I had spoken on a panel in the late seventies when asked from the floor to define "decadence." "When form overtakes and suppresses function," I answered reflexively. (Sometimes an angel can whisper into your ear.) That is modern edge, cutting-edge science fiction. Form has not only suppressed but has, in terms of most of the audience, stomped on function and has left it like a smashed-flat cartoon character, like a decapitated Roadrunner.

There are of course those who would disagree. I won't live long enough to apologize to them if they are right, so I will only write now: I am on your side. Cassandra *knew* she had a crappy job.

Next time maybe: Willie Stark's advice to Jack Burden in Penn Warren's *All the King's Men*. There is always something on everybody. Even George Lucas.

- February 2013: New Jersey
Copyright © 2013 by Barry Malzberg

Tina Gower won first place in a 2012 Writers of the Future *quarterly contest. This is her second professional fiction sale.* LATE-BREAKING NEWS: *On April 14, 17 days before this issue went live, Tina won the $5,000 Gold Prize at the 2013* Writers of the Future *ceremony*

TODAY I AM NOBODY

by Tina Gower

I am Amber when I see him again. I wake with auburn hair and green eyes, freckles across my skin, and decide to be Amber. The name fits the face in the mirror, and all day I do Amber things. Amber would love picking daisies in the meadow behind the reservation. Amber would wear her hair in two French braids. Amber would have a boyfriend with blond hair and one unruly lock that covers his left eye. When I see him, that perfect boy for Amber, I want him.

He works in the village, on the dusty grimy road that leads from the reservation to the back of the tannery. I am able to watch him scraping a hide for sale because he does not know Amber. He knew Rose. When I was Rose, I had olive skin with black hair. The roses were budding and I put one in my hair.

"How long will you be in town?" he had asked.

"Only until the roses bloom," I said. Truthfully, I didn't know then how quickly I would shed and change and become a new girl. The shaman didn't tell me how the medicine would work.

The corners of the boy's mouth twitched and his smile fell flat. "That's too bad. I like dark-skinned brunettes. Everyone in town is blond."

Amber doesn't have dark skin, so today I only watch while the young man (who is perfect for Amber) hangs the skins to dry. I hear wagon wheels squeak into the village with supplies from the East. The traders bring tea and preserves, waxes for candles when the long nights come. One trader hands a package of sweets to a girl my age. Her name is Nola. She will always be Nola, poor thing. The other girls do not recognize me anymore, although they knew me once.

✧

I walk home and cut through the glen. My hand skims along the wild grains and I pick one to chew absently. When I reach my tent by the creek, my pots and pans are scattered, my food supply is shredded and strewn along the bank.

I'm cleaning the mess when I hear the grumble of a bear. He swipes his paw at me before I see him, and I fall to the ground. The gravel smashes into my elbows and knees. The smell of pine and dust brings me to my senses. He swings at me again, and his paw leaves a scrape down my leg.

The injury burns. My breath is frozen in my chest and my palms are damp with sweat. I clutch a cast iron skillet and, with no other weapon, throw it at his head. While he rubs his face with a paw, I scamper and trip my way to the tallest pine and climb. He paces below.

My skin tingles and I feel an itch. The sensation multiplies until it's like a thousand insects burrowing into me. My skin peels. A wave of nausea crashes into me like the river against the rocks a few feet away. The change is happening too quickly. I hug the trunk, panting. A clump of Amber's hair falls to the bear. He bats at it and sniffs. Pieces of Amber melt away. When Amber is gone, the bear is gone, too.

I crawl back to the ruined tent and look in my mirror. A crack runs down the middle, but I can still see my new face in the reflection. I'm still pale, but my freckles are gone and I have blond hair.

The shaman's medicine doesn't work. I'm only half tribe and half white. Maybe I should never have agreed to the medicine. I don't fit in either world.

I stay at my campground on the reservation for the next few days. A blond will not do. The tanner sees too many blonds. "Everyone in town is blond," he told Rose. I spend the time cleaning the mess from the bear.

✧

Today I am Mia. My skin looks like porcelain and my eyelids look swollen. I have straight black hair. I run to the village to watch the young man in the tannery. Mia should have a boyfriend who works at the tannery, but he doesn't look at her. I am not Rose.

"Can I help you, Miss?" He asks.

"My name is Mia."

"Can I help you, Mia?" His eyes never leave the saddle he is brushing.

"No," I say, because I know now I'm not who he is looking for today.

I leave a rose for him at the table. The last one of the season. I watch him from a safe spot outside the window. He never touches the rose. I go back the next day and the next, but the rose doesn't move from its spot. It wilts and dries. One day it is gone.

✧

The bear comes to me in a dream and when he lifts his face I see the shaman. Her grey hair blends into the white patch of hair on the bear's neck and it is as if she is holding the bear up for me to see.

"I've brought you a bear," she says.

"I don't need a bear. I need friends, people to talk to. I'm lonely, and your medicine does not work."

She moves around me to light a fire and the bear flops to the ground like a pile of the tanner's skins. "Animal medicine takes a long time to work."

The wood smokes for a minute before the first flames lick the chilly night air. The pines that surround the campsite glow, but the forest beyond remains black.

"I asked for someone to love me and accept me. I didn't ask for animal medicine," I say.

My voice sounds muffled. My lips feel smashed against my teeth. I'm confused to find I'm talking into my arm. I rise and blink in the darkness of my tent. Outside the campfire smokes as if a fire was lit and died hours ago.

✧

Today I am Abigail. My skin is so dark it's black. My hair is also black, but curly and coarse. The tanner notices Abigail. His eyes follow me around the tannery, but his shoulders are tense, his lips are turned down in a frown. I finger a design on a small leather bag for sale. It is of a rose.

"Put that down." His hand is gripping a hammer so tight his knuckles are white. "That is not for you. Put that down."

He stomps towards me and I fumble the bag back to the display and run to the reservation. My heart beats so hard my throat hurts. My fingers feel numb where I held the bag meant for me. No, I remember, now. The tanner is correct; it's not for me. It's for Rose.

✧

Today I am nobody.

I do nothing. I sit and let the sounds of the creek drown out my thoughts. The leaves fall and regrow many times while I am nobody, doing nothing things. Every morning I am not Rose I am nobody. Some days I do not even check my mirror, searching for her.

✧

The roses are in bloom today, and I gather a few supplies to trade in town. Wild herbs and berries overflow in my baskets. The tanner is selling his hides two booths down from me. He stops for a moment to pick through my selection, and finds a few herbs to his liking. The sun streams through his blond hair, and I see one strand of silver. When he smiles I expect to feel warmth, but there is none. I wonder as he walks away who I am today. I never looked in the mirror.

✧

Today, I am Amber again. If I can be Amber then I can be Rose. I'm excited to discover this, and I dance around my camp. Maybe the medicine is working. Maybe I can force my body to change like I did with the bear. Maybe I can find a way to stay Rose.

I make plans.

✧

"Girl of many faces," the shaman called me. I walk the line between worlds. I schooled in the village, and the girls complimented me for my hand at mixing herbs to make pleasing scents, but no one bought them. In the reservation the women relied on me to plant the seeds for the next harvest, but criticized me for not planting in rows. Liked by all and loved by none. I was invisible in my efforts and visible only in my failures. So I became whatever people wanted me to be, and still nobody loved me. The shaman promised me the attention I deserved.

"You try to please everyone and you please no one, not even yourself," she said, and handed me a mirror. "The animal spirits have chosen to heal you and retrieve a lost part of your soul."

Then the day came when the people of the reservation moved to the South to follow the seasons. The shaman said I should stay behind and wait for my spirit animal's medicine.

The day after they left, I awoke to see Rose. Her hair shone a rich black-cocoa, not like my dull light brown. Her figure curved like a road that moves with the land, not like my straight narrow lines that short-cut to the ground.

I thought the spirit animals had made me into the woman I was meant to be. I thought the medicine had worked. But then I became sick: my skin peeled, my hair fell, and the part of me I thought of as "Rose"—the part of me I would learn to be—wilted away.

✧

Today I am finally Rose.

My hands tremble. This makes the basket quiver and the herbs shake. To be Rose, I jumped from a cliff by the river. After a dozen times and a dozen girls, fear of the height no longer changed me. I had to find a new danger. I fought a wolf, a badger, and thieves along the road. In the end, nothing scared me more than never being Rose again. She crept into me in my sleep.

I look in the broken mirror to be sure, but it's true. I am finally Rose.

I head straight to town, herb basket in hand. I do not stop until I'm at the tannery.

He brushes the skin of an animal and sees Rose.

"Hello," he says, smiling. "Can I help you?"

I smile and take a breath. I can finally give him back his Rose. I try to remember Rose. How did she smile? How did she hold her body? How did she speak? Was it soft or loud?

"I am Rose," I say.

He frowns. "Do I know you?"

The answer catches on my tongue. He looks at me, his forehead wrinkles, his eyelids lower to slits. He doesn't recognize Rose.

"I'm sorry, your name doesn't sound familiar," he says. "Do you have a request to place? I'm afraid I don't have any orders for Rose."

For the first time I notice the lines on his face around his mouth. When I come into town he is always here.

I nod, my voice deserting me. I want to hide and not be Rose. The tanner doesn't know Rose anymore.

He doesn't know me. He *never* knew me.

✧

When I arrive the camp is a mess. The bear has returned and shredded my tent beyond repair.

That night I sleep in the rain, huddled under a few gathered branches. The tanner is gone to me, so I wonder who I am supposed to be. I plant herbs for the harvest and find no pleasure in it. I gather a few seasonal plants to make tea and find no pleasure in that either.

The only thing that brings me pleasure is watching the rain drain into the river, and speculating where it leads. I'm soaked in water. I'm connected to the water and the water to the river and the river to the ocean, and I feel relief to be part of something.

✧

Today I am me. I do not know my hair color or the tone of my skin.

I've always wanted to see the ocean, so I pack. I've wanted to see the leaves turn in the valleys below the mountain. I'm planning things I've never planned before because I didn't know my life was my own. I feel whole; the animal medicine is working.

I stop by the tannery on my way out of town and leave a gift.

I peek through the window before turning away, and I see him glance in the broken mirror. I wonder who he will see. What animal will the spirits bring to the tanner?

The road out of town is damp from a mist of rain over the night. I walk until my feet are tired, and then I rest. I stare into the sky, finding shapes in the clouds. I see a rabbit. When I look again it's a dog, then a cow with horns, and, last, a bear. I fall asleep gazing at the clouds, assured that when I wake, no matter what shape or color I wear, I will still be me.

Original (First) Publication
Copyright © 2013 by Tina Gower

Catherine Lucille Moore made her professional debut with the classic "Shambleau" in 1933, created Northwest Smith and Jirel of Joiry, and alone and in tandem with husband Henry Kuttner produced a series of classic stories that are still being read and reprinted.

HAPPILY EVER AFTER

by C. L. Moore

Cinderella and the Prince were married with a great ceremony. No one had approved from the first, and now more often than not there was a gleam of I-told-you-so behind the King's spectacles, and the Queen's three chins quivered with bitter satisfaction as her predictions were realized one by one. For Cinderella and the Prince were not happy. No one had really expected them to be. You cannot pluck a kitchen girl from the cinders and set a crown on her head and let it go at that; small feet are not the only prerequisite of a princess.

To tell the truth, the step-sisters had played a large part in what happened. Cinderella never realized it, but if Darmar and Igraine, with their hauteur and their high-nosed, high-bred faces, had not led her out of the cinders and disdainfully acknowledged her as sister, the Prince might have never done what he did. But after he had made that rash proclamation about the slipper he had to carry it out, particularly with the herald bawling the news to the very doorstep at the time. And then, of course, she was quite charming.

For a while, to do her justice, he was not sorry. Nothing could have been more bewitching than the Princess Cinderella in her billowing skirts, with the gold crown on her head. She had some secret difficulty in keeping it there, and used to practice before the mirror at night, but she never learned to manage the thing with true dignity. Once, when she bent to pick up a dropped handkerchief, it fell off and rolled across the floor. Now, a princess born would never have stooped for the handkerchief in the first place. Poor Cinderella blushed to her ears, and the ladies-in-waiting tittered among themselves.

There were other things. She had a healthy appetite, and the delicacies of the royal table were far insufficient to her needs. She ate and ate until the court stared, and yet she was never satisfied. Her pretty fingers hesitated among the forks, and her full-throated laughter rang almost strident above the polite titters of the court. Once she had laughed so hard that her stays split, to the immense embarrassment of everyone concerned. And sometimes, sitting still in the audience hall, the chill of its shadows penetrated to her warm bourgeois blood, and her mind turned longingly to the cinders and the lentils boiling on the crane above the fire.

She who had never had an idle moment before suddenly found herself plunged into a vast *ennui*—nothing to do but preen before the mirror and walk the garden paths, her crown tilted at a precarious angle, while hawk-eyes on every side waited for her least mistake as a signal for lifted brows.

One afternoon Cinderella disappeared. For hours they searched. It was the Prince himself who found her at last. Far off in a corner of the castle was an old tower room where odds and ends of things were kept—seven-league boots somewhat run down at the heels, a cloak of darkness with threadbare seams, magic mirrors with cracked faces, and miscellaneous charms that somehow didn't seem to work very well any more. Under the window stood a spinning wheel that had once spun gold out of straw. The treadle had cracked years ago, it creaked when it moved, and here in the dusty attic it had stood for years. Cinderella had found it, and here she sat in the dusty sunlight under the window, spinning and spinning gold. The shadows were full of it, and all about her slippers shining masses gleamed in the muted sunlight. The famous small foot trundled happily away at the protesting treadle, the curly head bent over the wheel and shining gold ran out between her fingers as she worked. The crown tilted over her eyes at its most rakish angle.

"Cinderella!" The Prince's voice was harsh.

She started guiltily, and the crown fell from her curls and rolled across the dusty floor. "Cinderella—spinning in the attic! Look at that crown!"

Blushing, she retrieved the crown and balanced it on her head.

"Oh, I'm sorry—" she cried. "I–I didn't mean—"

"There is nothing for you to say, Cinderella. For all I know I may find you scrubbing floors tomorrow. Have you no sense of values? You are a princess, don't you understand? A princess! There's dust on your nose!—Now don't cry! Princesses never cry. Here—stop—Cinderella!"

"Yes," meekly.

"Stay here till I can find someone to dust you off. If you should be seen like this—now *don't* cry!"

The Prince went out hastily.

Cinderella sat under the window in silence, with magic heaped about her feet. Slowly all the gold slid out between her fingers until they were empty. Her eyes began to brim. She hid her face behind her hands and wept. The attic was still but for the Princess sitting and weeping with her gold crown on her head; and the tears flashed out between her fingers.

Presently behind her hands a light began to shine. Startled, she lifted her wet face. The attic was radiant, and in the midst of the light her Fairy Godmother stood.

"Cinderella, child, why do you weep?"

It was the same question she had asked in the kitchen at home, long ago.

"Because they scold me," sobbed the Princess. "Because I'm miserable! Oh, Godmother, Godmother, take me home!"

The Fairy smiled, and the radiance brightened until Cinderella's eyes were blinded with light. She put up her hands to shut it out. There was a deep silence.

After a while, when the quiet had become unendurable, she uncovered her eyes. It was dark—warmly dark. She sat before the kitchen fire again, snug in the cinders.

"Why—why—" Cinderella dug her fists into her eyes, and then, somehow, was yawning, stretching like a kitten. No crown trembled precariously on her ruffled curls. She yawned again, luxuriantly, sniffing the boiling lentils that swung above the fire. She laughed a happy little gurgle deep in her throat, and settled down among the warm cinders.

Brad R. Torgersen was a Campbell, Nebula and Hugo nominee in 2012, has become a mainstay at Analog, *and is currently putting the finishing touches on his first novel.*

THE FLAMINGO GIRL

by Brad R. Torgersen

Elvira was seven feet of naked avian loveliness. The tiny feathers sprouting from her skin formed a luxurious layer of bright-pink, velvet-soft plumage, and her unblinking eyes stared at the ceiling with an expression of surprise. The bed upon which her body lay was a confused mess of satin blankets and pillows, with not a hint of whom else might have been with her, or why that person had resorted to murder.

"Señor Soto," said a voice behind me. I turned, and beheld another seven-foot beauty, this one parrot-green. Her wings flexed and ruffled with agitation, and her sapphire-blue eyebrows hunched over a fear-filled gaze. Looking up into her face—we unmodified humans are generally shorter than Specials—I asked her what I could do for her.

"The other women are very nervous, Señor," she said. "They are wanting to know what has happened. Madam Arquette asked me to ask you what to tell them."

"And you are?" I said.

"Josefina," said the green bird-woman.

"You may tell them that Elvira is dead, and that housekeeping is free to enter and clean the Flamingo Suite as soon as the city's public mortician has removed the body."

"There isn't going to be an investigation?"

"That's for the police to decide. They'll be here shortly. I imagine that they'll want to question a few people, so make sure none of the customers leave before that happens."

In truth, the cops wouldn't give a damn about another dead Special. It was unlikely they'd interrogate anyone at all. The Aerie was a busy waypoint on Hollywood Boulevard, in a city that spared little budget for true law enforcement. I and three other guards were what laughably passed for security at the Aerie—our presence being a formality so that Madam Arquette could claim to be honoring her adult merchant commission with the Greater Los Angeles Commerce Bureau.

"The Madam will not be pleased," said Josefina.

"Then perhaps the Madam should have listened to me when I warned her about cutting her private security expenses again. All the reputable adult businesses on the Boulevard hire triple our number."

Josefina's wings rustled violently.

"Look," I said to her, "I'm sorry I can't do more. I really am."

I attempted to move past Josefina. She thrust out a wing that blocked my way.

"But you used to be a policeman," she said with quivering indignation. "You were hired because of your experience. If you can't help us now, what good are you?"

I stepped back, looked at the anger in her eyes, and felt the full weight of my fifty years settle on my shoulders. I had asked myself that same question ten times a day since coming to the Aerie. Once upon a time, I'd been an okay cop in the Long Beach supermetro. But when Carlita had left me, and taken the kids, and sold the house…whatever ties had been keeping me in Long Beach seemed to evaporate. I'd retired early, and immediately sought the job with the least amount of real responsibility I could find, as far away from Carlita as possible.

I just looked at Josefina, a sympathetic frown on my face. "The police will be here soon, and they will handle this. It's out of my purview."

Eventually her wing withdrew, and small tears began to stain the lime-colored down around Josefina's eyes.

"Look," I said, "if you really want to find out who did this, give the cops something to go on. I know the Madam has in-house rules about customer confidentiality, but this time I think there needs to be an exception. City corporate policy says they can't make her release her records, and knowing the Madam, I doubt she'd sacrifice her reputation on the strip for a single dead girl—"

"I will get the police what they need," Josefina said, suddenly standing stiff.

"Will the Madam know about it?" I asked.

"Would it bother you if she didn't?"

No, I had to admit, it wouldn't.

"You're taking this kind of hard," I said. "Was Elvira a friend?"

"No, Señor Soto. She was my younger sister."

☼

Twenty-four hours later I got a text from Josefina asking me to meet her in West Hollywood. No indication why, just that she needed me urgently. An address was attached. I checked in with the branch office of the security firm I worked for, and clocked out for an extended lunch break.

Josefina's apartment block was in what the supermetro called the Special District. Most of the Specials in Greater Los Angeles tended to congregate there—where everyone could be uniformly bizarre together. The sidewalk out front was replete with walking and talking cats, dogs, birds, wolves, rabbits, and other Specials who had had their human DNA artificially adapted to take on various other species' characteristics.

Entering the block I passed a man whose fur was striped like a skunk's, though thankfully he didn't smell like one. If he cared that a Normal—the Specials' word for everyone else in the world—was going into his apartment complex, he didn't show it.

I took the elevator up to the tenth floor and found the door with number 1036, tapped the little button in the middle of the door, and waited while the tiny camera inside the button surveyed me.

The door handle clicked, and I was beckoned into Josefina's home, microscopic as it was. I'd seen student studios with more square footage. But it was clean, and smelled gently of ginger and orange peel.

"Señor," she said respectfully. I took off my sun hat and nodded at her.

Josefina immediately pressed a thumb drive into my hand.

"It is all here," she said quietly. I noticed that she had on a plain-patterned traditionally-cut dress, with holes in the back for her wings, and no shoes. Her ankles and feet were the same color as the rest of her. Bright green.

"What is this?" I said.

"I tried to give it to the police, but they didn't want it. Nobody cares about Elvira."

"I told you, I—"

"*Por favor*, Señor Soto," Josefina said insistently. "There is no one else to do this. You must do it. Please! I don't have much money, but I can pay you for your time. I can—"

I raised a hand and patted it down through the air, pleadingly.

"Just tell me what I'll be looking at," I said, "before you go giving me any money."

"It's Elvira's schedule at the Aerie."

"There are names? Everyone who ever used your sister?"

"*Hired* her," Josefina corrected me. "Yes."

"I'll probably just need the names of the people she saw the night she died."

"But she was off that night, and there is no record of anyone having rented the suite or hiring Elvira."

"Then what was she doing there at all?"

"I do not know," Josefina said, eyes on the floor. Her wings had begun to tremble.

I slipped the thumb drive into a pocket and took her right hand in both of mine—the sensation of the tiny feathers on my bare palms was like mink pelt, but softer.

"It wasn't your fault," I said, flashing back to an almost identical scene in my supermetro days, when I'd had to both question and console a stricken mother whose son had died in a gang turf tumble.

"Of course it is," Josefina said. "It was my idea for her to come to the Aerie. I recommended her to the Madam. She was nervous about going Special, and I talked her into it. Mother and father never forgave me when I went Special, and they doubly hated it when Elvira came to work with me. I have no idea how much the whole family will hate me now."

"So why did you wind up at the Aerie in the first place?"

"It was my best option."

"I don't understand," I said.

"Señor Soto, you're not from East L.A.?"

"Not originally, no."

"But you are Raza?"

"I grew up in the barrios of Oakland. Joined the Army at 17. When I got out of the Army, I moved south and went to the police academy."

I remembered when I told my mother I'd joined supermetro's PD. She'd cried. But then, she'd cried when I'd joined the military, and when my brothers ran away, too. At least with me she'd known where I was and what I was doing. But it had still upset her a great deal. Always terrified I was going to get myself hurt, whether it was overseas, or here in California working Vice, or second-level Theft stuff, or the small army that ran herd on gangs.

I mumbled something to that effect.

"My mother was almost proud of being poor," Josefina said. "Our family had been in East L.A. for almost five generations, all in the same crappy little house. Elvira and me, we hated it. We wanted something better. But the schools in East L.A., what good are they? For you, the Army was your avenue out. For Elvira and I, just two poor sisters with homely faces and no education…"

I nodded my understanding—so far.

"Anyway, I got a cleaning job. They sent me all over. One day I got sent up to Madam Arquette's house in Beverly Hills. I'd never worked for a Special before, much less someone that rich. She's like a peacock, you know. Beautiful and grand and when I started asking questions, she told me how it works. If a girl will undergo Specialization and work in the Aerie, Madam will carry the cost. You pay it back over time, plus interest, and after that, you keep everything you earn, minus a house fee."

"But if you wanted to go into business for yourself—" I started to say, but Josefina cut me off.

"Look at me, Señor," Josefina stepped away a couple of paces and flared her wings wide, filling the tiny apartment, her hourglass silhouette accentuated through the thin fabric of the dress. "Men and women both will pay hundreds an hour to be with me. We have the richest clients in the entire city. People who want the Special experience. Crave it. A pro Normal girl in Long Beach, how much does she make, compared to that?"

Not much, I had to admit.

Josefina lowered and folded her wings.

"I didn't want to be just any working girl," she said. "I wanted to literally be a different person. Because someday, I want to have enough money of my own to leave Los Angeles on my own two feet, and not look back, and not need anyone else's help, and not have to take this…this part of me with me when I leave."

"Reversal of the Specialization is twice as expensive as the initial procedure," I said.

"I don't care. Once I've earned enough to pay the Madam off, I'll keep working until I can pay for the reversal, and get myself out of here to boot. When Elvira came to visit me and I told her about my plan, she'd wanted to come with me, but it would have been too expensive for both of us, so I told her she had to find a way to help with costs."

Josefina stopped, her face in her hands, wings gently shaking as she sobbed.

I felt my cheeks growing red.

"Look," I said, "I meant it before: Madam Arquette can't rely on just four men to keep her establishment free of trouble."

"But you're here, when you know you don't have to be," Josefina said, her nose sniffling.

"I didn't know your sister," I said, "But I don't like the idea of anyone killing a young woman and getting away with it."

She seemed to accept that explanation at face value, lame as it was.

"I can't make any promises," I said, reaching into my pocket and feeling the cool plastic of the thumb drive. "All I can tell you is that I'll take a look."

"Do what you can," Josefina said abruptly. "It's better than nothing."

"Yes, ma'am," I said, sticking out my hand, which she shook. Then she leaned down quickly and pecked me on the cheek.

How long had it been since a woman—*any* woman, Special or Normal—had done that to me? I felt my face redden all over again, then muttered a goodbye and ducked back out into the hallway.

The thumb drive turned out to contain all of Elvira's business calendar—every appointment going back to when she'd gotten out of the hospital, post-Specialization. The header on the calendar simply read FLAMINGO. Having met the Madam a few times I got the sense that she didn't bring on anyone new unless it was done on the Madam's terms, so Elvira was just filling the role assigned to her.

And while names were present, salient data beyond that was tough to come by. All financial transaction information had been stripped, as well as whether or not clients had been locals, celebrities, or even the rare tourist. If the schedule had ever contained details on what precisely Elvira had provided, in terms of customer care and needs—beyond what I already knew to be the case—that too was missing.

And Josefina had been right. Elvira was blacked out the day of her death. In fact, she was blacked out most of that week.

I mulled this over at my desk, back at the Aerie. If the Madam discovered I had this information—we guards were never ever allowed access to the scheduling software, for confidentiality purposes—it would cost me a lot more than my job. I quickly dumped the calendar to text, then erased the calendar, keeping only names and time blocks in ASCII format on the same thumb drive Josefina had given me. She was off for the rest of the week, a considerable concession from the Madam, given the circumstances, so I went about my usual work, only occasionally poking my head into the women's private rooms to ask a discrete question or two.

So far as anyone knew, Elvira had had no quarrels with the other Specials. In fact, the lot of them seemed heartbroken over the girl's death, and mournful in the extreme for her older sister. A community pot was being passed—I dropped in my share—and they were planning to have a silent moment in Elvira's memory when Josefina came back to work. Otherwise, business at the Aerie continued as usual. Clients came and went, their communications hushed and monosyllabic at the palatial registration desk—often from behind hoods or sunglasses or anything else that might obscure their faces from prying eyes, the Special fetish still being a somewhat controversial fetish, even in a city which had long ago abandoned any pretense of sexual propriety.

As I watched the clientele come and go from behind my own set of sunglasses, I realized that I didn't have much of a clue about what went on when the clients and the Specials met behind the closed doors of the suites. Oh, sure, I had plenty of educated assumptions. The Aerie had two-thirds female Specials and one-third male Specials, and if ever they "talked shop" it was done strictly between them, away from the ears of a Normal like me.

In many ways, I and the three other guards were like wallpaper or store window mannequins: unless our presence was called for—which was seldom—we kept our distance. The Specials did the same, and the clients ghosted to and fro with as low a profile as possible.

I examined the names I'd gotten from Josefina. I didn't know any of them, though I couldn't be sure any of them were actual names either. Fake names were as likely as anything, which was probably why the cops hadn't wanted the list in the first place. What good was a list of bogus identities?

Josefina came back to work. We never acknowledged that I'd been to her home.

I kept looking at the list of names throughout the next week, until I noticed one name that was down for numerous appointments in predictable succession, then abruptly stopped showing up.

I texted Josefina about this, and asked her if she knew the name. Or if Elvira had ever talked about this particular person. I got a text re-inviting me to Josefina's apartment, this time in the dinner hour.

☼

"What her real name is, I am not sure," Josefina said. She'd offered me a plate of grilled beef with peppers and onions, which I ate thankfully, not having had food since sipping a cup of bitter coffee at mid-morning.

"*Her?*" I said, somewhat surprised.

"She was an Anglo Normal, mid-forties."

"Did Elvira ever talk about this person?"

"Yes, because this woman never actually wanted sex."

"Is that unusual?"

"It happens. Some clients come in simply for the vicarious thrill of being around a Special. We're fascinating to them."

"This anglo Normal, she was one of these?"

"Yes. She would request Elvira in two-hour blocks. She adored real flamingos, apparently. She and Elvira would sit together on the bed of the suite, and the Anglo…she would stroke Elvira's body and wings affectionately, and just talk about her life. Her hectic middle-management work. Her grown sons. Her ex-husband, who apparently divorced her in disgust when he discovered she had a thing for Specials and had been surreptitiously using family funds to begin exploring the Special world on-line. That's how she found out about the Aerie, apparently, and when Madam Arquette put up the listing for The Flamingo Suite, this woman was an instant customer."

"So why'd she stop coming all of a sudden?"

"I don't know," Josefina said, nibbling at her own food.

"If this woman spent so much time talking to Elvira, did you sister ever talk back? I mean, about her own life?"

"I don't know, but I wonder. Elvira was only twenty. About the same age as this woman's children. Elvira always needed to trust people."

"Is it possible Elvira told this woman things she wouldn't tell you?"

"What do you mean?" Josefina's fork suddenly stopped moving.

"Not to question your relationship with your sister. It's just been my experience that siblings, even close siblings, don't always share everything with each other, whether they realize it or not. And as the saying goes, a man will tell things to a bartender he'd never tell his wife. This Anglo Normal, she's a question mark for me. She might know something which could tell us more about why Elvira died."

"Speaking of which," Josefina said, "the police tell me that an examination to determine exactly what killed Elvira is still pending. Does it normally take this long?"

"When there are no obvious wounds," I said, "things can get complicated. I called the coroner and made some polite inquiries. Elvira was a healthy young Special. Something was done to her, that much we can be certain of. What that something was is another matter entirely. Try to be patient. Meanwhile, is there any way possible for you to find out who this Anglo customer was? Does she come back to visit any of the other Specials, male or female?"

"I can try to find out tonight, when I am working."

We chewed in mutual silence for several minutes.

"If your daughter told you she wanted to go Special," Josefina said, "what would your reaction be?"

Now it was my fork that had suddenly stopped moving. My Angela was fifteen, and headstrong like Carlita. Last summer, Carlita had let Angela spend the summer with me, when it was my younger son Adam I'd wanted to have. I'd learned quickly it was because Angela was officially hell on wheels, and we'd scrapped it out for three months, before she'd finally gone home to Carlita in disgust—and with my blessing. I tried to imagine Angela showing up at my door in two more years, transformed into God knew what. *Hi Pop! It's me, your little girl!*

I must have visibly shuddered, because Josefina put her fork down and wiped her mouth, then stood up quickly.

"You can see yourself to the door."

"Wait, I'm sorry, I—"

"I'll see what I can find out for you about the Anglo. Goodnight, Señor."

My plate unfinished, I clumsily stood up and made my way out.

✼

I was making the mistake of giving a damn, that much was certain.

A smarter man probably would have quit the Aerie and gone to find a different job. But Josefina had shamed me, and now I felt like I owed her… something. Not sure what. Some kind of resolution, perhaps. I couldn't just walk away. That would have felt unmanly, and while I'd long ago given up certain pretensions to *machismo*, I was damned if I was going to let a woman almost half my age do what Josefina had done, whether she'd realized it when she asked the question or not. So I stewed my way through three days of shifts, until I thought my off-hours might coincide with Josefina's—and once again went to her apartment block in West Hollywood.

There was no answer at first. I almost turned and went home.

But the door popped, and Josefina opened it hesitantly.

"Yes?"

"The coroner sent me a report about Elvira," I said.

"And?"

"And I really think it would be best if I came in and we sat down."

Josefina eyed me closely, measuring my intent, then opened the door the rest of the way, allowing me into her single-room domain. Things weren't as clean as they'd been before. I wagered she'd not done any upkeep since the last time I'd visited. The same plate I'd eaten off of still sat half-submerged in cold soapy water in the kitchen sink.

"Tell me," Josefina said. It was practically a command.

"Near-instant anaphylactic shock," I said. "As a result of being exposed to concentrated bee venom."

"She was stung by a *bee*?"

"No. They found a small puncture wound on her neck, like what might be made by a microtubule. The plastic tip had broken off beneath the skin. Did you know she was allergic?"

"Yes, the whole family did. She was stung when we were kids, and had to be rushed to the emergency room. It almost killed her."

"Who else besides the two of you might have known?"

"I don't know. Maybe a few family friends from East L.A.?"

I scratched my head, thinking.

"So now the police will investigate it as murder," Josefina said.

"The file will be dropped down to homicide, homicide will see that it was a Special working the Boulevard, and the file will be quietly forgotten about."

"How can they do this?" Josefina said, balling her fists, her wings spasming. "She was a human being, for God's sake!"

"Supermetro jurisdictions track hundreds of potential homicides every day," I said. "More people die every year in the Greater Los Angeles area than died in the Army's entire invasion of Pakistan. The police prioritize, based on how easily a case might be solved, and how high-profile the victim happens to be. I hate to say it, but Specials barely register. Many cops don't even think of you as human anymore."

"You would know," Josefina snarled, her vehemence plain.

I felt my face flush. "Goddammit, I'm sorry I was such a *pendejo* when I was here the other night! Okay, alright, would I be thrilled if my daughter came home having gone Special? No. Frankly, it would freak me out."

Josefina turned away from me, but I grabbed her elbows with both arms and forced her to look at me—no small feat, given she had me by twelve inches and twenty-plus years.

"But she'd still be my daughter," I said, looking up into Josefina's enraged eyes with all of the sincerity I could muster, "and regardless of who or what she'd become, I'd never stop loving Angela with all my heart and soul. She's…she's the only decent thing I have left to show for myself! Her and Adam, my son."

Josefina's lips quivered, and tears openly flooded out into the feathers on her face, dropping across them to land on the lapels of my jacket.

She sank down to her knees, fists balled on my stomach, and began to sob into my chest. Almost reflexively I wrapped my arms around her head, again marveling at the incredible softness of the inhuman plumage that had replaced her hair. I found myself quietly whispering in Spanish, the same reassurances I had often given to Angela and Adam when they'd awaken screaming from a nightmare. Josefina's long arms circled the small of my back and almost crushed me as I held her, her wings gently and reflexively quivering along her back.

"We'll find who did this to Elvira," I said. "I promise you."

☼

Josefina went to work that night, and I went home to my own apartment in Culver City. After unsuccessfully trying to reach Carlita on her cell phone, and then Angela on *her* cell, I collapsed into bed feeling extraordinarily exhausted. I wondered—until sleep overtook me—about the Anglo woman who liked flamingos.

In the morning I appeared at the Aerie, prepared for another day of subtle poking and prodding, when one of the other security guys not so gently told me I was to report to Madam Arquette's office immediately. That there was trouble was obvious, so I grimaced and made my way up through the building until I reached the penthouse office suite, unofficially referred to by us guards as The Nest. I rapped on the frosted glass double doors that separated Madam Arquette's world from the reality outside it.

The doors parted, humming open on motorized hinges.

I saw Josefina, standing near Madam Arquette's desk, her head down towards the floor. She wouldn't look at me, though Madam Arquette herself stared across the room with the malice of a diving falcon. The Madam was naked except for her layer of plumage, her breasts dappled with blues and purples.

"Come in, Mister Soto," said the Madam in her characteristic French-laced accent.

I entered, realizing that I'd never actually been in the Nest proper before. Three walls were nothing but glass that looked out on the smog and bustle of the city. To our west we could see the heaped metal skyscape of Los Angeles, baking nicely in the advancing morning sun. I had to tear myself away from the unexpectedly impressive view when the Madam cleared her throat and indicated a huge leather chair in front of her desk, a feather-coated hand flourishing artfully.

I slowly but purposefully took a seat.

"Monsieur Soto," said the Madam, "Josefina here was caught snooping into the master schedule. It is forbidden by contract for any employee to research or view the schedule of any other employee. Our clientele demand the strictest discretion. What do you suggest be done about this matter?"

"Madam," I said, "Josefina was acting purely under my direction. I take full responsibility for the breach of company directive."

Madam Arquette simply stared at me, then stood up from her stool—her wings resplendent with emerald and sapphire feathering—and walked around her desk to stand imposingly over me.

"You are privately investigating the death of Elvira," the Madam said.

"Yes," I replied.

"You realize that if word were to get out that client information had been leaked to either a security firm or the police, the Aerie would be ruined."

"Yes."

"I could even bring civil charges against you and Josefina both for grossly and negligently violating your contracts. What do you have to say about that?"

I raised my hands out to my side, palms up, and said, "You have to do what you feel is the right thing, Madam."

She stared down at me, her eyes brilliantly lit up with fury, then turned and walked quickly to the wall of windows that looked out over the city, her very-high platform heels making *click-click* sounds on the polished simulated wood flooring.

"Elvira was not the first girl to die here," the Madam said, as if talking to the view outside the Aerie's top floor. "Before you came to work for me, Monsieur Soto, I always managed to have the matter dispensed with discretely and at great legal difficulty. It was unfortunate what happened in those cases, but I've spent twenty years building this business up from nothing, and I was not going to allow a few mishaps to ruin everything."

"Her sister was murdered," I said.

"Yes I know that," said the Madam.

"And that means nothing to you?"

"Do you take me for an animal?" the Madam said, spinning to face me, her wings rustling with tension. I elected not to give the first answer that came to my mind.

"I take you for a very focused businesswoman who has perhaps allowed the bottom line to get in the way of certain perspectives, about the people who work for you."

She seemed to evaluate that response, a tongue running along the inside of a cheek.

"And if I have lost these perspectives, as you say, Monsieur, what do you propose be done about it?"

"Give me information on one person, someone who saw Elvira many times, then suddenly stopped."

"Josefina has told me about her. I know of whom you speak, and she is a client of the highest social caliber. There is no way possible she is involved in this."

"But she might be someone who can tell us who is involved," I said.

"And what will this client think, when you show up at her doorstep, playing the investigator? The Aerie has an iron-clad reputation in this city. Our clientele expect the utmost privacy. Even one exception could destroy us."

"And if I went to the Beverly Hills press, starting rumors that the Aerie allows killers to come and go on its premises, without prejudice?" I said. "What do you think that will do to your excellent reputation?"

Madam Arquette eyed me coldly. Then she turned to Josefina.

"Leave us. You will do no more on this matter, or I will throw you out. Say nothing. To anyone. Is that understood? My quarrel is with the Monsieur now."

Josefina walked quickly out of the room.

The Madam walked over and rested her buttocks on the edge of her frosted-glass desk.

"You are an older man. Experienced. Why do you do this for a strange girl?"

"Because someone has to do it," I answered.

"Why?"

"Because some things just have to matter more than other things, and sometimes you can't just turn away and make something disappear. Josefina couldn't leave it alone, because it's her sister."

"And you can't leave Josefina alone, because…are there benefits I am not aware of? Security personnel are not allowed to solicit from the staff. That too is a violation."

"Bite your tongue!" I snapped. "She's young enough to be my daughter. And if you had stopped cutting back on security staffing when I told you to, maybe Elvira would still be alive, and we wouldn't be having this conversation right now!"

For the first time, the Madam's eyes dropped to the floor.

"I do not celebrate Elvira's death, whatever else you may think of me."

"Then prove it," I said. "Give me what I need to keep working on this. If it goes nowhere, that's my problem. But I've got an old cop's hunch, and I can't move on it without your help. Come on, Madam, show me that the Aerie's vaunted reputation is about more than just money."

Her eyes stayed on the floor for a very long time. Then she circled back around to the other side of her desk, sat on her stool, pantomimed some commands to the computer, and waited while a piece of hardcopy spat out of a nearby slim-line printer.

The Madam handed the copy across to me.

"Get out of my office."

I looked at the paper, then popped up out of the chair.

"With pleasure. Good day, Madam Arquette."

✧

The Madam had been right. The Anglo lady who liked flamingos was of the old-money Beverly Hills upper crust. I still didn't have a real name, but I had an address and I had contact information. The split with her husband had not affected her lifestyle to any great degree. Both were from wealthy families, and she still maintained a significant estate, one I'd be hard-pressed to visit with any degree of subtlety. So I did what I thought best. I sent her an anonymous text with an address of a public library, and attached a picture of a flamingo to it. Then I waited at the Frances Howard Goldwyn branch for her arrival at the date and time specified.

I was not disappointed. Her designer women's suit and expensive sunglasses gave her away against the backdrop of working-class readers who lined the aisles and sat at the computer terminals. I was off in a corner, a hard-bound Audubon edition on *Phoenicopteridae* displayed prominently. I saw her before she saw me, but when she saw the cover on the book, she bee-lined over and sat down.

"Who are you, and what's happened to Elly?"

"I am a family friend," I said, keeping my voice low to match hers. "And I am very sorry to say that Elly is dead."

The woman's hand shot to her mouth, the small purse in her other hand nearly falling to the floor.

"My God!" she said, genuinely and horribly startled.

"I need your help," I continued. "I used to be a police officer, and I'm handling this matter privately for Elly's family. I was hoping you could tell me about some of the last conversations you had with Elly when she was at the Aerie. Did she seem afraid of anyone, the last few times you were with her?"

"No," said the woman, slowly removing her sunglasses and reaching for a handkerchief in her purse. Tears had begun to flow down her face.

"Did she say anything about anyone at work? Someone who might have been bothering her?"

"No," said the woman.

"Did you and Elly have any trouble? Maybe, a fight of some kind?"

"We weren't like that. Elly was…she was *pure*. And beautiful. More beautiful than anything or anyone I have ever seen. Graceful and poetic, yet young and playful in the way only…I don't think I can explain it, Mister…"

"Rodriguez," I said. "Of the Los Taltos firm, out of Thousand Oaks."

"I've never heard of them," she said.

"Not many people have. We're small, because it allows us to be discrete. Please know that anything you tell me today is in the strictest confidence."

She nodded, blowing quietly into the handkerchief.

"So there was nothing amiss?" I said. "Nothing at all?"

"No."

"Then what stopped you from seeing Elly last month?"

The woman blew her nose one more time, and collected herself.

"I did it for Elly's sake. I could tell I was falling in love. Literally and truly. I was going to cross lines that would destroy Elly if I didn't take myself away. And I couldn't live with that. So one day I simply stopped making appointments."

"And you never saw her again after that?"

"No."

I sat back in my chair, trying to figure out what to ask next.

"Mister Rodriguez, who would hurt that girl?"

"I don't know," I said honestly.

We sat for several moments, the woman staring at the tabletop. Then she looked up at me, her red eyes mournful.

"There *is* one thing," she said.

"Yes?"

"Last time I was with Elly, she seemed distracted. Bothered. I asked her what was wrong, and she said her brother had called her from East Los Angeles, asking her to come home. She said they'd had an argument on the phone, then she'd laughed it off like it was no big deal. She and her brother had never gotten along, or so she said."

I mentally filed this away and waited for the woman to continue.

When she didn't, I finally stood up.

"You've been helpful," I said. "If you remember anything else, please contact me using this text address."

I handed her a plain white card with a number on it.

"Again, strictest confidence," I assured her.

She took the card and put her sunglasses back on.

"Mister Rodriguez," she said.

"Yes?"

"If you ever do find out what happened, please let me know?"

"I promise," I said. And meant it.

✧

Josefina's apartment was even messier than the last time.

"Antonio and Elvira never argued," she said as she handed me a cup of hot, lightly-sugared coffee. It was early morning, and she was just going to bed, while I was just getting ready to head back to the Aerie.

"The woman said they did," I told her. "And you told me that you thought there was no telling how much the family might hate you after Elvira came out and went Special."

"Yes, but I expected them to hate *me*, not her."

"Would they have hated either one of you enough to kill?"

"I could never think that…"

"But?"

"But the last time Papa and I spoke, he said I was dead to him."

"What about your brother?"

"Antonio and Papa always got along. Like father, like son."

"Where is Antonio now?"

"He left home to find work on the farms."

"Do you have an address?"

"No, but I'm sure my parents do."

"Then it's time for me to talk to your parents."

"*No!*"

"Their daughter is dead. The city has already sent the official notification. If my daughter had died like that, I'd sure as hell want someone to tell me why, or who had done it."

"No," she insisted.

"Josefina, do you really want to find out who killed your little sister?"

"Yes," she said.

"Then let me finish this."

✧

The barrios of East L.A. weren't a hell of a lot different from the barrios of Oakland. Row upon row of mid-20th century cheap housing that had slowly been churning through the hands of the poor over the last hundred years. The little bungalow I stopped at was a near carbon copy of the house where I'd grown up, and though they were older, the Aguilars were about what my mom and dad would have been—had my father not died young and left Mama to struggle in solitude.

Taking me for a city official—I neither confirmed nor denied that identity—the Aguilars welcomed me into the front room and offered me a cold glass of water.

"Never should have let her go," said Papa Aguilar, when I brought up the subject of Elvira. "It was bad enough when her older sister turned on the family."

"You had a falling out with Elvira's older sister?" I said innocently.

"She is a pervert!" Papa Aguilar said. "Ran off and turned herself into an animal who screws rich gringos. Disgusting!"

I swirled the icy water around in the scratched acrylic tumbler they'd given me.

"I'm sorry that things didn't turn out better for you and your daughters."

"You make it sound so neat and clean," he snorted.

Mama Aguilar placed a firm hand on his bicep, gave him a knowing look.

"We have lost both our daughters," Mama said. "Please forgive us if we are not as polite about it as we should be."

"Understandable," I said, and then took a swallow.

"At least we still have Antonio," Mama said.

"Your son?"

"Yes, he's been home from Santa Clara for a few months now. He's earned some money, now we're going to help him go back to school."

"What was he doing in Santa Clara?"

Mama led me into the kitchen, where she pulled a mason jar off the top of the refrigerator. It was filled with a viscous, golden substance. "Bee-keeping."

It took all my effort not to do a double-take.

Mama handed me the jar of honey, and I hefted it experimentally, choosing my next words very, very carefully.

"Did the coroner tell you exactly what caused Elvira's death?"

"Does it matter?" said Papa. "I got the notice. I crumpled it up and burned it without needing to read the fine print. Elvira was gone the moment she chose to follow her sister."

I carefully replaced the mason jar on top of the fridge.

"Mister Aguilar," I said, "did Antonio ever go visit either of his sisters after he came home?"

"No," he said.

"Are you sure?"

"Yes…Well, I can't imagine that he did." Papa's eyes narrowed. "What are you getting at?"

"If you had read the full text of the coroner's findings, you'd know that Elvira died because she'd been injected with *bee venom*."

Both of them froze in place, eyes narrowing at me, then slowly widening in comprehension.

"*La policía*…" Papa Aguilar breathed.

There was a slam as the back door opened and closed. Clomping footsteps came up the stairs, and a trim young man appeared at the other doorway to the kitchen.

Mama and Papa stared at me for an instant longer, then looked at their son, then back at me. Antonio's smile dropped, and he stared at me too.

"What's going on?" he said. "Who is this?"

"Rodriguez," I said. "I'm from the city. I need to talk to you about Elvira."

Maybe it was the way I'd said it. Maybe it was the fact that I still had the military-cropped haircut I'd kept since my Army days. Maybe he'd noticed the bulge of the stun gun I had in a holster tucked into the pit of my arm, under my suit jacket. Whatever it was, I never had a chance to get in another word before three things happened simultaneously:

Antonio, spinning and running back down the steps.

Mama screaming, "Antonio, *no!*"

Papa screaming, "*La policía!*"

I flew past the Aguilars and down the stairs, pleased that I could still be quick when I had to be. He never bothered to close the door as he sprinted across the patio, around the detached garage, and down the filthy, narrow street beyond. I skidded around the corner—my loafers were not quite as good on concrete as his athletic shoes—then shouted his name at the back of his head as he raced for the nearest intersection. I followed, sweating and cursing, but managing to keep an eye on him as I went around the corner. I saw him dodge two cars crossing to the other side, and kept running for the next intersection further south. I pulled the stunner out and kept pumping arms and legs, feeling the muscle memory exhilaration of pursuit. Just like old times. I wasn't the police, but I wasn't going to let Elvira's killer go, brother or no brother.

We crossed an alleyway, then crossed another street headed for a larger thoroughfare. People stopped or stepped out of our way as I ran, still shouting his name.

He stopped and turned once, just long enough to glare at me—the whites of his eyes large. Then he started running again, head still turned.

Across the thoroughfare, against traffic.

Cars skidded and honked as he slipped between two lanes.

The tow truck never saw him.

But I did, and it was too late.

☼

Antonio Aguilar lived just long enough to give a full confession in the hospital, before he passed. I stayed well clear of the Aguilars, figuring they'd be incited to murder if they spotted me. Police at the hospital knew me, and let me loiter around out of respect for the old days.

I was shocked when I saw Josefina arrive. Eyes darted to her, and stayed on her as she walked carefully through the hospital hallway, hands pensively clutching a purse in front of her as she padded along in canvas flats and a sensible, modest dress, holes cut in the back for her wings. She saw me, but didn't stop to say anything. I kept an eye on her as she approached her brother's room, spoke to the cops at the door, then passed inside.

Ten minutes later both she and her parents slowly walked out. All three of them appeared to be crying heavily. Josefina tried to hug her father. His arms just hung limply at his sides. When she tried to hug her mother, the older woman shakily reached her arms around her daughter, then squeezed with tentative enthusiasm.

The Aguilars went back into their son's room, and Josefina came back in my direction.

This time she did stop.

I stared up at her face, damp green fathers and all.

"I'm sorry," I said.

"We are all sorry," she said.

"I didn't mean for him to get hit."

"I know."

"I should have just let him run away."

"I do not think there was anywhere far enough for him to get away from the shame he felt, at Mama and Papa knowing what he had done for them."

"*For* them?"

"Papa said that Antonio said he did it for the honor of the family."

"So why didn't he try to kill both of you?"

"I don't know. Maybe after he saw what he'd done to his little sister, he lost his nerve. Papa is sick with himself. After I left home and joined the Aerie, Papa railed endlessly about what a disgrace I was, and then when Elvira left to join me...he railed against us both—how we had forever shamed the family. I think he didn't realize that Antonio would take it as much to heart as he did. Papa almost feels like he's the one who killed her. And Antonio now too."

I looked past Josefina's shoulder, to the shrinking old couple slumped against each other as they walked painfully down the opposite end of the corridor.

"What will they do now?"

"Bury Antonio and Elvira."

"And what will *you* do now?"

She stared at the purse in her hands, her fists balled around the straps.

"I will go back to work," she said.

I raised an eyebrow.

"What else can I do?" she said. "I cannot go home, and I don't have the money yet that I need to move on."

I cleared my throat uncomfortably, and scratched at my scalp.

"There are other things—"

"No, Señor Soto," she said firmly. "It was my choice to become Special, and it is my choice to finish my plan. My sister would have wanted that, even if my family did not."

"Will you be speaking with them again?"

"I don't know," she said. "I don't think so."

"Give it time," I said. "Give your Papa time. He will need you."

"He still partially blames me for all of this."

"Yes, and when he's a couple of years older and closer to his own grave, he will look at his pictures of you when you were a little girl, and he will wonder why he let himself come to hate you. Please, don't lock that door again."

She stared down at me, this time raising one of her own eyebrows.

"Fraternal compassion, Señor Soto?"

"More like one poor, stupid father apologizing for another poor, stupid father."

She regarded me for many quiet seconds, then she reached down to take up one of my hands in her marvelously soft one.

"*Por favor?*" she said.

"*Por favor,*" I said, squeezing her hand.

She let me escort her out of the hospital, and together we drove back to the Aerie.

Original (First) Publication
Copyright © 2013 by Brad R. Torgersen

COMING SOON FROM PHOENIX PICK

A NEW STELLAR GUILD BOOK

by

BRAD R. TORGERSEN
M. J. HARRINGTON
&
LARRY NIVEN

On sale November 30th, 2013

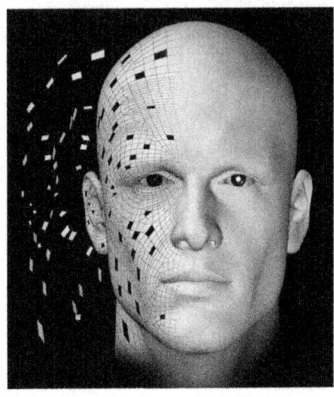

David Gerrold is a Hugo and Nebula winner, a bestselling novelist, and a television and movie writer. His Star Trek *episode, "The Trouble With Tribbles," was voted the most popular episode of that series.*

Wouldn't you love a pet dinosaur? I would. A dinosaur would make a great pet. Soft, cuddly, useful....

REX

by David Gerrold

"Daddy! The tyrannosaur is loose again! He jumped the fence."

Jonathan Filltree replied with a single word, one which he didn't want his eight-year-old daughter to hear. He punched the *save* key on his keyboard, kicked back his chair and headed toward the basement stairs with obvious annoyance. He resented these constant interruptions in the flow of his work.

"Hurry, Daddy!" Jill shouted again from the basement door. "He's chasing the stegosaurs! He's gonna get Steggy!"

"I warned you this was going to happen—" Filltree said angrily, grabbing the long-handled net off the wall. "No! Wait here," he snapped.

"That's not fair!" cried Jill, following him down the bare wooden stairs. "I didn't know he was going to get this big!"

"He's a meat-eater. The stegosaurs and the apatosaurs and all the others look like lunch to him. Get back upstairs, Jill!"

Filltree stopped at the bottom and looked slowly around the basement that his wife had demanded he convert into a miniature dinosaur kingdom for their spoiled daughter. Hot yellow lights bathed the cellar in a prehistoric ambience. A carboniferous smell permeated everything. He wrinkled his nose in distaste. For some reason, it was worse than usual.

The immediate problem was obvious. Most of the six-inch stegosaurs had retreated to the high slopes that butted up against the north wall, where they milled about nervously. Their bright yellow and orange colors made them easy to see. Quickly, he counted. All three of the calves and their mother were okay; so were the other two females; but they were all cheeping in distress. He spotted Fred and Cyril, but Steggy was not with the others. The two remaining males were emitting rasping peeps of agitation; and they kept making angry charging motions downslope.

Filltree followed the direction of their agitation. "Damn!" he said, spotting the two-foot-high tyrannosaur. Rex was ripping long strips of flesh off the side of the fallen Steggy and gulping them hungrily down. Already he was streaked with blood. His long tail lashed furiously in the air, acting as a counterweight as he bent to his kill. He ripped and tore, then rose up on his haunches, glancing around quickly and checking for danger with sharp bird-like motions. He jerked his head upward to gulp the latest bloody gobbet deeper into his mouth, then gulped a second time to swallow it. He grunted and roared, then lowered his whole body forward to again bury his muzzle deep in gore.

"Oh, Daddy! He's killed Steggy!"

"I told you to wait upstairs! A tyrannosaur can be dangerous when he's feeding!"

"But he's killed Steggy—!"

"Well, I'm sorry. There's nothing to do now but wait until he finishes and goes torpid." Filltree put the net down, leaning it against the edge of the table. The entire room was filled with an elaborate waist-high miniature landscape, through which an improbable mix of Cretaceous and Jurassic creatures prowled. The glass fences at the edges of the tables were all at least 36 inches high, and mildly electrified to keep the various creatures safely enclosed. Until they'd added Rex to the huge terrarium, they'd had one of the finest collections in Westchester, with over a hundred dinos prowling through the miniature forests. And every spring, the new births among the various herbivores usually added five to ten adorable little calves to their herds.

Now, the ranks of their menagerie had been reduced to only a few light-footed stegosaurs, some lumbering apatosaurs, two armored ankylosaurs, the belligerent triceratops herd, and the chirruping hadrosaurs. Most of those had survived only because their favorite grazing grounds were at one end of the huge U-shaped environment, and Rex's corral was all the way around at the opposite end. Rex wandered around the herbivore grounds only until he found something to attack. Like most of the mini-dinos, Rex didn't have a lot of gray matter to work with; he almost always attacked the first moving object he saw. In the six months since his installation in what Filltree had once believed was a secure corral, Rex had more than decimated the population of the Pleasant Avenue Dinosaur Zoo. He was now escaping regularly once or twice a week.

Slowly, Filltree worked his way around the table to the corral, examining all the fences carefully to see where and how the tyrannosaur might have broken through the barriers. He had thought for sure that the 30-inch-high rock-surfaced polyfoam bricks he had installed last week would finally keep the carnivore from escaping again to terrorize the more placid herbivores. Obviously, he had been wrong.

Filltree frowned as he studied the thick blockade. It had not been broken through in any place, nor had the tyrant-lizard dug a hole underneath it. The rocks were not chewed, but they were badly scratched in several places. Filltree leaned across the table for a closer look. "Mm," he said.

"What is it, Daddy? Tell me!" Jill demanded impatiently.

He pointed. The sides and tops of the bricks were sharply gouged. Rex had leapt up onto the top of the wall, surveyed the opposite side, and leapt down to feed. Judging from the numerous marks carved into the surface, today's outing was clearly not the first. "See. Rex can leap the fence. And that probably explains the mysterious disappearance of the last coelophysis too. This is getting ridiculous, Jill. I can't afford this anymore. We're going to have to find a new home for Rex."

"Daddy, no!" Jill became immediately belligerent. "Rexy is part of our family!"

"Rexy is eating up all the other dinosaurs, Jill. That's not very family-like."

"We can buy new ones."

"No, we can't. Dinosaurs cost money, and I'm not buying any new animals until we get rid of him. I'm sorry, kiddo; but I told you this wasn't going to work."

"Daddy, pleeeaase—! Rexy is my favorite!"

Jonathan Filltree took his daughter by the hand and led her back around to where Rexy was still gorging himself on the now unrecognizable remains of the much smaller stegosaur. "Look, Jill. This is going to keep happening, sweetheart. Rexy is getting too big for us to keep. It's all that fresh beef that you and Mommy keep feeding him. Remember what the dinosaur-doctor said? It accelerates his growth. But you didn't listen. Now, none of the other dinosaurs can escape him or even fight back. It isn't fair to them. And it isn't fair to Rexy either to keep him in a place where he won't be happy."

That last part was a complete fabrication on his part, and Filltree knew it even as he spoke it. If Rexy was capable of happiness, then he was probably very happy to be living in a place where he was the only carnivore and all of the prey animals were too small to resist his attacks. According to the genetic specifications, however, Rexy and the other mini-dinosaurs would have had to borrow the synapses necessary to complete a thought. Calling them stupid would have been a compliment.

"But—but, you can't! He'll miss me!"

Filltree sighed with exhaustion. He already knew how this argument was going to end. Jill would go to Mommy, and Mommy would promise to talk to Daddy. And then Mommy would sulk for two weeks because Daddy wanted her to break a promise to their darling little girl. And finally, he'd give in just to get a little peace and quiet again so he could get some work done. But he had to try anyway. He dropped to one knee in front of his daughter and put his hands on her shoulders. "We'll find a good place for him, Jilly, I promise." And even as he said it, he knew it was a promise he'd never be able to keep.

He knew he wouldn't be able to sell Rex. He'd seen the ads in the Recycler. There was no market for tyrant-lizards anymore—of any size. And Rexy was more than two feet high, and rapidly approaching the legal maximum of 36 inches. Rexy required ten pounds of fresh meat a week; he'd only eat dry kibble when the alternative was starvation. They still had half a bag of Purina Dinosaur Chow left from when they'd first bought him. The dinosaur would go for almost a week without eating before he'd touch the stuff, and even then he'd only pick at it.

Nor did Filltree think he'd even be able to give the creature away. The zoo didn't want any more tyrannosaurs, of *any* size. They were expensive to feed and they already had over a hundred of the little monsters, spitting and hissing and roaring—and occasionally devouring the smaller of their brethren.

At one time it had been fashionable to own your own miniature T. Rex; but the fad had passed, the tyrant-lizards had literally outgrown their welcome, the price of meat had risen again (due to the Brazilian droughts), and a lot of people—wearying of the smells and the bother—had finally dropped their pets off at the zoo or turned them over to the animal shelters. Because they were protected under the Artificial Species Act, the cost of putting a mini-dino down was almost prohibitive. Some thoughtless individuals had tried abandoning their hungry dinosaurs in the wild, not realizing that the animals were genetically traceable. The fines, according to the newspaper reports, had been astonishing.

"I promise you, Jilly, we'll find a place for Rexy where he'll be happy and we can visit him every week, okay?"

Jill shook his hands off, folded her arms in front of her, and turned away. "No!" she decided. "You're not giving Rexy away! He's my dinosaur. I picked him out and you said I could have him."

Filltree gave up. He turned back to the diorama. Rexy had stopped gorging himself and was now standing torpidly near his kill. Filltree grabbed the metal-mesh net and quickly brought it down over the dinosaur. Rexy struggled in the mesh, but not wildly. Filltree had learned a long time ago to wait until the tyrant-king had finished eating before trying to return him to his corral. He swung the net across the table, taking care to hold the dinosaur well away from him and as high as he could. Jill tried to reach up to grab the handle of the net, and instinctively he yanked it up out of her reach—but for just a moment, the temptation flickered across his mind to let her actually grab Rexy. Then he'd see how much she loved the little monster.

But…if he did, he'd never hear the end of it, he knew that—and besides, there was the danger that the mini-dino might actually do some serious damage. So he ignored Jill's yelps of protest and returned Rexy to his own kingdom. Temporarily at least. Then he went back and scooped up the bloody remains of poor Steggy and wordlessly tossed that into Rexy's domain as well.

"Aren't we going to have a funeral for Steggy?"

"No, we're not. We've had enough funerals. All it does is annoy the tyrannosaur. Let Rexy have his meal. It'll keep him from jumping the fence for another week or two. Maybe. I hope. Come on. I told you to stay upstairs. And you didn't listen. Just for that, no dessert—"

"I'm gonna tell Mommy!"

"You do that," he sighed tiredly, following her up the stairs—realizing that of all the animals in the house, the one he resented most was the one who was supposed to know better. She was eight and a half years old—at that age, they were supposed to be almost human, weren't they? He felt exhausted. He knew he wasn't going to get any more work done today. Not after Jilly finished crying to Mommy about Daddy threatening to get rid of poor little Rexy. "Rexy didn't mean to do anything wrong," he mimed to himself. "He was hungry because Daddy forgot to feed him last night."

Filltree both hated and envied Rexy. Jill gave all her attention and affection to the dinosaur, speaking to Daddy only when demanding something else for her collection of creatures. And Mommy was another one—she paid more attention to preparing the little tyrant's meals than to his. The dinosaur got fresh beef or lamb three times a week. He got soy-burgers.

For a long while, he'd been considering the idea of a separation—maybe even a divorce. He'd even gone so far as to log onto the Legal-Net website and crunch the numbers on their divorce-judgment simulator. Although Legal-Net refused to guarantee the accuracy of its legal software, lest they expose themselves to numerous lawsuits, the divorce-judgment simulator used the same Judicial Engine as the Federal Divorce Court, and was unofficially rated at ninety percent accuracy in its extrapolations.

All he wanted was a tiny little condo somewhere up in the hills, a place where he could sit and work and stare out the window in peace without having to think about tyrants, either the two-foot kind or the three-foot kind. Tyrant lizards, tyrant children— the only difference he could see was that the tyrant lizard only ate your heart out once and then it was done.

According to the simulator, he could afford the condo; that wasn't the problem. *Unfortunately*, also according to Legal-Net's Judicial Engine he could not afford the simultaneous maintenance of Joyce and Jill. The simulator gave him several options, none of them workable from his point of view. A divorce would give him freedom, but it would be prohibitively expensive. A separation would give him peace and quiet, but it wouldn't give him freedom— and he'd still have to keep up the payments on Joyce and Jill's various expensive habits.

Grunting in annoyance, he pulled the heavy carry cage out of the garage and lugged it awkwardly back down the basement stairs. Jilly followed him the whole way, whining and crying. He slipped easily into his robot-daddy mode, disconnecting his emotions and refusing to respond to even her most provocative assaults. "I don't love you anymore. You promised me. I'm not your daughter anymore. I'm gonna tell Mommy. I don't like you. You can go to hell."

"Don't tempt me. I might enjoy the change," he muttered in reply to the last remark.

Back downstairs, Filltree discovered that Rexy had not only finished his meal; he was already standing on top of the rock barrier again, lashing his tail furiously and studying the realm beyond. He looked like he was preparing to return to his hunting. At the opposite end of the room, the remaining stegosaurs were mooing agitatedly.

Rexy spotted them then. He turned sharply to glare across the intervening distance, cocking his head with birdlike motions to study them first with one baleful black eye, then the other. Perhaps it was just the shape of his head, but his expression seemed ominous and calculating. The creature's eyes were filled with hatred for the soft pink mammals who restricted him, as well as insatiable hunger for the taste of human flesh. Filltree wondered why he'd ever wanted a tyrannosaur in the first place. Rexy hissed in defiance, arching his neck forward and opening his mouth wide to reveal ranks of knife-sharp little teeth.

Filltree frowned. Was it his imagination or had the little tyrannosaur grown another six inches in the last six minutes? The creature seemed a lot bigger than he remembered him being. Of course, he'd been so angry at the little monster that he hadn't really looked at him closely for a while.

"He's awfully big. Have you been feeding him again?" he demanded of his daughter.

"No!" Jill said, indignantly. "We've only been giving him leftovers. Mommy said it's silly to waste food."

"In addition to his regular meals?"

"But, Daddy, we can't let him *starve*—"

"He's in no danger of starving. No wonder he's gotten so voracious. You've accelerated his appetite as well as his growth. I told you not to do that. Well…it's over now. We should have done this a long time ago." Filltree picked up the net and brought it around slowly, approaching Rexy from his blind side, taking great care not to alarm the two-foot tyrant king. The thing was getting large enough to be dangerous.

Rexy hissed and bit at the net, but did not try to run. Tyrannosaurs did not have it in their behavior to run. They attacked. They ate. If they couldn't do one, they did the other. If they couldn't do either, they waited until they could do one or the other. The creatures had the single-mindedness of lawyers.

Working quickly, Filltree caught Rexy in the net and swung him up and over the glass fence of the terrarium. He lowered the dinosaur into the open carry cage, turned the net over in one swift movement to tumble the creature out, lifted it away, and kicked the lid shut. He latched it rapidly before Rexy could begin bumping and thumping at it with his head. Jill watched, wide-eyed and resentful. She had stopped crying, but she still wore her cranky-face.

"What are you going to do with him?" she demanded.

"Well, he's going to spend tonight in the service porch where it's warm. Tomorrow, I'm going to take him to…the dinosaur farm, where he'll be a lot happier." To the animal shelter, where they'll put him down…for a hefty fee.

"What dinosaur farm? I never heard of any dinosaur farm."

"Oh, it's brand new. It's in…Florida. It's for dinosaurs like Rexy who've gotten too big to live in Connecticut. I'll put him on an airplane and send him straight to Florida. And we can visit him next year when we go to Disney World, okay?"

"You're lying—" Jill accused, but there was an edge of uncertainty in her tone. "When are we going to Disney World?"

"When you learn to stop whining. Probably when you're forty or fifty." Filltree grunted as he lifted the carry cage from behind. He could feel its center of gravity shifting in his arms as Rexy paced unhappily within, hissing and spitting and complaining loudly about being confined. The little tyrant was not happy. Jill complained in unison. *Neither* of the little tyrants were happy.

Somehow Filltree got the heavy box up the stairs and into the service porch. "He'll be fine there till tomorrow, Jill." In an uncharacteristic act of concession, he said, "You can feed him all the leftovers you want tonight. The harm has already been done. And you can say goodbye to him tomorrow before you go to school, okay?"

Jill grumped. "You're not fair!" she accused. She stomped loudly out of the service porch and upstairs to her bedroom for a four-hour sulk, during which time she would gather her strength for the daughter of all tantrums. Filltree waited until after he heard the slam of her door, then exhaled loudly, making a horsey sound with his lips. Considering the amount of agita produced, he wondered if he'd locked up the right animal.

Dinner was the usual resentful tableau. The servitors wheeled in, laid food on the table, waited respectfully, wheeled back, then removed the plates again. His wife glared across the soup at him. His daughter pouted over the salad. Not a word was said during the fish course. Instead of meat, there was soy-burger in silence again. Filltree had decided not to speak at all if he could possibly avoid it. Joyce couldn't start chewing at him if he didn't give her an opportunity.

Idly, he wondered how much meat it would take to accelerate Rexy's growth to six feet tall. The idea of Rexy stripping the flesh from Joyce's bones and gulping it hungrily down gave him an odd thrill of pleasure.

"What are you smiling about?" Joyce demanded abruptly.

"I wasn't smiling—" he said, startled at having been caught daydreaming.

"Don't lie to me. I *saw* you!"

"I'm sorry, dear. It must have been a gas pain. You know how soy-burger disagrees with me."

He realized too late his mistake. Now that the conversational gauntlet had been flung, picked up and flung back, Joyce was free to expand the realm of the discussion into any area she chose.

She chose. "You're being very cruel and unfair, you know that," she accused. "Your daughter loves that animal. It's her *favorite*."

Filltree considered the obvious response: "That animal gets more hamburger than I do. I'm the breadwinner in this family. I'd like to be treated as well as Rexy." He decided against it; that way lay domestic violence and an expensive reconciliation trip to Jamaica. At the very least. Instead, he nodded and agreed with her. "You're right. It is cruel and unfair. And yes, I know how much Jill loves Rexy." He tasted the green beans. They were underdone. Joyce had readjusted the servitors again.

"Well, I don't see why we can't rebuild the terrarium."

"It isn't the terrarium," Filltree pointed out quietly. "It's Rexy. He's been accelerated. Nothing we do is going to contain him anymore." He resisted the temptation to remind her that he had warned her about this very possibility. "If he gets any bigger, he's going to start being a hazard. I don't think we should take the risk, do you?" He inclined his head meaningfully in Jill's direction.

Joyce looked thwarted. Jonathan had hit her with an argument she couldn't refute. She pretended to concede the point while she considered her next move. Perhaps it was just the shape of her new coiffure, but her expression seemed ominous and calculating. Filltree wondered why he'd ever wanted to marry her in the first place.

His wife patted the tinted hairs at the back of her neck and smiled gently. "Well, I don't know how you intend to make it up to your daughter…but I hope you have something appropriate figured out." Both she and Jill looked to him expectantly.

Filltree met their gaze directly. He returned her plastic smile with one of equal authenticity. "Gee, I can't think of anything to take Rexy's place."

Joyce tightened her lips ever so delicately. "Well, I can. And I'm sure Jill can too, can't you sweetheart…?" Joyce looked to Jill. Jill smiled. They both looked to Daddy again.

So. That was it. Filltree recognized the ploy. Retreat on one battlefield, only to gain on another. Jamaica appeared inescapable. He considered his options. Option. Dead end. "You've already made the booking, haven't you?" His artificial smile widened even more artificially.

"I see," his wife said curtly. "Is that what you think of me…?" He recognized the tone immediately. If he said anything at all—*anything*—she would escalate to tactical nukes within three sentences. The *worst* thing he could say would be, "Now, sweetheart—"

Instead, he opened his mouth and said, "We can't go, in any case. I have research to do in Denver." This time, he amazed even himself. Denver? Where had *that* idea come from? "I'll be gone for a month. Maybe two. At least. I'm sorry if this ruins your plans, dear. I would have told you sooner, but I was hoping I wouldn't have to go. Unfortunately…I just heard this afternoon that no one else is available for this job." He spread his hands wide in a gesture of helplessness.

Joyce's mouth tightened almost to invisibility—then reformed itself in a deliberate smile. "I see," she said, in a voice like sugared acid. She refused to lose her temper in front of Jill. It was a bad role model, she insisted. She had declared that eight years ago, and in the past five, Jonathan Filltree had amused himself endlessly by seeing how close to the edge he could push her before she toppled over into incoherence. Tonight—with Denver—he had scored a grand slam home run, knocking it all the way out of the park and bringing in all three runners on base. "We'll talk about this later," she said with finality, her way of admitting that she was outflanked and that she had no choice but to retreat and regroup her energies while she reconnoitered the terrain. She would be back. But for the moment, the conversation was temporarily suspended.

"I'll be up late," Filltree said genially. "I have a report to finish. And I have to pack tonight too." He took a healthy bite of soy-burger. It was suddenly delicious.

Joyce excused herself to escort Jill upstairs to get her ready for bed. "But, Mommy, don't I get dessert…" the child wailed.

"Not while your Daddy is acting like this—"

Jonathan Filltree spent the rest of the evening, working quietly, almost enjoying himself, anticipating what it would be like to have a little quiet in the house without the regular interruption of Rexy's intolerable predations. If only he could get rid of Jill and Joyce as easily.

Filltree wondered if he should sleep on the couch in his office tonight, but then decided that would be the same as admitting a) that there had been a battle, and b) he had lost. He would not concede Joyce one inch of territory. Before heading upstairs, he took a look in at Rexy.

The tyrannosaur was worrying at the left side wall of the carry cage, scratching at it with first one foot, then the other, trying to carve an opening for itself. It bumped its head ferociously against the side; already the thick polymoid surface was deformed and even a little cracked. Filltree squatted down to get a closer look at the box, running his hands over the strained material. He decided that the damage inflicted was not sufficient to be worrisome; the carry cage would hold together for one more day. And one more day was all he needed.

He headed upstairs to bed, smiling to himself. It was a small victory, but a victory nonetheless. The knowledge that he'd be paying for it for months to come didn't detract from the satisfaction he took in knowing that he'd finally held the line on something. Today, Rexy; tomorrow, the soy-burger.

He was awakened by screaming—unfamiliar and agonized. Something was crashing through the kitchen. He heard the clattering of utensils. Joyce was sitting up in bed beside him, screaming herself, and clawing at his arm. "Do something!" she cried.

"Stay here!" he demanded. "See to Jill!" Wearing only his silk boxers, and carrying a cracked hockey stick as his weapon, he went charging down the stairs. The screaming was getting worse.

A male voice was raging, "Goddammit! Get it off of me! Help! Help! Anyone!" This was followed by the sound of someone battering at something with something. High-pitched shrieks of reptilian rage punctuated the blows.

Filltree burst through the kitchen door to see a man rolling back and forth across the floor—a youngish-looking man, skinny and dirty, in bloody T-shirt and blue jeans. Rexy had his mouth firmly attached to the burglar's right arm. He hung on with ferocious determination, even as the intruder swung and battered the creature at the floor, the walls, the stove. Again and again. The screaming went on and on. Filltree didn't know whether to strike at the burglar or at the dinosaur. The man had been bitten severely on both legs, and across his stomach as well. A ragged strip of flesh hung open. His shirt was soaked with blood. Gobbets of red were flying everywhere; the kitchen was spattered like an explosion.

The man saw Filltree then. "Get your goddamn dinosaur off of me!" he demanded angrily, as if it were Filltree's fault that he had been attacked.

That decided Filltree. He began striking the man with the hockey stick, battering him ineffectively about the head and shoulders. That didn't work—he couldn't get in close enough. He grabbed a frying pan and whanged the hapless robber sideways across the forehead. The man grunted in surprise, then slumped to the floor with a groan, no longer able to defend himself against Rexy's predacious assault. The tyrant-lizard began feeding. He ripped off a long strip of flesh from the fallen robber's arm. The man tried to resist, he flailed weakly, but he had neither strength nor consciousness. The dinosaur was undeterred. Rexy fed unchecked.

Behind him, Joyce was screaming. Jill was shrieking, "Do something! Daddy, he's hurting Rexy!"

Filltree's humanity reasserted itself then. He had to stop the beast before it killed the hapless man; but he couldn't get to the net. It was still in the service porch—and he couldn't get past Rex. The creature hissed and spit at him. It lashed its tail angrily, as if daring Filltree to make the attempt. As if saying, "This kill is mine!"

Filltree held out the frying pan in front of him, swinging it back and forth like a shield. The small tyrant-king followed it with its baleful black eyes. Still roaring its defiance, it snapped and bit at the frying pan. Its teeth slid helplessly off the shining metal surface. Filltree whacked the creature hard. It blinked, stunned. He swung the frying pan again and, reflexively, the dinosaur stepped back; but as the utensil swept past, it stepped right back in, biting and snapping. Filltree recognized the behavior.

The beast was acting as if it were in a fight with another predator over its kill.

Filltree swung harder and more directly, this time not to drive the creature back, but to actually hit it and hurt it badly. Rexy leapt backward, shrieking in fury. Filltree stepped in quickly, brandishing the frying pan, triumphantly driving the two-foot dinosaur back and back toward the service porch. As soon as Rexy was safely in the confines of the service porch, screaming in the middle of the broken remains of the carry cage, Filltree slammed the door shut and latched it—something went thump from the other side. The noise was punctuated with a series of angry cries. The door thumped a second time and then a third. Filltree waited, frying pan at the ready…

At last, Rexy's frantic screeching ebbed. Instead, there began a slow steady scratching at the bottom of the door.

When Filltree turned around again, two uniformed police officers were relievedly reholstering their pistols. He hadn't even heard them come in. "Is that your dinosaur, sir?"

Shaken, Filltree managed to nod.

"Y'know, there are laws against letting carnivores that size run free," said the older one.

"We'd have shot him if you hadn't been in the way," said the younger officer.

For a moment, Filltree felt a pang of regret. He looked at the fallen burglar. There was blood flowing freely all over the floor. The man had rolled over on his side, clutching his stomach, but he was motionless now, and very very pale. "Is he going to make it—?"

The older officer was bending to examine the robber. "It depends on the speed of the ambulance."

The younger cop took Filltree aside; she lowered her voice to a whisper. "You want to hope he doesn't make it. If he lives, he could file a very nasty lawsuit against you. We'll tell the driver to take his time getting to the E.R. …."

He looked at the woman in surprise. She nodded knowingly. "You don't need any more trouble. I think we can wrap this one up tonight." She glanced around the room. "It looks to me like the burglar tried to steal your dinosaur. But the cage didn't hold and the creature attacked him. Is that what happened?"

Filltree realized the woman was trying to do him a favor. He nodded in hasty agreement. "Yes, exactly."

"That's a mini-rex, right?" she asked, glancing meaningfully at the door.

"Uh-huh."

"Lousy pets. Great guard-animals. Do yourself a favor. If you're going to leave him running loose at night, get yourself a permit. It won't cost you too much, and it'll protect you against a lawsuit if anyone else tries something stupid."

"Oh, yes—I'll take care of that first thing in the morning, thank you."

"Good. Your wife and kid know to be careful? Those Rexys can't tell the difference between friend and foe, you know—"

"Oh, yes. They know to be *very* careful."

Later, after the police had left, after he had calmed down Joyce and Jill, after he had cleaned up the kitchen, after he had had a chance to think, Jonathan Filltree thoughtfully climbed the stairs again.

"I've made a decision," he said to his shaken wife and tearful daughter. They were huddled together in the master bedroom. "We're going to keep Rexy. If I'm going to be in Denver for two months, then you're going to need every protection possible."

"Do you really mean that, Daddy?"

Filltree nodded. "It just isn't fair for me to go away and leave you and Mommy undefended. I'm going to convert the service porch into a big dinosaur kennel, just for Rexy. Good and strong. And you can feed him all the leftovers you want."

"Really?"

"It's a reward," Filltree explained, "because Rexy did such a good job of protecting us tonight. We should give him lots and lots of hamburger too, because that's his favorite. But you have to promise me something, Jill—"

"I will."

"You must *never* open the kennel door without Mommy's permission, do you understand?"

"I won't," Jill promised insincerely.

Turning back to Joyce, Filltree added, "I promise, I'll finish up my work in Denver as quickly as possible. But if they need me to stay longer, will that be okay with you?"

Joyce shook her head. "I want you to get that thing out of the house tonight."

"No, dear—" Filltree insisted. "Rexy's a member of our family now. He's earned his place at the table." He climbed into bed next to his wife and patted her gently on the arm, all the time thinking about the high price of meat and what a bargain it represented.

Copyright © 1993 by David Gerrold

NANCY KRESS
at www.Phoenix Pick.com

Ralph Roberts is a jack of all trades in the lit biz. He has written and sold over 100 books, has sold 4 screenplays, and as a publisher he has produced over 300 titles. And if that isn't enough, he also runs an annual film festival.

GHOST IN THE MACHINE

by Ralph Roberts

Marcus Teague sat hunched over in the cramped confines of the 16-gigabyte USB thumb drive. The muscles on his mighty arms rippled as he cleaned his wizard's sword, running the polishing spell up and down the blade with precision. It might be all virtual, but he was buff with bulging biceps, a mighty chest, a narrow waist, bronzed skin, ready for *any* battle. The sleeveless T-shirt with its mystical symbols in hex and octal, and the Microsoft and Ubuntu certification badges, emphasized that.

"Looks like Bill could spring for a bigger ready room," he said, "maybe a 64-gig thumb drive or, better, a 120-gig solid state drive, huh?"

He looked up when Oscar did not answer.

The old man didn't look good—battered and bruised, moaning whenever he moved, flat on his back, exhausted. Troubleshooting hardware took it out of you. Blown power supplies, crashed hard drives, loose cables, and all those intermittent ills that kept Oscar in dark old machines for hours when no telling what was going to jump him.

When time permitted, Marcus went along to watch his friend's back. Besides, he enjoyed chopping up fanged viruses, stomping malware data-mining dwarves, tearing apart virus ogres, erasing script dragons, and all the rest of it. Bring on those Trojans in their virtual Greek armor. They were no match for the wiz!

Marcus shook his head. Oscar had insisted on keeping the same physique—he was the same old man now as the virtual-reality-helmet-wearing body laying currently on the broken-down couch in the littered backroom of Billal's Computer Repair. Billal's was maybe the most unprofitable computer shop in Chicago—but it had two things no other shop anywhere in the world had: it had him and Oscar. It also had Bill, who tried hard but was the most incompetent shop manager possible, and the shadowy, probably criminal partner, Al—who had bankrolled the place but was never around much. Well, scratch that last; Al hung out in the shop a lot more of late.

With some grunting, Oscar managed to roll over a little and looked at Marcus.

"Bill can't afford it. Shop's losing money, which suits that sleazebag Al just fine. He wants the secret of how we do this."

Marcus shrugged and went back to working on his sword. He just wanted to do his job. He liked it, even if minimum wage was all they got. He'd made all this work after Bill invented the concept. Coded it, debugged it, and was the first to try it. This was *his* baby! He'd given it birth—*virtual computer repair*. And, yes, he knew Al—who had to be connected to organized crime—was hot after this technology. That's why the gangster dribbled out only enough funds to keep the shop doors open.

"Marcus, what do you want out of life?" Oscar said.

Marcus thought about it and shrugged. "Enough money for me to upgrade my hardware at home and to find true love—in whichever order, but I want a 24-core CPU soon."

Oscar painfully laid flat again. "You won't get them things here."

A tone beeped and a work order with an IP address popped up on a tiny virtual screen.

"For me?" Oscar asked, his voice weary.

"Nope, it's for me—some guy's computer's running slow and probably full of nasty little beasts." He smiled enthusiastically, gave his sword one more pass with the polishing spell, and sheathed it. Grinning, he hoisted his backpack of diagnostic spells and the like.

Oscar gave him a disgusted look. "Don't enjoy it too much, and be *careful*. Something weirder than usual is going on out there."

Marcus carefully moved to the hatch. "You get a call, let me know where, Oscar, and don't hesitate to use that emergency abort utility I wrote for us. The red button: take it out, flip off the safety cover, press ABORT."

Oscar shook his head. "*No*, not that. You said yourself you weren't sure it would work. No telling what would happen to our real bodies. You said that."

Marcus shrugged. "Last resort, guy. Just don't get killed. That would mess up your real body even more. At least take some of those routines I built from the data in the Shaolin temple's computer."

Oscar shook his head despondently. "Haven't got the energy to use them, Marcus."

Worrying about his friend, Marcus flowed into the USB port that led to the shop's dinky server. A hand reached out to help him get to his feet. It was Beep, the USB driver.

"Thanks, Beep."

Beep.

"You have a good day, too, buddy."

The server itself was an old quad-core clunker he'd gotten off eBay for $50, for which Bill still owed him. But it had some memory, the latest version of Ubuntu, and gave him space to write and develop his spells and scripts. He always had been good at coding.

One-handed, Marcus air-typed up a large virtual screen with webcam, then smiled at his image. A mixture of Conan the Barbarian and King Arthur's Merlin the Magician—he could swing a sword or wave a wand with the best of them. Blond, blue-eyed, well-developed muscles—not a bit like his concave-chested, bespectacled, short, geeky body recumbent out there in the backroom.

A real chick magnet! Unfortunately, all the women who might be impressed were out there in the real world. He waved the screen away and headed for the cable modem port—no fast fiber optic or wireless connection for this cheap shop. Uploading was a pain. Slow!

He nodded to bits of software he passed; in this computer he knew them all and they trusted him. A bunch of little memory monkeys ran by carrying bits of this and bytes of that to here and there, ones and zeros flashing in their beady little eyes. "Hi, Marcus, hi Marcus," they chanted.

Passing the power supply, he patted one of the cables. Sparks playfully tickled his fingers. As a small boy he'd been fascinated with electricity and quickly made friends with it. That friendship often paid off in his current job. Whoa! *Current* job? He laughed.

Squeezing into the cable modem, he slowly climbed to the nearest intersection with one of Chicago's fiber optic backbones. This was the problem using just a regular cable connection. Fast download, yes, but slow upload. Servers needed a way to push data out quickly as well as pull it in.

Marcus broke out of the slow upload—like swimming through molasses—and stepped out on the crowded platform. All sorts of things shuffled around, waiting on the next train of data packets— email messages, SQL commands off to visit some database and retrieve info, lots of web URL queries, always rushing about to keep their human surfers sated.

He sensed the attack even before the monstrous Python script reared its ugly head over the railing at the back of the platform. He dived and rolled as a blast of red-hot electrons struck the spot where he had been.

He laid a *more* spell on it and didn't see anything to worry him in its code, so no use being nice. Marcus air-typed *rm dragon*. His erase code killed the process, wiped the Python file, and the fearsome towering head and body *poofed* into nothingness. At least he hoped it had. Erasing computer files was not always permanent. He was okay, but the attack had left behind a good deal of destruction. Its deadly breath, missing him, had killed a number of innocent pieces of software going about their legitimate duties.

Marcus knelt next to a whimpering, frightened jpeg—an image of a beautiful baby being sent by its proud mother to the baby's grandmother. Now that image would never arrive, fading away as he held it in his arms.

Sadly he stood, watching the surviving data constructs rush around in panic. This was just *wrong*! An attempt on him had destroyed good data, useful utilities and other programs—something very much against his principles. It was all a waste.

The attacking script had been crude but powerful. Someone or something out there was ruthless in its hatred of him. Well, *he* would see about that! He would make it his mission to hunt down this killer!

The train of data packet cars whizzed to a stop and all the data and snippets of code hurried to get on before another dragon could come along.

Marcus started to enter a car and a wall of stench hit his virtual nose. *Spam*! Of all things in the Internet universe he hated spam the most, spam and the evil humans who caused it to spew like so much sewage from their computers.

This packet was crammed to the ceiling with the slimy, stinky stuff. *All spam must die*! He donated them a couple of filter bombs from his backpack, ducking as tons of fragments blew through the packet's sides and more or less neatly landed in bit bins on the platform.

Satisfied, he moved to the next packet, boarded, and took a seat.

He called up a screen and scrolled the work order. *Hmmm*…An anonymous IP address—not usual, and it cost extra. Spammers, hackers, and other evil humans, they liked to have anonymous IPs. He had a bad feeling about this.

A tall black gentleman in a three-piece suit slid into the seat next to Marcus. He held out a check for four million dollars, smiling broadly.

Marcus tapped the certification patches on his T-shirt. "No phishing around here."

The software's eyes widened and he jumped up, motioning several of his kind to turn back. "Copper! Run! It's John Law!" he yelled in a Nigerian accent.

Several pieces of legitimate email nodded their thanks to Marcus. Phishing gave them all a bad name—almost as much as spam did.

A stream of porn oozed into the car. Marcus pointed to the next packet and they left. Porn was pretty mindless stuff, but it knew when the wiz was around.

Speaking of such stuff, Marcus turned around in his seat looking for Gwen. He had not seen her in a week or more. Gwen did some racy stuff, but she was a real woman and far from mindless. Some men paid a lot for interaction. She was the only other virtual human he'd seen down here besides himself and Oscar. They'd had some great conversations, riding together. He knew she hated what she had to do for a living. Certainly she didn't want her only family—her brother, who was an attorney with a big firm downtown—ever finding out.

Gwen's virtual body was as voluptuous as his was buff. She'd confided that her real body was a female geek, flat, not curvy. She even had a computer science degree and loved to code, but couldn't find a programming gig so was reduced to this—her face showed her disgust—"job." And she told him about her server—she also favored Ubuntu as her Linux of choice—and mentioned how she had backup virtual reality software on it. Even told him her real name, Gwendolyn Louise Baker.

Wow! Beautiful, *and* she knew computers and Linux, too? What…a…woman!

Marcus surprised himself by hugging her on their last ride. He didn't do well with girls, not nearly confident enough usually to initiate affection. What's more, she'd returned the hug! That was the last time he'd seen her.

✧

He landed after his wireless jump from the platform via a 40mb up-and-down connection at the IP address on his work order. It was a very fancy and powerful Internet connection with tons of bandwidth, but the port into the computer was foreboding—dark inside with a blackened ring around the port where a firewall had once flamed. No telling what had wandered in there. All the place needed was a sign: THIS IS A TRAP, DUFUS. COME RIGHT IN.

He pulled out his wand with his right hand and waved a work light sphere into existence with the other. With the bright light preceding him, Marcus confidently walked into the machine.

The first software he saw was a keyboard driver.

"Hey, guy, what computer is this?" he asked.

"CLACK, CLACK, CLACKITY, CLACK… busy…CLACK CLACK," the driver said. "Master types commands to kill you. CLACK CLACK *CLACKITY*."

A sudden *whoosh* and a wall of heat caused Marcus to whirl around. A white hot firewall now closed the exit port. He gestured at it to re-open a port—*any* port would do right now—but nothing happened.

The pounding of heavy boots caused him to spin again, this time to see heavily-armed and armored gigantic troll-like virus fighters bearing down on him waving swords, battle axes, and rifles with wicked-looking bayonets as long as the rifles.

"Gotta scoot, dude," the keyboard driver said, rushing off, CLACKing rapidly again.

Marcus groaned. These were no friendly McAfees or Nortons—rule-abiding, virus-squashing officers. No, *these* guys were coded on steroids. Mean, nasty, powerful! No *rm* spell would even scratch them.

He waved his wand and his most powerful *debug* spell sizzled out and hit the first troll. No effect. It *should* have slowed the monster down to a crawl and revealed its internal workings. After that, just tear out statements and variables and it was over. No problem, except, *nothing* happened.

He unlimbered his sword. Have to do this the old-fashioned way. Chop them into separate subroutines that would fizzle into oblivion.

The keyboard driver had returned, slipped to the back of the pack. There was rapid CLACKing and as the leading four trolls rushed him, their armor got thicker! Some human programmer was working real-time against him!

But the thicker armor added weight and the trolls' reactions were sluggish now as they struggled in slow motion to ram their bayonets through Marcus. Whoever this programmer might be, he was not very good.

Marcus chopped at the trolls with his sword. It wasn't easy, but big chunks were falling off.

CLACK, CLACK, CLACKITY, CLACK!

The programmer was fast on the uptake. The armor on all the trolls slimmed down and they duplicated until the memory around him was full of angry, hungry trolls with fast reflexes and anxious to taste his virtual blood.

However, their very numbers hampered getting at him and the computer's CPU was grinding down under the load. Suddenly the trolls were slow again, and so was the human programmer as he continued to duplicate them, adding yet more load.

Marcus chopped a few of them to bits, but he could sense the CPU wavering and—although his virtual body's code, written by him, was markedly more efficient, he felt like he was fighting in mush now. He didn't want to be here when the computer crashed, like in the next few milliseconds. Hell of a way to die for someone as good at coding as him—embarrassingly so, even.

He switched his sword to his left hand, parried a bayonet thrust while pulling the abort button from his pocket, flipping the safety cover off with his thumb. Holding his breath, he pressed it. *Click*!

☼

Marcus rolled through an open port on the old server in the shop's backroom, expanding to full size, and gracefully springing to his feet. He sheathed his sword and—

Bill—in his fifties, rotund, and bald as the proverbial billiard ball—was coming in holding a cup of coffee. He dropped both the cup and his jaw. The cup shattered, the brown fluid from it staining the ancient, already-discolored linoleum, but neither Marcus nor Bill noticed that.

"You…you're…" Bill said with several gasps.

Marcus was running his hands over his body. He *was* the steel-muscled, bronzed hero like his virtual self…except…it was now *real*!

He spun and looked at the ratty couch where his pencil-necked geek real-world body always rested. It was gone! The virtual reality helmet lay empty. Oscar's body was still on the other couch.

A sudden sheepish look came to his face.

"What?" Bill asked, dropping into a chair and grabbing a parts catalog to fan his face.

"I gotta pee," Marcus said. "That never happened down in the computer."

Bill weakly waved toward their small, filthy restroom.

In a couple of minutes, a bemused look on his face, Marcus returned.

"Everything big?" Bill said, guessing.

"Yeah," Marcus said, grinning. "*Yeah*!" Then he held up his hands. "We need to discuss everything and make a plan of action. I'm recalling Oscar."

He went over and seated himself in front of the server, his large fingers flying nimbly over the keys.

"Still got my computer skills," he said with a smile.

The smile faded as nothing happened.

"Something's wrong, Bill. I can't contact Oscar! That's bad! Better go in and rescue—"

"That won't be necessary," said an oily voice.

Marcus jumped to his feet and turned to see Al and two of his goons standing there. All three had large automatic pistols leveled at Bill and him. Al stepped forward and rammed the barrel of his weapon against Bill's ear. "Who's Conan the Barbarian over there? I didn't authorize you to hire anyone new. Where's that little wimp you used to have?"

Bill looked at Marcus. "Ah…he's gone."

"Well. Musclehead there isn't much smarter. Almost got him earlier, but he ran like a little girl. Not sure how, but he got out before the computer slagged itself."

"You're a lousy coder," Marcus said, which to him was about the worst insult you could hurl at someone.

"Haven't got time for you now. Get over there against the wall, flat on the floor."

Marcus complied, but he wasn't through talking. "Where's Oscar?"

"He and your little girlfriend Gwen are my virtual prisoners."

"Gwen?"

"Yeah, Gwen—I swiped Bill's code one day. Got it to work well enough to put her in the machine—most popular of my porn rentals, being interactive and all." He took the gun from Bill's ear long enough to wave it at Marcus. "*You* ruined that, getting all lovey-dovey with her. Now she wants out. But she ain't getting out!"

Marcus slapped his head with one hand. It hurt. "Encrypt sensitive software, stupid," he said in a disgusted mutter.

Al sneered. "So I'm taking Bill here. He's going to improve his code for me and I'm going to rule spam and porn all over the Internet." The gangster pointed at the server. "Bring that."

Marcus saw Bill, wide-eyed, shake his head. He didn't want Al to know that Marcus was really the one who had written the virtual insertion code. It was his idea, but only Marcus could make that idea work.

One of the goons put away his gun, went over, and turned the two gnarled knobs to the screws holding the server in the rack. He pulled it out, removed the cords, and stuck it under his arm.

Al pulled Bill out of his chair and pushed him over to the other goon, who grabbed his collar.

"You, on the floor there—you're fired, Conan. No severance or back pay. Consider yourself lucky to be alive."

Then they all left, slamming the front door resoundingly.

Marcus got up, the joy he'd felt in his new body now overwhelmed by despair and fear for his friends. He looked at Oscar's body and the virtual reality helmet on it. Somewhere Gwen's body was laying the same way.

He slammed a massive fist into his hand. Al was now in control of his only three friends in the world.

Marcus gently put a blanket over Oscar's body, then stooped and grabbed a few items out of his tool box on the floor. He left quickly, locking the shop and jogging toward his nearby apartment. *His server had a backup of everything on it!*

Too bad for Al. He was getting his friends back! Whatever it took, that's what he'd do.

As he passed two good-looking young women, he heard:

"Hot!"

"Wotta hunk!"

He grinned but ran faster. At least this new body stuff was working out. He wasn't even breathing hard.

✡

As he crossed the main room of his tiny one-bed/one-bath apartment, Marcus suddenly realized he could *hear* and, what's more, *sense* what was going on in the server he'd mounted in the small closet.

Wow! The powers of his virtual body had also been transferred to his physical, real-world body. He waved his fingers and a virtual terminal floated in the air in front of him.

Cool!

There was a crackling at an empty power socket. He waved at his friend, electricity. That was not new; he'd always been able to communicate with it.

He grinned at the glowing air terminal. It reminded him what one of his professors in tech school had been fond of saying: "Computer science is ninety percent theory and ten percent magic." Marcus was sure now the ten percent was a whole lot larger than that. And he was the wiz! It was a good feeling.

But that good feeling vanished almost immediately. Everything he now had would mean *nothing* to him if he couldn't save his three friends. Gwen, Oscar, and even Bill—they were all he had.

Waving his fingers at the terminal, Marcus made certain his server was still secure, the backup virtual reality program still ran, and all was in order for a rescue mission.

Then he slapped his head. He'd forgotten to grab his virtual reality helmet! But …

He opened the closet door. It just felt *right*, so he dived into the one open USB socket on the front panel and slid into the server. Two virus-chomping trolls were sitting on empty data containers, playing cards. They looked up at his entrance.

"Oh, hiya, Boss," one said. "All's secure."

Marcus nodded, clapped them on the shoulders, and motioned them to go back to playing. (Even software needed some relaxation.) He walked over to another data container and sat down to think, creating another virtual terminal.

A couple of ideas came. He implemented one of them, bringing up Oscar's virtual body configuration script. The old man had wanted to be the same down here as in the real world, but that was not working out too well. Marcus's fingers flew as he beefed Oscar up, giving him youth, muscles, various powers, including all the Shaolin temple Kung Fu routines. Marcus was very proud of those. You do a Bruce Lee on a nasty piece of software and it *stayed* down.

He then compiled the configuration file. He might not be able to easily find where Oscar was, but his virtual body regularly checked its configuration, and whoever was holding Oscar was going to have a surprise on their hands.

While he was at it, he set up a configuration file for Bill too. If Al threw him in a computer, there would be *two* mighty warriors, both yearning for Al's blood. Four, of course, counting him and Gwen—if only he could find her computer and modify her *config* file. It was now obvious to him that Al was her boss and the VR software they had was the early version Al had ripped off from Bill. Lot of improvements since then!

Now for the second part. None of this would probably work unless he could find and get into Al's computer, which was surely locked down and strongly protected against that very thing happening, but he had an idea.

Gwendolyn Louise Baker's address was easy to find, and not far away at all. Closer than going back to the shop and probably safer, since Al did not know about her computer. She'd told him that. Besides, as he'd already decided, he needed to update her virtual reality software.

"Be alert, guys," he said to the trolls and dived out the USB port.

☼

His *open* spell worked on her apartment door and his friend, electricity, kindly disabled the alarm system for him. He slipped in and relocked the door. The apartment was even smaller than his, and there she was (her body, that is), lying on her bed with the VR helmet on. She was a little chubby (she hadn't mentioned that), short, with not much of a figure, and as geeky as she said. But Marcus knew he loved her anyway.

Heart pounding, he found her server. Not bad. Old PowerEdge—20th generation—but those had plenty of reliability and capacity. He dived into the USB socket and was immediately challenged by three huge female virus-protection trolls, sharp swords poised.

"Halt! Password!"

"Er…" Marcus said, not wanting to hurt any of Gwen's software, but knowing he *had* to get through.

"Wait," one troll said, "that's *Marcus*!"

"She likes him," said the second.

"A *lot*," the remaining troll added.

His ears doing a virtual burn, Marcus quickly explained to them what he needed and how it would save Gwen.

The trolls nodded and lowered their swords.

"VR software starts at memory address 3ddff000," one said.

"We're alerting the CPUs to have a packet ready for you," said another.

"That way," said the third, pointing.

Marcus pounded down a long memory bus and came to the address. The CPUs were holding a refresh packet for him, and he jumped on it. But they made no objection to him first updating the VR software, throwing some Shaolin temple Kung Fu routines and other stuff into Gwen's *config* file, then recompiling it.

"Gwen's got a boyfriend! Gwen's got a boyfriend!" some of the memory monkeys were chanting.

Then it was onto the data packet and, clinging precariously to a couple of protruding bits, he whizzed along.

☼

Marcus flowed through the VR refresh port in Al's main server, the heavily-armored trolls ignoring this authorized traffic. He rolled off the packet, landing on his feet with poise as he entered a cordoned-off section of RAM serving as a cell for Gwen, Oscar, and Bill. He was *so* glad to see them! And he recognized the server he was in—it was the one from the shop.

"Miss me?" he said, grinning.

Gwen rushed over and threw her arms around him, resting her head on his shoulder. Oscar and Bill patted him on the back. Reluctantly he disengaged from Gwen.

"We've got to hurry," he said. "What's been happening here?"

"Not much," Gwen said. "Al's ignoring us. Ever since they got their new bodies, these two have been going over in the corner, looking at themselves, and chuckling a lot." She looked at Oscar and Bill. "It's just *virtual* size, guys."

"Er…no," Marcus said. "This is now my real body. We need to convert you guys so that you can help me demolish Al."

All three nodded at him. They *liked* that idea.

Marcus took out the red buttons he'd grabbed from his tool box. He handed one to each. "All set up. Flip up the cover, press ABORT." He held up his hand. "Not *yet*!"

Bill gently eased the cover closed again.

Marcus waved up a terminal and the screen showed the view outside the computer. Al and his two goons were there, eating pizza from a delivery box. *Hey, even disorganized criminals have to eat*, he acknowledged silently.

"Here's the plan," he said. "When Oscar and Bill press their buttons, they'll be up there with Al and his gorillas. Kung Fu the hell out of them, guys, before they can get their guns out. You know how now."

"What about me?" Gwen asked.

Marcus smiled at her. "Your button deposits you outside the server in your apartment. Your old body will be gone and *you* will be *you*."

Oscar, feeling his oats after years of being old and feeble, gave a wolf whistle.

Gwen stuck her tongue out at him but smiled.

"Then come back here and help us mop up. But… where is here?"

Marcus typed in the air and data streamed on his virtual terminal. "No encrypting of personal or business data for Al, hey?" He stopped the scrolling. "There! 6701 Greenview Avenue. Not too far from your apartment, Gwen. Let's do it!"

She nodded, opened the cover on her button, and hovered a finger over it reluctantly.

Marcus surprised himself again. "I love you. Press it, Gwen."

She looked at him, smiling radiantly, and did. *Whoosh!* She was gone.

He air-typed to the terminal and sent a video request out through the open refresh port. There she stood in her apartment, looking with awe at the image of her new body in a mirror.

"Move it, honey," he said.

Gwen jumped at his voice, but waved and ran out the door.

"So, are we waiting on her?" Bill asked.

"Nope. Press your buttons on three. One…two… *three*!"

They landed with silent grace, already in Kung Fu stances. Al and his two goons barely had time to drop their slices of pizza before they were disarmed and trussed up with electric cords ripped from a lamp, a fan, and the coffee maker.

Oscar and Bill took turns going to the restroom.

Marcus waved up a screen in the air, pulled over a chair, and then—with occasional suggestions from Bill or Oscar after they returned—demolished Al's porn and spam empires. He was especially careful to erase all mention of Gwen's work for Al. No need for her to be embarrassed during the investigations that were sure to come.

The office door slammed against the wall under a powerful *open* spell and Gwen stormed in, looking like an avenging goddess. Seeing the trussed-up gangsters, she slid to a halt.

"I'm sorry we didn't wait for you, Gwen," Marcus said, "but they were a pushover."

She shrugged.

"Now what?" Bill asked.

Gwen raised her hand. "I thought about that running over here."

They all noted that she was not a bit out of breath.

"My brother is a patent attorney with the biggest intellectual property firm in Chicago." She smiled. "You'll all be rich, and Marcus can make sure all this "—she ran her hands up and down her awesomely curvy body— "is used for the betterment of humanity."

"And software," Marcus added. "We're rich, Gwen—you too!" Oscar and Bill nodded enthusiastically. "Guess we should call the cops, huh?"

Gwen took his arm and gently pulled him toward the door.

"Let Bill and Oscar do that. I need you to check my computer." She smiled a smile that would melt steel and then temper it into something stronger than before.

Bill shrugged and winked.

"Race you back," Gwen yelled, already out the door.

Marcus pounded after her.

Oscar looked at Bill. "Big?"

"Huge," said Bill.

"I *love* computers," Oscar said.

Original (First) Publication
Copyright © 2013 by Ralph Roberts

Kristine Kathryn Rusch is the only person, living or dead, to win Hugos as both a writer and an editor. "Echea" won the HOMer Award and the Asimov's Readers Poll, *and was a Hugo, Nebula and Sturgeon nominee.*

ECHEA

by Kristine Kathryn Rusch

I can close my eyes and she appears in my mind as she did the moment I first saw her: tiny, fragile, with unnaturally pale skin and slanted chocolate eyes. Her hair was white as the moon on a cloudless evening. It seemed, that day, that her eyes were the only spot of color on her haggard little face. She was seven but she looked three.

And she acted like nothing we had ever encountered before.

Or since.

✧

We had three children and a good life. We were not impulsive, but we did feel as if we had something to give. Our home was large, and we had money; any child would benefit from that.

It seemed to be for the best.

It all started with the brochures. We saw them first at an outdoor cafe near our home. We were having lunch, when we glimpsed floating dots of color, a fleeting child's face. Both my husband and I touched them only to have the displays open before us:

The blank vista of the Moon, the Earth over the horizon like a giant blue and white ball, a looming presence, pristine and healthy and somehow guilt-ridden. The Moon itself looked barren, as it always had, until one focused. And then one saw the pockmarks, the shattered dome open to the stars. In the corner of the first brochure I opened, at the very edge of the reproduction, were blood-splotches. They were scattered on the craters and boulders, and had left fist-sized holes in the dust. I didn't need to be told what had caused it. We saw the effects of high-velocity rifles in low gravity every time we downloaded the news.

The brochures began with the Moon, and ended with the faces of refugees: pallid, worn, defeated. The passenger shuttles to Earth had pretty much stopped. At first, those who could pay came here, but by the time we got our brochures, Earth passage had changed. Only those with living relatives were able to return. Living relatives who were willing to acknowledge the relationship—and had official hard copy to prove it.

The rules were waived in the case of children, of orphans and of underage war refugees. They were allowed to come to Earth if their bodies could tolerate it, if they were willing to be adopted, and if they were willing to renounce any claims they had to Moon land.

They had to renounce the stars in order to have a home.

✧

We picked her up in Sioux Falls, the nearest star shuttle stop and detention center to our home. The shuttle stop was a desolate place. It was designed as an embarkation point for political prisoners and for star soldiers. It was built on the rolling prairie, a sprawling complex with laser fences shimmering in the sunlight. Guards stood at every entrance, and several hovered above. We were led, by men with laser rifles, into the main compound, a building finished almost a century before, made of concrete and steel, functional, cold and ancient. Its halls smelled musty. The concrete flaked, covering everything with a fine gray dust.

Echea had flown in on a previous shuttle. She had been in detox and sick bay; through psychiatric exams and physical screenings. We did not know we would get her until they called our name.

We met her in a concrete room with no windows, shielded against the sun, shielded against the world. The area had no furniture.

A door opened and a child appeared.

Tiny, pale, fragile. Eyes as big as the moon itself, and darker than the darkest night. She stood in the center of the room, legs spread, arms crossed, as if she were already angry at us.

Around us, through us, between us, a computer voice resonated:

This is Echea. She is yours. Please take her, and proceed through the doors to your left. The waiting shuttle will take you to your preassigned destination.

She didn't move when she heard the voice, although I started. My husband had already gone toward her. He crouched and she glowered at him.

"I don't need you," she said.

"We don't need you either," he said. "But we want you."

The hard set to her chin eased, just a bit. "Do you speak for her?" she asked, indicating me.

"No," I said. I knew what she wanted. She wanted reassurance early that she wouldn't be entering a private war zone as difficult and devastating as the one she left. "I speak for myself. I'd like it if you came home with us, Echea."

She stared at us both then, not relinquishing power, not changing that forceful stance. "Why do you want me?" she asked. "You don't even know me."

"But we will," my husband said.

"And then you'll send me back," she said, her tone bitter. I heard the fear in it.

"You won't go back," I said. "I promise you that."

It was an easy promise to make. None of the children, even if their adoptions did not work, returned to the Moon.

A bell sounded overhead. They had warned us about this, warned us that we would have to move when we heard it.

"It's time to leave," my husband said. "Get your things."

Her first look was shock and betrayal, quickly masked. I wasn't even sure I had seen it. And then she narrowed those lovely chocolate eyes. "I'm from the Moon," she said with a sarcasm that was foreign to our natural daughters. "We have no things."

☼

What we knew of the Moon Wars on Earth was fairly slim. The news vids were necessarily vague, and I had never had the patience for a long lesson in Moon history.

The shorthand for the Moon situation was this: the Moon's economic resources were scarce. Some colonies, after several years of existence, were self-sufficient. Others were not. The shipments from Earth, highly valuable, were designated to specific places and often did not get there. Piracy, theft, and murder occurred to gain the scarce resources. Sometimes skirmishes broke out. A few times, the fighting escalated. Domes were damaged, and in the worst of the fighting, two colonies were destroyed.

At the time, I did not understand the situation at all. I took at face value a cynical comment from one of my professors: colonies always struggle for dominance when they are away from the Mother country. I had even repeated it at parties.

I had not understood that it oversimplified one of the most complex situations in our universe.

I also had not understood the very human cost of such events.

That is, until I had Echea.

☼

We had ordered a private shuttle for our return, but it wouldn't have mattered if we were walking down a public street. I attempted to engage Echea, but she wouldn't talk. She stared out the window instead, and became visibly agitated as we approached home.

Lake Nebagamon is a small lake, one of the hundreds that dot Northern Wisconsin. It was a popular resort for people from nearby Superior. Many had summer homes, some dating from the late 1800s. In the early 2000s, the summer homes were sold off. Most lots were bought by families who already owned land there, and hated the crowding at Nebagamon. My family bought fifteen lots. My husband's bought ten. Our marriage, some joked, was one of the most important local mergers of the day.

Sometimes I think it was no joke. It was expected. There is affection between us, of course, and a certain warmth. But no real passion.

The passion I once shared with another man—a boy actually—was so long ago that I remember it in images, like a vid seen decades ago, or a painting made from someone else's life.

When my husband and I married, we acted like an acquiring conglomerate. We tore down my family's summer home because it had no potential or historical value, and we built onto my husband's. The ancient house became an estate with a grand lawn that rolled down to the muddy water. Evenings we sat on the verandah and listened to the cicadas until full dark. Then we stared at the stars and their reflections in our lake. Sometimes we were blessed with the Northern lights, but not too often.

This is the place we brought Echea. A girl who had never really seen green grass or tall trees; who had definitely never seen lakes or blue sky or Earth's stars. She had, in her brief time in South Dakota, seen what they considered Earth—the brown dust, the fresh air. But her exposure had been limited, and had not really included sunshine or nature itself.

We did not really know how this would affect her. There were many things we did not know.

✧

Our girls were lined up on the porch in age order: Kally, the twelve-year-old, and the tallest, stood near the door. Susan, the middle child, stood next to her, and Anne stood by herself near the porch. They were properly stair-stepped, three years between them, a separation considered optimal for more than a century now. We had followed the rules in birthing them, as well as in raising them.

Echea was the only thing out of the norm.

Anne, the courageous one, approached us as we got off the shuttle. She was small for six, but still bigger than Echea. Anne also blended our heritages perfectly—my husband's bright blue eyes and light hair with my dark skin and exotic features. She would be our beauty some day, something my husband claimed was unfair, since she also had the brains.

"Hi," she said, standing in the middle of the lawn. She wasn't looking at us. She was looking at Echea.

Echea stopped walking. She had been slightly ahead of me. By stopping, she forced me to stop too.

"I'm not like them," she said. She was glaring at my daughters. "I don't want to be."

"You don't have to be," I said softly.

"But you can be civil," my husband said.

Echea frowned at him, and in that moment, I think, their relationship was defined.

"I suppose you're the pampered baby," she said to Anne.

Anne grinned.

"That's right," she said. "I like it better than being the spoiled brat."

I held my breath. "Pampered baby" wasn't much different from "spoiled brat" and we all knew it.

"Do you have a spoiled brat?" Echea asked.

"No," Anne said.

Echea looked at the house, the lawn, the lake, and whispered. "You do now."

Later, my husband told me he heard this as a declaration. I heard it as awe. My daughters saw it as something else entirely.

"I think you have to fight Susan for it," Anne said.

"Do not!" Susan shouted from the porch.

"See?" Anne said. Then she took Echea's hand and led her up the steps.

✧

That first night we awakened to screams. I came out of a deep sleep, already sitting up, ready to do battle. At first, I thought my link was on; I had lulled myself to sleep with a bedtime story. My link had an automatic shut-off, but I sometimes forgot to set it. With all that had been happening the last few days, I believed I might have done so again.

Then I noticed my husband sitting up as well, groggily rubbing the sleep out of his eyes.

The screams hadn't stopped. They were piercing, shrill. It took me a moment to recognize them.

Susan.

I was out of bed before I realized it, running down the hall before I had time to grab my robe. My nightgown flapped around me as I ran. My husband was right behind me. I could hear his heavy steps on the hardwood floor.

When we reached Susan's room, she was sitting on the window seat, sobbing. The light of the full moon cut across the cushions and illuminated the rag rugs and the old-fashioned pink spread.

I sat down beside her and put my arm around her. Her frail shoulders were shaking, and her breath was coming in short gasps. My husband crouched before her, taking her hands in his.

"What happened, sweetheart?" I asked.

"I—I—I saw him," she said. "His face exploded, and the blood *floated* down."

"Were you watching vids again before sleep?" my husband asked in a sympathetic tone. We both knew if she said yes, in the morning she would get yet another lecture about being careful about what she put in her brain before it rested.

"No!" she wailed.

She apparently remembered those early lectures too.

"Then what caused this?" I asked.

"I don't *know!*" she said and burst into sobs again. I cradled her against me, but she didn't loosen her grip on my husband's hands.

"After his blood floated, what happened, baby?" my husband asked.

"Someone grabbed me," she said against my shirt. "And pulled me away from him. I didn't want to go."

"And then what?" My husband's voice was still soft.

"I woke up," she said, and her breath hitched.

I put my hand on her head and pulled her closer. "It's all right, sweetheart," I said. "It was just a dream."

"But it was so *real*," she said.

"You're here now," my husband said. "Right here. In your room. And we're right here with you."

"I don't want to go back to sleep," she said. "Do I have to?"

"Yes," I said, knowing it was better for her to sleep than be afraid of it. "Tell you what, though. I'll program House to tell you a soothing story, with a bit of music and maybe a few moving images. What do you say?"

"Dr. Seuss," she said.

"That's not always soothing," my husband said, obviously remembering how House's *Cat in the Hat* program gave Kally a terror of anything feline.

"It is to Susan," I said gently, reminding him. In her third year, she played *Green Eggs and Ham* all night, House's voice droning on and on, making me thankful that our room was at the opposite end of the hall.

But she was three no longer, and she hadn't wanted Dr. Seuss for years. The dream had really frightened her.

"If you have any more trouble, baby," my husband said to her, "you come and get us, all right?"

She nodded. He squeezed her hands, then I picked her up and carried her to bed. My husband pulled back the covers. Susan clung to me as I eased her down. "Will I go back there if I close my eyes?" she asked.

"No," I said. "You'll listen to House and sleep deeply. And if you dream at all, it'll be about nice things, like sunshine on flowers, and the lake in summertime."

"Promise?" she asked, her voice quavering.

"Promise," I said. Then I removed her hands from my neck and kissed each of them before putting them on the coverlet. Then I kissed her forehead. My husband did the same, and as we were leaving, she was ordering up the House reading program.

As I pulled the door closed, I saw the opening images of *Green Eggs and Ham* flicker across the wall.

☼

The next morning everything seemed fine. When I came down to breakfast, the chef had already placed the food on the table, each dish on its own warming plate. The scrambled eggs had the slightly runny look that indicated they had sat more than an hour—not even the latest design in warming plates could stop that. In addition, there was French toast, and Susan's favorite, waffles. The scent of fresh blueberry muffins floated over it all, and made me smile. The household staff had gone to great lengths to make Echea feel welcome.

My husband was already in his usual spot, e-conferencing while he sipped his coffee and broke a muffin apart with his fingers. His plate, showing the remains of eggs and ham, was pushed off to the side.

"Morning," I said as I slipped into my usual place on the other side of the table. It was made of oak and had been in my family since 1851, when my mother's people brought it over from Europe as a wedding present for my many-great grandparents. The housekeeper kept it polished to a shine, and she only used linen placemats to protect it from the effects of food.

There wasn't a scratch on it.

My husband acknowledged me with a blueberry-stained hand as laughter made me look up. Kally came in, her arm around Susan. Susan still didn't look herself. She had deep circles under her eyes which meant that *Green Eggs and Ham* hadn't quite done the trick. She was too old to get us—I had known that when we left her last night—but I hoped she hadn't spent the rest of the night listening to House, trying to find comfort in artificial voices and imagery.

The girls were still smiling when they saw me.

"Something funny?" I asked.

"Echea," Kally said. "Did you know someone owned her dress before she did?"

No, I hadn't known that but it didn't surprise me. My daughters, on the other hand, had owned only the best. Sometimes their knowledge of life—or lack thereof—shocked me.

"It's not an unusual way for people to save money," I said. "But it'll be the last pre-owned dress she'll have."

Mom? It was Anne, e-mailing me directly. The instant prompt appeared before my left eye. *Can you come up here?*

I blinked the message away, then sighed and pushed back my chair. I should have known the girls would do something that first morning. And the laughter should have prepared me.

"Remember," I said as I stood. "Only one main course. No matter what your father says."

"Ma," Kally said.

"I mean it," I said, then hurried up the stairs. I didn't have to check where Anne was. She had sent me an image along with the e-mail—the door to Echea's room.

As I got closer, I heard Anne's voice.

"…didn't mean it. They're old poops."

"Poop" was Anne's worst word, at least so far. And when she used it, she put so much emphasis on it the word became an epithet.

"It's my dress," Echea said. She sounded calm and contained, but I thought there was a raggedness to her voice that hadn't been there the day before. "It's all I have."

At that moment, I entered the room. Anne was on the bed, which had been carefully made up. If I hadn't tucked Echea in the night before, I never would have thought she had slept there.

Echea was standing near her window seat, gazing at the lawn as if she didn't dare let it out of her sight.

"Actually," I said, keeping my voice light. "You have an entire closet full of clothes."

Thanks, Mom, Anne sent me.

"Those clothes are yours," Echea said.

"We've adopted you," I said. "What's ours is yours."

"You don't get it," she said. "This dress is *mine*. It's all I have."

She had her arms wrapped around it, her hands gripping it as if we were going to take it away.

"I know," I said softly. "I know, sweetie-baby. You can keep it. We're not trying to take it away from you."

"They said you would."

"Who?" I asked, with a sinking feeling. I already knew who. My other two daughters. "Kally and Susan?"

She nodded.

"Well, they're wrong," I said. "My husband and I make the rules in this house. I will never take away something of yours. I promise."

"Promise?" she whispered.

"Promise," I said. "Now how about breakfast?"

She looked at Anne for confirmation, and I wanted to hug my youngest daughter. She had already decided to care for Echea, to ally with her, to make Echea's entrance into the household easier.

I was so proud of her.

"Breakfast," Anne said, and I heard a tone in her voice I'd never heard before. "It's the first meal of the day."

The government had fed the children standard nutrition supplements, in beverage form. Echea hadn't taken a meal on Earth until she joined us.

"You name your meals?" she asked Anne. "You have that many of them?" Then she put a hand over her mouth, as if she were surprised she had let the questions out.

"Three of them," I said, trying to sound normal. Instead I felt defensive, as if we had too much. "We only have three of them."

✿

The second night, we had no disturbances. By the third, we had developed a routine. I spent time with my girls, and then I went into Echea's room. She didn't like House or House's stories. House's voice, no matter how I programmed it, scared her. It made me wonder how we were going to link her when the time came. If she found House intrusive, imagine how she would find the constant barrage of information services, of instant e-mail scrolling across her eyes, or sudden images appearing inside her head. She was almost past the age where a child adapted easily to a link. We had to calm her quickly or risk her suffering a disadvantage for the rest of her life.

Perhaps it was the voice that upset her. The reason links made sound optional was because too many people had had trouble distinguishing the voices inside their head. Perhaps Echea would be one of them.

It was time to find out.

I had yet to broach the topic with my husband. He seemed to have cooled toward Echea immediately. He thought Echea abnormal because she wasn't like our girls. I reminded him that Echea hadn't had the advantages, to which he responded that she had the advantages now. He felt that since her life had changed, she should change.

Somehow I didn't think it worked like that.

It was on the second night that I realized she was terrified of going to sleep. She kept me as long as she could, and when I finally left, she asked to keep the lights on.

House said she had them on all night, although the computer clocked her even breathing starting at 2:47 a.m.

On the third night, she asked me questions. Simple ones, like the one about breakfast, and I answered them without my previous defensiveness. I held my emotions back, my shock that a child would have to ask what that pleasant ache was in her stomach after meals ("You're full, Echea. That's your stomach telling you it's happy.") or why we insisted on bathing at least once a day ("People stink if they don't bathe often, Echea. Haven't you noticed?"). She asked the questions with her eyes averted, and her hands clenched against the coverlet. She knew she should know the answers, she knew better than to ask my older two daughters or my husband, and she tried ever so hard to be sophisticated.

Already the girls had humiliated her more than once. The dress incident had blossomed into an obsession with them, and they taunted her about her unwillingness to attach to anything. She wouldn't even claim a place at the dining room table. She seemed convinced that we would toss her out at the first chance.

On the fourth night, she addressed that fear. Her question came at me sideways, her body more rigid than usual.

"If I break something," she asked, "what will happen?"

I resisted the urge to ask what she had broken. I knew she hadn't broken anything. House would have told me, even if the girls hadn't.

"Echea," I said, sitting on the edge of her bed, "are you afraid that you'll do something which will force us to get rid of you?"

She flinched as if I had struck her, then she slid down against the coverlet. The material was twisted in her hands, and her lower jaw was working even before she spoke.

"Yes," she whispered.

"Didn't they explain this to you before they brought you here?" I asked.

"They said nothing." That harsh tone was back in her voice, the tone I hadn't heard since that very first day, her very first comment.

I leaned forward and, for the first time, took one of those clenched fists into my hands. I felt the sharp knuckles against my palms, and the softness of the fabric brushing my skin.

"Echea," I said. "When we adopted you, we made you our child by law. We cannot get rid of you. No matter what. It is illegal for us to do so."

"People do illegal things," she whispered.

"When it benefits them," I said. "Losing you will not benefit us."

"You're saying that to be kind," she said.

I shook my head. The real answer was harsh, harsher than I wanted to state, but I could not leave it at this. She would not believe me. She would think I was trying to ease her mind. I was, but not through polite lies.

"No," I said. "The agreement we signed is legally binding. If we treat you as anything less than a member of our family, we not only lose you, we lose our other daughters as well."

I was particularly proud of adding the word "other." I suspected that, if my husband had been having this conversation with her, that he would have forgotten to add it.

"You would?" she asked.

"Yes," I said.

"This is true?" she asked.

"True," I said. "I can download the agreement and its ramifications for you in the morning. House can read you the standard agreement—the one everyone must sign—tonight if you like."

She shook her head, and pushed her hands harder into mine. "Could you—could you answer me one thing?" she asked.

"Anything," I said.

"I don't have to leave?"

"Not ever," I said.

She frowned. "Even if you die?"

"Even if we die," I said. "You'll inherit, just like the other girls."

My stomach knotted as I spoke. I had never mentioned the money to our own children. I figured they knew. And now I was telling Echea who was, in all intents and purposes, still a stranger.

And an unknown one at that.

I made myself smile, made the next words come out lightly. "I suspect there are provisions against killing us in our beds."

Her eyes widened, then instantly filled with tears. "I would never do that," she said.

And I believed her.

✡

As she grew more comfortable with me, she told me about her previous life. She spoke of it only in passing, as if the things that happened before no longer mattered to her. But in the very flatness with which she told them, I could sense deep emotions churning beneath the surface.

The stories she told were hair-raising. She had not, as I had assumed, been orphaned as an infant. She had spent most of her life with a family member who had died, and then she had been brought to Earth. Somehow, I had believed that she had grown up in an orphanage like the ones from the 19th and 20th centuries, the ones Dickens wrote about, and the famous pioneer filmmakers had made Flats about. I had not realized that those places did not exist on the Moon. Either children were chosen for adoption, or they were left to their own devices, to see if they could survive on their own.

Until she had moved in with us, she had never slept in a bed. She did not know it was possible to grow food by planting it, although she had heard rumors of such miracles.

She did not know that people could accept her for what she was, instead of what she could do for them.

My husband said that she was playing on my sympathies so that I would never let her go.

But I wouldn't have let her go anyway. I had signed the documents and made the verbal promise. And I cared for her. I would never let her go, any more than I would let a child of my flesh go.

I hoped, at one point, that he would feel the same.

✡

As the weeks progressed, I was able to focus on Echea's less immediate needs. She was beginning to use House—her initial objection to it had been based on something that happened on the Moon, something she never fully explained—but House could not teach her everything. Anne introduced her to reading, and often Echea would read to herself. She caught on quickly, and I was surprised that she had not learned in her school on the Moon, until someone told me that most Moon colonies had no schools. The children were home-taught, which worked only for children with stable homes.

Anne also showed her how to program House to read things Echea did not understand. Echea made use of that as well. At night, when I couldn't sleep, I would check on the girls. Often I would have to open Echea's door, and turn off House myself. Echea would fall asleep to the drone of a deep male voice. She never used the vids. She simply liked the words, she said, and she would listen to them endlessly, as if she couldn't get enough.

I downloaded information on child development and learning curves, and it was as I remembered. A child who did not link before the age of ten was significantly behind her peers in all things. If she did not link before the age of twenty, she would never be able to function at an adult level in modern society.

Echea's link would be her first step into the world that my daughters already knew, the Earth culture denied so many who had fled to the Moon.

After a bit of hesitation, I made an appointment with Ronald Caro, our Interface Physician.

Through force of habit, I did not tell my husband.

✡

I had known my husband all my life, and our match was assumed from the beginning. We had a warm and comfortable relationship, much better than many among my peers. I had always liked my husband, and had always admired the way he worked his way around each obstacle life presented him.

One of those obstacles was Ronald Caro. When he arrived in St. Paul, after getting all his degrees and licenses and awards, Ronald Caro contacted me. He had known that my daughter Kally was in need of a link, and he offered to be the one to do it.

I would have turned him down, but my husband, always practical, checked on his credentials.

"How sad," my husband had said. "He's become one of the best Interface Physicians in the country."

I hadn't thought it sad. I hadn't thought it anything at all except inconvenient. My family had forbidden me to see Ronald Caro when I was sixteen, and I had disobeyed them.

All girls, particularly home-schooled ones, have on-line romances. Some progress to vid conferencing and virtual sex. Only a handful progress to actual physical contact. And of those that do, only a small fraction survive.

At sixteen, I ran away from home to be with Ronald Caro. He had been sixteen too, and gorgeous, if the remaining snapshot in my image memory were any indication. I thought I loved him. My father, who had been monitoring my e-mail, sent two police officers and his personal assistant to bring me home.

The resulting disgrace made me so ill that I could not get out of bed for six months. My then-future husband visited me each and every day of those six months, and it is from that period that most of my memories of him were formed. I was glad to have him; my father, who had been quite close to me, rarely spoke to me after I ran away with Ronald, and treated me as a stranger.

When Ronald reappeared in the Northland long after I had married, my husband showed his forgiving nature. He knew Ronald Caro was no longer a threat to us. He proved it by letting me take the short shuttle hop to the Twin Cities to have Kally linked.

Ronald did not act improperly toward me then or thereafter, although he often looked at me with a sadness I did not reciprocate. My husband was relieved. He always insisted on having the best, and because my husband was squeamish about brain work, particularly that which required chips, lasers and remote placement devices, he preferred to let me handle the children's interface needs.

Even though I no longer wanted it, I still had a personal relationship with Ronald Caro. He did not treat me as a patient, or as the mother of his patients, but as a friend.

Nothing more.

Even my husband knew that.

Still, the afternoon I made the appointment, I went into our bedroom, made certain my husband was in his office, and closed the door. Then I used the link to send a message to Ronald.

Instantly his response flashed across my left eye.

Are you all right? he sent, as he always did, as if he expected something terrible to have happened to me during our most recent silence.

Fine, I sent back, disliking the personal questions.

And the girls?

Fine also.

So you linked to chat? again, as he always did.

And I responded as I always did. *No. I need to make an appointment for Echea.*

The Moon Child?

I smiled. Ronald was the only person I knew, besides my husband, who didn't think we were insane for taking on a child not our own. But I felt that we could, and because we could, and because so many were suffering, we should.

My husband probably had his own reasons. We never really discussed them, beyond that first day.

The Moon Child, I responded. *Echea.*

Pretty name.

Pretty girl.

There was a silence, as if he didn't know how to respond to that. He had always been silent about my children. They were links he could not form, links to my husband that could not be broken, links that Ronald and I could never have.

She has no interface, I sent into that silence.

Not at all?

No.

Did they tell you anything about her?

Only that she'd been orphaned. You know, the standard stuff. I felt odd, sending that. I had asked for information, of course, at every step. And my husband had. And when we compared notes, I learned that each time we had been told the same thing—that we had asked for a child, and we would get one, and that child's life would start fresh with us. The past did not matter.

The present did.

How old is she?

Seven.

Hmmm. The procedure won't be involved, but there might be some dislocation. She's been alone in her head all this time. Is she stable enough for the change?

I was genuinely perplexed. I had never encountered an unlinked child, let alone lived with one. I didn't know what "stable" meant in that context.

My silence had apparently been answer enough.

I'll do an exam, he sent. *Don't worry.*

Good. I got ready to terminate the conversation.

You sure everything's all right there? he sent.

It's as right as it always is, I sent and then severed the connection.

☼

That night I dreamed. It was an odd dream because it felt like a virtual reality vid, complete with emotions and all the five senses. But it had the distance of vr too—that strange sense that the experience was not mine.

I dreamed I was on a dirty, dusty street. The air was thin and dry. I had never felt air like this. It tasted recycled, and it seemed to suck the moisture from my skin. It wasn't hot, but it wasn't cold either. I wore a ripped shirt and ragged pants, and my shoes were boots made of a light material I had never felt before. Walking was easy and precarious at the same time. I felt lighter than ever, as if with one wrong gesture I would float.

My body moved easily in this strange atmosphere, as if it were used to it. I had felt something like it before: when my husband and I had gone to the Museum of Science and Technology in Chicago on our honeymoon. We explored the Moon exhibit, and felt firsthand what it was like to be in a colony environment.

Only that had been clean.

This wasn't.

The buildings were white plastic, covered with a filmy grit and pockmarked with time and use. The dirt on the ground seemed to get on everything, but I knew, as well as I knew how to walk in this imperfect gravity, that there wasn't enough money to pave the roads.

The light above was artificial, built into the dome itself. If I looked up, I could see the dome and the light, and if I squinted, I could see beyond to the darkness that was the unprotected atmosphere. It made me feel as if I were in a lighted glass porch on a starless night. Open, and vulnerable, and terrified, more because I couldn't see what was beyond than because I could.

People crowded the roadway and huddled near the plastic buildings. The buildings were domed too. Pre-fab, shipped up decades ago when Earth had hopes for the colonies. Now there were no more shipments, at least not here. We had heard that there were shipments coming to Colony Russia and Colony Europe, but no one confirmed the rumors. I was in Colony London, a bastard colony made by refugees and dissidents from Colony Europe. For a while, we had stolen their supply ships. Now, it seemed, they had stolen them back.

A man took my arm. I smiled up at him. His face was my father's face, a face I hadn't seen since I was twenty-five. Only something had altered it terribly. He was younger than I had ever remembered him. He was too thin and his skin filthy with dust. He smiled back at me, three teeth missing, lost to malnutrition, the rest blackened and about to go. In the past few days the whites of his eyes had turned yellow, and a strange mucus came from his nose. I wanted him to see the colony's medical facility or at least pay for an autodoc, but we had no credit, no means to pay at all.

It would have to wait until we found something.

"I think I found us free passage to Colony Latina," he said. His breath whistled through the gaps in his teeth. I had learned long ago to be far away from his mouth. The stench could be overpowering. "But you'll have to do them a job."

A job. I sighed. He had promised no more. But that had been months ago. The credits had run out, and he had gotten sicker.

"A big job?" I asked.

He didn't meet my gaze. "Might be."

"Dad—"

"Honey, we gotta use what we got."

It might have been his motto. *We gotta use what we got.* I'd heard it all my life. He'd come from Earth, he'd said, in one of the last free ships. Some of the others we knew said there were no free ships except for parolees, and I often wondered if he had come on one of those. His morals were certainly slippery enough.

I don't remember my mother. I'm not even sure I had one. I'd seen more than one adult buy an infant, and then proceed to exploit it for gain. It wouldn't have been beyond him.

But he loved me. That much was clear.

And I adored him.

I'd have done the job just because he'd asked it.

I'd done it before.

The last job was how we'd gotten here. I'd been younger then and I hadn't completely understood.

But I'd understood when we were done.

And I'd hated myself.

"Isn't there another way?" I found myself asking.

He put his hand on the back of my head, propelling me forward. "You know better," he said. "There's nothing here for us."

"There might not be anything in Colony Latina, either."

"They're getting shipments from the U.N. Seems they vowed to negotiate a peace."

"Then everyone will want to go."

"But not everyone can," he said. "We can." He touched his pocket. I saw the bulge of his credit slip. "If you do the job."

It had been easier when I didn't know. When doing a job meant just that. When I didn't have other things to consider. After the first job, my father asked where I had gotten the morals. He said I hadn't inherited them from him, and I hadn't. I knew that. I suggested maybe Mother, and he had laughed, saying no mother who gave birth to me had morals either.

"Don't think about it, honey," he'd said. "Just do."

Just do. I opened my mouth—to say what, I don't know—and felt hot liquid splatter me. An exit wound had opened in his chest, spraying his blood all around. People screamed and backed away. I screamed. I didn't see where the shot had come from, only that it had come.

The blood moved slowly, more slowly than I would have expected.

He fell forward and I knew I wouldn't be able to move him, I wouldn't be able to grab the credit slip, wouldn't be able to get to Colony Latina, wouldn't have to do the job.

Faces, unbloodied faces, appeared around me.

They hadn't killed him for the slip.

I turned and ran, as he once told me to do, ran as fast as I could, blasting as I went, watching people duck or cover their ears or wrap their arms around their heads.

I ran until I saw the sign.

The tiny prefab with the Red Crescent painted on its door, the Red Cross on its windows. I stopped blasting and tumbled inside, bloody, terrified, and completely alone.

☼

I woke up to find my husband's arms around me, my head buried in his shoulder. He was rocking me as if I were one of the girls, murmuring in my ear, cradling me and making me feel safe. I was crying and shaking, my throat raw with tears or with the aftereffects of screams.

Our door was shut and locked, something that we only did when we were amorous. He must have had House do it, so no one would walk in on us.

He stroked my hair, wiped the tears from my face. "You should leave your link on at night," he said tenderly. "I could have manipulated the dream, made it into something pleasant."

We used to do that for each other when we were first married. It had been a way to mesh our different sexual needs, a way to discover each other's thoughts and desires.

We hadn't done it in a long, long time.

"Do you want to tell me about it?" he asked.

So I did.

He buried his face in my hair. It had been a long time since he had done that, too, since he had shown that kind of vulnerability with me.

"It's Echea," he said.

"I know," I said. That much was obvious. I had been thinking about her so much that she had worked her way into my dreams.

"No," he said. "It's nothing to be calm about." He sat up, kept his hand on me, and peered into my face. "First Susan, then you. It's like she's a poison that's infecting my family."

The moment of closeness shattered. I didn't pull away from him, but it took great control not to. "She's our child."

"No," he said. "She's someone else's child, and she's disrupting our household."

"*Babies* disrupt households. It took a while, but you accepted that."

"And if Echea had come to us as a baby, I would have accepted her. But she didn't. She has problems that we did not expect."

"The documents we signed said that we must treat those problems as our own."

His grip on my shoulder grew tighter. He probably didn't realize he was doing it. "They also said that the child had been inspected and was guaranteed illness-free."

"You think some kind of illness is causing these dreams? That they're being passed from Echea to us like a virus?"

"Aren't they?" he asked. "Susan dreamed of a man who died. Someone whom she didn't want to go. Then 'they' pulled her away from him. You dream of your father's death—"

"They're different," I said. "Susan dreamed of a man's face exploding, and being captured. I dreamed of a man being shot, and of running away."

"But those are just details."

"*Dream* details," I said. "We've all been talking to Echea. I'm sure that some of her memories have woven their way into our dreams, just as our daily experiences do, or the vids we've seen. It's not that unusual."

"There were no night terrors in this household until she came," he said.

"And no one had gone through any trauma until she arrived, either." I pulled away from him now.

"What we've gone through is small compared to her. Your parents' deaths, mine, the birth of the girls, a few bad investments, these things are all minor. We still live in the house you were born in. We swim in the lake of our childhood. We have grown wealthier. We have wonderful daughters. That's why we took Echea."

"To learn trauma?"

"No," I said. "Because we could take her, and so many others can't."

He ran a hand through his thinning hair. "But I don't want trauma in this house. I don't want to be disturbed anymore. She's not our child. Let's let her become someone else's problem."

I sighed. "If we do that, we'll still have trauma. The government will sue. We'll have legal bills up to our eyeballs. We did sign documents covering these things."

"They said if the child was defective, we could send her back."

I shook my head. "And we signed even more documents that said she was fine. We waived that right."

He bowed his head. Small strands of gray circled his crown. I had never noticed them before.

"I don't want her here," he said.

I put a hand on his. He had felt that way about Kally, early on. He had hated the way an infant disrupted our routine. He had hated the midnight feedings, had tried to get me to hire a wet-nurse, and then a nanny. He had wanted someone else to raise our children because they inconvenienced him.

And yet the pregnancies had been his idea, just like Echea had been ours. He would get enthusiastic, and then when reality settled in, he would forget the initial impulse.

In the old days we had compromised. No wet nurse, but a nanny. His sleep undisturbed, but mine disrupted. My choice, not his. As the girls got older, he found his own ways to delight in them.

"You haven't spent any time with her," I said. "Get to know her. See what she's really like. She's a delightful child. You'll see."

He shook his head. "I don't want nightmares," he said, but I heard capitulation in his voice.

"I'll leave my interface on at night," I said. "We can even link when we sleep and manipulate each other's dreams."

He raised his head, smiling, suddenly looking boyish, like the man who proposed to me, all those years ago. "Like old times," he said.

I smiled back, irritation gone. "Just like old times," I said.

☼

The nanny had offered to take Echea to Ronald's, but I insisted, even though the thought of seeing him so close to a comfortable intimacy with my husband made me uneasy. Ronald's main offices were over fifteen minutes away by shuttle. He was in a decade-old office park near the Mississippi, not too far from St. Paul's new capitol building. Ronald's building was all glass on the river side. It stood on stilts—the Mississippi had flooded abominably in '45, and the city still hadn't recovered from the shock—and to get to the main entrance, visitors needed a lift code. Ronald had given me one when I made the appointment.

Echea had been silent during the entire trip. The shuttle had terrified her, and it didn't take long to figure out why. Each time she had traveled by shuttle, she had gone to a new home. I reassured her that would not happen this time, but I could tell she thought I lied.

When she saw the building, she grabbed my hand. "I'll be good," she whispered.

"You've been fine so far," I said, wishing my husband could see her now. For all his demonizing, he failed to realize she was just a little girl.

"Don't leave me here."

"I don't plan to," I said.

The lift was a small glass enclosure with voice controls. When I spoke the code, it rose on air jets to the fifth floor and docked, just like a shuttle. It was designed to work no matter what the weather, no matter what the conditions on the ground.

Echea was not amused. Her grip on my hand grew so tight that it cut off the circulation to my fingers.

We docked at the main entrance. The building's door was open, apparently on the theory that anyone who knew the code was invited. A secretary sat behind an antique wood desk, dark and polished until it shone. He had a blotter in the center of the desk, a pen and inkwell beside it, and a single sheet of paper on top. I suspected that he did most of his work through his link, but the illusion worked. It made me feel as if I had slipped into a place wealthy enough to use paper, wealthy enough to waste wood on a desk.

"We're here to see Dr. Caro," I said as Echea and I entered.

"The end of the hall to your right," the secretary said, even though the directions were unnecessary. I had been that way dozens of times.

Echea hadn't, though. She moved through the building as if it were a wonder, never letting go of my hand. She seemed to remain convinced that I would leave her there, but her fear did not diminish her curiosity. Everything was strange. I suppose it had to be, compared to the Moon where space—with oxygen—was always at a premium. To waste so much area on an entrance wouldn't merely be a luxury there. It would be criminal.

We walked across the wood floors past several closed doors until we reached Ronald's offices. The secretary had warned someone because the doors swung open. Usually I had to use the small bell to the side, another old-fashioned affectation.

The interior of his offices was comfortable. They were done in blue, the color of calm, he once told me, with thick easy chairs and pillowed couches. A children's area was off to the side, filled with blocks and soft toys and a few dolls. The bulk of Ronald's clients were toddlers, and the play area reflected that.

A young man in a blue work suit appeared at one of the doors, and called my name. Echea clutched my hand tighter. He noticed her and smiled.

"Room B," he said.

I liked Room B. It was familiar. All three of my girls had done their post-interface work in Room B. I had only been in the other rooms once, and had felt less comfortable.

It was a good omen, to bring Echea to such a safe place.

I made my way down the hall, Echea in tow, without the man's guidance. The door to Room B was open. Ronald had not changed it. It still had the fainting couch, the work unit recessed into the wall, the reclining rockers. I had slept in one of those rockers as Kally had gone through her most rigorous testing.

I had been pregnant with Susan at the time.

I eased Echea inside and then pulled the door closed behind us. Ronald came through the back door—he must have been waiting for us—and Echea jumped. Her grip on my hand grew so tight that I thought she might break one of my fingers. I smiled at her and did not pull my hand away.

Ronald looked nice. He was too slim, as always, and his blond hair flopped against his brow. It needed a cut. He wore a silver silk shirt and matching pants, and even though they were a few years out of style, they looked sharp against his brown skin.

Ronald was good with children. He smiled at her first, and then took a stool and wheeled it toward us so that he would be at her eye level.

"Echea," he said. "Pretty name."

And a pretty child, he sent, just for me.

She said nothing. The sullen expression she had had when we met her had returned.

"Are you afraid of me?" he asked.

"I don't want to go with you," she said.

"Where do you think I'm taking you?"

"Away from here. Away from—" she held up my hand, clasped in her small one. At that moment it became clear to me. She had no word for what we were to her. She didn't want to use the word "family," perhaps because she might lose us.

"Your mother—" he said slowly and as he did he sent *Right?* to me.

Right, I responded.

"—brought you here for a check-up. Have you seen a doctor since you've come to Earth?"

"At the center," she said.

"And was everything all right?"

"If it wasn't, they'd have sent me back."

He leaned his elbows on his knees, clasping his hands and placing them under his chin. His eyes, a silver that matched the suit, were soft.

"Are you afraid I'm going to find something?" he asked.

"No," she said.

"But you're afraid I'm going to send you back."

"Not everybody likes me," she said. "Not everybody wants me. They said, when they brought me to Earth, that the whole family had to like me, that I had to behave or I'd be sent back."

Is this true? he asked me.

I don't know. I was shocked. I had known nothing of this.

Does the family dislike her?

She's new. A disruption. That'll change.

He glanced at me over her head, but sent nothing else. His look was enough. He didn't believe they'd change, any more than Echea would.

"Have you behaved?" he asked softly.

She glanced at me. I nodded almost imperceptibly. She looked back at him. "I've tried," she said.

He touched her then, his long delicate fingers tucking a strand of her pale hair behind her ear. She leaned into his fingers as if she'd been longing for touch.

She's more like you, he told me, *than any of your own girls.*

I did not respond. Kally looked just like me, and Susan and Anne both favored me as well. There was nothing of me in Echea. Only a bond that had formed when I first saw her, all those weeks before.

Reassure her, he sent.

I have been.

Do it again.

"Echea," I said, and she started as if she had forgotten I was there. "Dr. Caro is telling you the truth. You're just here for an examination. No matter how it turns out, you'll still be coming home with me. Remember my promise?"

She nodded, eyes wide.

"I always keep my promises," I said.

Do you? Ronald asked. He was staring at me over Echea's shoulder.

I shivered, wondering what promise I had forgotten.

Always, I told him.

The edge of his lips turned up in a smile, but there was no mirth in it.

"Echea," he said. "It's my normal practice to work alone with my patient, but I'll bet you want your mother to stay."

She nodded. I could almost feel the desperation in the move.

"All right," he said. "You'll have to move to the couch."

He scooted his chair toward it.

"It's called a fainting couch," he said. "Do you know why?"

She let go of my hand and stood. When he asked the question, she looked at me as if I would supply her with the answer. I shrugged.

"No," she whispered. She followed him hesitantly, not the little girl I knew around the house.

"Because almost two hundred years ago when these were fashionable, women fainted a lot."

"They did not," Echea said.

"Oh, but they did," Ronald said. "And do you know why?"

She shook her small head. With this idle chatter he had managed to ease her passage toward the couch.

"Because they wore undergarments so tight that they often couldn't breathe right. And if a person can't breathe right, she'll faint."

"That's silly."

"That's right," he said, as he patted the couch. "Ease yourself up there and see what it was like on one of those things."

I knew his fainting couch wasn't an antique. His had all sorts of diagnostic equipment built in. I wondered how many other people he had lured on it with his quaint stories.

Certainly not my daughters. They had known the answers to his questions before coming to the office.

"People do a lot of silly things," he said. "Even now. Did you know most people on Earth are linked?"

As he explained the net and its uses, I ignored them. I did some leftover business, made my daily chess move, and tuned into their conversation on occasion.

"—and what's really silly is that so many people refuse a link. It prevents them from functioning well in our society. From getting jobs, from communicating—"

Echea listened intently while she lay on the couch. And while he talked to her, I knew, he was examining her, seeing what parts of her brain responded to his questions.

"But doesn't it hurt?" she asked.

"No," he said. "Science makes such things easy. It's like touching a strand of hair."

And then I smiled. I understood why he had made the tender move earlier. So that he wouldn't alarm her when he put in the first chip, the beginning of her own link.

"What if it goes wrong?" she asked. "Will everybody—die?"

He pulled back from her. Probably not enough so that she would notice. But I did. There was a slight frown between his eyes. At first I had thought he would shrug off the question, but it took him too long to answer.

"No," he said as firmly as he could. "No one will die."

Then I realized what he was doing. He was dealing with a child's fear realistically. Sometimes I was too used to my husband's rather casual attitude toward the girls. And I was used to the girls themselves. They were much more placid than my Echea.

With the flick of a finger, he turned on the overhead light.

"Do you have dreams, honey?" he asked as casually as he could.

She looked down at her hands. They were slightly scarred from experiences I knew nothing about. I had planned to ask her about each scar as I gained her trust. So far, I had asked about none.

"Not anymore," she said.

This time, I moved back slightly. Everyone dreamed, didn't they? Or were dreams only the product of a linked mind? That couldn't be right. I'd seen the babies dream before we brought them here.

"When was the last time you dreamed?" he asked.

She shoved herself back on the lounge. Its base squealed from the force of her contact. She looked around, seemingly terrified. Then she looked at me. It seemed like her eyes were appealing for help.

This was why I wanted a link for her. I wanted her to be able to tell me, without speaking, without Ronald knowing, what she needed. I didn't want to guess.

"It's all right," I said to her. "Dr. Caro won't hurt you."

She jutted out her chin, squeezed her eyes closed, as if she couldn't face him when she spoke, and took a deep breath. Ronald waited, breathless.

I thought, not for the first time, that it was a shame he did not have children of his own.

"They shut me off," she said.

"Who?" His voice held infinite patience.

Do you know what's going on? I sent him.

He did not respond. His full attention was on her.

"The Red Crescent," she said softly.

"The Red Cross," I said. "On the Moon. They were the ones in charge of the orphans—"

"Let Echea tell it," he said, and I stopped, flushing. He had never rebuked me before. At least, not verbally.

"Was it on the Moon?" he asked her.

"They wouldn't let me come otherwise."

"Has anyone touched it since?" he asked.

She shook her head slowly. Somewhere in their discussion, her eyes had opened. She was watching Ronald with that mixture of fear and longing that she had first used with me.

"May I see?" he asked.

She clapped a hand to the side of her head. "If it comes on, they'll make me leave."

"Did they tell you that?" he asked.

She shook her head again.

"Then there's nothing to worry about." He put a hand on her shoulder and eased her back on the lounge. I watched, back stiff. It seemed like I had missed a part of the conversation, but I knew I hadn't. They were discussing something I had never heard of, something the government had neglected to tell us. My stomach turned. This was exactly the kind of excuse my husband would use to get rid of her.

She was laying rigidly on the lounge. Ronald was smiling at her, talking softly, his hand on the lounge's controls. He got the read-outs directly through his link. Most everything in the office worked that way, with a back-up download on the office's equivalent of House. He would send us a file copy later. It was something my husband insisted on, since he did not like coming to these appointments. I doubted he read the files, but he might this time. With Echea.

Ronald's frown grew. "No more dreams?" he asked.

"No," Echea said again. She sounded terrified.

I could keep silent no longer. *Our family's had night terrors since she arrived*, I sent him.

He glanced at me, whether with irritation or speculation, I could not tell.

They're similar, I sent. *The dreams are all about a death on the Moon. My husband thinks—*

I don't care what he thinks. Ronald's message was intended as harsh. I had never seen him like this before. At least, I didn't think so. A dim memory rose and fell, a sense memory. I had heard him use a harsh tone with me, but I could not remember when.

"Have you tried to link with her?" he asked me directly.

"How could I?" I asked. "She's not linked."

"Have your daughters?"

"I don't know," I said.

"Do you know if anyone's tried?" he asked her.

Echea shook her head.

"Has she been doing any computer work at all?" he asked.

"Listening to House," I said. "I insisted. I wanted to see if—"

"House," he said. "Your home system."

"Yes." Something was very wrong. I could feel it. It was in his tone, in his face, in his casual movements, designed to disguise his worry from his patients.

"Did House bother you?" he asked Echea.

"At first," she said. Then she glanced at me. Again, the need for reassurance. "But now I like it."

"Even though it's painful," he said.

"No, it's not," she said, but she averted her eyes from mine.

My mouth went dry. "It hurts you to use House?" I asked. "And you didn't say anything?"

She didn't want to risk losing the first home she ever had, Ronald sent. *Don't be so harsh.*

I wasn't the one being harsh. He was. And I didn't like it.

"It doesn't really hurt," she said.

Tell me what's happening, I sent him. *What's wrong with her?*

"Echea," he said, putting his hand alongside her head one more time. "I'd like to talk with your mother alone. Would it be all right if we sent you back to the play area?"

She shook her head.

"How about if we leave the door open? You'll always be able to see her."

She bit her lower lip.

Can't you tell me this way? I sent.

I need all the verbal tools, he sent back. *Trust me.*

I did trust him. And because I did, a fear had settled in the pit of my stomach.

"That's okay," she said. Then she looked at me. "Can I come back in when I want?"

"If it looks like we're done," I said.

"You won't leave me here," she said again. When would I gain her complete trust?

"Never," I said.

She stood then and walked out the door without looking back. She seemed so much like the little girl I'd first met that my heart went out to her. All that bravado the first day had been just that, a cover for sheer terror.

She went to the play area and sat on a cushioned block. She folded her hands in her lap, and stared at me. Ronald's assistant tried to interest her in a doll, but she shook him off.

"What is it?" I asked.

Ronald sighed, and scooted his stool closer to me. He stopped near the edge of the lounge, not close enough to touch, but close enough that I could smell the scent of him mingled with his specially blended soap.

"The children being sent down from the Moon were rescued," he said softly.

"I know." I had read all the literature they sent when we first applied for Echea.

"No, you don't," he said. "They weren't just rescued from a miserable life like you and the other adoptive parents believe. They were rescued from a program that was started in Colony Europe about fifteen years ago. Most of the children involved died."

"Are you saying she has some horrible disease?"

"No," he said. "Hear me out. She has an implant—"

"A link?"

"No," he said. "Sarah, please."

Sarah. The name startled me. No one called me that anymore. Ronald had not used it in all the years of our reacquaintance.

The name no longer felt like mine.

"Remember how devastating the Moon Wars were? They were using projectile weapons and shattering the colonies themselves, opening them to space. A single bomb would destroy generations of work. Then some of the colonists went underground—"

"And started attacking from there, yes, I know. But that was decades ago. What has that to do with Echea?"

"Colony London, Colony Europe, Colony Russia, and Colony New Delhi signed the peace treaty—"

"—vowing not to use any more destructive weapons. I remember this, Ronald—"

"Because if they did, no more supply ships would be sent."

I nodded. "Colony New York and Colony Armstrong refused to participate."

"And were eventually obliterated." Ronald leaned toward me, like he had done with Echea. I glanced at her. She was watching, as still as could be. "But the fighting didn't stop. Colonies used knives and secret assassins to kill government officials—"

"And they found a way to divert supply ships," I said.

He smiled sadly. "That's right," he said. "That's Echea."

He had come around to the topic of my child so quickly it made me dizzy.

"How could she divert supply ships?"

He rubbed his nose with his thumb and forefinger. Then he sighed again. "A scientist on Colony Europe developed a technology that broadcast thoughts through the subconscious. It was subtle, and it worked very well. A broadcast about hunger at Colony Europe would get a supply captain to divert his ship from Colony Russia and drop the supplies in Colony Europe. It's more sophisticated than I make it sound. The technology actually made the captain believe that the rerouting was his idea."

Dreams. Dreams came from the subconscious. I shivered.

"The problem was that the technology was inserted into the brain of the user, like a link, but if the user had an existing link, it superseded the new technology. So they installed it in children born on the Moon, born in Colony Europe. Apparently Echea was."

"And they rerouted supply ships?"

"By imagining themselves hungry—or actually being starved. They would broadcast messages to the supply ships. Sometimes they were about food. Sometimes they were about clothing. Sometimes they were about weapons." He shook his head. "Are. I should say are. They're still doing this."

"Can't it be stopped?"

He shook his head. "We're gathering data on it now. Echea is the third child I've seen with this condition. It's not enough to go to the World Congress yet. Everyone knows though. The Red Crescent and the Red Cross are alerted to this, and they remove children from the colonies, sometimes on penalty of death, to send them here where they will no longer be harmed. The technology is deactivated, and people like you adopt them and give them full lives."

"Why are you telling me this?"

"Perhaps your House reactivated her device."

I shook my head. "The first dream happened before she listened to House."

"Then some other technology did. Perhaps the government didn't shut her off properly. It happens. The recommended procedure is to say nothing, and to simply remove the device."

I frowned at him. "Then why are you telling me this? Why didn't you just remove it?"

"Because you want her to be linked."

"Of course I do," I said. "You know that. You told her yourself the benefits of linking. You know what would happen to her if she isn't. You know."

"I know that she would be fine if you and your husband provided for her in your wills. If you gave her one of the houses and enough money to have servants for the rest of her life. She would be fine."

"But not productive."

"Maybe she doesn't need to be," he said.

It sounded so unlike the Ronald who had been treating my children that I frowned. "What aren't you telling me?"

"Her technology and the link are incompatible."

"I understand that," I said. "But you can remove her technology."

"Her brain formed around it. If I installed the link, it would wipe her mind clean."

"So?"

He swallowed so hard his Adam's apple bobbed up and down. "I'm not being clear," he said more to himself than to me. "It would make her a blank slate. Like a baby. She'd have to learn everything all over again. How to walk. How to eat. It would go quicker this time, but she wouldn't be a normal seven-year-old girl for half a year."

"I think that's worth the price of the link," I said.

"But that's not all," he said. "She'd lose all her memories. Every last one of them. Life on the Moon, arrival here, what she ate for breakfast the morning she received the link." He started to scoot forward and then stopped. "We *are* our memories, Sarah. She wouldn't be *Echea* anymore."

"Are you so sure?" I asked. "After all, the basic template would be the same. Her genetic makeup wouldn't alter."

"I'm sure," he said. "Trust me. I've seen it."

"Can't you do a memory store? Back things up so that when she gets her link she'll have access to her life before?"

"Of course," he said. "But it's not the same. It's like being told about a boat ride as opposed to taking one yourself. You have the same basic knowledge, but the experience is no longer part of you."

His eyes were bright. Too bright.

"Surely it's not that bad," I said.

"This is my specialty," he said, and his voice was shaking. He was obviously very passionate about this work. "I study how wiped minds and memory stores interact. I got into this profession hoping I could reverse the effects."

I hadn't known that. Or maybe I had and forgotten it.

"How different would she be?" I asked.

"I don't know," he said. "Considering the extent of her experience on the Moon, and the traumatic nature of much of it, I'd bet she'll be very different." He glanced into the play area. "She'd probably play with that doll beside her and not give a second thought to where you are."

"But that's good."

"That is, yes, but think how good it feels to earn her trust. She doesn't give it easily, and when she does, it's heartfelt."

I ran a hand through my hair. My stomach churned.

I don't like these choices, Ronald.

"I know," he said. I started. I hadn't realized I had actually sent him that last message.

"You're telling me that either I keep the same child and she can't function in our society, or I give her the same chances as everyone else and take away who she is."

"Yes," he said.

"I can't make that choice," I said. "My husband will see this as a breach of contract. He'll think that they sent us a defective child."

"Read the fine print in your agreement," Ronald said. "This one is covered. So are a few others. It's boilerplate. I'll bet your lawyer didn't even flinch when she read them."

"I can't make this choice," I said again.

He scooted forward and put his hands on mine. They were warm and strong and comfortable.

And familiar. Strangely familiar.

"You have to make the choice," he said. "At some point. That's part of your contract too. You're to provide for her, to prepare her for a life in the world. Either she gets a link or she gets an inheritance that someone else manages."

"And she won't even be able to check to see if she's being cheated."

"That's right," he said. "You'll have to provide for that too."

"It's not fair, Ronald."

He closed his eyes, bowed his head, and leaned it against my forehead. "It never was," he said softly. "Dearest Sarah. It never was."

☼

"Damn," my husband said. We were sitting in our bedroom. It was a half an hour before supper, and I had just told him about Echea's condition. "The lawyer was supposed to check for things like this."

"Dr. Caro said they're just learning about the problem on Earth."

"Dr. Caro." My husband stood. "Dr. Caro is wrong."

I frowned at him. My husband was rarely this agitated.

"This is not a technology developed on the Moon," my husband said. "It's an Earth technology, pre-neural net. Subject to international ban in '24. The devices disappeared when the link became the common currency among all of us. He's right that they're incompatible."

I felt the muscles in my shoulders tighten. I wondered how my husband knew of the technology and wondered if I should ask. We never discussed each other's business.

"You'd think that Dr. Caro would have known this," I said casually.

"His work is in current technology, not the history of technology," my husband said absently. He sat back down. "What a mess."

"It is that," I said softly. "We have a little girl to think of."

"Who's defective."

"Who has been used." I shuddered. I had cradled her the whole way back and she had let me. I had remembered what Ronald said, how precious it was to hold her when I knew how hard it was for her to reach out. How each touch was a victory, each moment of trust a celebration. "Think about it. Imagine using something that keys into your most basic desires, uses them for purposes other than—"

"Don't do that," he said.

"What?"

"Put a romantic spin on this. The child is defective. We shouldn't have to deal with that."

"She's not a durable good," I said. "She is a human being."

"How much money did we spend on in-the-womb enhancement so that Anne's substandard IQ was corrected? How much would we have spent if the other girls had had similar problems?"

"That's not the same thing," I said.

"Isn't it?" he asked. "We have a certain guarantee in this world. We are guaranteed excellent children, with the best advantages. If I wanted to shoot craps with my children's lives I would—"

"What would you do?" I snapped. "Go to the Moon?"

He stared at me as if he had never seen me before. "What does your precious Dr. Caro want you to do?"

"Leave Echea alone," I said.

My husband snorted. "So that she would be unlinked and dependent the rest of her life. A burden on the girls, a sieve for our wealth. Oh, but Ronald Caro would like that."

"He didn't want her to lose her personality," I said. "He wanted her to remain Echea."

My husband stared at me for a moment, and the anger seemed to leave him. He had gone pale. He reached out to touch me, then withdrew his hand. For a moment, I thought his eyes filled with tears.

I had never seen tears in his eyes before.

Had I?

"There is that," he said softly.

He turned away from me, and I wondered if I had imagined his reaction. He hadn't been close to Echea. Why would he care if her personality had changed?

"We can't think of the legalities anymore," I said. "She's ours. We have to accept that. Just like we accepted the expense when we conceived Anne. We could have terminated the pregnancy. The cost would have been significantly less."

"We could have," he said as if the thought were unthinkable. People in our circle repaired their mistakes. They did not obliterate them.

"You wanted her at first," I said.

"Anne?" he asked.

"Echea. It was our idea, much as you want to say it was mine."

He bowed his head. After a moment, he ran his hands through his hair. "We can't make this decision alone," he said.

He had capitulated. I didn't know whether to be thrilled or saddened. Now we could stop fighting about the legalities and get to the heart.

"She's too young to make this decision," I said. "You can't ask a child to make a choice like this."

"If she doesn't—"

"It won't matter," I said. "She'll never know. We won't tell her either way."

He shook his head. "She'll wonder why she's not linked, why she can only use parts of House. She'll wonder why she can't leave here without escort when the other girls will be able to."

"Or," I said, "she'll be linked and have no memory of this at all."

"And then she'll wonder why she can't remember her early years."

"She'll be able to remember them," I said. "Ronald assured me."

"Yes." My husband's smile was bitter. "Like she remembers a question on a history exam."

I had never seen him like this. I didn't know he had studied the history of neural development. I didn't know he had opinions about it.

"We can't make this decision," he said again.

I understood. I had said the same thing. "We can't ask a child to make a choice of this magnitude."

He raised his eyes to me. I had never noticed the fine lines around them, the matching lines around his nose and mouth. He was aging. We both were. We had been together a long, long time.

"She has lived through more than most on Earth ever do," he said. "She has lived through more than our daughters will, if we raise them right."

"That's not an excuse," I said. "You just want us to expiate our guilt."

"No," he said. "It's her life. She will have to be the one to live it, not us."

"But she's our child, and that entails making choices for her," I said.

He sprawled flat on our bed. "You know what I'll choose," he said softly.

"Both choices will disturb the household," I said. "Either we live with her as she is—"

"Or we train her to be what we want." He put an arm over his eyes.

He was silent for a moment, and then he sighed. "Do you ever regret the choices you made?" he asked. "Marrying me, choosing this house over the other, deciding to remain where we grew up?"

"Having the girls," I said.

"Any of it. Do you regret it?"

He wasn't looking at me. It was as if he couldn't look at me, as if our whole lives rested on my answer.

I put my hand in the one he had dangling. His fingers closed over mine. His skin was cold.

"Of course not," I said. And then, because I was confused, because I was a bit scared of his unusual intensity, I asked, "Do you regret the choices you made?"

"No," he said. But his tone was so flat I wondered if he lied.

☼

In the end, he didn't come with Echea and me to St. Paul. He couldn't face brain work, although I wished he had made an exception this time. Echea was more confident on this trip, more cheerful, and I watched her with a detachment I hadn't thought I was capable of.

It was as if she were already gone.

This was what parenting was all about: the difficult painful choices, the irreversible choices with no easy answers, the second-guessing of the future with no help at all from the past. I held her hand tightly this time while she wandered ahead of me down the hallway.

I was the one with fear.

Ronald greeted us at the door to his office. His smile, when he bestowed it on Echea, was sad.

He already knew our choice. I had made my husband contact him. I wanted that much participation from Echea's other parent.

Surprised? I sent.

He shook his head. *It is the choice your family always makes.*

He looked at me for a long moment, as if he expected a response, and when I did nothing, he crouched in front of Echea. "Your life will be different after today," he said.

"Momma—" and the word was a gift, a first, a never-to-be repeated blessing—"said it would be better."

"And mothers are always right," he said. He put a hand on her shoulder. "I have to take you from her this time."

"I know," Echea said brightly. "But you'll bring me back. It's a procedure."

"That's right," he said, looking at me over her head. "It's a procedure."

He waited just a moment, the silence deep between us. I think he meant for me to change my mind. But I did not. I could not.

It was for the best.

Then he nodded once, stood, and took Echea's hand. She gave it to him as willingly, as trustingly, as she had given it to me.

He led her into the back room.

At the doorway, she stopped and waved.

And I never saw her again.

✡

Oh, we have a child living with us, and her name is Echea. She is a wonderful vibrant creature, as worthy of our love and our heritage as our natural daughters.

But she is not the child of my heart.

✡

My husband likes her better now, and Ronald never mentions her. He has redoubled his efforts on his research.

He is making no progress.

And I'm not sure I want him to.

She is a happy, healthy child with a wonderful future.

We made the right choice.

It was for the best.

Echea's best.

My husband says she will grow into the perfect woman.

Like me, he says.

She'll be just like me.

She is such a vibrant child.

Why do I miss the wounded sullen girl who rarely smiled?

Why was she the child of my heart?

"Echea" by Kristine Kathryn Rusch was first published in Asimov's Science Fiction Magazine, *July 1998.*

Copyright © 1999 by Kristine Kathryn Rusch

KEVIN J. ANDERSON
at www.PhoenixPick.com

Gio Clairval is an Italian-born writer and translator. After living most of her life in Paris, she recently moved to Edinburgh, Scotland. Her fiction has appeared in Weird Tales, Fantasy Magazine, Postscripts, *and elsewhere.*

SPARKLER

by Gio Clairval

Howard's mother loved her pet because it glowed in the dark. Howard thought it was a silly reason to love something, but old Mrs. Apperson, withered and sickly, was in no position to be too picky about what cheered her up.

Every night Howard came home from work to find the creature curled up in his mother's lap as she watched her favorite films from Earth. The sparkler looked like a spiky poodle, with the occasional flicker of grass-green or lavender bursting from its asymmetrical ears. She'd named it Galin Naadam, the Mongolian words for "fireworks." Galin, for short.

The sparkler's sudden light always startled Howard. Each time Galin puffed light, he'd jump out of his chair. He began to hate the creature, but he knew better than to complain about the one thing his mother loved other than himself.

The pet grew rapidly. Two months ago it was the size of a chick. Now, when it walked on its hind legs, it could reach the top of the table.

Every night, Mrs. Apperson would say: "How was your day? I made you *Khorkhog*."

"I'll get it, Mom," Howard always answered.

But she never listened. Instead, she stood up, pressing Galin to her chest with skeletal arms, and trudged to the kitchen, limping noticeably. The doctors had refused to operate on a ninety-three-year-old woman in her precarious condition.

"You should go out tonight," she would tell him. Since they'd emigrated from Turini 34, he rarely left home to go anywhere except to his place of work. He preferred to keep to himself. He liked the lab because he worked alone.

One night, when he got home, his mother lay unconscious on the floor. Galin was tugging futilely at her, trying to lift her onto the couch.

"Help!" cried the creature.

Howard's jaw dropped. He'd heard the rumours that sparklers could speak, but he'd dismissed them as the idle fancies of unscientific minds.

He slid his arms under his mother's armpits and lifted her while Galin rushed to lift her feet, and together they moved her onto the couch.

"She hurts," it said in a thin voice, echoing his mother's Mongolian accent. It looked considerably larger than when Howard had left in the morning.

Howard summoned the medics, whose verdict was that she was so fragile, her condition so advanced, that there was no sense rushing her to the hospital. Better to tranquilize her and let her die painlessly in surroundings she loved.

Howard's hands grew cold. "You'll be all right, Mom," he lied when they had left. "I'll call a nurse, and she'll bring some medication that'll ease your pain."

"I don't need a nurse," she snapped. "Galin can take care of me."

"Don't be silly," said Howard.

A shadow fell across his face, and he looked up. The sparkler towered above him, head touching the ceiling. Howard gripped the armrests.

"Don't worry," Mom said. "It happens. Sometimes they grow bigger."

Howard stared at the sparkler. "Not like *this*."

"When needed…" Galin raised a paw fractionally, a curious expression on its misshapen muzzle.

"I don't know about this," said Howard dubiously. He'd always taken good care of his mother. How could a pet do better than her own son? "It looks dangerous."

His mother smiled. "Oh, no, dear. Sparklers are harmless. It says so on the galaxynet."

"But—"

"You were going to send me to die in a hospital with strangers. I'm asking you to let me stay here with the people I love."

"*People?* It's not a *person*, Mom!"

"People come in all colors and sizes," replied his mother. "So surely they can come in all shapes as well."

"Thank you, Mom," said Galin, and spirals of light burst out of every pore. Howard shielded his eyes and tried not to think about this alien creature calling his mother "Mom."

☼

Within days Galin began to have trouble squeezing through the doorways between the rooms—but Mrs. Apperson, who had seemed to be on Death's doorstep, showed signs of improvement.

Howard watched in wonderment as his mother kept getting stronger and Galin kept getting bigger.

"He's helping me, Howard. He needs to be big to take all my illness and digest it."

Howard threw his arms up. "Nonsense! And don't call it 'he.'"

Within a week Galin was so large he became confined to the garden.

It's getting out of hand, Howard thought one morning. "I wish you'd *stop growing*!" he said aloud.

Galin hung its head. "As you. Wish."

That day, Howard took a syringe from the lab, filled with *taloxenin*, a potent poison. On his way home, he stopped to buy the most placid Xialong cat he could find—an acceptable replacement pet.

As the conveyor approached his district, a rocket shot upwards. The passengers screamed, but the rocket dissolved before touching the top of the dome above the city, and a shower of stars followed. And rings, clovers of light, a ball with glittering streamers, radial lines tracing a spider's leg, and fragments like tiny fish swimming away. The cat screeched in terror and bolted off before he could stop it.

Howard ran home under a rain of powdery flashes.

His mother sat on the threshold, clapping her hands at each explosion of light. Galin shone with slow-burning stars of every imaginable color, the meaning of its Mongolian name more appropriate than ever.

"It's like New Year's Eve in Ulaanbaator!" Mrs. Apperson cried.

"Did…Galin help you out of bed?"

"I can walk without help." She looked healthier than she had for years.

Howard hid the syringe behind a potted *Calpurnia*. *Later*, he thought.

"I love you, Mom," said Galin, its voice weaker than usual. The spiky fur hung limp from its body.

Howard stepped forward and clumsily hugged the massive neck. Galin's head fell on its chest, imprisoning Howard's arms.

My God, thought Howard. *It's dying so that she can live.*

The sparkler's skin grew cold. Its light faded.

"Grow, please, my brother," Howard whispered. "Glow."

Original (First) Publication
Copyright © 2013 by Gio Clairval

WANT FREE EBOOKS?

Join the 'list' at Phoenix Pick

We give away a free ebook every month

www.PhoenixPick.com

Over the decades, Bruce McAllister's short fiction has been a finalist for both the Hugo and the Nebula. His "ESP in war" novel, Dream Baby, *is considered a classic of its type.*

CHILD OF THE GODS

Bruce McAllister

So they've given me these two big wings, but also these pathetic legs because (so they tell me) I won't be needing legs when I fly. Makes sense—up to a point. I need to walk on this world they've made for me, too. That's part of being who I am for them, and they don't seem to get it. I'm supposed to be their "child," the "Child of the Gods." That's what they've engineered this new body of mine to be, but it's not as ideal as it sounds. I'm alone (I think someone else is being groomed to join me, but who knows?), and in their grand plan they've neglected a few things. It makes life in this body they've given me a living hell, even if the world is Earth-like.

I've never seen them. They arrived in the usual B-movie way—telepathic message from An Incredibly Advanced Alien Race—and chose two human beings to be "special." That's how they put it. One was me. The other was a woman, I think. We weren't in any position to argue. They just took us. "We will treat them as children," they announced. "We will help them be as innocent and happy as children should be—as all our children are."

Was I excited to be chosen—an out-of-shape (not proud of it), 45-year-old yogurt distributor from Kansas City, unhappily divorced, no living children, an obsession with sports memorabilia, and bored with the grind? "Worried" would be the better word. How, I asked myself, would aliens (advanced or not) define "special"? How would they even define "child"? I could end up gray matter in a cyborg ship or a yappy pet with ten heads.

So here I am. The stars call like a bad habit, and I find myself, even when asleep, heading out there, flapping and flapping, pain shooting through my bones, and then, airless, falling like Icarus. But my lungs are happier up there than down here, where it hurts to breathe. It's bad planning, as if they don't get what a body is about.

So I do a lot of coughing when I walk, and my legs feel like the legs of an 80-year-old, about as useful as a pterodactyl's must have been. I try to feel the sun on my skin—that would be nice (the Child of the Gods gets a tan)—but the nerves are missing. They've given me this raging heart, this heat machine, so I won't be cold when I'm flying up where I shouldn't be flying; but the tradeoffs are hell.

I don't have a mouth because I haven't been given one. My lips are like a wound that's healed. I'd ask them why, but I can't. They've given me a body that doesn't need food, so I don't need a mouth, but every day words flutter like mad butterflies in my throat and I want to let them loose.

I've been given four arms with webbed fingers on each hand. My arms, easily confused, get tangled with my wings when I try to fly. When the wings finally catch the wind, the arms calm down. But for that moment flying feels impossible.

It's a shitty situation.

What I've found on this planet, this kingdom of mine—the one they've given me—looks pretty impressive, however: forests, deserts, lakes, mountains, seas, valleys, rivers, and meadows; insects, birds, and animals of all types. When the little things are near me (tree or animal), I can't see them. They're blurred. But when I stand in a valley at night and look at a distant mountain, I see a scampering mole snatched up by an owl with a hungry hiss, fur floating down like a slow song from the tree as it eats. It's beautiful.

If I hover over the ocean as dawn breaks and I look toward shore, I see perfectly, miles away, the red eyes of the birds with their stick-like legs and long bills pecking at the mud for tiny crab-like things. And the eight legs of the crab-like things kick frantically as the birds swallow them. And the lice move happily through the tiniest of feathers on those birds' heads. I don't know why, but for some reason this makes me happy.

Maybe it's because I can't see what's near me that I can't see the Gods, that I can't tell whether the voices I hear (if I'm really hearing them) are mine or theirs. But maybe it's that I haven't looked *far enough*—beyond mountains, beyond seas. That's what it feels like (because they want me to?): *That I haven't looked far enough.*

"Why did you make me this way?" I ask, and it's my voice all right—the one my ex heard every morning for years, the one my sales staff had to put up with. It's mine, but it sounds like someone else's voice and someone else's life.

The engines of the stars rumble. I don't know how else to put it. It's nothing I would have known in Kansas City, in that body I had. I don't know that words can say it.

The night turns red and blue—the *universe* turns red and blue—in my eyes, which are closed.

They answer with the voices of the moles, birds, lice, rocking sea, timeless mountains and light that dwells in the darkness within the light. It sounds, if it has a sound, like my own voice, the one I once had and might have if I had a mouth to emit one.

"*We did not make you,*" the voices say.

"You are the Gods and I am your child. Of course you made me…"

The engines race.

"You were *given* to us," the voices say. "You were given to us the way you are. There was no planet called Earth. There was no Missouri, no dairy product to be distributed and consumed, no little boy—your son—who died at the birthday party that day, filling you with a grief that drove others away. All of that was a dream you brought with you when you were given to us." The voices pause. "You have been with us *forever*, given to us in the beginning the way you are."

"But you are *the Gods*," I say again, the words coming as if from a child. "If you did not make me," I continue, my voice my son's, "who is there for me so that I might mean as much as the little crabs the birds eat on the mud, or the lice on their heads, or sand on the shore? Who is there in the darkness within the light to make the words fluttering in my throat mean what they might mean were you the Gods who made me?"

A voice that must be theirs, not mine, answers: "We make of the universe what we are given—what no one else wants. We take it and make it ours."

Looking down at the world, I see that it's true. How the jaw of a wildcat with funny ears and a single eye in its forehead opens, yawning. How an ape with hooves and a bleeding hand picks up a stone despite the pain and looks at it with a plan. How in the mountain range across the sea the tallest mountain collapses and in its fire a million insects, birds and animals vaporize, but none of this matters because others will come. They always come.

"What am *I* then?" I hear myself ask, the litany like a new religion.

"There are no mirrors here yet," the voices are saying, "because we haven't been given them. But we can show you what you would see were you to look in one."

I kick near the stars, high above the planet that's mine, wings tiring, and cry:

"But I can't see up close!"

"*Yes, you can,*" the moles shout back, speaking for the Gods and everything else as the little crab-like things whisper, "*Yes, you can. Just look—*"

They're right, of course. I can see. I look, and as I do, the Gods show themselves, and I see at last what I am, and I know why.

"So that I am yours. Really yours."

Yes, Child, they answer.

It is done.

"*But what about* her?" *I want to ask—that other voice, that other me, the old, fading dream. "The second one you chose? Brittany or Tiffany—some silly name like that. When is she coming and will she look like me?"*

But I don't. They'll tell me it's a dream, and I barely remember the question.

Original (First) Publication
Copyright © 2013 by Bruce McAllister

The late Charles Sheffield was a master of hard science fiction. He also served as the President of the Science Fiction and Fantasy Writers of America and of the American Astronautical Society. He won the Nebula and Hugo for his novelette "Georgia on My Mind," which is included in his collection Georgia on My Mind and Other Places, *as is the following story.*

THE FEYNMAN SALTATION

by Charles Sheffield

The worm in the apple; the crab in the walnut…Colin Trantham was adding fine black bristles to the crab's jointed legs when the nurse called him into the office.

He glanced at his watch as he entered. "An hour and a quarter the first time. Forty minutes the second. Now he sees me in nine minutes. Are you trying to tell me something?"

The nurse did not reply, and Dr. James Wollaston, a pudgy fifty-year-old with a small mouth and the face of a petulant baby, did not smile. He gestured to a chair, and waited until Trantham was seated on the other side of his desk.

"Let me dispose of the main point, then we can chat." Wollaston was totally lacking in bedside manner, which was one of the reasons that Colin Trantham liked him. "We have one more test result to come, but there's little doubt as to what it will show. You have a tumor in your left occipital lobe. That's the bad news. The good news is that it's quite operable."

"Quite?"

"Sorry. Completely operable. We should get the whole thing." He stared at Trantham. "You don't seem surprised by this."

Colin pushed the drawing across the table: the beautifully detailed little crab, sitting in one end of the shelled walnut. "I'm not an idiot. I've been reading and thinking cancer for weeks. I suppose it's too much to hope it might be benign?"

"I'm afraid not. It is malignant. But it appears to be a primary site. There are no other signs of tumors anywhere in your body."

"Wonderful. So I only have cancer once." Trantham folded the drawing and tucked it away in his jacket breast pocket. "Am I supposed to be pleased?"

Wollaston did not answer. He was consulting a desk calendar and comparing it with a typed sheet. "Friday is the twenty-third. I would like you in the night before, so we can operate early."

"I was supposed to go to Toronto this weekend. I have to sign a contract for a set of interior murals."

"Postpone it."

"Good. I was afraid you'd say cancel."

"Postpone it for four weeks." Wollaston was pulling another folder from the side drawer of his desk. "I propose to get you Hugo Hemsley. He and I have already talked. He's the best surgeon east of the Rockies, but he has his little ways. He'll want to know every symptom you've had from day one before he'll pick up a scalpel. How's the headache?"

The neurologist's calm was damping Colin's internal hysteria. "About the same. Worst in the morning."

"That is typical. Your first symptom was colored lights across your field of vision, sixty-three days ago. Describe that to me…."

✧

The muffled thump on the door was perfunctory, a relic of the days when Colin Trantham had a live-in girlfriend. Julia Trantham entered with a case in one hand and a loaded paper bag held to her chest with the other, pushing the door open with her foot and backing through.

"Grab this before I drop it." She turned and nodded down at the bag. "Bought it before I thought to ask. You allowed to drink?"

"I didn't ask, either." Colin examined the label on the bottle. "Moving up in the world. You don't get a Grands Echézeaux of this vintage for less than sixty bucks."

"Seventy-two plus tax. When did you memorize the wine catalog?"

"I'm feeling bright these days. When a man knows he is to be hanged in a fortnight, it concentrates his mind wonderfully."

"No points for that. Everybody quotes Johnson." Julia Trantham pulled the cork and sniffed it, while her brother was reaching up into the cabinet for two eight-ounce glasses.

"You're late." Colin Trantham placed the thin-stemmed goblets on the table and watched as Julia poured, a thin stream of dark red wine. His sister's face was calm, but the tremor in her hand was not. "The plane was on time. You went to see Wollaston, didn't you, before you came here?"

"You're too smart for your own good. I did."

"What did you find out?"

Julia Trantham took a deep breath. Colin had always been able to see through her lies, it would be a mistake to try one now. "It's a glioblastoma. A neuroglial cell tumor. And it's Type Four. Which means—"

"I know what it means. As malignant as you can get." Colin Trantham picked up his glass, emptied it in four gulps, and walked over to stand at the sink and stare out of the kitchen window. "Christ. You still have the knack of getting the truth out of people, don't you? I had my little interview with Dr. Hemsley, but he didn't get as honest as that. He talked procedure. Day after tomorrow he saws open my skull, digs in between the hemispheres, and cuts out a lump of my brain as big as a tennis ball. Local anesthetic—he wants me conscious while he operates."

"Probably wants you to hold tools for him. Like helping to change a car tire. Sounds minor."

"Minor for him. He gets five thousand bucks for a morning's work. And it's not his brain."

"Minor operation equals operation on somebody else."

"One point for that. Wish it weren't my brain, either. It's my second favorite organ."

"No points—that's Woody Allen in Sleeper. You're all quotes today."

Colin Trantham sat down slowly at the kitchen table. "I'm trying, Julia. It's just not…easy."

The casual brother-sister jousting shattered and fell away from between them like a brittle screen. Julia Trantham dropped into the seat opposite. "I know, Colin. It's not easy. It's awful. My fault. I'm not handling this well."

"Not your fault. Everybody's. Mine too, same problem. You go through life, build your social responses. Then you get a situation they just don't cover. Who wants to talk about dying, for Christ's sake?" There was a long silence, but the tension was gone. Colin Trantham stared at his older sister's familiar face, unseen for half a year. "I'm scared, Julie. I lie awake at night, and I think, I won't make old bones."

Little brother, hurt and crying. We're grown-ups now. We haven't hugged in twenty years. "Social responses. I'm supposed to say, don't be scared, Col, you'll be fine. But while I say it I'm thinking, you're scared, no shit? Of course you're scared. Me, I'd be petrified. I am petrified."

"Will you stay until the operation's over?"

"I was planning to. If it's all right with you, I'll hang around until you're out of the hospital. Write up a paper on extinct invertebrates that I've had in the mill for a while." She poured again into both glasses, emptying the bottle. "Any girlfriend that I need to know about, before I embarrass her by my drying panty hose?"

"Rachel. Just a now-and-again thing." Colin Trantham picked up the empty bottle and stared at the layer of sediment left in the bottom, divining his future. "Should we have decanted it? I hardly tasted that first glass. I'll try to sip it this time with due reverence." The raw emotion was fading, the fence of casual responses moving back into position. "No problem with Rachel. If she finds you here with me I'll just pretend you're my sister."

✣

The waiting room was empty. Julia dithered on the threshold, possessed by conflicting desires. She wanted news, as soon as it was available. She also wanted a cigarette, more than she had ever wanted one, but smoking was forbidden anywhere in the hospital.

Dr. Wollaston solved her problem before she could. He approached along the corridor behind her and spoke at once: "Good news. It went as well as it possibly could go."

The nicotine urge was blotted out by a rush of relief.

"Minimum time in the operating room," the neurologist went on. "No complications." He actually summoned a smile. "Sedated now, but he wanted you to see this. He said that you would know exactly what it means."

He held out a piece of paper about five inches square. At its center, in blue ink, a little figure of a hedgehog leered out at Julia, cheeks bulging. She could feel her own cheeks burning. "That's me—according to Colin. Private family joke."

"Drawn right after the operation, when Hemsley was testing motor skills. Astonishing, I thought."

"Can I see him?"

"If you wish, although he might not recognize you at the moment. He should be sleeping. Also"—a second of hesitation, picking words carefully—"I would appreciate a few minutes of your time. Perhaps a glass of wine, after what I know has been a trying day for you. This is"—Julia sensed another infinitesimal pause—"primarily medical matters. I need to talk to you about your brother."

How could she refuse? Walking to the wine bar, Julia realized that he had talked her out of seeing Colin, without seeming to do so. Typical James Wollaston, according to Colin. Gruff, sometimes grumpy; but smart.

His eyes were on her as they settled in on the cushioned round stools across a fake hogshead table, and she took out and lit a cigarette.

"How many of those a day?"

"Five or six." Julia took one puff and laid down the burning cigarette in the ashtray. "Except I'm like every other person who smokes five—a pack lasts me a day and a half."

"You're going to regret it. It's murder on your skin. Another ten years and you'll look like a prune."

"Skin? I thought you were going to tell me about my heart and lungs."

"For maximum effect, you have to hit where it's least expected. You ought to give it up."

"I was going to. I really was. But you know what happened? Since Mother died, Colin and I have called each other every week."

"Sunday midday."

"That's right. How'd you know?"

"I know a lot about you and Colin."

"Then you know Colin's not one for overstatement. He hadn't said a word about…all this. When the evidence was in, he hit me with it all at once. It floored me. I'd got up that morning determined that I was through, that was it for cigarettes. I'd just thrown a near-full pack away." She laughed shakily. "Looks like I picked a hell of a day to quit smoking."

"That's from Airplane. No points, I think your brother would say."

"My God. You really do know a lot about us."

"When it was clear to me that Colin might have a serious problem, I put him through my biggest battery of tests, checking his memory and his reflexes and his logical processes. We also went over all his background. As a result I know a great deal about you, too, your background, what you do." He paused. "I even understood about the hedgehog, though it didn't seem the best time and place to mention it. Anyway, how's the paleontology business?"

"Just scratching out a living. Sorry. Programmed response. In a very interesting state. You see, every few years there's a major upheaval—facts, or theories. New radioactive dating, punctuated equilibrium, Cretaceous extinctions, mitochondrial DNA tracking, the reinterpretation of the Burgess Shale. Well, it seems we're in for another one. A biggie."

"So I have heard."

"You have? Well, not from Colin, that's for sure."

"True. I read it."

"Fossils bore him stiff. He says that Megatherium was an Irish woman mathematician."

A moment's thought. "Meg O'Theorem?"

"That's her. He was all set to be a mathematician or a physicist himself, 'til the drawing and painting bug took hold. He's the talented one, you know—I'm just the one who wrote papers and stayed in college forever. Anyway, first he started to paint in the evenings, and then—" She stopped, drew breath, and shook her head. "Sorry, doctor. I'm babbling. Nerves. You wanted to talk."

"I do. But I like to listen, too—unless you're in a big hurry?"

"Nothing in the world to do but sit here and listen."

Wollaston nodded. The wine had arrived and he was frowning at the label. "I hope this isn't too lowbrow. It's certainly not the Grands Crus that you and your brother like to sample. It's a naive domestic burgundy without any breeding, but I think you'll be amused—"

"—by its presumption. No points. But I get one for finishing the line."

"I need practice, or I'll never be a match for the two of you." He poured the first splash of wine, and in that instant seemed to become a younger and more vulnerable person. "A successful operation. That was the first stage. It is now behind us. Did your brother discuss with you what might happen next?"

Julia shook her head. Colin had not raised the subject, nor had she. Somehow it had not seemed significant before the operation. "Chemotherapy?"

"Not with the conventional antimetabolites. They have difficulty crossing the blood-brain barrier. The normal next step would be radiation. But a glioblastoma is fiercely malignant. Bad odds. I want to try something that I hope will be a lot better. However, I wanted to obtain your reaction before I discussed it with Colin." Another pause, words chosen carefully. Julia nodded her internal approval. A good, cautious doctor. "I'd like to put him onto an experimental protocol," continued Wollaston. "An implanted drug-release device inside the brain itself, with a completely new drug, a variable delivery rate, and an internal monitor sensitive enough to respond to selected ambient neurotransmitter levels. It's tiny, and there will be no need to reopen the skull to install it."

He was not looking at her. Why not? "Price isn't an issue, Dr. Wollaston, unless it's out of this world. We have insurance and money. What are the side effects?"

"No consistent patterns. This is too new. And the implant would be done free, since your brother would be part of a controlled experiment. But"—the kicker, here it came, he was finally looking into her eyes—

"Colin would have to fly to Europe to get it. You see, it's not yet FDA approved."

"He'd have to stay there?"

His surprise was comical. "Stay there? Of course not. He could fly over one night, have the implant performed the next day, and as soon as the surgeon there approved his release he'd turn right around and come back. But I'm not sure how Colin will react to the idea. What do you think? It doesn't have FDA approval, you see, so—"

"I don't think. I know. Colin doesn't give a tinker's damn about the FDA. He'll do it." Julia stubbed out her cigarette, burned its whole length unnoticed in the ashtray. "Of course he'll do it. Colin wants to live."

She took a first sip of wine, then two big gulps. "What next?"

"On medical matters? Nothing. I'm done. More wine. Relax. Your turn to talk." He was smiling again. "I hope you don't have to run off right away." Julia was staring all around her. His smile vanished. "Do you?"

Julia was still scanning the wine bar. "Where are all the waiters? You know, I didn't eat one thing all day. I'm absolutely famished. How do you order food in this place?"

☼

Walking back to Colin's apartment through the mellow April evening, Julia Trantham was filled with guilt. Ten hours ago a malignant tumor the size and shape of a Bartlett pear had been removed from the brain of her brother. He was lying unconscious, gravely ill. While she…

For the past three hours she had managed to forget Colin's condition—and in the company of James Wollaston she had enjoyed herself hugely.

☼

Concorde, Heathrow to Dulles; seventy thousand feet, supersonic over open ocean.

Colin Trantham sat brooding in a left-side window seat, staring out at blue-black sky and sunlit cloud tops. The plane was half-empty, with no one between him and the aisle. Occasional curious looks from flight attendants and other passengers did not bother him. He was beyond that, accepting their stares as normal, just as he accepted the head bandages and bristly sprouting hair. If his appearance were enough to stir curiosity, what would people say if they knew what sat inside his head?

Maybe they would be as unimpressed as he had been. Colin had been shown the device before its insertion, and seen nothing to suggest its powers: a swollen iridescent disk no bigger than his fingernail, surrounded by the hollow legs of sensors and drug delivery system. Super-beetle. An unlikely candidate to be his savior. He felt nothing, but according to the London doctors it had set to work at once. The battle was going on now. Deep within his skull, bloated with slow poison, the scarab was stinging the crab's microstases in silent conflict.

And the chance that it would succeed? No one would give him odds. Bad sign.

"Make a note of thoughts that strike you as unusual." Wollaston, on their last meeting before Colin flew to England, had maintained his imperturbability. "We can watch your stomach at work, or your gall bladder. But you're the only one who knows how normally your brain is functioning. Record your dreams."

"My dreams? Doctor Wollaston, even before I got sick, my dreams never made much sense."

"They don't have to. Remember what Havelock Ellis said: 'Dreams are real while they last; can we say more of life?' I want to know about them."

Colin was beginning to agree. Dreams and life, life and dreams; he had felt like telling Wollaston that his whole life had become one waking dream, on that morning when a headache came and grew and would not go. Since then nothing had been real. The pain had gone with the operation, but in its place was a continuous foreboding. Never glad confident morning again. He did not recall a real dream of any kind since the operation. And he did not want to write notes on his condition; he wanted it never to have happened.

The flight attendant had paused by Colin's row of seats and was staring at him questioningly. He did not want to talk to her; to avoid it he stared again out of the window. The sun was visible in the dark sky, farther toward the rear of the plane. At Mach Two they were outpacing it. Time was running backward. Call back yesterday, bid time return.

Colin shivered at a slow stir of movement, deep within his brain. Something there was waking from long sleep. He stared straight at the sun. His pupils contracted, his hands relaxed. Fully awake, he began to dream.

✧

I was standing on a flat shore, watching the sea. Or maybe I was sitting, I can't tell because I had no sense of feeling of legs and arms. I just knew I was there. Enjoying the sunshine on my bare back, feeling good. More than good, absolutely terrific. Cold, perfect day, I could feel the blood running in my veins. Something must have died a mile or so offshore, or maybe it was a school of fish, because thousands of flying things were swooping and turning and settling. I decided I would swim out there and see for myself …

Julia Trantham looked up from the third sheet. "Does it just go on like this for all the rest? Because if it does, I can't help. It's not specific enough."

"I know." Wollaston nodded. "It would have been nice if you could have said, hey, that's where we spent my fourteenth summer. But I didn't expect it would ring any particular bells. Keep reading, if you would—I want you to have the context for something else."

"And I thought you asked me here for dinner."

He did not reply. She went on in silence until she reached the last page, then looked up with raised eyebrows. "So?"

He took four pages of 20" x 14" unlined paper from a folder and slid them across the table. "Colin found what he had written as unsatisfactory as you do. He says he's an artist, not a writer. Pictures, not words. What do you make of these?"

The drawings were sepia ink on white background. Julia glanced for a few seconds at the first couple of sheets and put them aside, but the other two occupied her for a long time. James Wollaston watched her closely but did not speak or move.

"If you tell me these are all Colin's, I'll have to accept that they are." She tapped the first two pages, spread out on the table of Wollaston's dining room. "But these ones sure don't look like it."

"Why not?"

"Not detailed enough." She picked up one of the sheets. "When you ask Colin to draw something, he draws it exactly. It's not that he lacks imagination, but he never cheats. Once he's seen it, he can draw it. And he sees more than you or I."

"He didn't see these. He dreamed them."

"You're the one who's been telling me that dreams are as real as anything else. Anyway, compare the first two pages with the others. These must be birds, because they're flying. But they're cartoon birds, vague wings and bodies and heads, almost as though Colin didn't care what they looked like. And now look at these other two, the tidal shellfish and crabs and worms. Precise. Every joint and every hair drawn in. See this? It's *Pecten jacobaeus*—a scallop. Look at the eyes on the fringed mantle. You could use it as a textbook illustration. That's Colin's trademark. Same with the two lugworms. You can tell they're different species. But those first two pages are just wrong." She paused. "You don't see it, do you?"

"I can't argue with you." Wollaston stared at the pages as though he were seeing them for the first time. He had taken off his tie and draped it over a chair back, and now he picked it up and rolled it around his forefingers.

"But you don't like it," said Julia, "what I said about the first two sheets?"

"I do not."

"It's a bad sign?"

"I don't know. I know it's not a good sign. In Colin's situation the best change in behavior is no change."

"Do you think it's coming back?"

"I'd love to say, no, of course not. But I don't know. God, I hate to keep saying it to you. I don't know, I don't know. But it's the truth." He came closer, half a step nearer than convention permitted. "Julia, I wish I could say something more definite. It could be the treatment—new drug, new protocol, new delivery system."

"But you don't think it is."

"I think these drawings may be the effects of the treatment." He slid the sheets back into the folder. "But they're not the whole story. I go more by look and sound and sense. My gut feel says it's something more than side effects. I think Colin has problems. How long are you staying?"

"I've been wondering. I could stay the whole summer. It's late to do it, but if I moved fast I could even make part of next year a sabbatical. Should I?"

She was tense, hearing the question behind the question, not sure she wanted to hear the answer.

"I think you should." James Wollaston looked more miserable than an objective physician had a right to look. "I think you should stay, until—well, stay as long as you can."

✡

The northern bedroom of the ground floor apartment had been converted to a studio, its bare expanse of window looking out onto a paved courtyard where weeds pushed up between cracked stones. The studio lay at the end of a corridor, far from the entrance to the apartment. Julia stood and listened as she came through the front door.

Total silence. That was odd. For the past three months her arrival had always produced a call of "Hi!" and a quick appearance in the kitchen to discuss dinner plans. He must be really deep into his work.

She slipped off her shoes and stole along the corridor.

Colin was in the studio, standing at the easel with his back half-turned to her. He was working in acrylics, and she saw a vivid flash of colors on the big board. She studied him as she came in. The hair on the back of his head had regrown completely, it must be two inches long now; but he was terribly thin, just gaunt bones, and the skin on his temple had a pale, translucent look. She saw that the food on the tray table beyond the easel was untouched. He must have eaten nothing since she left, over ten hours ago.

"Col?"

He did not seem to hear. He was painting furiously, brush strokes as rapid and sure as they had ever been. She came to his shoulder to examine the picture, but before she reached the easel she glanced up at his face. His gray eyes were unnaturally bright, and there was a smile of exquisite pleasure on his gaunt face. But it was not for Julia. He did not know that she was there. He was smiling away into some private space.

"Colin!" She touched his arm, suddenly frightened. The brush strokes faltered, the moving hand slowed. He blinked, frowned, and turned toward her. "Julie—" he said. "I'm through one barrier. It's wonderful, but now there's another. Bigger. I can't see a way past it yet." His hand jerked up and down, a quick chopping movement with the paint brush. "Like a wall. If I can just get through this one…"

The expression of ecstasy was replaced by surprise. He swayed and groaned, his lips drawing back from his teeth. Julia saw his gums, pale and bloodless, and the veinless white of his eyes. The brush fell to the floor. She grabbed for his arm, but before she could catch him he had crumpled forward, pawing at the painting and easel before falling heavily on top of them.

✡

"I don't care what you tell Colin. I want your prognosis, no matter how bad it looks."

It was long after working hours. Julia Trantham was sitting at one end of the uncomfortable vinyl-covered couch in the doctor's reception room. Her face was as pale as her brother's had been, twenty-four hours earlier.

"At the moment Colin doesn't want to hear anything. Doesn't seem to care. That's not as unusual as you might think." Wollaston had been standing, but now he came to sit next to her. "People hide from bad news."

"And it is bad news. Isn't it?"

"It's very bad. And it's not a surprise." He sighed and leaned his head on the smooth yellow seat back. At dinner he had switched to martinis instead of the usual wine. Julia could see the difference. He was more talkative than usual, and he needed her to be an audience.

"I wonder what it will be like a hundred years from now," he went on. "The physicians will look back and think we were like medieval barbers, trying to practice medicine without the tools. All the cancer treatments except surgery are based on the same principle: do something that kills the patient, and hope it kills the cancer a bit faster. The antimetabolite drugs—like the ones in Colin's implant—kill cancer cells when the cells divide. But a few resistant ones survive, and they go on and multiply. I've seen it a thousand times. You start chemotherapy, and at first the patient does well, wonderfully well. Then over the months…the slip back starts."

"That's what's happened to Colin—even with this new experimental treatment?"

He was nodding, eyes closed and the back of his head still against the couch. "Experimental treatments are like lotteries. You have to play to win. But you don't win very often." He reached out blind and groped for her hand. "I'm sorry, Julia. We're not winning. It's back. Growing fast. I can't believe the change since the last CAT scan."

"How long, Jim?"

"I don't know. Pretty quick. Colin can come out of the hospital if he wants to, keeping him in won't help. A hospice might be better. A day or two, a few weeks, a month. Nobody knows."

"And there's no other treatment you can try?"

He said nothing. Julia stared across at the wall, where Wollaston had hung one of Colin's postoperative drawings, a lightning sketch of half a dozen lines that was clearly a picture of some kind of bird feeding her chick, the beak inside the little one's gaping bill and halfway down its throat.

"When did Colin draw the picture on the wall there?"

"About two weeks ago." Wollaston stirred. "It's wonderful, isn't it? Have you seen all the others—the ones he's done since the operation?"

"I haven't seen any. It's a habit we got into years ago. I wouldn't look at Colin's work when he was getting ready for a show or a delivery until the end, then I'd give him my opinion of the whole thing. He didn't like me in his studio."

"Maybe it's just as well. Some of the recent ones have been…strange."

"You mean he's losing his technique? God, to Colin that would be worse than dying."

"No. The technique is terrific. But the animals don't look right. For instance, he drew a pair of seals. But their flippers were too developed, too much like real legs. And there was one of a zebra, except it wasn't quite a zebra, more like a funny okapi. I wondered at first if the pictures could tell me something about what's going on in Colin's head, but they haven't. I'd say he's feeling strange, so he's drawing strange." He patted her hand. "I know, Julia, 'Colin draws just what he sees,' don't say it."

"Real legs, you say? And there's wing claws on that bird, that's what's odd. But it's not a baby hoatzin."

The hand was pulled from his. There was a rapid movement of the couch next to him. Wollaston opened his eyes. "Julia?"

But she was no longer by his side. She was over at the wall, gazing with total concentration at Colin's drawing. When she turned, her mouth was an open O of confusion and surmise.

✧

"There they are." Julia Trantham patted a stack of papers, boards, and canvases. They were in Wollaston's office, with the big wooden desk swept clear and the table lamp on its highest setting. "Every one we could find. But instead of grouping according to medium and size, the way you usually would, I've rearranged them to chronological order. There are eighty-nine pictures here, all signed and dated. The top one is the first drawing that Colin made when he was flying back from England. The last one is the painting he was working on in his studio when he passed out. I want you to look through the whole stack before you say anything."

"If you say so." James Wollaston was humoring her, knowing she had been under terrible stress for months. It was close to midnight, and they had spent the last hour collecting Colin Trantham's pictures, pulling them from medical records and apartment and studio. Julia would not tell him what game she was playing, but he could see that to her it was far more than a game. He started carefully through the heap; pen and ink drawings, charcoal sketches, oils and acrylics and pencils.

"Well?" Julia was too impatient to wait for him to finish. She was staring at him expectantly although he was on only the tenth picture.

"Did he always draw nothing but nature scenes?" said Wollaston. "Just plants and animals?" He was staring at sheet after sheet.

"Mostly. Colin is a top biological illustrator. Why?"

"You insist he drew from life, from what he had seen. But in these pictures that doesn't seem to be true."

"Why not?" Julia pounced on him with the question.

"Well, I recognize the first drawings, and they're terrific. But this—" he held out the board he was examining "—it looks wrong."

"It's not wrong. That's a member of Castoroidinae—a rodent, a sort of beaver. Keep going. What's that one?"

"Damned if I know. Like a cross between a horse and a dog—as though Colin started by drawing a horse's head, then when he got to the body and legs he changed his mind."

"You were right about the horse. That's Hyracotherium. To the life. Keep going."

But Wollaston had paused. "Are you sure? It looks strange to me, and I have a pretty good grounding in comparative anatomy."

"I'm sure you do." Julia took a painting from the stack. They were less than halfway through the heap. Her hands were trembling. "Current anatomy, Jim. But I specialize in paleoanatomy. Colin has been drawing real plants and animals. The only thing is, some of them are extinct. The Castoroidinae were giant beavers, big as a bear. They were around during the Pleistocene. Hyracotherium's a forerunner of the horse;, it flourished during the Lower Eocene, forty or fifty million years ago. These pictures are consistent with our best understanding of their anatomy based on the fossil record."

She was shaking, but Wollaston did not share her excitement. "I'll take your word for it, Julia. But I want to point out that none of this is too surprising, given your own interests and the work you do."

"That's not true!" Julia fumbled out a cigarette, lit it, and inhaled hard enough to shrivel the bottom of her lungs. "It's more than surprising, it's astonishing. I told you the first time we had a drink together, what I do bores Colin stiff. He doesn't know beans about it and he doesn't care. There's no way he got these drawings from me. And do you realize that these pictures are in reverse chronological order? Fossil dating is a tricky business, I'm the first to admit that; but in this set, the more recently Colin did them, the older the forms represented."

"What are you saying, Julia?" The concern in Wollaston's voice was for sister more than brother. "If you're suggesting…what it sounds like you're suggesting, then it's nonsense. And there's a perfectly rational explanation."

"Like what?"

He reached forward, removed the cigarette from her fingers, and stubbed it out. "Julia, the longer you study the human brain, the more astonishing it seems. You say that what you do bores Colin. Probably true. But do you think that means he didn't even hear you, when you talked and talked paleontology all these years? Do you think he never picked up one of your books? They're scattered all over the apartment, I've seen them there myself. It's no wonder you recognize what Colin has been painting—because you put all those ideas into his head yourself."

"I didn't, Jim. I know I didn't. And here's why." She was turning the stack, moving down toward the bottom. "Now we're beyond the K-T barrier—the time of the late Cretaceous extinction. See this?"

The painting was in subdued oils, browns and ochers and dark greens, crowded with detail. The viewpoint was low to the ground, peering up through a screen of ferns. In the clearing beyond the leafy cover crouched three scaly animals, staring at a group of four others advancing from the left. The sun was low, casting long shadows to the right, and there was a hint of morning ground mist still present to soften outlines.

"Saurischians. Coelurosaurs, I'd say, and not very big ones." Julia pointed to the three animals in the foreground. "The pictures we were looking at before were all Tertiary or later. But everything beyond that is Cretaceous or earlier. I'd place this one as middle Jurassic, a hundred and sixty million years ago. No birds, no flowering plants. I know those three animals—but the four behind them are completely new to me. I've never seen anything like them. If I had to guess I'd say they're a form of small hadrosaur, some unknown midget relative of Orthomerus. That flat hulk, way over in the background, is probably a crocodile. But look at the detail on the coelurosaurs, Jim. I couldn't have told Colin all that—I couldn't even have imagined it. Look at the scales and wrinkles and pleats in the mouth pouch, look at the eyes and the saw-toothed brow ridges—I've never seen those on any illustration, anywhere. The vegetation fits, too, all gymnosperms, cycads, ginkgoes, and conifers."

James Wollaston laughed, but there was no suggestion from his face that he found anything funny. He was sure that Julia Trantham was practicing her own form of denial, of reality avoidance. "Julia, if you came in to see me as a patient and said all that, I'd refer you for immediate testing. Listen to yourself!"

But she had moved to the final drawing, smeared where Colin Trantham had fallen on top of it before it was dry. "And this is earlier yet." She was talking quietly, and not to Wollaston. He stared at her hopelessly.

"Something like Rutiodon, one of the phytosaurs. But a different jaw. And there on the left is Desmatosuchus, one of the aëtosaurs. I don't recognize that other one, but it has mammalian characteristics." She looked up. "My God, we must be back near the beginning of the Triassic. Over two hundred million years. These are thecodonts, the original dinosaur root stock. He's jumping farther and farther! Jim, I'm scared."

He reached out for her, and she clung to him and buried her face in his jacket. But her words were perfectly clear: "First thing in the morning, I've got to see Colin."

✧

What James Wollaston had heard with incredulity, Colin Trantham listened to with a remote and dreamy interest. Julia had taken one look at him, and known that no matter what the neurologist might say, Colin would never be leaving the hospital. It was not the IVs, or the bluish pallor of his face. It was something else, an impalpable smell in the air of the room that made her look at her brother and see the skull beneath the skin.

Whatever it was, he seemed oblivious to it. He was grinning, staring at her and beyond her, his face filled with the same ecstasy that she had seen in the studio. His conversation faded in and out, at one moment perfectly rational, the next jumping off in some wild direction.

"Very interesting. The implant and the drugs, of course, that's what's doing it. Has to be." From his tone he might have been talking of a treatment applied to some casual acquaintance. "Did you know, Julia, if I were a bird I'd be in much better shape than I am now? Good old Hemsley operated on me, and he got most of it. But he must have missed a little bit—a bit too much for the implant to handle. Poor little scarab, can't beat the crab. But if I'd been a bird, they could have cut away the whole of both cerebral hemispheres, and I'd be as good as ever. Or nearly as good. Wouldn't know how to build a nest, of course, but who needs that?"

And then suddenly he was laughing, a gasping laugh that racked his chest and shook the tubes leading into his fleshless arms.

"Colin!" The fear that curiosity had held at bay came flooding back, and Julia was terrified. "I'll get the nurse."

"I'm fine." He stopped the strained laughter as quickly as he had started it and his face went calm. "Better than fine. But I'm a robot now. I, Robot."

She stared at him in horror, convinced that the final disintegration of mind was at hand.

"You know what I mean, Julie." Now he sounded rational but impatient. "Don't go stupid on me. Remember what Feynman said, in physics you can look on any positron as an electron that's traveling backward in time. You tell me I've been jumping backward—"

"Jim says that's nonsense. He says I'm talking through my hat."

"Jim?"

"Dr. Wollaston."

"So it's Jim, is it. And how long has that been going on?" He narrowed his eyes and peered up at her slyly. "Well, you tell Jim that I agree with you. I'm going backward, and I can prove it. And according to Feynman that means the electrons in my brain are positrons. I've got a positronic brain. Get it?" He laughed again, slapping his skinny hands on the bedsheets. "Positronic brain. I'm a robot!"

"Colin, I'm getting the nurse. Right now." Julia had already pressed the button, but no one had appeared.

"In a minute. And you know how I can prove it? I can prove it because I feel absolutely wonderful."

His face had filled again with that strange bliss. He reached out and held her hand. "Remember how it felt when you were four years old, and you woke up in the morning, and you knew it was your birthday? That's how it used to be, all the time for all of us. But ontogeny recapitulates phylogeny: immature forms pass through the evolutionary stages of their ancestors. And that applies to feelings as well as bodies. Little kids feel the way all the animals used to feel, a long time ago. That's the way I am when I'm there. Fantastic, marvelous. And the farther I go, the better it gets. You looked at my pictures. If I've been going back, how far did I get?"

Julia hesitated. She was torn. Half of her wanted to believe her brother, to see more of those marvelously detailed drawings and to analyze them. The other half told her she was dealing with a mind already hopelessly twisted by disease.

"Your last picture shows the period of the earliest dinosaurs. They're all thecodonts, nothing that most people would recognize. The fossil record is very spotty there. We don't know nearly as much about them as we'd like to."

"And what would be next—going backward, I mean?"

"The Permian. No dinosaurs. And at this end of the Permian, over ninety percent of all the lifeforms on earth died off. We don't know why."

He was nodding. "The barrier. I can feel it, you know, when I'm trying to jump. I went through one, when all the dinosaurs died off. This one is bigger. I've been trying to fight my way through. I'm nearly there, but it's taking every bit of energy I have."

"Col, anything that tires you or upsets you is bad. You need rest. Why are you climbing imaginary walls?"

"You don't know the feeling. If I could jump all the way back, right to the first spark of life, I bet the intensity of life force and joy would be just about too much to stand. I'm going there, Julie. Across the barrier, into the Permian, all the way to the beginning. And I'm never coming back. Never."

As though on cue, the thin body arched up from the bed, arms flailing. The mouth widened to a rictus of infernal torment and breath came hoarse and loud. Julia cried out, just as the nurse appeared. Wollaston was right behind her.

"Grand mal." He was bending over Colin, grabbing at a rubber spatula and pushing it into the mouth just as the teeth clenched down. "Hold this, nurse, we don't want him swallowing his tongue."

But the spasm ended as quickly as it had started. Colin Trantham lay totally at ease, his breath slow and easy. His face smoothed, and the fixed grin faded. In its place came a look of infinite calm and blissful peace.

"Dr. Wollaston!" The nurse was watching the monitors, her hand on Colin's pulse. "Dr. Wollaston, we have arrhythmia. Becoming fainter."

Wollaston had the hypodermic with its six-inch needle in his hand, the syringe already filled. It was poised above Colin Trantham's chest when he caught Julia's eye.

She shook her head. "No, Jim. Please. Not for one month more pain."

He hesitated, finally nodded, and stepped away from the bed.

"Dr. Wollaston." The nurse looked up, sensing that she had missed something important but not sure what. She was still holding Colin Trantham's wrist. "I can't help him. He's going, doctor. He's going."

Julia Trantham moved to grip her brother's other hand in both of hers.

"He is," she said. "He's going." She leaned forward, to stare down into open eyes that still sparkled with a surprised joy. "He's going. And I'd give anything to know where."

Afterword to "The Feynman Saltation"

Anthony Trollope said, "A genius must wait for inspiration. I am not a genius, so I write every day."

I am not a genius, and I don't write every day, either, but there is one guaranteed way to get a story from me. You ask me for one, on some specialized subject, and my brain juices start to flow at once.

This story began with a letter from Robert Silverberg, asking if I had a dinosaur story for a new book he was editing. I didn't, and at the time I was not writing anything because I was busy reading deeply about parasitic diseases and cancer treatment. I also know nothing about dinosaurs.

Naturally, I wrote back at once and said yes; I gave him my proposed title, "The Feynman Saltation," and I started to write. But I could not get my mind far away from the morbid fascinations of glioblastomas and chemotherapy and antimetabolite drugs. If this tale seems to be more about cancer than dinosaurs, you now know why.

Paul Cook is the author of eight books of science fiction, and is currently both a college instructor and the editor of the Phoenix Pick Science Fiction Classics line.

BOOK REVIEWS

by Paul Cook

The Cassandra Project
by Jack McDevitt & Mike Resnick
Ace Science Fiction 2012
Hardcover, 400 pages
ISBN: 978-1937008710

Two of our most successful writers have joined to produce a taut political and scientific thriller in *The Cassandra Project.*

The novel opens with the travails of Jerry Culpepper, a seasoned PR expert at NASA who yearns for the good old days when America had a space program. Now, it's shutting down completely. Culpepper moves on to work for a multi-billionaire (picture a cross between a visionary such as Richard Branson and a good ole boy who understands how the system—and money—actually works: someone such as Lyndon Johnson). But before all this happens, we, the readers, discover that Neil Armstrong and Buzz Aldrin might not have been the first humans on the moon in 1969. Instead, Culpepper discovers redacted photos of the far side of the moon as well as other missing data that suggest a cover-up during the presidency of Richard Nixon. (Watergate figures into this novel. Imagine that!) Nevertheless, *some-*

thing was found on the far side of the moon and has been suppressed for more than fifty years by every administration. But what was it? "Bucky" Blackstone wants to fund his own moon mission and find out and Jerry Culpepper is on board. *The Cassandra Project* never lags and is engaging to the very end. In fact, it practically rushes to its conclusion.

A personal note—What drew me to the novel was its main conceit: that there was "something" on the dark side of the moon and that NASA sent two missions to examine it before Armstrong and Aldrin flew the "official" mission to the moon. When I was eleven, I went on the Rocket to the Moon ride at Disneyland in Anaheim, California. This would have been about 1961. You sat in a seat that leaned back and felt the theater rumble as the rocket took off, and you saw the voyage through an overhead screen. Disney animation wasn't all that good, but the thrill for an eleven-year-old was to circle the moon and see the Captain fire a flare on the far side of the moon to show the audience the rectangular remains of "something" built there and abandoned a long time ago. This is what science fiction is about: that sense of wonder.

We're all grown up now, and that sense of wonder has virtually been hammered out of all of us. But it's the character of Jerry Culpepper that drives the novel. He's the one with a real sense of wonder and he still has pride in a space program that used to provide that same thrill to a whole world. Now the space program is gone but McDevitt and Resnick manage to evoke just enough to make *The Cassandra Project* worth your time…especially if there's an eleven-year-old trapped inside you or you remember Disneyland of old.

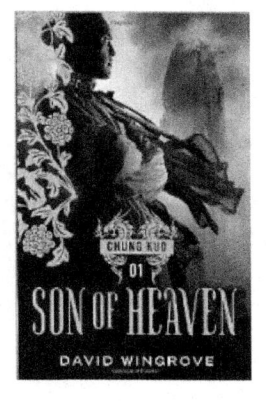

✧

Son of Heaven
by David Wingrove
Atlantic Books 2012
Paperback: 442 pages
ISBN: 978-1848875265

Reviewed here is the newly-released trade paperback edition of the original UK hardbound publication of David Wingrove's *Son of Heaven*, which originally came out in 2011. *Son of Heaven* is the first of six projected novels that form a prequel to his extraordinary Chung Kuo series that started in 1989 and concluded in 1999. Those first novels are:

The Middle Kingdom (1989)
The Broken Wheel (1990)
The White Mountain (1992)
The Stone Within (1993)
Beneath the Tree of Heaven (1994)
White Moon, Red Dragon (1994)
Days of Bitter Strength (1997)
The Marriage of the Living Dark (1999)

These books were major science fiction bestsellers in the UK but hardly received much traction in the US when they appeared—or at least any traction critically other than a few measly book reviews. If you haven't discovered this series, then you're in for a treat. China hasn't been the focus of much science fiction in the past. Here it is, full bore. The series Chung Kuo (or China) chronicles the rise and fall of a future world dominated by a highly-advanced China which had earlier caused the downfall of the West in the middle of the 21st century. This China has created a fantastic world-smothering City, but despite its power, it is riddled with palace intrigues and a resurgence of the groups (racial, ethnic, and political) who are actively being suppressed by China's iron rule. Despite the huge cast of the original characters and the unfamiliarity American readers might have with Chinese names and terms, the Chung Kuo series is very readable. It is written with both lyricism and an attention to visual detail. Wingrove is a master writer and a master storyteller, as the original series amply demonstrated. I hope that first series will return to print soon as this new one unfolds.

With this new series, Wingrove is pulling a George Lucas, telling the story of how this future China came about. Unlike Lucas' prequels to the first three *Star Wars* movies, this new series seems to actually work and requires none of the knowledge of the middle books (now numbered 7-14). *Son of Heaven*, the inaugural novel in this new series, tells the story of Jake Reed, a man who is working in a high-tech London as a financial wizard. It's 2085 and he discovers that China's main computer wizard is clandestinely at work to wreck the entire global financial system. Which he does. And it throws the world into barbarism and chaos. Anyone familiar with the world-wrecking novels of British writer John Christopher (Sam Youd), who wrote *The Long Winter*, *The Ragged Edge*, and *No Blade of Grass*, will find much of Wingrove's post-apocalyptic Wessex familiar (but not derivative).

What makes matters worse is that as Reed is keeping his little village safe from refugees and brigands, they observe to the east a strange white "wall," like a line of glaciers, appearing along the horizon. This is the City being built out of nano-particles, super-cement, and indestructible steel. Then there are the odd blimp-like airships with Chinese dragon insignias flying in the distance: China is literally covering the surface of the earth with a fantastic white city that's building itself on its own. Behind it all is Tsao Ch'un, the current Chinese ruler, who wants to destroy every aspect of Western Civilization. Jake Reed gets caught up in this conquest and thus the series begins.

The novel does stand on its own, but such is Wingrove's skill that we do want to see how this turns out, what else China has in mind to conquer. Wingrove knows his science fiction and he creates sympathetic characters who have deep family concerns as well as broader cultural worries. This would also include one Chinese general who has a strong moral streak, a man who is probably to be further tested as the series progresses (as well as Jake Reed).

Son of Heaven is actually a quick read and the series, taken together, stands a good chance of becoming science fiction's equivalent of *War and Peace*. It's *that* good.

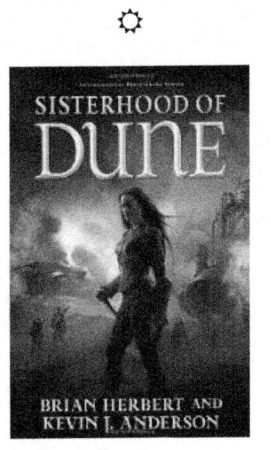

☼

Sisterhood of Dune
by Brian Herbert and Kevin J. Anderson
Tor Science Fiction 2012
Hardcover: 496 pages
ISBN: 978-0765322739

Sisterhood of Dune is the opening work in a trilogy that predates the Dune series at the conclusion of the Battle of Corrin where all thinking machines (and a whole bunch of human beings) were destroyed. Faykan Butler has taken the name of Corrino and has pronounced himself as the first Emperor of a new order—the Imperium. *Sisterhood* starts in the backwash of the Corrin conflict where disorder rules the roost and all kinds of minor groups and partisans fight to find their place in this new society.

The novel follows the Butlerians, led by Manford Torondo, as they further their jihad to destroy all technology, and the Bene Gesserit, which is just starting to evolve, led by the Reverend Mother Raquella Berto-Anirul, who is working on a human breeding program (which will lead to Paul Atreides, of course). The Emperor, meanwhile, has his hands full juggling palace intrigues, dealing with the Suk school, the rise of the Swordmaster school, and the Mental adepts, always an interesting group. One of the most interesting tropes in this novel is the rise of the Navigators, probably the most important class of (altered) humans in the entire *Dune* series. I personally found their story the most enthralling (mostly because I know where it's going to lead and how important the Navigators will be).

Sisterhood of Dune is really a fine read, falling squarely into the space opera category, moving perhaps a bit faster than the original Frank Herbert books in this series—probably because it's less philosophical than the original novels, less talky. Herbert fils *and* Anderson write with both passion and skill, and the action is non-stop. All the tropes and conceits that run through Frank Herbert's original trilogy are here and the authors don't much violate Frank Herbert's original creation.

The real issue here is whether or not these books add anything to the series or perhaps whether they should exist at all. The former notion is probably not germane or relevant. Readers read these books because they take us back to the original universe and all of the original intrigues. Franchising is nothing new in science fiction and novels-in-franchise such as the *Star Wars* novels and the *Star Trek* books are a case in point. True, neither Brian Herbert nor Kevin Anderson *are* Frank Herbert and thus cannot write like him. Still, none of that is to the point, nor should it be. Herbert and Anderson have wisely made their *Dune* books their own and really make no effort to write in Frank Herbert's style. (And we can be thankful that they don't enter the heads of their characters where we are privy to their every thought. There are hardly any italics in this book, and for that both authors deserve medals.)

Brian Herbert and Kevin J. Anderson are entertainers and they are very skilled at what they do. And in *Sisterhood of Dune*, they deliver. If you're a purist and don't think anyone should touch Frank Herbert's masterpiece, then there's nothing here for you. If, however, you're looking for a few hours with a fine adventure story, you really can't go wrong with *Sisterhood of Dune*.

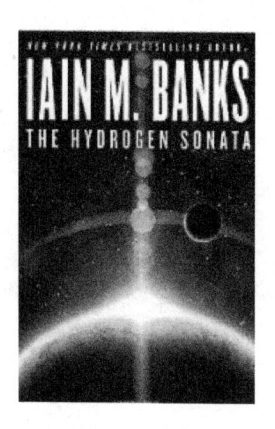

✧

The Hydrogen Sonata
by Iain M. Banks
Orbit 2012
Hardcover: 528 pages
ISBN: 978-0316212373

The Hydrogen Sonata is one of Iain M. Banks' Culture novels wherein an ancient civilization called the Gzilt are about to Sublime and a number of entities want to participate: either to scavenge when the Gzilt disappear (to God-knows-where), or to exact revenge before they go, or to capture an ancient criminal whose mind is downloaded into a mysterious cube. Then there is Vyr Cossont, a four-armed beauty who plays an eleven-stringed instrument something like a harp (she's attempting to learn how to play "The Hydrogen Sonata," an unplayable masterpiece that makes for a nice recurring trope to the novel).

Part of the problem for Ms. Cossont is that no one knows where civilizations go when they Sublime and there's evidence to suggest that it might be nowhere at all. It might just be a hoax. Ms. Cossont, who is a member of both the Culture and the Gzilt, has a personal problem, however. She doesn't want to Sublime and quite a few Ship Minds (who actually run the ships which the races of the Culture travel on) are more than just a little bit interested in the Gzilt civilization and why everyone is racing there to get a piece of the action or a piece of the pie.

This is one of Banks' superior Culture novels and it's written with great humor, for both the milieu it embraces and the diverse cast of characters involved. I was especially taken with the Ship Minds who have minds of their own and seem to be more curious about the Gzilt than the humans. Their conversations break up the action in the book and it's clear that Banks was having a dandy time writing *The Hydrogen Sonata*.

I think right now that Banks and Alastair Reynolds own the space opera. Others have mastered it as well but few have created a galaxy-wide semi-organized melange of cultures as Banks, cultures and characters which still, after eleven or so novels, still surprise and entertain. One trope I enjoyed in *The Hydrogen Sonata* was the Girdle City—a city about two-hundred kilometers high that circles the Gzilt world at the equator. Millions of people live in the Girdle City. One scene (actually two) centers around a floating palace, something like a giant Zeppelin that travels the hollow core of the Girdle city. It's a classic BDO (Big Dumb Object) I'll never forget.

The Hydrogen Sonata was a delight from start to finish. And to Banks' credit, it's a stand-alone novel, not part of a continuous series or the beginning, middle, or end of a serial work. You can read it without knowing anything at all about the Culture stories because Banks so ably fills you in as you go with just enough information to allow for it to make sense *and* to make you want to read more Culture novels. I'm already on board.

✧

The Devil's Nebula
by Eric Brown
Abaddon Books 2012
Mass Market: 352 pages
ISBN: 9781781080238

I picked up *The Devil's Nebula* by British writer Eric Brown for two reasons, maybe three. First of all I had seen Brown's books at my local Barnes & Noble bookstore for a while now and hadn't really paid any attention to them. He's had no real press here in America as far as I can tell even though he's quite accomplished. Brown has written nineteen novels and has published easily half a dozen short story collections. So I thought I'd give him a try. Secondly, I have never heard of Abaddon Books and I was impressed with their stylish logo on the spine and the book's great cover art work. Thirdly, perhaps most importantly, so many American publishers are consolidating and eating up smaller publishers (and shrinking their own midlist in the process) that the print venues for fiction are shrinking. Thus, I am an advocate for the smaller presses or publishing houses that are taking up a lot of the slack. (And many thanks to Barnes & Noble for stocking a wide array of publishers in their SF and Fantasy section. If we didn't have access to these other publishers, I'd only be reviewing the major writers in the field from just the major publishers…which would be something of a drag.)

The Devil's Nebula is a stand-alone novel in a milieu called Weird Space—but this is not a dark fantasy novel nor is it horror. The "weird" gets explained fully later in the novel. *The Devil's Nebula* involves the Expansion, a vast but loosely-organized confederacy of worlds. Within the Expansion are a few malcontents who've fallen between the cracks, so to speak. Ed Carew is the captain of a small band of misfits who are captured and sent into the domain of an evil race called the Vetch (nice name, that) to look into what was behind a distress signal sent from a lost colony fifty or so years earlier. Carew and his cadre have to go into the Devil's Nebula or get executed on the spot by their Expansion overlords. When Carew and crew arrive at the source of the distress signal, they find that the original colonists have been enslaved by some Lovecraftian nightmares and the book details Carew's efforts at freeing the survivors of the original colonial effort.

As I said a moment ago, this is not a fantasy or horror novel. The aliens are merely creepy in a Lovecraftian way and how they interact with the colonists is one of the cleverest tropes I've read in science fiction. I'd say it's rather daring of Brown to even suggest it. The novel itself reads like one of the military novels of David Drake or David Weber, but there's much less emphasis of military hardware and fighting and more on the very human situation the colonists find themselves in. *The Devil's Nebula* is carefully written, expertly paced, and full of surprises. I am doubly thankful that this book was a stand-alone, but I think we'll be seeing a lot of Ed Carew and his team and more of Weird Space.

Views expressed by guest or resident columnists are entirely their own.

Greg Benford is a Nebula winner and a former Worldcon Guest of Honor. He is the author of more than 30 novels and 6 books of non-fiction, and has edited 10 anthologies.

THE REAL FUTURE OF SPACE

by Gregory Benford

Space Opera Meets the Accountants

Space opera is big these days. Myriad authors send us into distant futures where vast interplanetary or interstellar societies struggle, their cause manned (nearly always; not womanned) by masters of vast ships that sail to operatic destinies.

Since the term was invented in 1941 by Bob ("Wilson") Tucker, space opera has had a grandiosity we pedestrian scientists could long for but seldom believe. Lately, however, developments in our rather plodding space program have provoked in me some hope that such futures make sense.

The best argument against space is its cost. The price of getting into orbit ($1 million per person-mass to reach low Earth orbit) is so high that few commercial ventures make sense. So far, only communications satellites at geosynchronous orbit have made economic sense. They have lowered the cost of intercontinental calls by orders of magnitude.

Yet space opera boasts giant spacecraft and huge space colonies. Who pays for them?

Another way to pose the problem is, what would a viable, economic space program look like at the end of the 21st century?

The British have acquired a taste for the recent style of space opera—note Iain M. Banks's series, Ken MacLeod, Colin Greenland's *Take Back Plenty*, Peter Hamilton's popular mega-scale space operas, and more recently Alastair Reynolds and Charles Stross—all working with futures fragrant of gargantuan techno-sizzle. Interestingly, all these authors and futures are somewhat vaguely socialist. In this they contrast with the sober, often nostalgic near-future looks at the space program by Stephen Baxter, notably *Titan*.

A greatly expanded economy will surely be necessary to afford the vast space resources beloved of epic drama. Real-world moderate, welfare-state socialism, as seen in Europe, can afford no grand space operas. Europe has no manned space program at all. The investment for economic benefit is too steep—hundreds of billions just to set up a single solar-power satellite in near-Earth orbit, for example. The second such satellite would cost far less, of course, since the infrastructure would be done—but that first step is a killer.

Unless one envisions a society with limitless wealth (say, by matter duplication using the transporter, that Star Trek staple), there will always be limits. And the sad lesson of most advanced societies is that they get fat and lazy. Both anarchist and libertarian societies may avoid this, because they aren't top-down socialist. But nobody knows that, because they haven't been tried.

In these operatic futures the classic criticism of left-socialist economics has gone unanswered: that markets provide far greater information flow than do top-down, directed economic systems. Through prices, each stage from raw materials to finished product has an added cost attached, as an increased price to the next step. This moves economic information through great distances and over time, which feeds back to the earlier stages, all working toward higher efficiency. Classical socialism ends up starved for feedback. Committees or commissars are not enough to replace the ever-running detail of prices.

Politics does not offer simple maps, but one should distinguish between the Banks/Reynolds/Stross pole and the MacLeod pole. The BRS pole seems Libertarian/anarchist, and by Libertarianism I mean anarchism with a police force and a respect for contract law. MacLeod is the closest thing to a true classical socialist, as in *The Stone Canal*. But even MacLeod is all over the board. Though socialism was his earliest fancy, he experiments with multiple social structures. In later works he espouses variants of libertarianism and anarchism, and even occasional capitalism.

The BRS pole is very muscular, quite capable of militarism and imperialism when necessary (consider Banks's *Use of Weapons*). Socialism isn't just cradle-to-grave security here. Contracts count for a lot (Reynolds's *Revelation Space*), and mild anarchism is often the preferred social structure of the major protagonists. In Charles Stross's *Singularity Sky* the aliens are capitalists who value everything in trade in terms of its information content, a breath of hip economics.

The whiff of welfare socialism in these novels contrasts with the bright, energetic atmosphere. This calls into question whether advanced socialist societies could plausibly support grandiose space-operatic futures.

In some ways, popular socialist thinking parallels Creationism. Unable to imagine how order and increasing complexity can arise from unseen competitive mechanisms, socialists fall into the belief that advanced societies must come from top-down direction—often, in practice, from a sole master thinker, the Chairman-for-life so common in totalitarian states. In politics, everybody is entitled to their own opinion. But not everybody is entitled to their own facts—especially not in economics.

In sf, economic dodges began well before *Star Trek*'s moneyless economy. Idealists have always hated mere money. It seems so, well, *crass*. Still, with no medium of exchange, there is no way to allocate scarce resources, so inevitably politics and brute force dictate outcomes.

Typically in such regimes, one can still amass wealth, just by owning things. To avoid state controls and taxes, barter returns—presto, we're back in the Middle Ages.

Money isn't the object of people's lives, it's just how we keep score. Money measures economic matters. Without it, we can't see what works and what doesn't.

Few in sf ever go beyond this simple truth. Certainly *Trek* seems oblivious to it.

Granted, there are still too many future societies where one doesn't even get to see how the plumbing works, let alone the economy. However odd the future will be, it surely won't be a repeat; economics evolves. The leftish space operas of recent years have plenty of quantum computers and big, Doc Smith-style planet-smashing weaponry, but the hard bits of real economics they swerve around. Maybe because they haven't any real answers, or aren't interested. Opera isn't realism.

Though New Wave sf had a leftist tinge, it had no real political/economic agenda. The common association of hard sf with libertarian ideas, on the other hand, may have sprung from a root world view. Science values the primacy of the individual mind, which can do an experiment (thought experiments, as with Einstein, or real ones) to check any prevailing theory.

This heroic model lies deep in Western culture. Individual truth and a respect for facts is the fulcrum of libertarian theory. Of course, anarchist societies (not socialist), as in Ursula LeGuin's *The Dispossessed*, can depict the struggle of the lone physicist against the collective, received wisdom. But *The Dispossessed*'s logic is not about economics—it is a deeply felt story about a single man's sacrifice and discovery. The social satires of Pohl and Kornbluth have more bite, and probably more useful truth for today. *The Space Merchants* by its title foretells much we may learn from.

I speak first of economics because it is something of a science, with its own Nobel Prize, and it influences the science of space—real space, not the sf operas—quite crucially. In the end, the accountants want to know who is going to pay for all this, and why.

What possible economic motive could a spacefaring society have?

Mining the Sky

Motives answer needs.

Within a century we are going to start running out of two essentials: metals and energy. Within about 50 years most of our oil reserves will be gone—farewell, SUVs! The Middle East will cease to be a crucial tinderbox, simply because countries there will be poor and doomed. Most policy makers know this but seldom speak of it in public—half a century is unimaginably long for a politician.

I will deal with the vast problems of energy supply in my next column. Less well recognized is that many metal ore deposits in the crust of the earth will be mined out within a century. Of course, substitute materials can be and have been found. But some are crucial and to substitute something else changes the world for the worse.

My favorite example of this is oysters. In Dickens novels you can read of poor people forced to eat oysters, then a cheap, easily found, but somewhat lower-class food, while the rich ate beef Wellington. Now we gobble down McDonald's burgers and oysters are a fancy appetizer. Sure, we're well fed—but I prefer oysters, which as a boy I ate for breakfast in my fisherman family, little appreciating my luxury.

Technology can help us greatly in the uplifting of humanity—the great task confronting us. A century ago, aluminum was a rare metal more costly than silver; now we toss it away in soft drink cans—then recycle it. But inevitably the poor nations' growing demand will overburden our demand on the Earth's crust and we will surely run short of the simplest metals, even iron.

As it turns out, both metals and energy are available in space in quantities that we will desperately need.

We also need a clean environment. Mining for metals comes second to fossil fuel extraction in its environmental polluting impact. Coal slag is the #1 water pollutant in the U.S., with runoff from iron mines the second.

Detailed analysis shows that metals brought from the asteroids will be competitive with dwindling Earthly supplies. Better, by refining them in space, we prevent pollution, particularly of another scarce resource—water.

There is money to be made in that sky. An ordinary metal-rich asteroid a kilometer in diameter has high-quality nickel, cobalt, platinum and iron. The platinum-group metals alone would be worth $150 billion on Earth at present prices. Separating out these metals takes simple chemistry done every day in Earthly refineries, using carbon and oxygen compounds for the processing steps. Such an asteroid has plenty carbon and oxygen, so the refining could be done while we slowly tug it toward a very high Earth orbit—a task taking decades.

Steam Rockets

Crucial in all this is the shipping cost, so attention focuses on how to move big masses through the deep sky.

Certainly not with chemical rockets, which have nearly outlived their role in deep space.

Liquid hydrogen and oxygen meet in the reaction chambers of our big rockets, expelling steam at about 4.1 km/sec speeds. That is the best chemical rockets can do, yet to get to low Earth orbit demands a velocity change of about 9 km/sec—over twice what the best rockets can provide without paying the price of hauling lots of added fuel to high altitude, before burning it. This means a 100-ton launch vehicle will deliver only about 8 tons to orbit—the rest goes to fuel and superstructure.

Moving around the inner solar system, which takes a total velocity change of 20 or 30 km/sec, is thus a very big deal. Current systems can throw only a few percent of their total mass from ground to Mars, for example. Big velocity changes ("delta-V" in NASAspeak) of large masses lies far beyond any chemical method. To get from Earth to the biggest asteroid, Ceres, takes a delta-V of 18.6 km/sec, which means the payload would comprise only half of one percent of the vehicle mass.

Using chemical rockets to carry people or cargo anywhere in deep space was like the Europeans discovering and exploring North America using birch bark canoes—theoretically possible, but after all, the Indians did not try it in reverse, for good reason.

For thirty years NASA ignored the technology that can answer these challenges. In the late 1960s both the US and the USSR developed and ran nuclear rockets for hundreds of hours. These achieved double the exhaust velocity of the best chemical rockets, in the 9 km/sec range. These rockets pump ultra-cold liquid hydrogen past an array of ceramic plates, all glowing hot from the decay of radioactive fuel embedded within. The plume does not carry significant radioactivity.

Those early programs were shut down by nuclear-limiting treaties, appropriate for the Cold War but now out of date. We will need that technology to venture further into space. NASA has gingerly begun building more of the nuclear-electrical generators they ran many missions with, including the Voyagers (still running after over a quarter of a century, and twice as far away as is Pluto) and the Viking landers on Mars. These are simple devices powered by the decay of two pounds of plutonium dioxide, yielding 250 watts of heat. Indeed, simply heating spacecraft in the chill of space is the everyday use for small radioactive pellets, which were embedded into every spacecraft headed outward from Earth orbit.

Even this tentative step back to the past seems to acutely embarrass NASA. They elaborately describe how safe the technologies are, because we live in a Chicken Little age, spooked by tiny risks.

Far bigger accidents have already happened. Four large nuclear reactors have fallen from orbit, none has caused any distribution of radioactive debris. In fact, a Soviet reactor plunged into the Canadian woods and emitted so little radioactivity we could never find it. Embedded in tough ceramic nuggets, the plutonium cannot be powdered and inhaled.

Beyond this return to our past capabilities, NASA is considering building a nuclear-driven ion rocket. This will yield exhaust velocities (jetting pure hydrogen) of 250 km/s—a great improvement. But the total thrust of these is small, suitable only for long missions and light payloads.

Using hydrogen as fuel maximizes exhaust velocity (for a given temperature, lighter molecules move faster). And we can get hydrogen from water, wherever it can be found. We've discovered from our Mars orbiters that Mars has plenty of ice within meters of the surface. Comets, the Jovian ice moons—all are potential refueling stations.

But holding hydrogen at liquid temperatures demands heavy technology and careful handling. Water is easier to pump, but provides only a third the exhaust velocity. Many believe that ease of handling will drive our expansion into space to use not more exotic fuels, but plain old… water.

Living Off the Land

What could our space program be like right now, if we hadn't shut down the nuclear program? The road not taken could already have led us to the planets.

The key to the solar system may well be nuclear rockets—*nukes* to friend and foe alike. The very idea of them had of course suffered decades of oblivion, from the early 1970s until the early days of the 21st century. Uranium and plutonium carry over ten thousand times as much energy per gram as do chemical rockets, such as liquid hydrogen burning liquid oxygen.

So in the end, advanced rockets may well be steam rockets, all the way from the launch pad to

Pluto. Chemical boosters can get a nuke rocket into orbit, where it turns on. Whether with liquid hydrogen married to liquid oxygen, or with water passing by slabs of hot plutonium, they all flash into plumes of steam.

Real space commerce demands high energy efficiency. Realization of this returned to NASA in 2002, with the hesitant first steps of its nuclear Project Prometheus (bureaucracy loves resplendent names).

The first rush of heavy Mars exploration will probably prove the essential principle: refuel at the destination. Live off the land. Don't haul reaction mass with you. Nuclear rockets are far easier to refuel because they need only water—easy to pump, and easy to find, if you pick the right destination. Nearly all the inner solar system is dry as a bone, or drier. If ordinary sidewalk concrete were on the moon, it would be mined for its water, because everything around it would be far drier.

Mars is another story. It bears out the general rule that the lighter elements were blown outward by the radiation pressure of the early, hot sun, soon after its birth. This dried the worlds forming nearby, and wettened those further out—principally the gas giants, whose thick atmospheres churn with ices and gases. Mars has recently proved to be wet beneath its ultraviolet-blasted surface. Without much atmosphere, its crust has been sucked dry by the near-vacuum. Beneath the crust are thick slabs of ice, and at the poles lie snow and even glaciers. So explorers there could readily refuel by melting the buried ice and pumping it into their tanks.

The moons of Jupiter and the other gas giants are similar gas stations, though they orbit far down into the gravitational well of those massive worlds, requiring big delta-V to reach. Pluto, though, is a surprisingly easy mission destination. Small, deeply cold, with a large ice moon like a younger twin, it is far away but reachable with a smaller delta-V.

Of course, there are more sophisticated ways to use water. One could run electricity through it and break off the oxygen, saving it to breathe, and then chill the hydrogen into liquid fuel. That would be the most efficient fuel of all for a nuclear rocket.

But the equipment to keep hydrogen liquefied is bulky and prone to error—imagine the problems of pumps that have to operate in deep space at 200 degrees below zero, over periods of years. An easier method would be to use that hydrogen to combine with the Martian atmosphere, which is mostly CO_2, carbon dioxide. Together they make oxygen and methane, CH_4, both easy to store. Burning them together in a nozzle gives a fairly high-efficiency chemical rocket. A utility reactor on Mars could provide the substantial power needed for this.

Still, that would demand an infrastructure at both ends of the route. Genuine exploration—say, a mission to explore the deep oceans of Jupiter's moon Europa—would need to carry a large nuclear reactor for propulsion and power, gathering its reaction mass from the icy worlds.

NASA is studying an expedition to Europa using a nuclear-driven ion rocket, which would carry its own fuel. It will have to fire steadily for *seven* years to get to Europa, land and begin sending out rovers. Testing the reliability of such a long-lived propulsion scheme demands decades of work, effectively putting off the mission until the 2020s.

Far better would be a true nuclear fission rocket throwing hot gas out the back. If it could melt surface ice on Europa and tank up with water, it could then fly samples back to us.

The true use of a big nuclear reactor opens far more ambitious missions. The real job of studying that deep ocean is boring through the ice layer, which is quite possibly miles thick, and maybe even hundreds of miles. No conceivable drill could do it. But simple hot water could, if piped down and kept running, slowly opening a bore hole. Hot water has been tried in Antarctica and it works.

To test for life on Europa would demand that we send a deep-sea-style submarine into those dark, chilly waters. To power it we could play out a thick, tough power cord, just as do the undersea robot explorers that now nose about in the hulks of the *Titanic* and the *Bismarck*—power cord tens of kilometers long. Only nuclear can provide such vast powers in space.

Dreadnoughts of Space

Space is big. Moving asteroids and other large masses demands scale. This leads to a future using *big* nukes.

The payload would be a pod sitting atop a big fuel tank, loaded probably with ordinary water, which in turn would feed into the reactor. Of course, for manned flights the parts have to line up that way, because the water in the tank shields the crew from the reactor and from the plasma plume in the magnetic nozzle. To even see the plume, and diagnose it, they will need a rearview mirror floating out to the side. The whole stack will run most of its trajectory in zero-G, when the rocket is off and the reactor provides onboard power.

A top thick disk would spin to create centrifugal gravity, so the crew could choose what fractional G they would wish to live in. Perhaps forty meters in diameter, looking like an angel food cake, it would spin lazily around. The outer walls would be meter-thick and filled with water for radiation shielding. Nobody could eyeball the outside except through electronic feeds.

Plausible early designs envision a ship a hundred meters long, riding a blue-white flare that stretches back ten kilometers before fraying into steamy streamers. Plasma fumes and blares along the exhaust length, ions and electrons finding each other at last and reuniting into atoms, spitting out a harsh glare. This blue pencil points dead astern, so bright that, leaving Earth orbit, it could be seen from the ground by naked eye.

Ordinary fission nuclear power plants are quite good at generating electrical power but they are starved for the neutrons that slam into nuclei and break them down. That is why power reactors are regulated by pulling carbon rods in and out of the "pile" of fissionable elements—the carbon can absorb neutrons, cooling the whole ensemble and preventing overheating.

The next big revolution in nukes would then come with the invention of practical thermonuclear *fusion* machines.

Fusion slams light nuclei like hydrogen or helium together, also yielding energy, as in the hydrogen bomb. Unlike fission, fusion is rich in hot particles but has trouble making much energy.

Most spaceflight engineers have paid little attention to fusion, believing—as the skeptics have said for half a century—that controlled fusion power plants lie twenty years ahead, and always will. Fusion has to hold hot plasma in magnetic bottles, because ordinary materials cannot take the punishment. The most successful bottle is a magnetic doughnut, most prominently the Russian-inspired Tokamak.

To make it into a rocket, let the doughnut collapse. Fusion rockets are the opposite of fusion electric power plants—they work by letting confinement fail. Ions fly out. Repeat, by building the doughnut and starting the reaction again.

The rocket engine core is this come-and-go doughnut, holding the plasma, then letting it escape down a magnetic gullet that shapes the plasma into a jet out the back. Rather than straining to confine the fusing, burning plasma, as our so-far-unsuccessful power plant designs do, a rocket could just relax the magnetic bottle.

So these fusion nukes are a wholly different sort of vehicle. They can promise far higher exhaust velocities than the fission nukes.

Leaving high Earth orbit, such ships will not ignite their fusion drives until they are well outside the Van Allen belts, the magnetic zones where particles are trapped—or otherwise the spray of plasma would short out innumerable communications and scientific satellites ringing the Earth. (This actually happened in 1962, when the USA project Starfish Prime set off a hydrogen bomb in the Van Allen belts. People have trouble believing anybody ever did this, but those were different days, indeed. The ions and electrons built up charge on our communications satellites, most of which belonged to the Department of Defense, and electrically shorted them out. Presto, billions of dollars lost in surveillance satellites gone dead within the first hour. A colossal embarrassment, never repeated.)

The Long Prospect

So will we have a space operatic future? If that means huge spacecraft driven by spectacular engines, maybe so. Interstellar flight lies beyond the technologically foreseeable, alas.

But the rest of the space opera agenda depends on your political prognostications. Will Iain Banks's anarchist/socialist empire arise from remorseless economic forces? Or perhaps Robert Heinlein's libertarian frontier?

Currently we're "developing" space mostly with tax dollars that go into hugely inefficient projects like the International Space Station, which does very little research. We now pay the Russians to deliver our crews and Elon Musk's SpaceX to deliver freight. What we need is *Ad Astra, Contra Bureaucratica*. The private opening of space will drive forward now, as low-orbit tourism and the first efforts to carry out repair and resource gathering like asteroid mining, at much greater distances. Still, this is a mere toe in the ocean.

Humanity's current dilemma is exploding populations amid, and *versus*, environmental decay and dwindling resources. Of course we've dodged most of the bullets, thanks to the engineers and scientists. But we cannot count on them forever to solve our social problems.

Rick Tumlinson, a leading space advocate, put it this way:

Ultimately, nearly anything you want to do in a "sustainable" world will be something someone else cannot—and that will mean limits. Limits to when and where and how you travel, how much you consume, the size of your home, the foods you eat, the job where you work, even how long you are allowed to live… Yet Earth's population continues to grow.

Quite Heinleinesque. Robert Zubrin, an eloquent exponent of space as the last and greatest frontier, puts it eloquently:

We see around us now an ever more apparent loss of vigor of American society: increasing fixity of the power structure and bureaucratization of all levels of society; impotence of political institutions to carry off great projects; the cancerous proliferation of regulations affecting all aspects of public, private and commercial life; the spread of irrationalism; the balkanization of popular culture; the loss of willingness by individuals to take risks, to fend or think for themselves; economic stagnation and decline; the deceleration of the rate of technological innovation and a loss of belief in the idea of progress itself. Everywhere you look, the writing is on the wall.

This is a neat way to summarize the agenda of an entire culture: the space frontier revolutionaries. They tend to be Heinleiner-style libertarians. It galls them that the future of space still lies in government hands.

I've been talking about the nuts and bolts of moving large masses around the solar system, for exploration or economics. But the ultimate agenda is one that has lain at the core of our society for centuries: the promise that expanding spatial horizons in turn opens those enlightening horizons of the mind that have made the modern age.

Many concepts will fail, and staying the course will require leadership.

Consider how John F. Kennedy voiced the goals of the Apollo program:

We choose to go to the Moon in this decade, and to do the other things, not because they are easy, but because they are hard. Because that goal will serve to organize and measure the best of our energies and skills.

Copyright 2004 (revised 2013) by Gregory Benford

www.PhoenixPick.com

PHOENIX PICK PRESENTS

This is where the publisher gets to showcase one of Phoenix Pick's hidden gems.

Ursula K. Le Guin's *The Left Hand of Darkness* inspired a whole sub-genre of SF related to gender issues. The following excerpt is from a work that continues that tradition with a finely constructed tale of a group of humans marooned on an alien planet.

Descendants of the long-stranded group struggle with mutations and infertility, and the small community faces certain extinction unless a cure can be found.

Anais is a community doctor desperately looking for a cure. She also has a secret—she suffers from a strange sexual deformity. Then her world is turned inside out when she discovers the same deformity on a preserved corpse of a long-extinct race.

What is the connection? And can she find the answer to this mystery that has reached back from time to haunt both her and the colony struggling to survive against impossible odds?

The story is told with a unique style, employing multiple voices, including those of the extinct race. But all the strands, modern and ancient, come together to form a beautiful, intricately crafted story that makes us question the meaning of identity, self and of life itself.

Shahid Mahmud, Publisher

Please note the following is an excerpt, not a complete story

PART I: DISCOVERIES

CONTEXT: Elena Koda-Schmidt

The autumn day was as hot as any in recent memory. The temperature was nearly 10°C, and Elena paused to unbutton her sweater and wipe away the sweat that threatened to drip into her eyes. Near the tree line bordering the river a kilometer away, the dark waters of a pond glittered in the sun: Tlilipan, it was called, "the place of black water." The peat-stained shallow lake was the last vestige of a much larger parent, now just a marshy wetland. Further down the peat bog, Elena could see Faika Koda-Shimmura and Aldhelm Martinez-Santos—they were kissing, a long, oblivious embrace that made Elena feel vaguely jealous, watching. Faika was ten and had reached her menarche.

Elena suspected that her brother Wan-Li was going to be disappointed when she told him. Wan-Li had spent the night in the Koda-Shimmura compound with Faika a few days before. It seemed he hadn't quite made the impression he'd thought he had. Elena remembered her own menarche year, and how she'd experimented with her new sexual freedom.

The cart was nearly full of peat; Elena leaned her shovel against the wheel and rubbed her protruding stomach with calloused hands. She loved the swelling, surprising curve of her belly, loved the weight of it, the feeling of being centered and rooted. Her roundness made her believe that, despite the odds, *her* baby would be perfect. *Her* baby would live and give her grandchildren to dandle on her knee when she was past childbearing herself. She stroked the hard sphere of her womb and the baby kicked in response. Elena laughed.

"Now you be still, little one. It's bad enough without you stomping on my bladder. Mama's still got a lot of work to do before we get home."

With a sigh, Elena picked up the shovel and prepared to attack the peat once more. She was working an old face, several feet down in the bog where the peat was rich, thick and as dark as old Gerard's face. She lifted the spade.

Stopped.

A flap of something leathery and brown like stained wood protruded from the earth, about a foot up on the wall of the ancient marsh. Elena crouched down, grunting with the unaccustomed bulk of her belly. She peered at the fold of leather, prodding it with the tip of her shovel to pull a little more out of the moss.

Elena gasped and dropped the shovel. Protruding from the appendage, squashed and compressed by the weight of centuries of peat, was a hand with four fingers, the tip of each finger a wide knob capped with a recessed claw. The shock sent Elena stepping backward. The shovel's handle tangled between her legs, tripping her. She put her hands out instinctively to protect her stomach. She grunted with the impact, and the handle slammed against her knee. For a moment, she just lay there, taking inventory. The child jumped inside her, and she breathed again.

"Faika—" she began, but the shout came out entangled in the breath. She thought of how she must look, sprawled in the wet dirt and staring at the apparition in the peat, and laughed at herself.

"What a sight!" she told the child in her womb. "You'd think your mother was sure the boggin was going to get up and walk out of there," she said. She stood, brushing uselessly at her stained trousers and grimacing with the bruised, protesting knee.

As she stood, she saw movement from the corner of her eye. A figure shifted in the small stand of globe-trees a hundred meters away. "Faika? Aldhelm?" Elena called, but the shadowy form—almost lost in tree-shadow—moved once more, and she knew it wasn't either of the two. She could feel it, watching, staring at her. *A grumbler?* she thought, wondering if the rifle was still in the cart, but in the instant she glanced away to check the weapon, the shadow was gone.

There was no one there. The sense of being observed was gone.

Elena shivered, hugging herself. "Baby, your mother's seeing ghosts now," she said. She glanced back at the hand hanging from the peat. "I think I just saw your *kami*," she told it. "Don't worry, I'm not going to do anything nasty to you. I'll leave that to Anaïs. Knowing her, she'll *enjoy* it."

She took a deep breath, and looked again at the copse of trees. "Faika! Aldhelm!" Elena shouted. "If you two can stop fondling each other for a minute or so, I think you should come here and look at this."

VOICE: Anaïs Koda-Levin the Younger

"So…are you pregnant yet, Anaïs?"

I hate that question. I always have the wrong answer.

No. I'm not.

"Give it a rest, Ghost."

"Everything's still the same, is it? You *are* still trying, aren't you? If we could only get you up here so we could *see*.…"

I felt the old emotional garbage rising with Ghost's questioning: the anger, the bitterness, the self-loathing. I forced the gorge down, packing the filth down behind that internal wall, but it was an effort. Our ancient steel surgical instruments, worn to a satin patina by over a century of use and constant sterilization, beat a raucous percussion on the tray I was holding. "Ghost—"

"Sorry, Anaïs. No need to get irritated. As the repository of Mictlan's history..."

There are times when I wish I knew programming well enough to tone down Ghost's assertiveness. "Shut up, Ghost."

This time around, Ghost looked like an old blind man, hunched over an ornate glass cane that was as swirled and frosted as a Miccail stele. His sightless, ice-blue eyes stared somewhere past my right shoulder into the back corner of the coldroom lab. The outline of his body sparkled and flared disconcertingly, and his legs were implanted in the polished whitewood planking past his ankles.

"Ghost, Hui and I put a new floor in here since the last time. You look like you're wading in wood, and it's really disconcerting. Can you shift your image up about a dozen centimeters?"

"Oh, now that we're on the subject of sex and reproduction, you want to change it? Anaïs, I know it's no comfort to you, but if it were possible to reach the *Ibn Battuta*, a resonance scan or even an ultrasound would answer a lot of questions, and we could—"

"Drop it, Ghost. Drop it right now."

This time, I made no effort to hide the anger. Ghost reminded me too much of the sympathy, the false reassurances given to me by my sibs, by my *mam* Maria. They look into my room and see my clothing draped carefully over the huge mirror (which had once belonged to Rebecca Koda-Levin herself), the shirts and pants arranged so that the mirror reflects nothing, and they don't understand the significance of what they're seeing.

The old man sighed. The image, sparking, raised up until the soles of his feet were almost even with the floor. "Better?"

"It'll do."

"You're going to have to describe what you're seeing," Ghost said. "Since you've had the ill grace not to put a video feed in here."

"Quit complaining." My voice was muffled through the gauze mask I was tying behind my head, and my breath clouded in the cold air. "We put the feed in; the line was bad. No one's had a chance to *fix* it yet—it's not exactly high priority. Maybe next time."

"But I'm curious *now*," Ghost persisted. "I don't have much time this orbit. Come on—you're as slow as your Geema."

I sniffed. A strand of hair had made an escape from the surgical cap; I brushed it out of my eyes. "Maybe that's why they named me for her, huh?"

The retort was weak but it was the best I had at the moment. I turned back to the examination table and its strange contents. The bog body Elena had found lay there like a man-sized, crumpled bag of leather—which, in essence, it was. The acidic chemical stew of the peat had tanned and preserved the skin, but the skeletal structure and most of the interior organs had dissolved away. Over the last several days, in scraps of time between other, more pressing duties, I'd carefully cleaned away the worst of the peat clinging to the outside of the body, still hunched into its centuries-old fetal position. Now, like a gift, I was ready to unwrap the present given us by the bog.

Every time I'd looked at the body, I'd felt the same rush of adrenaline I felt now, a sense of standing in front of something...I don't know...maybe *sacred* is the best word. Old and venerable, certainly. I was almost inclined to believe Elena's tale about seeing a *kami* watching her when she'd found it.

After all, it was the bones of this race's dead that had given rise to the name given to the planet: Mictlan, suggested by the lone Mexican crewmember of the *Ibn Battuta*. Mictlan was the Aztec land of the dead, where the god Quetzalcoatl found the bones of humankind—and now, where the bones of another dead culture had been found. The race itself were christened the Miccail—"the Dead," in the Nahuatl language. In the years following, a few Miccailian burial sites had been explored. Not that the excavations told us much about the Miccail, since they cremated their dead before they buried the calcined and charred bones—a rite we'd borrowed from them for our own dead. The strange, whorled spires the Miccail had left behind on the northern continent, sticking out of Mictlan's rocky soil like faerie cathedrals of dull glass and carved with images of themselves, had been photographed and documented; it was from these that we learned the most about the extinct race. More would have been done, probably, but the near destruction and crippling of the *Ibn*

Battuta not six months after the colonists' arrival and the resultant death of nearly all the crew members had suddenly, radically, and permanently shifted everyone's priorities.

Basically, it was more important to scrape an existence from Mictlan than to try to decipher the mystery of our world's previous inhabitants.

I suppose I could appreciate my ancestors' sentiments. Priorities hadn't changed much in the century since the accident. Survival was still far more important than any anthropological exploration. No one wanted Mictlan to harbor the scattered bones of *two* extinct, sentient races. I suppose we have the deliberate uncuriosity of the matriarchs and patriarchs to thank for our being here at all.

For one reason or another, though, I don't seem to be much like them. In so many ways…

"Are you ready to record, Ghost?"

"I'd have much more to analyze with video."

I waited. A moment later, Ghost sighed. The ancient's body dissolved into static for a moment, then returned as a young woman in an *Ibn Battuta* officer's uniform, though a fanciful, brightly-colored scarf was tied over her eyes like a blindfold. The voice changed also, from an elderly male quaver to a female soprano. "Recording into *Ibn Battuta* memory. Audio only log: 101 September 41. The voice is Anaïs Koda-Levin the Younger, Generation Six. Go ahead, Anaïs."

I gave Ghost a sidewise look, swearing—as I had a few hundred times before—that I'd never understand why Gabriela had programmed her AI with such a quirky sense of humor and strange set of idiosyncrasies. "All right. This is another examination of the Miccail body found in the peat bog—and this will be very cursory, I'm afraid, since I'm on duty in the clinic tonight. Ghost, you can download my previous recordings from the Mictlan library."

"It's already done. Go on, Ana, you have my undivided attention."

I knew that wasn't true—there were still three other working projectors scattered among the compounds, and Ghost was no doubt talking with people at each of them at the moment, as well as performing the systems work necessary to keep our patchwork and shrinking network of century-old terminals together, but it was a nice lie. I shook my hair back from my eyes once more and leaned over the table.

Imagine someone unzipping his skin, crumpling it up, and throwing the discarded epidermis in a corner like an old suit—that's what the corpse looked like. On its side, the body was drawn up like someone cowering in fear, the right arm folded around its back, the left thrown over the right shoulder like a shawl. The head was bowed down into the chest, crushed flat and turned to the left. I could see the closed lid of the right eye and the translucent covering of the central "eye" high on the forehead. A mane of dark, matted hair ran from the back of the bald, knobbed skull and halfway down the spine.

I gently pulled down the right leg, which was tucked up against the body. The skin moved grudgingly; I had to go slowly to avoid tearing it, moistening the skin occasionally with a sponge. Tedious work.

"Most of the body is intact," I noted aloud after a while, figuring that Ghost was going to complain if I didn't start talking soon. "From the spinal mane and the protrusions around the forehead, it's one of the type Gabriela designated as 'Nomads.' If I recall correctly, she believed that since the carvings of Nomads disappear from the Miccail's stelae in the late periods, these were a subspecies that went extinct a millennium or so before the rest of the Miccail."

"You've been studying things you've been told to stay away from."

"Guilty as charged. So that makes the body—what?—two thousand years old?"

"No later than that," Ghost interrupted, "assuming Gabriela's right about the stelae. We'll have a better idea when we get the estimates from the peat samples and measurements. Máire's still working on them."

"Sounds fine. I'll check with her in the next few days."

I was lost in the examination now, seeing nothing but the ancient corpse in front of me. A distant part of me noted that my voice had gone deeper and more resonant, no longer consciously pitched high—we all have our little idiosyncrasies, I suppose. "Two thousand or more years old, then. The body evidently went naked into the lake that later became the bog—there's no trace of any clothing. That may or may not be something unusual. The pictographs on the Miccail stelae show ornate costumes in daily use, on the Nomads as well as the rest, so it's rather strange that this one's naked.…Maybe he was swimming? Anyway, we're missing the left leg a half meter down from the hip and…"

The right leg, boneless and twisted, lay stretched on the table. Fragments of skin peeled from the stump of the ankle like bark from a whitewood. "…the right foot a few centimeters above the ankle. A pity—I'd like to have seen that central claw on the foot. Looks like the leg and foot decayed off the body sometime after it went into the lake. Wouldn't be surprised if they turn up somewhere else later."

I straightened the right arm carefully, laying it down on the table, moving slowly from shoulder to wrist. "Here's one hand—four fingers, not five. Wonder if they counted in base eight? These are really long phalanges, though the meta-carpals must have been relatively short. The pads at the end of each digit still have vestiges of a recessed claw—would have been a nasty customer in a fight. There's webbing almost halfway up the finger; bet they swam well. And this thumb…it's highly opposed and much longer than a human's. From the folds in the skin, I'd guess that it had an extra articulation, also."

I grunted as I turned the body so that it rested mostly on its back. "There appears to be a large tattoo on the chest and stomach—blue-black lines. Looks like a pictogram of some sort, but there's still a lot of peat obscuring it, and I'll have to make sure that this isn't some accidental postmortem marking of some kind. I'll leave that for later…"

The remnant of the left leg was folded high up on the stomach, obscuring the tattoo. I lifted it carefully and moved it aside, revealing the groin. "Now *that's* interesting…"

"What?" Ghost asked. "I'm a blind AI, remember?"

I exhaled under the surgical mask, resisting the urge to rise to Ghost's baiting. "The genitalia. There's a scaly, fleshy knob, rather high on the front pubis. I suppose that's the penis analogue for the species, but it doesn't look like normal erectile tissue or a penile sheath. No evidence of anything like testicles—no scrotal sac at all. Maybe they kept it inside."

"They're aliens, remember? Maybe they didn't *have* one."

I accepted Ghost's criticism with a nod. She was right—I was lacing some heavy anthropomorphism into my speculations. "Maybe. There's a youngpouch on the abdomen, though, and I haven't seen any Mictlanian marsupialoids where both sexes *had* the pouch. Maybe in the Miccail both male and female suckled the young." I lifted the leg, turning the body again with an effort. "There's a urethra further down between the legs, and an anus about where you'd expect it—"

I stopped, dropping the leg I was holding. It fell to the table with a soft thud. I breathed. I could feel a flush climbing my neck, and my vision actually shivered for a moment, disorientingly.

"Anaïs?"

"It's…" I licked suddenly dry lips. Frowned. "There's what looks to be a vaginal opening just below the base of the spine, past the anus."

"A hermaphrodite," Ghost said, her voice suddenly flat. "Now there's synchronicity for you, eh?"

I said nothing for several seconds. I was staring at the body, at the soft folds hiding the opening at the rear of the creature, not quite knowing whether to be angry. Trying to gather the shreds of composure. *Staring at myself in the mirror, forcing myself to look only at that other Anaïs's face, that contemplative, uncertain face lost in the fogged, spotted silver backing, and my gaze always, inevitably, drifting lower.…*

The Miccail body was an accusation, a mockery placed just for me by whatever gods ruled Mictlan.

"Gabriela speculated about the sexuality of the Nomads," Ghost continued. "There were notes in her journals. She collected rubbings of some rather suggestive carvings on the Middle Period stelae. In fact, in a few cases she referred to the Nomads as 'midmales' because the stelae were ambiguous as to which they might be. It's all scanned in the database—call it up."

"I've read some of Gabriela's journals—the public ones, anyway. Gabriela said a lot of strange things about the Miccail—and everything else on this world. Doesn't make her right."

"Give poor Gabriela a break. No one else was particularly interested in the Miccail after the accident. The first generation had more pressing problems than an extinct race. As an archeologist/anthropologist she was—just like you, I might add—a dilettante, a rank amateur."

"And she was your lead programmer, right? That explains a lot about *you*."

"It's also why I'm still working. Ana, I'm running out of time here."

"All right."

I took another long breath, trying to find the objective, aloof Anaïs the bog body had banished. The leg had fallen so that the tattered end of the ankle hung over the edge of the table. I placed it carefully back into position and didn't look at the trunk of the body or the mocking twinned genitals. Instead, I moved around the table, going to the Nomad's head. Carefully, I started prying it from the folded position it had held for centuries.

"Looks like she...he..." I stopped. Ghost waited. My jaw was knotted; I forced myself to relax. *Do this goddamn thing and get it over with. Put the body back in the freezer and forget about it.* "She didn't die of drowning. There's a large wound on the back of the skull. Part crushing, part cutting like a blunt axe, and it probably came from behind. I'll bet we'll find that's the cause of death, though I guess it's possible she was thrown into the lake still alive. I'm moving the head back to its normal position now. Hey, what's this...?"

I'd lifted the chin of the Miccail. Trapped deep in the folds of the neck was a thin, knotted cord, a garrote, pulled so tightly against the skin that I could see that the windpipe had closed under the pressure. "He was strangled as well."

"He? I thought it was a she."

I exhaled in exasperation. "*Goddamn* it, Ghost..."

"Sorry," Ghost apologized. She didn't sound particularly sincere. "Axed, strangled, *and* drowned," Ghost mused. "Wonder which happened first?"

"Somebody really wanted him dead. Poor thing." I looked down at the flattened, peat-darkened features, telling myself that I was only trying to see in them some reflection of the Miccail's mysterious life. This Miccail was a worse mirror than the one in my room. Between the pressure-distorted head and the long Miccail snout, the wide-set eyes, the light-sensitive eyelike organ at the top of the head, the nasal slits above the too-small, toothless mouth, it was difficult to attribute any human expression to the face. I sighed. "Let's see if we can straighten out the other arm—"

"Ana," Ghost interrupted, "you have company on the way, I'm afraid—"

"Anaïs!"

The shout came from outside, in the clinic's lobby. A few seconds later, Elio Allen-Shimmura came through the lab doors in a burst. His dark hair was disheveled, his black eyes worried. The hair and eyes stood out harshly against his light skin, reddened slightly from the cold northwest wind. His plain, undistinguished features were furrowed, creasing the too-pale forehead under the shock of bangs and drawing the ugly, sharp planes of his face even tighter. He cast a glance at the bog body; I moved between Elio and the Miccail. Some part of me didn't want him to see, didn't want anyone to see.

Elio didn't seem to notice. He glanced quickly to the glowing apparition of Ghost. "Is that you, Elio?" Ghost asked. "I can't see through this damn blindfold." Ghost grinned under the parti-colored blindfold.

Elio smiled in return, habitually, an expression that just touched the corners of his too-thin lips and died. "It's me." Something was bothering Elio; he couldn't stand still, shuffling from foot to foot as if he were anxious to be somewhere else. I'd often noticed that reaction in my presence, but at least this time I didn't seem to be the cause of it. Elio turned away from Ghost. "Anaïs, has Euzhan been in here?"

"Haven't seen her, El." *Your Geeda Dominic doesn't exactly encourage your Family's children to be around me, I wanted to add, but didn't.* With my own Family having no children at the moment, if I had a favorite kid in the settlement, it would be Euzhan, a giggling, mischievous presence. Euzhan liked me, liked me with the uncomplicated trust of a child; liked me—I have to admit—with the same unconscious grace that her mother had possessed. It was impossible not to love the child back. I began to feel a sour stirring in the pit of my stomach.

"Damn! I was hoping..." Elio's gaze went to the door, flicking away from me.

"El, what's going on?"

He spoke to the air somewhere between Ghost and me. "It's probably nothing. Euz is missing from the compound, has been for an hour. Dominic's pretty frantic. We'll probably find her hiding in the new building, but…"

I could hear the forced nonchalance in Elio's voice; that told me that they'd already checked the obvious places where a small child might hide. A missing child, in a population as small as ours, was certainly cause for immediate concern—Dominic, the current patriarch of the Allen-Shimmura family, would have sent out every available person to look for the girl. Elio frowned and shook his head. "All right. You're in the middle of something, I know. But if you do see her—"

His obvious distress sparked guilt. "This has waited for a few thousand years. It can certainly wait another hour or two. I'll come help. Just give me a few minutes to put things away and scrub."

"Thanks. We appreciate it." Elio glanced again at the Miccail's body, still eclipsed behind me, then gave me a small smile before he left. I was almost startled by that and returned the smile, forgetting that he couldn't see it behind the mask. As he left, I slid the examining table back into the isolation compartment, then went to the sink and began scrubbing the protective brownish covering of thorn-vine sap from my hands.

"A bit of interest there?" Ghost ventured.

"You're blind, remember?"

"Only visually. I'm getting excellent audio from your terminal. Let me play it back—you'll hear how your voice perked up—"

"Elio's always been friendly enough to me, that's all. I'm not interested; he's *definitely* not, or he hides it awfully well. Besides, El is…" *Ugly*, I almost said, and realized how that would sound, coming from me. *His eyes are nice, and his hands. But his face—the eyes are set too close together, his nose is too long and the mouth too large. His skin is a patchwork of blotches. And the one time we tried…* "At least he doesn't look at me like…like…" I hated the way I sounded, hated the fact that I knew Ghost was recording it all. I hugged myself, biting my lower lip. "Look, I really don't want to talk about this."

Ghost flickered. Her face morphed into lines familiar from holos of the Matriarchs: Gabriela. "Making sense of an attraction is like analyzing chocolate. Just enjoy it, and to hell with the calories."

The voice was Gabriela's, too: smoky, husky, almost as low as mine.

"You're quoting."

"And you're evading." A line of fire-edged darkness sputtered down Ghost's figure from head to foot as the image began to break up. "Doesn't matter—I'm also drifting out of range. See you in three days this time. I should have a longer window then. Make sure you document everything about the Miccail body."

"I will. You get me those age estimates from Máire's uploads when you can."

"Promise." Static chattered in Ghost's voice; miniature lightning storms crackled across her body. She disappeared, then returned, translucent. I could see the murdered Nomad's body through her. "Go help Elio find Euzhan."

"I will. Take care up there, Ghost."

A flash of light rolled through Ghost's image. She went two-dimensional and vanished utterly.

CONTEXT: Bui Allen-Shimmura

"Bui, Geeda Dominic wants you. Now." Bui felt his skin prickle in response, like spiders scurrying up his spine. He straightened up, closing the vegetable bin door. Euzhan wasn't there, wasn't in any of her usual hiding places. Bui looked at Micah's lopsided face, and could see that there was no good news there. He asked anyway. "Did anyone find her?"

Micah shook his head, his lips tight. "Not yet," he answered, his voice blurred with his cleft palate. "Geeda's sent Elio out to alert the other Families and get them to help search."

"*Khudda.*" Bui didn't care that *da* Micah heard him cursing. The way Bui figured it, he couldn't get into any more trouble than he was already in. If he found Euzhan now, he might just kill the girl for slipping away while he was responsible for watching her. It wasn't fair. He'd be ten in half a year. At his age, he should have been out working the fields with the rest, not babysitting.

"How's Geeda?" he asked Micah.

"In as foul a mood as I've ever seen. You'd better get up there fast, boy."

Bui's shoulders sagged. He almost started to cry, sniffing and wiping his nose on his sleeve. "Go on," Micah told him. "Get it over with."

He went.

Geeda Dominic was in the common room of the Allen-Shimmura compound, staring out from the window laser-chiseled from the stone of the Rock. A dusty sunbeam threw Dominic's shadow on the opposite wall. Bui noticed immediately that no one else from the Family was in the room. That didn't bode well, since the others sometimes managed to keep Dominic's infamous temper in check. "Geeda?" Bui said tremulously. "Micah said you—"

Dominic was the eldest of the Allen-Shimmura family, a venerable eighty, but he turned now with a youth born of anger. His cane, carved by the patriarch Shigetomo himself, with a knobbed head of oak all the way from Earth, slashed air and slammed into Bui's upper arm. Surprise and pain made Bui cry out, and the blow was hard enough to send him sprawling on the rug.

"*Hakuchi!*" Dominic shouted at him, the cane waving in Bui's face like a club. "You fool!"

Bui clutched his arm, crying openly now. "Geeda, it wasn't my fault. Hizo, he'd fallen and skinned his knees, and when I finished with him, Euzhan—"

"Shut up!" The cane *whoomped* as it slashed in front of his face. "You listen to me, boy. If Euzhan is hurt or…or…" Bui knew the word that Dominic wouldn't say. *Dead*. Fear reverberated in Bui's head, throbbing in aching syncopation with the pain in his arm. "You better hope they find her safe, boy, or I'll have you goddamn shunned. I swear I will. No one will talk to you again. You'll be cast out of the Family. You'll find your own food or you'll starve."

"No, Geeda, please…" Bui shivered.

"Get out of here," Dominic roared. His hand tightened around the shaft of his cane, trembling. "Get out of here and find her. Don't bother coming back until you do. You understand me, boy?"

"Yes, Geeda Dominic. I'm…I'm sorry…I'm awful sorry…" Bui, still sobbing, half crawled, half ran from the room.

Dominic's cane clattered against the archway behind Bui as he went through.

VOICE: Anaïs Koda-Levin the Younger

"Euzhan! Damn, it, child.…" I exhaled in frustration, my voice hoarse from calling. Elio sagged tiredly near me. He rubbed the glossy stock of his rifle with fingers that seemed almost angry. "It's getting dark," he said. "It's near SixthHour. She'll come out from wherever she's hiding as soon as she notices. She always wants the light on in the creche, and she'll be getting hungry by now. She'll be out. I know it."

Elio wasn't convincing even himself. There was a quick desperation in his voice. I understood it all too well. All of us did. Our short history's full of testimonials to this world's whims—as our resident historian, Elio probably understood that better than I did.

Mictlan had not been a kind world for the survivors of *Ibn Battuta*. Two colonies—one on each of Mictlan's two continents—had been left behind after the accident that had destroyed most of the mothership. The colonies quickly lost touch with each other when a massive, powerful hurricane raked the southern colony's continent in the first year of exile, and they never resumed radio contact with us or with Ghost on the *Ibn Battuta*.

Another storm had nearly obliterated our northern colony in Year 23, killing six of the original nine crewmembers here. I suppose that was our historical watershed, since that disaster inalterably changed the societal structure, giving rise to what became the Families. Local diseases mutated to attack our strange new host bodies, stalking the children especially—the Bloody Cough alone killed two children in five by the time they reached puberty. I know: I see the bodies and do the autopsies. There are the toothworms or the tree-leapers or the grumblers; there are the bogs and the storms and the bitter winters; there are accidents and infections and far, far too many congenital defects. Most of them are bad enough that nature itself takes care of them: miscarriages, stillbirths, nonviable babies who are born and die within a few days or a few months—which is why none of the Families will name a child before his or her first birthday. I also know the others—the ones who lived but who are marked with the stamp of Mictlan.

I knew *them* very well.

The rate of viable live births—for whatever reason: a side effect of the LongSleep, or some unknown factor in the Mictlan environment—was significantly lower among the ship members and their descendants than for the general population of Earth. Just over a century after being stranded on Mictlan, our human population nearly matched the year; there'd been no growth for the last quarter of a century. Too many years, deaths outnumbered births.

Mictlan was not a sweet, loving Motherworld. She was unsympathetic and unremittingly harsh.

I knew that Elio's imagination was calculating the same dismal odds mine was. This was no longer just a child hiding away from her *mi* or *da*, not this late, not this long.

Euzhan was four. I'd seen the girl in the clinic just a few days ago—an eager child, still awkward and lisping, and utterly charming. Ochiba, Euzhan's mother, had once been my best—hell, one of my only—friends. What we'd had....

Anyway, Euzhan had been a difficult birth, a breech baby. All of Ochiba's births were difficult; her pelvis was narrow, barely wide enough to accommodate a baby's head. On Earth, she would have been an automatic cesarean, but not here, not when any major operation is an open invitation for some postoperative infection. I could have gone in. Ochiba told me she'd go with whatever I decided. Ochiba had delivered three children before—with long, difficult labors, each time. I made the decision to let her go, and she—finally—delivered twelve hours later.

But Ochiba's exhaustion after the long labor gave an opportunistic respiratory virus its chance—Ochiba died three days after Euzhan's birth on 97 LastDay. Neither Hui Koda-Schmidt, the colony's other "doctor," nor I had been able to break the raging fever or stop the creeping muscular paralysis that followed. Our medical database is quite extensive, but is entirely Earth-based. On Mictlan-specific diseases, there's only the information that we colonists have entered, and I was all too familiar with that. Ghost had been out of touch, the *Ibn Battuta*'s unsynchronized orbit trapping the AI on the far side of Mictlan. I don't have the words to convey the utter helpless impotence I'd felt, watching Ochiba slowly succumb, knowing that I was losing someone I loved.

Knowing that maybe, just maybe, my decision had been the reason she died.

I'd been holding Ochiba's hand at the end. I cried along with her Family, and Dominic—grudgingly—had even asked me to speak for Ochiba at her Burning.

A damn small consolation.

Euzhan, Ochiba's third named child, was especially precious to Dominic, the head of Family Allen-Shimmura. Euz was normal and healthy. As we all knew too well, any child was precious, but one such as Euzhan was priceless. The growing fear that something tragic had happened to Euzhan was a black weight on my soul.

"Who was watching Euz?"

"Bui," Elio answered. "Poor kid. Dominic'll have him skinned alive if Euz is hurt."

Nearly all of the Allen-Shimmura family were out searching for Euzhan now, along with many from the other Families. The buildings were being scoured one more time; a large party had gone into the cultivated fields to the southeast of the compound and were prowling the rows of white-bean stalks and scarlet faux-wheat. Elio and I had gone out along the edge of Tlilipan. I'd been half-afraid we'd see Euzhan's tiny footprints pressed in the mud flats along the pond's shore, but there'd been nothing but the cloverleaf tracks of skimmers. That didn't mean that Euzhan hadn't fallen into one of the patches of wet marsh between the colony and Tlilipan, or that a prowling grumbler hadn't come across her unconscious body and dragged her off, still half-alive, to a rocky lair along the river....

I forced the thoughts away. I shivered under my sweater and shrugged the strap of the medical kit higher on my shoulder. I've never been particularly religious, but I found myself praying to whatever *kami* happened to be watching.

Just let her be all right. Let her come toddling out of some forgotten hole in the compound, scared and dirty, but unharmed.

The sun was prowling the tops of the low western hills, the river trees painting long, grotesque shadows which rippled over the bluefern-pocked marshland. Not far away was the pit where we'd dug the

Miccail body from the peat. Behind the trees, the chill breeze brought the thin, faint sound of voices from below the Rock, calling for Euzhan. I turned to look, squinting back up the rutted dirt road. There, a tall blackness loomed against the sky: the Rock. The first generation had carved a labyrinth of tunnels in the monolithic hill of bare stone perched alongside the river; from the various openings, we'd added structures that poked out like wood, steel, and glass growths on the stone, so that the Families lived half in and half out of the granite crag. Now, in its darkness, the familiar lights of the Family compounds glistened.

The Rock. Home to all of us.

"Let's keep looking," I told Elio. "We still have time before it gets too dark."

Elio nodded. Where his light skin met the dark cloth of his shirt there was a knife-sharp contrast that stood out even in the dusk. "Fine. We should spread out a bit...."

Elio looked so forlorn that I found myself wanting to move closer to him, to hug him. As much as I might have denied it to Ghost, the truth was that Elio was someone I genuinely liked. Maybe it was because he was so plain, with that pale, blotchy skin, his off-center mouth and wide nose, and his gawky, nervous presence. Elio was not one of the popular men, not one of those who spend every possible night in some woman's room, but we talked well, and I liked the way he walked and the fact that one side of his mouth went higher than the other when he smiled. I liked the warmth in his voice.

He was tapping the rifle stock angrily, staring out into the marsh. I touched his arm; he jerked away. Under the deep ridges of his brows, his black eyes glinted. I could read nothing in them, couldn't tell what he was thinking. "Let's go find Euz," I said.

The light had slid into a deep gold, almost liquid. The sun was half lost behind slopes gone black with shadow. If we were going to continue searching, we'd have to go back soon for lights. Elio and I moved slowly around the marsh's edge, calling Euz's name and peering under the low-hanging limbs of the amberdrop trees, brushing aside the sticky, purplish leaves. Darkness crept slowly over the landscape, the temperature dropping as rapidly as the sun. The marsh steamed in the cooling air, the evening fog already cloud-thick near the river. Our breaths formed small thunderheads before us. Neither of the moons—the brooding Longago or its smaller, fleeter companion Faraway—were up yet. At the zenith, the stars were hard, bright points set in satin, though a faint trace of deep blue lingered at the horizon. Near the compound, outside the fences, someone had lit a large bonfire; the breeze brought the scent of smoke.

"El? It's way past SixthHour, and it's getting too dark to see...."

"All right," Elio sighed. "I guess we might as well—"

Before he could finish, a grumbler's basso growl shivered the evening quiet, sinister and low. "Over there," I whispered, pointing. Elio unslung the rifle. "Come on."

I moved out into the wet ground, and Elio followed.

The grumblers were scavengers, nearly two meters in height, looking like a cut-and-paste, two-legged hybrid of great ape and Komodo dragon, though—like the Miccail and several other local species—they were probably biologically closer to an Earth marsupial than anything else. They walked upright if stooped over, their clawed front hands pulled close, slinking through the night. They were rarely seen near our settlement, seeming to fear the presence of the noisy humans. Sometimes alone, sometimes running in a small pack, they were also generally quiet—hearing one meant that the creature was close, and that it had found something. Grumblers were thieves and scavengers, snatching the kills of other, smaller predators or pouncing on an unsuspecting animal if it looked tiny and helpless enough. I hated them: they were ugly, cowardly, and mean beasts. They invariably ran if challenged.

If one had crept this close to the compound, then it had spotted something worth the danger to itself. Elio and I ran.

The grumbler was leaning over something in a small hollow, still mewling in its bass voice. Hearing us approach, it stood upright, turning its furred snout toward us and exposing double rows of needled teeth. The twinned tongue that was common in Mictlanian wildlife slithered in the mouth. Straggling fur swung under its chin like dreadlocks. Shorter fur cradled the socket of the central lens—

like that of the Miccail—placed high in the forehead. The grumbler glared and cocked its head as if appraising us.

It growled. I couldn't see what it had been crouching over, but the grumbler appeared decidedly irritated at having been disturbed. The long, thin arms sliced the air in our direction, the curved slashing claws on the fingers extended. They looked sharper and longer than I remembered.

"Shoo!" I shouted. "Get out of here!" I waved my arms at it The few times I'd met grumblers before, that had been enough; they'd skulked away like scolded children.

This one didn't move. It growled again, and it took a step toward us.

"Hey—" Elio said behind me. He fired the rifle into the air once. The percussive report echoed over the marsh, deafening. The grumbler jumped backward, crouching, but it held its ground. It snarled now, and took a step forward. I waved at it again.

"Ana…" Elio said warningly.

The grumbler gave him no time to say more.

It leaped toward me.

Improvisation, my great-grandmother Anaïs has often told me, is not just for musicians. Of course, Geema Ana usually says that when she's decided to use coarse red thread rather than thin white in the pattern she's weaving. I don't think she had situations like this in mind. Or maybe she did, since she was talking about using the materials at hand for your task. For the first time in my life, I demonstrated that I had that skill: I swung my medical bag.

The heavy leather hit the creature in the side of the head and sent it reeling down into the marsh on all fours. The bag broke open, the strap tearing as the contents tumbled out. Shaking its ugly head, the dreadlocks caked with mud, the grumbler snarled and hissed. It gathered itself to leap again. I doubted that the now-empty bag was going to stop it a second time, and I had the feeling that I'd pretty much exhausted my improvisational repertoire.

Elio fired from his hip, with no time to aim. A jagged line of small scarlet craters appeared on the grumbler's muscular chest, and it shrieked, twisting in midair. The grumbler collapsed on the ground in front of me, still slashing with its claws and snapping.

Elio brought the rifle to his shoulder, aimed carefully between the eyes that glared at him in defiance, and pulled the trigger.

The grumbler twitched once and lay still. Its eyes were still open, staring at death with a decided fury.

"What was *that* all about?" I said. I could hardly hear over the sound of blood pounding in my head.

"I don't know. I've never seen one do that before." Elio still hadn't lowered the rifle, as if he were waiting for the grumbler to move again. His face was paler than usual, with a prominent red flush on the cheeks. I could see something dark huddled on the ground where the grumbler had been.

"Elio! There she is!"

I ran.

Euzhan was unconscious, lying on her back. "Oh, God," Elio whispered. I knew he was staring at the girl's blouse—it was torn, and blood darkened the cloth just above the navel. I knelt beside her and gently pulled up the shirt.

The grumbler's claws had laid Euzhan open. The gash was long and deep, exposing the fatty tissue and tearing into muscles, though thankfully it looked like the abdominal wall was intact. "Damn…" I muttered; then, for Elio's benefit: "It looks worse than it is." Euzhan had lost blood; it pooled dark and thick under her, but the wound was seeping rather than pulsing—no arterial loss. I allowed myself a quick sigh of relief: we could get her back to the clinic, then. Still, she'd lost a lot of blood, and the unconsciousness worried me.

I quickly probed the rest of body, checked the limbs, felt under the head. There was a swelling bump on the back of her skull, but other than that and the grumbler's wound, Euzhan appeared unharmed. As I tucked the girl's blouse back down, her eyes fluttered open. "Anaïs? Elio? I'm awful cold," Euzhan said sleepily. I smiled at her and stroked her cheek.

"I'm sure you are, love. Here, Anaïs has a sweater you can wear until we get you back." Euzhan nodded, then her eyes closed again. "Euzhan," I said quietly but firmly. "Euz, no sleeping now, love. I need you to stay awake and talk to me. Do you understand?"

Long eyelashes lifted slightly. Her breath deepened. "Am I going to die, Ana?"

I could barely answer through the sudden constriction in my throat. "No, honey. You're not going to die. I promise. You lay there very still now, and keep those pretty eyes open. I need to talk to your *da* a second."

"I think we found her in time," I told Elio, covering Euzhan in my sweater. "But we need to move quickly. We have to get her back to the clinic where I can work on her. What I've got in the kit isn't going to do it. Go get us some help. We'll need a stretcher."

Elio didn't move. He stood there, staring down at Euzhan, his eyes wide with worry and fear. I prodded him. "I need you to go now, El. Don't worry—she'll be fine."

That shook him out of his stasis. Elio nodded and broke into a run, calling back to the settlement as he ran.

She'll be fine, I'd promised him.

I hoped I was going to be right.

CONTEXT: Faika Koda-Shimmura

"They found Euzhan, Geema Tozo." Faika was still breathing hard from the exertion of climbing the stairs to Geema's loft in the tower. Faika, who'd been part of those searching near the old landing pad, had been with the group that helped bring Euzhan back to the Rock. She was still buzzing from the excitement.

Tozo lifted her head from the fragrant incense burning in an ornate holder set on top of a small Miccail stele Tozo used as an altar, but she didn't turn toward Faika. She kept her hands folded together in meditation, her breathing calm and centered, a distinct contrast to Faika's gasping. Several polished stones were set around the base of the stele. Tozo reached out and touched them, each in turn. "I know," she said. "I felt it. She's hurt but alive."

Geema Tozo's tone indicated that her words were more statement than question. But then Tozo always said that she actually talked with the *kami* that lived around the Rock. There were others who were devout, but Tozo lived *Njia*—The Way—as no one else did; at least it seemed so to Faika's somewhat prejudiced eyes. Faika was sure that when the current Kiria, Tami, chose a replacement this coming LastDay, Tozo would be the next Kiria. Faika was a little disappointed that her news wasn't quite the bombshell she'd hoped, but she was also proud that her Geema could know it, just from listening to the voices in her head.

"They took her to the clinic?" Tozo asked. She turned finally. Her face was a network of fine wrinkles, like a piece of paper folded over and over, and the eyes were the brown of nuts in the late fall. Both her hands (and her feet, as Faika knew from seeing Tozo in the Baths) were webbed with a thin sheath of pink skin between the fingers, and the lower half of her face was squeezed together in a faint suggestion of a snout. Faika thought Tozo looked like some ancient and beautiful aquatic animal.

"*Hai*," Faika answered. "Anaïs and Elio found her, and Anaïs was taking care of her. There was a lot of blood. A grumbler—"

"I know," Geema Tozo said, and Faika nodded. The incense hissed and sputtered behind Tozo, and she closed her eyes briefly. "There's trouble coming, Faika. I can feel it. The *kami*, the old ones, are stirring. Anaïs…" Tozo sighed.

"Come help me up, child," she said to Faika, extending her hand. "Let's go downstairs. I can smell Giosha's dinner even through the incense, and my stomach's rumbling. What's done is done, and we can't change it."

INTERLUDE: KaiSa

KaiSa stood on the bluff that overlooked the sea. As Kai expected, BieTe was there: the OldFather for the local settlement. He was squatting in front of the *nasituda*, (See Appendix 'A' for a detailed glossary of terms) the Telling Stone. In one hand he held a bronze drill, in the other was the chipped bulk of his favorite hammerstone. The salt-laden wind ruffled his hair. The sound of his carving was loud in the morning stillness, each note brilliant and distinct against the rhythmic background of surf, separated by a moment of aching silence and anticipation: *T-ching. T-ching. T-ching.* Bie was wearing his ceremonial red robes: the *shangaa*. Flakes of the translucent pale crystal of the stone had settled in his lap, like spring petals on a field of blood.

Bie must have heard Kai's approach, but he gave no sign. KaiSa sniffed the air, fragrant with brine and crisp with the promise of new snow, and opened ker mouth wide to taste all the glorious scents. "The wind is calling the new season, OldFather," ke said. "Can't you hear it?"

Bie grimaced. He snorted once and bared the hard-ridged gums of his mouth in a wide negative without turning around. *T-ching. T-ching.* "I hear—" *T-ching.* "—nothing."

Bie put down the hammerstone. He blew across the carving so that milky rock powder curled into the breeze and away. He stood, lifted his *shangaa* above the hips and carefully urinated on the column. Afterward, he wiped away the excess with the robe's hem to join the multitude of other stains there, a ceremonial three strokes of the cloth: for earth, for air, for water. Where Bie's urine had splashed onto the newly-carved surface, the almost colorless rock slowly darkened to a vivid yellow-orange, highlighting the new figures and matching the other carvings on the stele, while the weathered, oxidized surface of the Telling Stone remained frosty white. Kai could read the hieroglyphic, pictorial writing: the glyph of the OldFather, the wavy line that indicated birth, the glyph of other-self, the slash that made the second figure a diminutive, and the dark circle of femininity.

I, BieTe, declare here that a new female child has been born.

"I decided to take a walk after the birth," Kai said. "Has MasTa named the child?"

"I've not heard her name. Mas said that VeiSaTi hasn't spoken it yet."

Where there should have been joy, there was instead a hue of sullenness in Bie's voice, and Kai knew that ke was the cause of it. Kai nodded. "Mas will give the child strength." Then, because ke knew that it would prick the aloofness that Bie had gathered around himself, ke added: "Mas is a delight, very beautiful and very wise. We're both lucky to enjoy her love."

Kai could see Bie's throat pulse at that. "I know what you're thinking," Bie said. "I know why you came to find me. You're telling me you want to go." Bie's gaze, as brown as the stones of the sea-bluff, drifted away from Kai down to the surging waves, then back. "But I don't want you to leave."

Kai knew this was coming, though ke had hoped that this time it would be different, that for once ker love and affection might emerge unmarred and free of the memory of anger or violence. But—as with most times before—ker wish would not be granted. Kai's mentor JaqSaTu had warned ker of this years ago, when Kai was still bright with the optimism of the newly initiated.

Jaq handed Kai a paglanut and closed ker fingers around the thin, chitinous shell. "Each time, you will think your hands have been filled with joy, but you will be wrong." Jaq told ker. Ke increased the pressure on Kai's fingers, until the ripe nut had broken open. The scent of corruption filled Kai's nostrils—all but one small kernel of the nut was rotten. Jaq plucked the good kernel from the mess in Kai's hand and held it in front of ker. "You will learn to find the nourishment among the rot, or you will starve."

Kai looked at the weathered, handsome face of Bie OldFather, at the creased, folded lines ke had caressed and licked in the heat of lovemaking, and ke saw that Bie's love had hardened and grown brittle.

"I'm only a servant of VeiSaTi," Kai answered softly and hopelessly. "BieTe, please, you don't want to anger a god. I love you. My time here has been wonderful and for that I wish I could stay, but I have my duty." Kai indicated ker own *shangaa*, dyed bright yellow from the juices of pagla root: VeiSaTi's favored plant, that the god had spewed upon the earth so that all could eat. "Mas has her child. HajXa and CerXa will deliver soon. I have given your people all that a Sa can."

A cloud, driven fast by the high wind, cloaked the sun for a moment before passing. The *brais*, the Sun's Eye high on their foreheads, registered the quick shift in light and both of them crouched instinctively as if ready to flee from a diving wingclaw. Kai watched the scudding clouds pass overhead for a few seconds, then glanced back at Bie. His face was as hard as the Telling Stone, as unyielding as the bronze drill he'd used to carve it. "You should not leave yet," he said. "Tonight, we will give thanks to VeiSaTi for the new child. You must be here for the ceremony."

"And then I may go?"

BieTe didn't answer. He was staring at the Telling Stone, and whatever he was thinking was hidden.

He picked up the hammerstone from the ground and hefted it in his hand. "You'll walk back with me now," he said.

There didn't seem to be an answer to that.

BieTe left Kai almost as soon as they reached the village, going off to examine the pagla fields. His mood had not improved during their walk, and Kai was glad to be left alone. Ke went into the TeTa dwelling. "MasTa?" ke called softly.

"In here, Kai."

Kai slid behind the curtain that screened the sleeping quarters. "I'm so happy for you," ke said. "May...may I see?"

MasTa smiled at Kai. Almost shyly, she unfastened the closures of her *shangaa*, exposing her body. Sliding a hand down her abdomen, she opened the muscular lip of her youngpouch and let Kai peer inside. The infant, eyes still closed and entirely hairless, not much longer than Kai's hand, was curled at the bottom of the snug pocket of Mas's flesh. Her mouth was fastened on one of Mas's nipples, and her sides heaved in the rapid breath of the newborn as she suckled. "She's beautiful, isn't she?" Mas whispered.

Kai reached into the warm youngpouch and stroked the child gently, enjoying the shiver ker daughter gave as ke touched her. "Yes," ke sighed. "She's beautiful, yes." Reluctantly, ke took ker hand from the pouch and stroked Mas's cheek with fingers still fragrant and moist from the infant. Ke fondled the tight, red-gold curls down her neck. "After all, she's yours."

Mas laughed at that. She let the youngpouch close, fastened her *shangaa* again, and reclined on the pillows supporting her back.

"Tired?" Kai asked.

"A little."

"Then rest. I'll leave you alone to sleep."

"No, Kai," Mas said. "Please."

"All right." Kai settled back into the nest of pillows piled in the sleeping room. For what seemed a long time, ke simply watched Mas, enjoying the way the sunlight burned in her hair and burnished the pattern of her skin as it came through the open window of the residence. As ke gazed at her, ke could feel that part of ker did indeed want to stay, to watch this child of kers and Mas and Bie grow, to see her weaned from the pouch when the weather turned warm again, to listen to her first words and watch the reflection of kerself in the new child's eyes. Mas must have guessed what ke was thinking, for she spoke from her repose, her eyes closed against the sun.

"I know that you must leave. I understand."

"I'm glad someone does." Kai said it as unharshly as ke could.

Her large eyes opened, that surprising flecked blue-green that was so rare and so striking. A knitted covering tied around her head shielded her *brais* from the afternoon glare. "Bei loves you as much as I do. Maybe more. He told me once that you have made him feel whole. He's afraid, Kai. That's all. He's afraid that when you leave, you'll take part of him with you."

"I'm leaving behind far more of myself than I'm taking," Kai answered. Ke stroked ker own belly for emphasis. "I'm leaving behind your child, and Haj and Cer's. I've given you VeiSaTi's gift. Now I must give it to others."

"Why?" Mas asked. Her bright, colorful eyes searched ker face.

"Now you sound like BieTe," Kai said, and softened ker words with a laugh. "I'm a Sa. I've been taught the ways of the Sa. After I leave, other Sa will come here."

"And if they don't?"

"You'll still have children," Kai said, answering the question ke knew was hidden behind her words. "With BieTe alone."

"I had three other children before you came," Mas said. "Only one lived, a male. Bie sent him away." Mas averted her eyes, not looking at Kai, and her skin went pale with sadness. Kai's own brown arms whitened in sympathy. "The others...well, my first one lived only a season. The other, a female, was wild and strange. She never learned to talk, and she was fey. She would attack me when I was sleeping, or kill the little meatfurs just to watch them die. A wingclaw took her finally, or that's what BieTe told me. I...I found it hard to mourn."

"Mas—" Kai leaned forward to hold Mas, but she bared her gums.

"Don't," Mas said. "Don't, because you'll only make me miss you more. You'll only make it harder." Mas brought her legs up. Arms around knees, she hugged herself, as if she was cold. "The sun's almost down. Bie will be starting the ceremony soon. I need to sleep, so I'll be ready."

"I understand," Kai said....*the smell of the rotten paglanut, breaking in ker hand...*"I understand. I...I'll see you then."

Reaching forward, ke patted the youngpouch through her *shangaa*. "Sleep for a bit. Rest." Ke rose and went to the door of the chamber. Stopping there, ke looked back at her, at the way she watched ker.

"I love you, MasTa," ke said.

She didn't smile. "I love you also," she said. "But I wish I didn't."

VOICE: Anaïs Koda-Levin the Younger

"Clean Euzhan up and get her into a bed," I told our assistants. "She should be waking up in about ten minutes or so—let Hui or me know if she isn't responding. Hayat, we're going to need more whole blood, so after you get Euzhan comfortable, round up three or four of her mi, da, or sibs and get some. Ama, if you'd take charge of the cleanup...."

As they rolled Euzhan away to one of the clinic rooms, I went to the sink and scrubbed the blood and thorn-vine sap from my hands. Hui shuffled alongside me, using the other spigot. When I'd finished drying, I leaned back against the cool wall, frowning through the weariness. Hui shook water from his hands, toweled dry, and tossed the towel in the hamper as I watched his slow, deliberate motions.

I knew what he was going to say before he said it. We'd been working together for that long.

"You did what you could, Anaïs. Now we wait and see." Hui stretched out one ancient forefinger and tapped me gently under the chin. "We can't do anything else for her right now."

"Hui, you saw how close that was." I shivered at the memory. "The descending oblique was nearly severed. If those claws had dug in a few millimeters deeper..."

"But they didn't, and Euzhan will fight off infections or she won't, and we'll do what we need to do, whatever happens. Ana, what did I tell you when you first started studying with me?"

That finally coaxed a wan, grudging smile through the fog of exhaustion. "Let's see... 'Is that expression normal for you, child, or does catatonia run in your family?' Or how about: 'I'm afraid to let you handle a broom, much less a scalpel.' Oh, and I couldn't forget: 'I'm sure you have *some* qualities, or they wouldn't have sent you to me. Let's hope we manage to stumble across them before you kill someone.'" I shrugged. "Those were some of the milder quotes that I can recall. I was sure you were going to send me home and tell my family that I was hopeless."

Hui snorted. The wrinkles around his almond eyes pressed deeper as he grinned. "I very nearly did. You have a good memory, Anaïs, but a selective one. You've forgotten the one important thing."

"And what was that?"

I could see myself in his dark eyes. I could also see the filmy white of the cataracts that were slowly and irrevocably destroying his vision. Not that Hui would ever complain or even admit it, though I'd noticed—silently—that he'd passed nearly all the surgery to me in the past year. "I once told you that no matter how good you were, you are only a tool in the hands of whatever *kami* inhabits this place. You're a very good tool, Anaïs, and you have done all the work that you're capable of doing for the moment. Be satisfied. Besides, it's no longer you that I'm hounding; it's Hayat and Ama." His forefinger tapped me under my chin once more. "Come on, child."

"I'm not a child, Hui."

"No, you're not. But I still get to call you that. Come on. Dominic will be going apoplectic by now, and we can't afford that at his age."

Hui was right about that. As we came through the doors into the clinic's waiting room, half of the Allen-Shimmura family surged forward toward us, with patriarch Dominic at the fore. I avoided him and tried to give a reassuring smile to Andrea and Hizo, Ochiba's other two children, both of them standing close behind the bulwark of Dominic.

"Well?" the old man snapped. He was as thin as a thorn-vine stalk, and as prickly. His narrow lips were surrounded by furrows, his black, almost pupilless eyes were overhung by folds. His voice had gone to wavering with his great age, but was no less edged for that. The grandson of Rebecca Allen, he was one of the few people left of the third generation. My Geema Anaïs once described Dominic as being like a strip of preserved meat: too salty and dry to decay, and too tough to be worth chewing. "How is she?"

I noticed immediately that Dominic was looking at Hui rather than me, even though the patriarch was aware that I had been in charge of the surgery.

Hui noticed it as well. He was wearing what I thought of as his "go ahead and make your mistake" face, the expressionless and noncommittal mask he wore when one of his students would look up quizzically while making an incision. Hui leaned against the wall and folded his arms over his chest. "Anaïs did the surgery. All I did was assist." He said nothing more. The silence stretched for several seconds before Dominic finally sniffed, glared at Hui angrily, and turned his sour gaze on me.

"Well?" he snapped once more.

"Euzhan's fine for the moment." I found it easier, after the first few words, to put my regard elsewhere. I let my gaze wander, making eye contact with Euzhan's *mi* and *da*, and favoring Elio with a transient smile. "We cleaned up the wound—nothing vital was injured, but we had to repair more muscle damage than I like. She's going to need therapy afterward, but we'll work out some schedule for that later. Actually, she should be waking up in a few minutes. She's going to be groggy and in some pain—Hui's already prepared painkillers for her. Dominic, I'll leave it to you. It would be good if there were some familiar faces around her when she comes out of the anesthetic. But no more than two of you, please."

Dominic's grim expression relaxed slightly. He allowed me a fleeting, brief half-smile. "Stefani, come with me. KaWai, take the rest of the Family home and get them fed. Tell Bui that he's been damned lucky. Damned lucky." With those abrupt commands, he left the room with his shuffling, slow walk that still somehow managed to appear regal. The rest of the family murmured for a few minutes, thanking me and Hui, and then drifted from the clinic into the cold night. Eventually, only Hui and myself were left.

"He really doesn't like you, does he?"

That garnered a laugh that might have come from the eastern desert. "You noticed."

"So what's the problem between the two of you?"

"What do you *think* is the problem?" I answered shortly, hating the bitterness in my voice but unable to keep the emotion out. "He knows about me, just like you do. 'Poor Anaïs—from what I've heard, there's no chance *she's* going to have children. And what about her and Ochiba? Don't you think they were just a little too *close*...'"

I stopped. Blinked. I was staring at the wall behind Hui, at the pencil and charcoal sketch of Ochiba I'd done years before, while she was pregnant with Euz. Hui had taken the piece without my knowledge from the desk drawer into which I'd stuffed it. He'd matted and framed the drawing, then placed it on the clinic wall as a Naming Day gift. *Don't ever be timid about your talents,* he'd said. *Gifts like yours are too rare on this world to be hidden. And don't hide your feelings, either, girl—those are also far too rare.*

Well, Hui, that's a wonderfully idealistic statement, but it doesn't fit into this world we've made for ourselves. There are some things that are better left stuffed in the drawer.

"You can't let him intimidate you," Hui said. "I don't care how old and venerated he is..."

"That's *khudda*, Hui, and we both know it. What Dominic says, goes—and that's true even for the other Families, too. With the exception of Vladimir Allen-Levin and Tozo Koda-Shimmura, Dominic's the Eldest, and poor Vlad's so senile—" I cut off my own words with a motion of my hands. "Hui, we don't need to talk about this. Not now. It's really not important. Euzhan should be coming around about now. Why don't you go back and check on her? Dominic would be more comfortable if you were there."

He didn't protest, which surprised me. Hui touched my shoulder gently, pressing once, then turned. I sat in one of the ornate clinic chairs (carved by my *da* Derek when Hui had declared me "graduated" from his tutelage) and leaned my head back, closing my eyes. I stayed there for several minutes until I heard Dominic and Hui's voices, sounding as if they were heading back into the lobby. I didn't feel like another round of frigid exchanges with Dominic, so I rose and walked into the coldroom lab.

It was warmer there than in his presence.

I set the pot of thorn-vine sap over the bunsen to heat, put on a clean gown and mask, then scrubbed my hands. I plunged still-wet hands into the warm, syrupy goo, then raised them so that the brown-gold, viscous liquid coated my fingers and hands, turning my hands until the sap covered the skin evenly. After it dried, I pulled out the gurney holding the Miccail body. I stared at it (*him? her?*) for a time, not really wanting to work but feeling a need to do something. I straightened the legs, examining again the odd, inexplicable genitalia.

"Ana?"

The voice sent quick shivers through me. I felt my cheeks flush, almost guiltily, and I turned. "*El. Komban wa.* I thought you'd left."

"Went out to get some air." Elio stepped into the room. "I, ummm, just wanted to thank you. For Euzhan. Dominic, he…he should have told you himself, but I know that he's grateful, too."

"He didn't need to thank me. Besides, Euzhan's rather special to me, too."

"*I* know. But Dominic still shouldn't have been so rude." Not many in his Family dared to criticize Dominic to anyone else; the fact that Elio did dampened some of my irritation with him. Elio tugged at the jacket he wore, pulling down the cloth sleeves. "So that's your bogman, huh? Elena told me about how she found it. Pretty ugly."

"Give the poor Miccail a break. You'd be ugly too if you sat in a peat bog for a couple thousand years. It's hell on the complexion."

Elio grinned at that. "Yeah, I guess so. Might give me some color, though. Couldn't hurt." He leaned forward for a closer look, and I felt myself interposing between Elio and the Miccail, as I had earlier. Elio didn't seem to notice. After another glance at the body, he moved away.

"You planning to become the next Gabriela?" he asked, then blushed, as he realized that he'd given the words an undercurrent he hadn't intended. "I mean, you work too much, Ana," he said quickly. "You're always here. When's the last time you did a drawing or went to a Gather?"

Ages. The answer surfaced in my mind. *Far too long.* But I couldn't say any of the words. I only shrugged. "Elio, if I'm going to get anything done…"

"Sorry," he said reflexively. "I understand."

He didn't leave. He watched as I worked patiently on the hand I'd uncovered earlier, straightening the fingers and the ragged webbing between them. When, sometime later, he cleared his throat, I looked up.

"Listen," Elio said. "When you're done here, do you have plans? I thought, well, we haven't been together in a long time…"

Two years. I haven't been with anyone in almost two years. "El…" The unexpected proposition sent guilty thoughts skittering through my mind. *You're the last of the Koda-Levin line, unless Mam Shawna gets pregnant again—and she's already showing signs of menopause. If they heard that you turned someone down, after all this time—*

And then: *Ochiba would tell you to do it. You know she would.*

"El, I just don't know."

"Think about it," he said. Muscles relaxed in his pale face; he gave a faint smile. "It's not because of today," he told me. "Just in case that's what you're thinking."

It had been, of course. Anaïs: the charity fuck. "No. Of course not."

"That's good. It's just that I haven't seen you much recently with all your work, and being with you today, even under the circumstances, I'd forgotten how much I enjoyed talking with you."

I wondered whether he'd also forgotten the miserable failure the last time we tried to make love.

"I'm sorry, Ana. I don't know what the problem is," he said, even though we both knew well enough. I kissed away the apology, pretending that I didn't care. I think I even managed to smile.

I was fairly certain he'd only asked me as a favor to Ochiba.

"No," I said. "It's me. Not you. It's fine. Don't worry about it." But we both had, and Elio had slipped away from my bed as quickly as he could, pleading an early morning appointment we both knew was a fiction.

I had spent the rest of the night alternating between tears and anger.

"Elio, I'm afraid tonight…well, it wouldn't be good. I'm tired, and I was planning to stay here, just in case Euz needs some help." I lifted my sap-stained fingers. "I was hoping to get some of this work done, also." The excuses came too fast and probably one too many; I saw in his face that he realized it too.

Guilt warred with anxiety over the battleground of conscience and won an entirely Pyrrhic victory.

"El, I'm sorry. It's just that I…." I stopped, deciding that there wasn't much use in trying to explain what I didn't fully understand myself. And there was the guilt of turning down an opportunity when I'd yet to become pregnant and those chances seemed to come less and less. "Anyway, I *can* do this some other time, and chances are Euz is going to be fine. Give me a bit, just to make sure that Euz is stabilized and to clean up again…"

I wasn't sure what it was I saw in his face. "Sure. Good. I'll come by then. At your Family compound?"

I nodded. We were being so polite now. "I'll meet you in the common room."

"Okay. See you then." Awkwardly, he leaned over and kissed me. His lips were dry, the touch almost brotherly, but I enjoyed it. Before I could pull his head down to me again, he straightened. Cold air replaced his warmth. "See you about NinthHour?"

"That would be fine."

After Elio had left, I halfheartedly cleaned some of the clinging peat from the folds of the Miccail's face. "What were you like?" I asked the misshapen, crushed flesh. "And do you have any advice for someone who isn't sure she just made the right decision?"

The ancient body didn't answer. I sighed and went to the sink to scrub my hands.

CONTEXT: Ama Martinez-Santos

There were times that Ama regretted having been apprenticed to Hui. However, Geema Kyra had given her no choice in the matter, and an elder's word was always law. Hui was never satisfied—no matter how fast Ama moved or how well she did something, Hui always pointed out how she could have done it faster, better, or more effectively another way. Hayat was given the same harsh treatment, but that didn't lessen the impact. Ama was fairly certain that it was not possible to satisfy Hui.

And then there was Anaïs. She was just fucking weird. A good doctor, yes, and at least she'd give out a crumb of praise now and then, but she was… strange. The way she used all her free time lately examining that nasty body Elena had found….

Anaïs had told her to put the Miccail's body back in the coldroom. Ama threw a sheet over the thing before she moved it—she couldn't stand to see the empty bag of alien flesh; she hated the earthy smell of the creature and the leathery, unnatural feel of its skin. The thing was creepy—it didn't surprise Ama that it had been killed.

Ama had heard her *mi* and *da* talking—there was a nasty rumor that Anaïs and Ochiba had been lovers, though as Thandi always pointed out, Ochiba had died after giving birth to Euzhan, so if Anaïs was a *rezu*, then it hadn't stopped Ochiba from sleeping with men. Ama sometimes wondered what it would be like, making love to another woman….

She shivered. That was a sure way to be shunned. That's what had happened to Gabriela—the second and final time she had been shunned. .

Ama wheeled the gurney into the coldroom. She slid the bog body into its niche and hurried out of the room.

She didn't look back as she turned out the lights. Afterward, she scrubbed her hands at the sink in the autopsy room, twice, even though she knew that would make her late changing Euzhan's dressings and Hui would yell at her again.

VOICE: Anaïs Koda-Levin the Younger

Most of my erotic memories don't involve fucking. I suppose the wet piston mechanics of sex never aroused me as much as other things. Smaller things. More intimate things. I can close my eyes and remember…at one of the Gathers, dancing the whirlwind with a few dozen others out on the old shuttle landing pad, when I noticed Marshall Koda-Schmidt watching from the side in front of the bonfire. I was twelve and just a half year past my menarche, which had come much later than I'd wanted. Marsh was older, much older—one of the fifth generation—and in my eyes appeared to be far more sensual than the gawky boys my own age. He stood there, trying to keep up a conversation with Hui over the racing, furious beat of the musicians. I kept watching him as I danced, laughing as I turned and pranced through the intricate steps, and I noticed we both had the same stone on our necklaces. I thought that an omen. During one of the partner changes, there was suddenly an open space between us, and Marsh looked up from his conversation out to the dance. His gaze snared mine; he smiled. At that moment, one of the logs fell and the bonfire erupted into a coiling, writhing column of bright fireflies behind him. I was caught in those eyes, those older and, I thought, wiser eyes. I couldn't take my eyes off him, and every time I looked, it seemed he was also watching me. I smiled; he laughed and applauded me. I felt flushed and giddy, and I laughed louder and danced harder, sweating with the energy even in the night cold, stealing glances toward Marshall. We smiled together, and as I danced, I felt I was dancing with him. For him. To him…

…Chi-Wa's fingers stroking my bare shoulder and running down my arm, my skin almost electric under his gentle touch, inhaling his warm, sweet breath as we lay there with our mouths open, so close, so close but not quite touching. When his hand had traversed the slope of my arm and slipped off to tumble into the nest of my lap, our lips finally met at the same time…

…sitting with Ochiba at the preparation table in the Allen-Shimmura compound's huge kitchen, peeling sweet-melon for the dessert. We were just talking, not saying anything important really, but the words didn't matter. I was intoxicated by the sound of Ochiba's voice, drunk on her laugh and the smell of her hair and the sheer familiar presence of her. I'd just finished cutting up one of the melons and Ochiba reached across me to steal a piece. She sucked the fruit into her mouth in exaggerated mock triumph while the orange-red juice ran down her chin in twin streaks. For some reason, that struck us both as hilarious, and we burst into helpless laughter. Ochiba reached over and we hugged, and I was so aware of her body, of the feel of her against me, of how soft her breasts seemed under the faux-cotton blouse. Then the confusion hit, making me blush as I realized that what I was feeling was something I wasn't prepared or expecting to feel, and knowing by the way Ochiba's embrace suddenly tightened around me that she was feeling it as well, and was just as frightened and awed by the emotions as I was…

Moments. Those fleeting seconds when the sexual tension is highest, when you're alone in a universe of two where nothing else can intrude.

Of course, then reality usually hits. After the Gather, I turned down two other offers of company and went back to my compound alone, with one last smile for Marshall. I left my outer door open, certain that Marshall would come to me that night, but he never did.

Chi-Wa was so involved in his own arousal and pleasure that I quickly realized that I was nothing more than another anonymous vessel for his glorious seed.

And Ochiba, the only one of them who was truly important to me…well, in another year she was dead.

Tonight, I was keeping reality away with a glass of *da* Joel's pale ale, and trying to stop thinking that it was late and that I wished I'd just told Elio no. There was no one else in the common room; Che, Joel, and Derek had all grinned, made quick excuses, and left when I'd mentioned that I was staying up because Elio was coming over. I requested the room to play me Gabriela's *Reflections on the Miccail* and leaned back in the chair as the first pulsing chords of the dobra sounded. The chair was one of *da* Jason's creations, with a padded, luxurious curved back that seemed to wrap and enfold you—very womblike, very private: I'd never known Jason, who had died when I was very young, but his was my favorite listening chair. The family pet, a verrechat Derek had rescued from a spring flood five years before, came up and curled into my lap. I stroked the velvety, nearly transparent skin of the creature, and watched its heart pulse behind the glassy muscles and porcelain ribs. I shut my eyes and let the rising drone of the music carry me somewhere else. I barely heard the clock chiming NinthHour.

"I never thought Gabriela was much of a composer."

"She'd have agreed with you," I answered. "And I think you're both wrong. She was a fine composer; the problem was that she just wasn't much of a musician. You have to imagine what she was trying to play rather than what actually came out. Hello, Elio."

I told the room to lower the music and pulled the chair back up. The verrechat glared at me in annoyance and went off in search of a more stable resting place. Elio gave me an uncertain smile. "You looked so comfortable, I almost didn't want to interrupt."

"Sorry. Music's my meditation. I spend more time here than's good for me."

He nodded. I nodded back. Great conversationalists, both of us. I should have kept the music up. At least we could have both pretended to be listening to it. "Any change in Euzhan?" he asked at last, just as the silence was threatening to swallow us. I hurried into the opening, grateful.

"When I left, she was sleeping. Hui's keeping her doped up right now. When I left, Dominic was still there, but Hui was trying to convince him that camping out in the clinic wasn't going to help. I'm not sure he was making much progress."

"Geeda Dominic can be pretty strong-willed."

"Uh-huh. And water can be pretty wet."

Elio grinned. The grin faded slowly, and he was just Elio again. We both looked at each other. "Umm," he began.

If you're going through with this, then do it, I told myself. "Elio, let's go to my room," I said, trying to make it sound like something other than "And get this over with." I was rewarded with a faint smile, so maybe Elio wasn't as reluctant as I'd thought. I'd been planning to let him back out now, if that's what he wanted, figuring that if this *was* simply a guilt fuck, we were both better off without it—for most women I knew, sex simply for the sake of sex was something you did the first year or two after menarche. By then, you'd gone through most of the available or interested males on Mictlan. In my case, that hadn't been too many, not after the first time around. Since then, with one glorious and forbidden exception, the only regular liaison I've had has been with Hui's speculum and some cold semen, once a month.

Even that hasn't worked out.

All that was long ago. Forget it. The voice wasn't entirely convincing, but I held out my hand, and Elio took the invitation without hesitating. Tugging on my fingers, he pulled me toward him, and this time he kissed me. There was a hunger in the kiss this time, and I found parts of me awakening that I thought had been dead.

I suddenly wanted this to work, and that increased my nervousness. I wondered if he could tell how scared I was.

Elio either sensed that fright, or he'd learned a lot since the last time. In my admittedly noncomprehensive experience, men tended to go straight for the kill, shedding clothes on the way so they didn't snag them on rampant erections. Maybe that was just youthful exuberance, but I'd spent many postcoital hours crying, believing that the quickness and remoteness was because they wanted to get the deed done as fast as possible. Because it was *me*. "Just doing my duty, ma'am. Have to make sure that we increase the population, after all. Nothing personal."

Except that sex is always personal and always intimate, no matter what the reasons for it might be. In the midst, I might look up to see my partner's eyes closed, a look almost of pain on his face as he thrust into me, and I knew he was gone, lost in imagined couplings with someone else.

Not *with* me. Never *with* me. Never together.

Elio pulled away. I breathed, watching him. He was still here. "This way," I said, and led him off.

I'd done some quick housekeeping before he'd come, and the room actually looked halfway neat except for the mirror, as always draped in clothing. Through the folds I caught a reflection of someone who looked like me, her face twisted in uncertain lines.

When I closed the door and turned, Elio was closer to me than I expected, and I started, leaning back against the jamb. He touched my cheek, stroked my hair. As *his* hand cupped the back of my head, he pulled me into him, his arms going around me. Neither of us had said anything. I leaned my head against his shoulder. He continued to stroke my hair.

I wondered what he was thinking, and when I turned my head up to look, he kissed me again: gently, warmly, his lips slightly parted. This time the kiss was longer, more demanding, and I found myself opening my mouth to him, pulling his head down even further. His hands dropped from my shoulders; his fingers teased my nipples through my blouse, and they responded to his touch, ripening and making me shudder.

When we finally broke apart again, his pale eyes searched mine with soft questions. I reached behind us and touched the wall plate, the lights gliding down into darkness as I did so. "I can't see, Ana."

"You don't need to."

"I'd like to look at you."

"Elio…"

A pause. Silence, He waited.

Biting my lower lip, I touched the plate again, letting the lights rise to a golden dimness. I stepped deliberately away from him. Standing in front of my bed, I undid the buttons of my blouse, of my pants. I held the clothes to me, hugging myself, then took a breath and let them fall to the floor. I stood before Elio, defiantly naked. I shivered, though the room wasn't cold.

I knew what he was seeing. I might keep my mirror covered, but I knew.

Under a wide-featured face, he saw a woman's body, with small breasts and flared hips. Extending below the triangle of pubic hair, though, there was something wrong, something that didn't belong: a hint of curved flesh.

An elongated, enlarged clitoris, Hui had told my mother, who noticed it at birth: a paranoid, detailed examination of every newborn child is Mictlan's birthright. *A slight to moderate hermaphrodism. I doubt that it's anything to stop her from reaching her Naming. Everything else is female and normal. She may never notice.*

Maybe Hui would have been right had everything stayed as it was when I was a child. I certainly paid no attention to my small deformity, nor did anyone else. I didn't seem much different from the other little girls I saw. After menarche, though….My periods from the beginning were so slight as to be nearly unnoticeable and the pale spottings weren't at all like the dark menstrual flow of the other women. I also began to notice how sensitive I was there, how the oversized nub of flesh had begun to change, to swell until the growth protruded well past my labial folds, pushing them apart before ducking under the taut and distended clitoral hood.

Over the years, even after menarche, the change continued. The last time I glanced at a mirror, I thought I looked like an effeminate and not particularly pretty young man with his penis tucked between his legs, pretending to be a woman.

Elio's gaze never drifted that low. I noticed, and tried to pretend that it didn't matter. I wanted to believe that it didn't matter. He took a step toward me. He cupped my breasts in his hands, his skin so pale against mine. I fumbled with his shirt, finally getting it open and sliding it down his shoulders. Elio was thin, though his waist rounded gently at the belt line.

His skin was very warm.

I pulled him into bed on top of me…and sometime later…later…

No, I'm sorry. I can't say. I won't say.

JOURNAL ENTRY: Gabriela Rusack

I was a slow learner when it came to the difference between love and sex. Oh, I knew that people could enjoy sex without being in love with the person they're with at the moment. God knows I experienced that myself often enough…and often enough kicked myself in the morning for paying attention to whining hormones.

As I grew older, I slowly realized that the reverse was also a possibility—I could be in love with someone and *not* have sex with them, if that wasn't in the cards. I needed friends more than I needed lovers, and I found that sex can actually destroy love.

Lacina was my college roommate, and my friend. At the time, I was still mainly heterosexual, though I'd already had my first tentative encounters with women. I think Lacina suspected that I was experimenting, but we never really talked about it. I dated guys and slept with some of them, just as she did, so if on rare occasions a girlfriend stayed overnight, she just shrugged and said nothing. One Friday night in my junior year, neither of us had a date. We were drinking cheap wine and watching erotic holos in our apartment, and the wine and the holos had made us both silly and horny. I remember putting my arm around Lacina, playfully, and how sweet her lips were when I finally leaned over to kiss her, and her breathy gasp when I touched her breasts….We tumbled into my bed and I made love to her, and showed her how to make love to me. But the next morning, when the wine fumes had cleared….

After that night, it was never the same between us. There was a wall inside Lacina that had never been there before, and she flinched if I'd come near her or touch her. I don't know why she retreated. I don't know what old guilt I'd tapped; afterward, it wasn't a subject on which she'd allow discussion. She pretended that our night together had never happened. She pretended that things were the same as they had been, but they weren't, and we both knew it. At the end of the semester, she moved out.

No, sex and love are basically independent of each other. Not that it matters for me, not anymore. My closest friends are dead, and those here on Mictlan that I thought were friends won't talk to me at all anymore.

No more sex. No more love. I spend my remaining days with the only passion I have left, the only passion allowed me: the cold and dead Miccail.

Now if sex, love, and passion are intricate, varied, and dangerous for us, then the sexuality of the Miccail must have been positively labyrinthian. I can only imagine how convoluted their relationships were, with the midmale sex complicating things. I wonder *how* they loved, and I try to decipher the answer from the few clues left: the stelae, the crumbling ruins, the ancient artifacts. I wonder why this world saw fit to add another sex into the biological mix, but the past holds its secrets too well.

What frightens me is that I'm certain it's important for us to know. The Miccail died only a thousand years ago. With all the artifacts, all the structures they left behind, none of them we've found are any younger than that. From what I've been able to determine, the collapse and decline of the Miccail began another thousand years before their extinction, possibly linked with the rapid disappearance of the midmales, all mention of whom vanish from the stelae at that point. One short millennium later—barely a breath in the life of the world and the Miccail's own long history—and the Miccail were gone, every last one.

It's almost as if Something didn't like them.

And now *we're* here, filling our lungs and our bodies with Mictlan-stuff. Yes, we sampled and tested Mictlan's air, water and soil, let it flow through the assorted filters and gauges until the machines stamped the world with their cold imprimatur. The proportion of gases was within our body tolerances. We could taste the winds of this world and live. Our lungs would move, the oxygen would flow in our blood. But Mictlan is not Earth. The atmosphere of a world holds its own life, and life moves within it.

So we take a deep breath of Mictlan and we bring the alien presence into our lungs because we have no choice. We will slowly become Mictlan. Mictlan will become us.

And the Something that obliterated the Miccail will take a long look at us: because we are here, because we breathe, because we drink the water and eat the plants.

I wonder if that Something will like us better than it did the Miccail.

INTERLUDE: KaiSa

After leaving MasTa, Kai had gone directly to ker rooms in the TeTa house and packed the few belongings which were truly kers into ker traveling pouch: the well-used grinding stones for herbs and potions which JaqSa had given ker as a parting gift the first time ke'd left the sacred Sa island called AnglSaiye; the parchment book of medicines, written in the private language of the Sa with the sacred inks only the Sa knew how to make; the relic of VeiSaTi which was ker authorization to move freely outside the island; the tools of sacrifice. Ke left behind the fine anklet BieTe had carved for ker from redstone, with crystalline images of BieTe and MasTa's sacred animals set in the swirling, ornate patterns. Keeping the jewelry would only remind ker of Bie and Mas, and of the children ke had helped to sire here.

It was painful enough to leave. It was even more painful to have to remember.

Kai shouldered ker pack and pushed open the door. A hand pushed ker back inside: NosXe, one of BieTe's adopted sons. Kai stumbled and fell backward, striking ker left shoulder hard on the flagstone floor. "My father said you would try to leave," Nos grumbled. "You don't know how much BieTe and MasTa care for you, KaiSa."

"I know all too well, Nos," Kai answered. "And if I didn't love them in return, I wouldn't be leaving now. Cycles from now, if you become Te, you will understand that. Tell me, Nos, did BieTe or MasTa send you here?"

NosXe didn't have to answer; the grim stubbornness on his face told Kai that the young son of Bie had acted on his own. Kai rubbed ker sore shoulder, knowing it would shame Nos even more to see that he had injured a Sa.

"I thought not. Your Ta and Te know that it's the curse of Sa to always travel, to leave those they love most. Your Ta and Te know that no matter how much they would like me to stay, I cannot. And they cannot make me stay, not without raising the wrath of VeiSaTi Kerself. Is that what you're willing to risk, Nos? Are you willing to defy a god?"

Always before, that had worked. It was the threat of VeiSaTi's anger that kept all Sa safe. Kai thought that the warning, a doctrine taught to all of the CieTiLa—The People—from childhood, had worked now. Still rubbing ker shoulder, ke got to ker feet and started to walk out past the grim-faced Nos, who still blocked the doorway. But as ke brushed past, Nos reached out with a hand and grabbed Kai's shoulder with his right hand, his talons slightly extended.

"No," Nos started to say, but Kai had already reacted.

Kai slapped ker left hand on top of Nos', claws out. At the same time, ke turned ker hip back and brought ker right arm on top of Nos', dropping ker weight. Cloth tore on Kai's shoulder, but Nos howled in pain as his wrist was torqued. The much larger Xe collapsed to his knees to escape the pressure, and Kai completed the pin, taking the struggling Nos down to the floor. Holding Nos' wrist with one hand, ke reached out with ker long fingers and pressed them on either side of Nos' neck, just below the ears—closing the arteries. Nos' struggles became weaker; a few seconds later, he went limp.

Kai released the pin. Ke checked to make sure that Nos was still breathing, then stood. "The Sa are also taught to protect those they love," Kai told the unconscious Nos. "That is another thing you must learn. What you love most is also the most dangerous to you."

Ke stepped over Nos. Ke found that now that it was over, ke was shaking from the sudden encounter. The settlement of BieTe and MasTa, which had once seemed so peaceful and welcoming, now frightened ker.

Ke walked away, almost at a run.

BieTe had started the ceremonial fire on the bluff over-looking the sea. KaiSa could see the smear of dark smoke against the twilight sky and the silhouetted figures of BieTe's people as they moved in the preliminary dance of welcome to the new infant. But Kai saw them only in the distance.

Ke moved quickly from the settlement into the woods. A few of the Je and Ja saw ker, but—under the bonds of servitude and at the bottom of the social structure of the CieTiLa—there was no chance that any of them would, like NosXe, challenge Kai's right to go where ke wanted, whenever ke wanted. One of the Ja watched as ke moved away from the cluster of wood and stone buildings; Kai knew that the word would get to BieTe, either from the Ja or from NosXe, as soon as he returned to the ceremony, but by that time it would be too late.

I'm sorry that it had to be this way, Kai told the distant image of the fire. *BieTe, MasTa, I'm sorry to miss the ceremony for my own daughter, but in your hearts, you understand. You must understand, You know the laws as well as I do. A Sa must give ker Gift to all CieTiLa, and that means I must hurt the two of you,*

It means I must hurt myself.

KaiSa put ker back to the fire, to BieTe and MasTa, and to ker daughters and sons, and moved into the forest.

Under the canopy of sweet-leaves, the twilight quickly shifted to full night. The wind was from the west, shivering the leaves with its chill and bringing the scent of flowers. A wingclaw called from its night roost high in one of the trees, the creature's ululating whoop raising the hairs on Kai's arms. The phosphorescent mosses on the many-trunked trees framed the darkness, and the double moons were up, Chali just setting, though Quali was well above the horizon in the east, bright enough that ke could almost see the colors of the leaves. The sound of ker feet shushing through the fallen leaves seemed the loudest sound, though the rhythmic *kuh-whump* of the slickskins calling for their mates in a nearby pond was a constant backdrop.

It was tempting to stop, to try and listen to the voice of VeiSaTi in the rustling and chirping of the world, but there was no time for that now.

Kai knew that there was a wayhouse not far distant. Until ke had actually made the decision to leave, ke had given no thought to where ke might go next. Now, ke determined to stop for the rest of the night at the wayhouse. Ke lengthened ker stride, falling into ker quick walking pace.

When Quali had reached the zenith, its silver light painting the edges of the leaves, Kai came upon the High Road and the wayhouse. The High Road was the main artery through the CieTiLa lands, a trail of flagged stone, a path between all the settlements of the CieTiLa designed by the legendary Sa leader NasiSaTu over six *terduva* ago, and completed by ker successors after NasiSaTu's sacrificial death. The various segments of the road were maintained by the Te and Ta of the lands through which they passed, part of the payment for the services of the mendicant Sa order.

The *nasituda* set in front of the wayhouse declared it to be on the border of the territory of GaiTe and CiTa. For the first time since ke had left, Kai felt ker muscles relax fully, releasing a tension ke hadn't even known ke'd been holding. A light from an oil lamp glimmered behind the translucent window, made from the *brais* of one of the huge but slow thunderbeasts: someone else was already in the wayhouse. Kai gave a low, warbling call of greeting as ke approached the building, waited the polite sequence of sixteen slow breaths, then entered, brushing aside the thunderbeast hide door covering.

The wayhouse was built along typical CieTiLa lines: a large common room where travelers could talk and eat; a small kitchen to the left for food preparation and storage, and three tiny sleeping cubicles to the right. The privacy curtain was drawn on one of those, and a Sa poked ker head out as Kai entered, rubbing ker eyes sleepily.

"Kai?"

"AbriSa!"

Abri tumbled out of the low sleeping cubicle and ran to Kai. The two Sa embraced, laughing. Kai had come to the island some time after Abri's arrival, and the older youth had been one of Kai's mentors, comforting the disoriented and frightened child of three cycles and helping to teach Kai the intricate structure of Sa life. It was Abri who, when Kai had taken First Vows, had taken an inked needle to Kai's chest and marked ker with the symbol of AnglSaiye. Kai's debt to Abri had been paid long ago, when Kai had kerself taken one of the arriving children as ker special project, passing along the knowledge Abri had given ker. Abri had left the AnglSaiye sanctuary long before Kai had been given JaqSaTu's blessing and ker own sanction to begin ker travels through the CieTiLa lands. Kai held Abri at arm's length, looking at ker. Ke could see the cycles and the pain of many separations in ker face, in the flesh-hewn valleys of experience VeiSaTi had etched there.

"Where are you traveling to, Abri?" Kai asked when they finally pulled apart. *Where are you going? Where have you been?* Those were the eternal questions of Sa meeting on the road.

"Actually, I was looking for you, among others."

"For me? You're joking. Why?"

Abri didn't answer. Instead, ke pulled away from Kai, and the furrows in ker face deepened as ke frowned. "Let me fix some *kav*. You looked tired," ke said.

Kai watched Abri as ke went into the kitchen and poured the bittersweet, herbal brew into two wooden mugs. "I've been on the island for the past two cycles," ke said as ke placed the pottery jug back into the coldbox sunk into the kitchen's floor. Ke brought the mugs out and handed one to Kai. Ke sipped carefully—"once for TeTa, again for XeXa, and last for Jeja," three being the sacred number of VeiSaTi—then sank down onto one of the large pillows at the edge of the eating pit. "There have been disturbing rumors, Kai," ke said finally. "I'm just one of several who have been sent out by JaqSaTu to bring all Sa back to the island."

The words sent the *kav* swirling, almost spilling from the mug as Kai started. *To bring all the Sa back to AnglSaiye,* bring all of us back from our journeys....It was something that had never been done before, in all the cycles upon cycles written down on the *nasitudas* set on AnglSaiye's shores. It was something Kai could very nearly not comprehend. "I don't understand…"

"You will, when you get back there." Abri sipped ker *kav* once more, staring into the brown depths of the mug. "I really can't say more, except to say that it is becoming a dangerous world for Sa."

Kai, remembering BieTe and MasTa, and ker departure of only a few hours ago, opened hard-ridged lips in a grin. "Love is always dangerous, AbriSa. I have the bruises to prove it."

But Abri didn't share in the jest. Abri's dark, expressive eyes regarded Kai's, and there was pain in ker gaze.

"This is different, Kai," ke said. "This is something no Sa has faced before."

END OF EXCERPT

Dark Water's Embrace copyright © 1998, 2009 Stephen Leigh. All rights reserved. This book may not be copied or reproduced, in whole or in part, by any means, electronic, mechanical or otherwise without written permission from the publisher except by a reviewer who may quote brief passages in a review.

Available from Amazon.com, BN.com or by special order through your local bookstore.

Ebook version is available at www.PhoenixPick.com or your favorite online store.

SERIALIZATION:
Dark Universe

(Continued from Issue One)

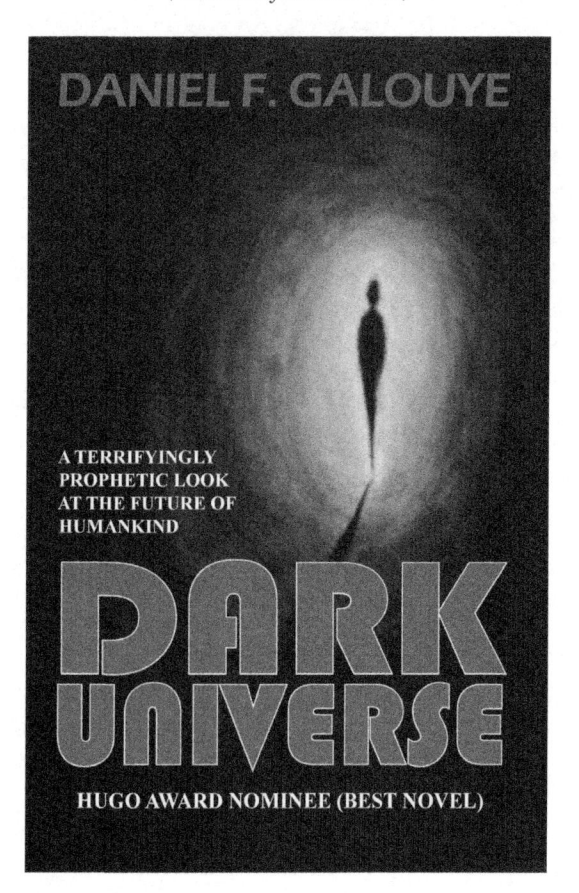

DARK UNIVERSE
by Daniel Galouye
Phoenix Pick, 2010
Trade Paperback: 182 pages. *Kindle, Nook, More*
ISBN: 978-1-60450-487-3

Dark Universe Copyright © 1961 Daniel F. Galouye. All rights reserved. This book may not be copied or reproduced, in whole or in part, by any means, electronic, mechanical or otherwise without written permission from the publisher except by a reviewer who may quote brief passages in a review.

Excerpt is reprinted here by permission of the Publisher and the Estate's literary agent.

Dark Universe

(Continued from Issue One)

CHAPTER SIX

"...We therefore humbly invoke the guidance of Light Almighty as we rededicate ourselves under new leadership."

Survivor Averyman, as Senior Elder, was bringing his speech to a close. He paused and listened out over the Assembly.

Standing behind him, Jared too heard the silence, relieved only by the soft flow of many tense breaths. It was an anxious stillness, rather than one that bore respect for the Investiture Ceremonies.

Nor could he himself muster much attention for the Elder's words. His thoughts were overburdened with bitterness. It wasn't as much that Light had broken the covenant as it was that He had decided on so ruthless a means of making that fact clear.

That the Prime Survivor was gone forever from the worlds of man was, for Jared, a tragedy. On several occasions over the past two periods he would have gone charging defiantly up the passageway had it not been for the remote possibility that the loss of his father was only temporary, to test the sincerity of his repentance. A more practical reason he hadn't tried to track down the monster was that Protectors had been stationed at the entrance.

He sneezed and sniffled, evoking a disdainful pause in Survivor Averyman's speech. After a moment, the Elder resumed:

"We must not expect from our new Prime Survivor the forehearing and wisdom that we came to associate with his late father. For what *could* compare with an understanding deep enough to hear ahead to the imminent necessity of preparing his successor?"

Jared listened impatiently over toward the guarded entrance. There was yet another reason he couldn't go plunging beyond the Barrier in search of his father. That would only call the wrath of the Elders down on his head and they would make Romel the Prime Survivor—a development which could bring only chaos to the world.

Someone nudged him forward and he found himself standing in front of the Guardian of the Way.

"Repeat after me," Philar said solemnly, "'I swear that I will bend all effort to the Challenge of Survival, not only for myself but in behalf of every individual in the Lower Level.'"

Struggling through the vow, Jared interrupted his flow of words with a sniffle.

"'I dedicate myself,'" the Guardian went on, "'to the needs of all who depend upon me and I will do whatever I can to draw aside the Curtain of Darkness—so help me Light!'"

Jared punctuated the final word with a sneeze.

Investiture over, he remained in front of the Official Grotto receiving perfunctory handshakes.

Romel was the last to approach. "Now the fun begins," he said facetiously. The words were not as relaxed as they might have been, though, and they offered no clue as to what expression was silenced by the obscuring veil of hair.

"I'll need a lot of help," Jared admitted. "It won't be easy."

"I didn't think it would." Romel wasn't successfully concealing his envy. "Of course, the first thing will be to finish the hearing."

Interrupted by Investiture, the hearing wasn't Jared's concern, however. It was being conducted by the Elders, who were even now filing back into the Official Grotto. And there was no doubt that its mention had been subtly intended to lead to something else. For a moment Jared could almost hear the familiar *hiss* of the swish-rope.

"Do you suppose," Romel continued, unnecessarily loud, "that the monster that got the Prime Survivor was anything like the one you heard in the Original World?"

There it was—the tightening of the coils around his ankles. Romel wasn't going to let anyone forget Jared had violated the Barrier taboo. Slack was being taken on the rope. The violent tug would come later.

"I wouldn't know," he rapped out, following the last of the witnesses into the Official Grotto.

A portable caster had been set in operation and Jared, taking his place at the meeting slab, concentrated on its *clicks* as modified by the persons in the recess. All the Elders were in their places while the witnesses were grouped off to one side.

"I believe we were listening to Survivor Metcalf," Elder Averyman said. "He was telling us what he heard."

A lean, nervous man came forward and stood beside the slab. Quite audibly, his fingers enmeshed, squirmed against one another, freed themselves and locked again.

"I couldn't catch its sound too clearly," he apologized. "I was just coming from the orchard when I heard you and the Prime Survivor shouting. I picked my impression of the thing off the echoes from your voices."

"And what did it sound like?"

"I don't know. Something about the size of a man, I suppose."

It was disconcerting the way the witness kept moving his head from side to side. He was a fuzzy-face and the rippling motion of the hair streaming down in front reminded Jared of the fluttering flesh of the Original World monster.

"Did you hear its face?" Averyman asked.

"No. I was too far away."

"What about an—uncanny sound?"

"I don't recall anything like a *silent* sound, like some of the others heard."

Metcalf was a fuzzy-face. So was Averyman, as were two others who had testified. And not one of those four had gotten psychic impressions of a roaring silence, Jared remembered. Even in the Upper Level none of the fuzzy-faces had heard the incredible, inaudible noise made by the monsters.

Jared cleared his throat, and swallowed painfully, coughed several times and gripped his neck. He'd never felt like *this* before.

Averyman dismissed the witness and called another.

By now, the two periods of hearings had become tedious. After all, there were really only two categories of witnesses—those who had heard the supernatural sound and those who hadn't.

More important, as far as Jared was concerned, was the personal matter of his growing uncertainty. He wasn't so sure now that the monsters were a punishment for his defiance of the Barrier. That the horrible menace had *not* ended with his sincere atonement could mean only one of two things: Light would accept *no* degree of repentance, or his visit to the Original World had not, after all, aggravated the monsters.

Then he drew attentively erect as a third possibility suggested itself: Suppose he was right about Light and Darkness being *physical* things. Suppose, in his search for the two, he had almost uncovered a significant truth. And suppose the monsters, assuming that they were opposed to his success, were aware of how close he had come. Wouldn't they do everything possible to discourage him?

A violent sneeze snapped his head back and elicited a reproving silence from Averyman, who had been in the middle of a question.

The new witness was a young boy whose excited account left no doubt that *he* had heard the impossible sounds.

"And how would you describe these—sensations?" Elder Averyman completed the question.

"It was like a lot of crazy shouts that kept bouncing against my face. And when I put my hands over my ears I kept on hearing them."

The child's head had been turned toward Averyman and Jared couldn't hear the details of his face. But suddenly it seemed vitally important that he should know the boy's characteristic expression. So he went around the slab, seized his shoulders and held him with his features fully exposed to the portable caster.

It was as he had expected—the child's eyes were wide open.

"You have something you'd like to say?" Averyman asked, not quite concealing his resentment over the interruption.

"No—nothing." Jared returned to his place.

The boy was an open-eyed type. Jared, himself, was open-eyed. Three other witnesses had fallen into the same category. And *all* of them had felt the strange sensations!

Was it as he had guessed once before—that the silent sound might in some way be connected with the eyes, provided they were exposed? And now he recalled how strangely his own eyes had reacted during the Excitation of the Optic Nerve Ceremony. The weird rings of noise had clearly seemed to be dancing beneath his lids, hadn't they?

But what significance could be drawn from all this? If the eyes were intended only for feeling

Light, then why was it they could also sense the evil of the monsters? He was both excited and confused by the flood of inspirational questions. And he was annoyed that the same inspiration would produce none of the answers.

Since the eyes seemed to be the common element between Divinity and Devil, he asked himself queasily, could Light be in some sort of evil conspiracy with the monsters?

There! He had entertained the sacrilegious thought! And he braced himself for the wrath of the Almighty.

But, instead, there came only a direct question from Elder Averyman: "Well, Jared—rather, Your Survivorship—you've heard these various descriptions. How do they compare with your impressions of that monster in the Original World?"

He decided to play it a bit shrewder. "I'm not so sure I heard a monster. You know how your imagination can run away with you." There was no sense in calling attention to his experience with the creature. Nor did he hear where he could gain anything by telling them about the beings that had invaded the Upper Level.

"Eh? What?" Elder Haverty inquired. "You mean you *didn't* hear a monster in the Original World? You *did* go there, didn't you?"

Jared tried to clear his throat, but the painful roughness persisted. "Yes, I went there."

"And a lot has happened since then," Survivor Maxwell reminded. "We've lost some hot springs. A monster has carried off the Prime Survivor. Do you suppose you're to blame for those misfortunes?"

"No, I don't think so." Why incriminate himself?

"Some think you might be," Averyman said stiffly.

Jared sprang up. "If this is an attempt to remove me from—"

"Sit down, son," Maxwell urged. "Elder Averyman said we had to make you Prime Survivor. But there's nothing to keep us from easing you out if we think that's best."

"The question," Haverty repeated, "is whether you're the cause of all that's happened to this world."

"Of course I'm not! Those first three hot springs went dry long before I crossed the Barrier!"

There was a speculative silence around the slab. But Jared was more surprised than any of them by the truth he had spontaneously spoken. It had opened his ears to a whole flood of realization.

"Don't you understand?" He leaned tensely over the slab, letting sound from the portable caster play over his face so the others could hear his sincerity. "What's happening now *couldn't* be because I went across the Barrier! The Upper Level's having the *same troubles!* They lost some boiling pits and one of their Survivors turned up missing before I even went to the Original World!"

"We'd be more likely to believe that," Averyman pointed out cynically, "if you'd told us about it earlier."

"I didn't realize I had crossed the Barrier *after* those things had happened. And I figured that if I told you about them you'd only be more certain I was to blame."

"Eh?" Haverty put in. "How do we know you're telling the truth about the Upper Level having trouble too?"

"Get the Official Escort to ask about it when they take me back up there."

Jared felt like a Survivor who had been freed from the depths of Radiation. He had cast off shackles of superstition that would have thrown a curtain of fear over the rest of his life.

His relief was almost boundless—knowing that his trip to the Original World to hunt for Darkness and Light had not provoked the vengeance of an aggrieved Almighty Power. It meant there was no dire necessity of relinquishing that search. Of course, he wouldn't be able to devote as much effort to the quest as he had planned—not with his Prime Survivorship a reality and with Unification hanging over his head. But, at least, he could go on with it.

A depression that he had known for many periods melted away before his exuberance. He would have felt like shouting had it not been for the fact that his throat was bothering him again.

He sneezed and his head started throbbing.

A few moments later Elder Maxwell sneezed too, then sniffled.

Abruptly there was a disturbance in the world outside and Jared tensed as he caught a whiff of the monster's stench.

Someone swept into the grotto and quickly placated, "Don't be alarmed by the smell." The voice was Romel's. "It's coming from something in my hand—

something the monster dropped when it carried off the Prime Survivor."

Jared intercepted the *clicks* from the portable caster as they echoed against the object his brother was displaying. It was the cloth he had buried in the passageway. Romel was firming his grip on that imaginary swish-rope. And Jared waited for the tug that would jerk him off his feet.

The elders had had time to study the reeking object, and Maxwell asked, "Where did you get this thing?"

"I listened to Jared hide it. And I dug it up."

"Why would he do a thing like that?"

"Ask *him*." But before Maxwell could, Romel went on, "I think he was covering up for the monster. Don't get me wrong now. Jared's my brother. But the interest of the Lower Level comes first. That's why I'm exposing this conspiracy."

"That's ridiculous—" Jared began.

"Eh? What?" Haverty interrupted. "Conspiracy? What conspiracy? Why should your brother conspire with the monster? How *could* he conspire with it?"

"He stole off and met it in the Original World, didn't he?"

Echoes fetched only the impression of hair hanging down over Romel's face. But Jared knew that the smile concealed beneath the veil was as sardonic as it had been each time the swish-rope accomplished its mischievous purpose during an earlier era.

"I hid the cloth," he began, "because—"

But Haverty persisted. "What would he gain by conspiring with a monster?"

There was yet another tug to be had from the swish-rope. "He's Prime Survivor now, isn't he?" Romel reminded with a laugh.

Jared lunged up. But two Elders halted his charge.

"That kind of outburst," Averyman assured, "only makes the accusation seem more reasonable."

Jared relaxed before the slab. "I hid the cloth because I wanted to study it later. I couldn't very well bring it into the world without having to answer the same questions I'm answering now."

"Reasonable," Averyman grumbled. "And what about this matter of conspiring with the monster?"

"Would you say I'd have anything to gain if a monster kidnapped a Zivver?"

"Not personally, no."

He told them about the invasion of the Upper Level by the two monsters.

"And why didn't you say anything about this before?" Averyman asked somewhat indignantly after he had finished.

"For the same reason I've already given—I didn't realize then that I *wasn't* responsible for what was happening."

After a moment Maxwell warned, "We certainly intend to check that story about the Zivver being carried off by monsters."

"If you find out I'm lying, give me any length of sentence in the Punishment Pit."

Averyman rose. "I think this hearing has taken up enough time for one period."

"Hearing? Compost!" Jared swore. "Let's quit sitting on our hands and go after the Prime Survivor!"

"Easy now," Haverty soothed. "We don't want to do anything rash. We may be dealing with Cobalt and Strontium themselves."

"But they'll be back!"

"At which time we'll rely both on the Protectors we've posted at the entrance and on the Guardian for Exorcism."

It was a stupid position born of deaf superstition. But Jared heard that he wouldn't be able to budge them from it.

✧

Later that period he withdrew to the Fenton Grotto to work on a formula for reallocating the remaining manna husk output among Survivors and livestock. Hunched over the sandbox, he brushed the writing area smooth and began all over again with his stylus. But a violent sneeze swept the surface clean and he threw the instrument down in disgust.

He pushed the box aside and laid his head on the slab. Not only were the sniffles driving him out of his mind, but he also felt as though his head were stuffed with warm, moist wool. He'd had fever before, but not like this. Nor had he ever heard of anyone else being sick in this manner.

Leading his thoughts away from physical discomfort, he took cheer from the still unbelievable realization that no Divine Being stood in the way of his quest for Light. The monsters might resent his seeking Darkness and Light. But they could be resisted—if he could only find some way to get around their sleep-dealing powers.

It was tantalizing, too, how everything seemed to point toward some vast and incomprehensible pattern into which were woven so many material and immaterial things. What was the obscure relationship between the eyes and Light, Light and Darkness, Darkness and the Original World, the Original World and Radiation? The apparent linkage extended to the Twin Devils then, in a great circle, back again to the eyes and the Light-Darkness arrangement.

He found himself recalling Cyrus, the Thinker, who spent his time meditating in his grotto at the other end of the world. He remembered that gestations ago he had heard the old man express some novel ideas on Darkness. Perhaps it was those philosophic sessions that had suggested the search for Darkness—*and* Light—in the first place. And Jared knew he must talk with the Thinker again—soon.

The curtains parted, admitting Many, one of the new Survivors.

"For a P.S. of only a few heartbeats' experience," he chided, "you've sure carved out a chunk of trouble for yourself—popping off before the Elders about chasing after the monster."

Jared laughed. "Guess I should have kept my mouth shut."

Many perched on the slab beside him and sneezed. "The Guardian hit the dome when he heard about it. He says now he's sure Romel would make a better P.S."

"After I hear my way clear with this hot-springs emergency, I'll straighten him out."

"He's saying the way you acted at the hearing proves you haven't atoned. And he's predicting more misfortune for the world."

As though Many's words had also been a cue for fulfillment of Guardian Philar's prophesy, distressed voices began filtering through the curtain.

Plunging outside, Jared snagged one of the men who were racing by. "What's all the commotion?"

"The river! It's running dry!"

Even before he reached the bank, the central caster's *clacks* fetched a composite of the situation. The river had fallen so alarmingly below its normal level that the liquid softness of its reflected sound was completely hidden in the echo void of the bank. And there came only the enfeebled gurgling of water around rocks that had never before been exposed.

A terrified scream shrilled from the direction of the main entrance and, without breaking stride, Jared altered course.

With the central caster behind him, he began getting a better impression of what lay ahead. The Protectors stationed at the mouth of the passageway were in a state of agitated disorder.

"Monster! Monster!" someone over there was shouting.

Then Jared checked his charge as the entire tunnel abruptly began roaring with the soundless noise of the monsters. The sensations he received were like Effective Excitation amplified a thousandfold. But now there were no fuzzy half rings of inaudible sound touching his eyeballs, as in the Optic Nerve Ceremony. Instead, the screaming silence was like a detached, impersonal thing—something associated not with any part of himself, but rather with the mouth of the tunnel!

It was more than that, however. The noiselessness leaked off, much like valid sound, and touched many things—the dome, the wall on his right, the hanging stones beside the entrance.

Starting forward again, he threw his hands in front of his face. The distant, whispering roar of Effective Excitation left him immediately. Then that *proved* it—the uncanny stuff that came from monsters *did* inflict its weird pressure *on his eyes!*

Spared the confusing sensations, he concentrated now on the echoes coming from ahead. There was no monster in the entrance. That one had been there only a few beats earlier was borne out by the loitering scent. And his ears picked out the tubular object that lay on the floor of the tunnel. Even from this distance he could hear it was like the one Della had found in the Upper Level.

Just as he reached the entrance, one of the Protectors raised a rock over his head and raced toward the tube.

"No! Don't!" Jared shouted.

The guard hurled the rock.

Eyes exposed again, Jared reached down for the remains of the object. It was warm and it rattled and tinkled when he shook it.

He noticed, too, that there were no more traces of the screaming silence.

CHAPTER SEVEN

Living alone and served his necessities by the widowed women of the Lower Level, Cyrus spent his time immersed in himself. When the opportunity to speak materialized, however, his tongue diligently set about the task of making up for long stretches of idleness.

Now, for instance, the Thinker was holding forth on many subjects, seemingly all at the same time:

"Jared Fenton. *Prime Survivor* Jared Fenton, mind you! Back for another session—just like we used to have gestations ago."

Jared shifted impatiently on the bench beside him. "I wanted to ask about—"

"But I'm afraid you've got your work cut out for you—what with the hot springs trickling out and those monsters running around the passages. Have you decided what's to be done about the river going dry? And that thing the monster left behind yesterperiod—what do you suppose it was?"

"It seems to me that—"

"Hold it! I'd like to think this thing out a bit."

Jared was more than grateful for the few moments' silence. It brought relief to his pounding head, which threatened to split like a manna shell each time he coughed. He'd had fever before—when he was bitten by a spider, for instance. But it was never like this.

Cyrus' grotto was shielded from most of the world's sounds by the thick drapery that hung in its entrance. But the recess was so small that Jared had no trouble concentrating on the echoes from his words to hear how much the Thinker had changed.

How fortunate it was the old man had never developed a preference for protecting his face with a curtain of hair. For now he was completely bald. And the wrinkles, deposited by a lifetime of muscular tension to insure closed eyes, were etched even more deeply.

"I was just considering," Cyrus said, explaining his silence, "whether the monster could have purposely left that thing in the entrance. And I'm convinced it did. What do you think?"

"It sounded that way to me."

"What do you suppose its purpose was?"

Jared listened to the fervent supplications of the Litany of Light from the Revitalization Ceremony across the world. Audible, too, was the conversation of his Official Escort, waiting outside to take him to the Upper Level.

"That's one of the things I wanted to talk about," he said finally. "Tell me about—Darkness."

"Darkness?" There was the sound of Cyrus' chin wedging itself between thumb and forefinger. "We used to talk a lot about that, didn't we? What is it you'd like to know?"

"Is it possible Darkness can be connected with"—Jared hesitated—"the eyes?"

After a few beats the other said, "Not that I can hear—not any more than with the knee or little finger. Why do you ask?"

"I figure it might be close to Light in some way or other."

Cyrus weighed the proposition. "Light Almighty—infinite goodness. Darkness—infinite evil, according to the beliefs. The principle of relative opposites. You can't have one without the other. If there were no Darkness, then Light would be everywhere. Yes, I suppose you could say there is a negative relationship. But I don't hear where the eyes would fit into the composite."

Coughing, Jared rose and swayed against the dizzying effects of his fever. "Have you ever felt Effective Excitation?"

"In the Optic Nerve Ceremony? Yes. Many gestations ago."

"Well, in Effective Excitation you're supposed to be feeling Light. And if the existence of Light depends in a negative way on the existence of Darkness, then the eyes must also be designed to feel Darkness."

Jared listened to the other rub his face in deep thought. "Sounds logical," the Thinker conceded.

"If one found Darkness, do you suppose he might also find—"

But Cyrus wouldn't let his running thoughts be repressed. "If we're going to talk about Darkness as a material concept, let's ask ourselves: What *is* Darkness? We find it could—now mind you, I say *could*, because it's just an idea—could be a universal medium. That means it exists everywhere—in the air about us, in the passageways, in the infinite rocks and mud."

Jared's fever turned into a sudden chill, but he kept his attention on the other's words.

"Point number two," Cyrus went on, his voice now reflecting against a second upthrust finger. "If it's so universal then it must be completely undetectable through the senses."

Disappointed, Jared sank back on the bench. If the Thinker were correct, he could *never* expect to find Darkness. "Then why would it exist at all?"

"It might be the medium by which sound is transmitted."

They were both silent awhile.

"No Jared. I don't think you could ever expect to find Darkness anywhere in this universe."

Eagerly, Jared asked, "Would there be less Darkness beyond infinity?"

"If you have our so-called Paradise in mind, then we can forget about Darkness as a *physical* medium. In that case I would say—yes, there must be less Darkness in Paradise since Paradise is supposed to be full of Light."

"What's your composite of Paradise?"

The Thinker laughed. "If you've an ear for the beliefs, you'll have to admit it must have been wonderful. Man was supposed to be godlike. Thanks to the presence everywhere of Light, it was possible to know what lay ahead *without* smelling or hearing it. Nor did we have to go about feeling things. It was as though our senses were all rolled up into one and could be projected many times the distance that even the strongest voice carries."

Jared sat there thinking how uninspiring had been this visit to Cyrus. He hadn't even gotten encouragement in his quest for Light.

"Your Escort's waiting," the Thinker reminded.

"One more question: How do you explain the Optic Nerve Ceremony?"

"I don't know. It bothers me too. And Light knows I've done enough thinking about it. But here's something: Effective Excitation *could* be some sort of normal body function."

"In what way?"

"Close your eyes—*real tight*. Now—what do you hear?"

"There's a roaring noise in my ears."

"Right. Now, suppose for generations we had to live in a place where there was no sound. Nobody now alive would have ever heard anything. But perhaps the legend of sound has been passed down—through a touch language, let's say."

"I don't hear what—"

"Can you imagine that there might now be such a thing as an Excitation of the Hearing Nerve Ceremony? That's what you just did when you tightened your facial muscles. And there might now be a Guardian of the Way who would make you squinch up your face and feel the Great Sound Almighty."

Jared rose excitedly. "Those rings of silent sound we feel during Effective Excitation—you mean they might have a connection with something people once *did* with their eyes?"

He plainly caught Cyrus' shrug as the Thinker said, "I mean nothing. I'm merely posing a theoretical question."

The old man's breathing became shallow with meditation.

Jared stepped toward the curtain, then paused and listened back in the direction of the Thinker. Long ago he had believed he might find less Darkness in the Original World and recognize it for what it was. But Cyrus had concluded Darkness was a universal medium which couldn't be sensed.

Wasn't it possible, however, that Light could have a canceling effect—could *erase* some of the Darkness? And if one were lucky enough to hear the cancellation taking place, might he not get a clue as to the nature of both Light and Darkness?

Then something vastly more important occurred to him: Cyrus had said the presence of Light Almighty in Paradise made it possible for man to "know what lay ahead *without* smelling or hearing it"!

Wasn't that exactly what the Zivvers could do? Was it that the Zivvers, too, shared some peculiar relationship with Light—a relationship which they themselves probably didn't even suspect?

He had already sensed an intrinsic association among Light, Darkness, the eyes, the Original World and the Twin Devils. Now it seemed he would have to include the Zivvers with that group. For, whenever they zivved, there must be less of something around them as a result of that zivving—just as there was less silence when a normal person listened to noise. And that lessness, in the Zivvers' case, might well be the lessness he was seeking—a lessness of Darkness!

Recalling that Della was a Zivver, he was suddenly anxious to return to the Upper Level so he could keep an ear on her and perhaps hear what there was less of in her vicinity whenever she zivved.

Jared brushed the curtain aside.

"Good-bye, son—and good luck," Cyrus called, then sneezed.

✧

Jared dismissed his Official Escort at the last bend before the entrance to the Upper Level. There would be no need for them to wait for the runner who had come ahead, since it had been decided that the man would remain here for a while.

In a way, he was glad to get rid of the others. The Captain had kept on complaining of a sore throat and another of the crew had coughed so much it was hard to hear the tones of the clickstones.

Moreover, those who had no complaint over personal discomfort had been on edge over the fact that they thought they detected the scent of the monster from time to time. Jared himself could smell nothing—not with his nose stopped up the way it was. Nor could he hear very much, since the general stuffiness in his head seemed to have extended to his ear passages too.

Shivering with a chill, he sounded his stones for maximum volume and staggered on down the passageway, wishing all the while that he'd reported in to the Injury Treatment Grotto instead of going on with Declaration of Unification Intentions.

He rounded the sweeping curve and paused, listening ahead. There was brisk activity up there—rock being cast down on top of rock, methodically but swiftly. Voices—the voices of two men mumbling in desperate tones, swearing and invoking the name of Light Almighty.

Rattling his pebbles more intently, he listened to the *clicks* echo against the men as they darted about collecting rocks and depositing them in a heap against one wall of the Upper Level entrance.

Then he realized he was *hearing silent sound—in front of the pair*! It was attached to the wall.

The small bundle of frozen echoes seemed to be plastered there and the men were frantically covering it up with stones. One of them belatedly heard Jared's presence, shouted fearfully and bolted back into the world.

"It's only Fenton—from the Lower Level," the other called.

But it was audible that the man didn't intend to return.

Jared started forward and drew back, dismayed. Again he was certain the screaming silence wasn't reaching him through his ears. He was *actually* hearing (if that was the word for it) the stuff with his eyes! He proved that much by turning his head the other way; he instantly became altogether unaware of its presence.

When he turned back, the bundle of soundless noise was gone—*completely*. And it seemed significant that he had heard the man put the final rock on the pile, thereby finishing the echo barrier.

"You'd better get inside," the other warned, "before the monster comes back!"

"What happened?"

Reflections of his words fetched a composite of the man raising a trembling hand to wipe perspiration off his face. "The monster didn't take anyone this time. It only stayed out here swabbing the wall with—"

He screamed and shook his head violently in front of him. Then he plunged deafly down the passage, sobbing, "Light Almighty!"

Jared readily heard what had frightened the other. The palm of his hand was full of the roaring silence!

He advanced curiously on the rock pile. But a seizure of coughing drove home the realization of how sick he was and he stumbled on into the Upper Level World.

There was nobody at the entrance to meet him this time, so he used the *clacks* of the central caster to sound his way to the Wheel's grotto. He found

Anselm pacing behind the curtain and muttering to himself, grim-voiced and tense.

"Come in, my boy—rather, Prime Survivor," the Wheel invited. "Wish I could say I'm glad to have you back."

He returned to his pacing and Jared dropped miserably down on a bench. He cupped his feverish face in his hands.

"Sorry to hear about your father, my boy. I was shocked when the runner told me. We've had three people taken by the monsters since you left."

"I came back," Jared said weakly, "to Declare Unification In—"

"Unification Intentions—compost!" Anselm boiled over as he faced Jared with hands on his hips. "At a time like this you've got *Unification* on your mind?"

When Jared didn't answer, he said, "Sorry, my boy. But we're on edge up here—with monsters running all over the place and hot springs drying up. Five more boiled out yesterperiod. I understand you've been having the same trouble."

Jared nodded, not particularly caring whether the Wheel heard.

Anselm mumbled some more and said, "Unification! Didn't the runner tell you I'd decided to put things off until we can do something about all these other complications?"

"I haven't heard the runner. Where is he?"

"I sent him back early this period."

Jared slumped on the bench, his body boiling like a turbulent spring. The runner had already left but hadn't reached the Lower Level. And they hadn't passed him on the way up. Only ominous significance could be attached to the fact that several members of the Official Escort—those with clear noses, at least—had told of smelling the lingering scent of the monster in the passageway.

His lungs convulsed in a coughing spell and when he finished he was aware the Adviser had entered the grotto and was standing there listening intensely down at him.

"Well, Fenton," Lorenz said bluntly, "what do *you* make of all this monster business?"

Jared trembled with another chill. "I don't know what to think of it."

"I've told the Wheel what *I* think: The Zivvers have gone back to their old tricks. They're taking Survivors as slaves. And they're in league with the Twin Devils to accomplish their purpose."

"And I say that's ridiculous," put in Anselm. "We even *heard* the monsters take a Zivver!"

"How do we know that wasn't something they *wanted* us to hear?"

Anselm snorted. "If the Zivvers are going to start taking slaves again, they'd just *do* it."

Lorenz was silent. But it was an adamant silence. It was readily audible he was going to insist the monsters and Zivvers were working together. And Jared could understand why: if the Adviser intended to accuse him of being a Zivver, he was going to make certain the accusation also included indirect blame for the presence of the monsters.

"I'm sure Della will want to hear your decision on Unification, my boy." Anselm took the Adviser by the arm and swept the curtain aside. "I'll send her in."

Jared coughed, spanned his steaming forehead with a trembling hand and shivered.

A short while later the girl entered and drew in a sharp breath as she stood with her back against the curtain.

"Jared!" she exclaimed with deep concern. "You're boiling! What's wrong?"

He was surprised at first that she could hear his fever all the way across the grotto. But fever was heat. And heat was the stuff Zivvers zivved, wasn't it?

"I don't know," he managed.

For a moment he had almost generated interest in the fact that she was here and zivving. And that now was his chance to listen closely and perhaps hear whether there was a lessness of something around her *while* she zivved. But his purpose faded away in another jarring shiver.

Della closed the curtain securely behind her and came over. He turned his head and coughed and she knelt before him, feeling the heat in his arms and face. And he heard her features twist with concern.

But she pushed the expression aside for something that was evidently more urgent. "Jared, I'm sure the Adviser knows you're a Zivver!" she whispered. "He hasn't come out and said so, but he keeps reminding everybody how remarkable your senses are!"

Jared swayed forward, caught himself and sat there trembling and perspiring, his head roaring, spinning.

"Don't you hear why he made you shoot at that target among the hot springs?" she went on. "He *knows* what too much heat does to a Zivver! He was just trying to find out if you—"

The girl's words faded into oblivion as he toppled forward off the bench.

✡

When finally he awoke, there was the waning taste in his mouth of medicinal mold and the vague memory of having been forced to swallow the mushy substance several times.

Too, he sensed that during the entire period—or was it longer?—he had lain semiconscious in the Wheel's grotto, Kind Survivoress had tried to force her way back into his delirious dreams. Perhaps she had even succeeded. But he could recall neither her successful intrusion nor the dreams themselves.

Now he felt only an inner calm and comfort. His throat was smooth again and the pounding fever had left his head. Even if he was not entirely well, he felt certain that only a full return of his strength stood in the way of complete recovery.

Gradually, he became aware of restrained breathing at the other end of the grotto and recognized the rhythm and depth of the breaths as Della's.

There was the firm, supple sound of thigh and calf muscles working together as she paced—nervously, he could tell by the erratic steps—to the curtain and back again.

Then she came abruptly over to the slumber ledge and shook him desperately. "Jared, wake up!"

He could tell from the urgency in her voice that she had been trying to arouse him for some time.

"I'm awake."

"Oh, thank Light!" Some of her hair had come out of the band that held it tightly behind her head and had fallen across her face. She brushed it aside and he got a clearer impression of smooth, precise features that were taut with solicitude.

"You've got to get out of here!" she went on in a strained whisper. "The Adviser's convinced Uncle Noris you're a Zivver! They're going to—"

There was the sound of nearby conversation in the outside world and Jared heard the soft current of air swirl around her face as she jerked her head toward the curtain, then back again,.

"They're coming!" she warned. "Maybe we can slip out before they get here!"

He tried to rise but fell back down, weak and puzzled, as he suddenly realized the girl didn't customarily bend an ear toward an interesting noise, as everyone else did. She always kept her face pointed directly at anything that held her attention. Which meant she didn't ziv with her ears! But, then, what *did* she ziv with?

The voices outside came more clearly through the curtain now.

Adviser: "Of *course* I'm dead certain he's a Zivver! As good a marksman as he is, he couldn't hit a simple stationary target in the manna orchard. And you know as well as I do that Zivvers are confused by excessive heat."

Wheel: "It *does* seem incriminating."

Adviser: "And what about Aubrey? We sent him out to cover that silent sound the monster left on the wall outside. That was two periods ago and he's been missing ever since. Who was the last one to hear him?"

Wheel, coughing hoarsely: "Byron says that when he ran back into the world, Fenton was still out there with Aubrey."

Adviser, sneezing: "There you are! And if you need any more proof that Fenton's a Zivver who has conspired with the monsters, you have one of our basic beliefs to go by."

Wheel: "The one that says any Survivor who consorts with Cobalt or Strontium will become deathly sick."

They stepped deliberately toward the grotto entrance.

Wheel, with a sniffle: "What'll we do with him?"

Adviser: "The Pit'll hold him for the moment." Another sneeze. "Being a Zivver, he'll be worth something as a hostage, no doubt."

When they drew the curtain aside Jared heard several armed Protectors taking their posts outside the grotto.

Wheel Anselm came and stood beside Jared, edging Della aside. "Has he made any wakeful noises yet?"

"He's not a Zivver!" she pleaded. "Let him alone!"

Jared heard that her face was turned directly toward the Wheel. And again he caught the fleeting impression of her hand brushing hair away from her forehead—away from her eyes, actually.

And now he remembered that just before she had handed him the tubular object the monsters had left behind, she had brought it up before her and held it on a level with her face.

It was her *eyes* that she was zivving with!

Anselm seized his arm and shook him roughly. "All right—up off that ledge! We can hear you're awake!"

Feebly, Jared struggled to his feet. Lorenz seized his other arm, but he shook off the grip.

"Protectors!" the Adviser shouted anxiously.

And the guards hurried in.

CHAPTER EIGHT

Although he hadn't thought it possible, the Upper Level Punishment Pit was worse than the one in Jared's own world. It occurred to him that it would be hard to imagine a more terrible penalty for wrongdoing. As a detention facility, it was escapeproof. The ledge on which he lay was fully two body lengths below the surface. And it was much narrower than his shoulders, so that an arm and leg had to dangle over the abyss.

Lowered there by rope, he lay motionless for hundreds of heartbeats—until his limbs had become numb. Then, cautiously, he had dropped one of his clickstones into the hole. It had fallen—fallen—fallen. And many breaths later, after he had given up hope of listening to the impact, there was the faintest *kerplunk* he had ever heard.

From remote distances came the sounds of late period activity—children at play after their Familiarization session, manna shells scraping slabs during mealtime, and a staccato frequency of coughs.

Eventually, the echo caster was turned off for the sleep period and, still later, Della came.

On a cord she lowered a shell filled with food. Then she lay with her head overhanging the mouth of the Pit.

"I almost convinced Uncle Noris you couldn't be a Zivver," she whispered disappointedly, "until that epidemic got him excited all over again."

"That sneezing and coughing?"

The steady flow of her voice wavered as she nodded her head. "They ought to be taking mold, like we did. But Lorenz's telling them it won't work against Radiation sickness."

She fell silent and he let the manna shell clatter against the wall of the Pit. Intercepting the sharp echoes, he quickly put together a composite of the girl's features. And even more than before, he liked what he heard.

The general configuration was soft and confident. Her hair, slicked back from her forehead, had a pleasant sound and gave her face a sleek, delicate tonal balance. Somehow the total impression had much in common with the wistful music she had stroked from the hanging stones. And he fully heard now how desirable she was for Unification.

He brought another shelled crayfish to his mouth, but paused when he realized that even now she must be zivving. Again he let the bowl strike rock to produce more sounding echoes. And he heard that her face was directed fixedly toward him. He could almost feel the intense steadiness of her eyes.

Now was hardly the time, though, to listen for whatever happened to the things about her whenever she zivved. If there was a lessening of something or other, he certainly wouldn't be able to detect it while clinging precariously to the ledge.

Nevertheless, he did seize upon one fact that had, at the moment, become clear: since both Darkness and Light were probably connected with the eyes—perhaps especially with a Zivver's eyes—then the lessness he was listening for would no doubt have a measurable effect on the eyes.

Wait! There *was* something—back in the Wheel's grotto, when Della had bent over him to shake him awake. Some of her hair had fallen over her face. And when she had brushed it aside, wasn't there then *less hair* before her eyes?

He slumped with a tinge of futility. No—Darkness couldn't be as simple a thing as hair. That would be too ironic—listening for something he had known all his life. Anyway, Cyrus had said Darkness was universal, everywhere. That meant he would have to listen over a broad area, all around the girl.

"Jared," she said tentatively. "You're not—I mean you and the monsters aren't—"

"I haven't had anything to do with them."

Her breath escaped with a relieved sound. "Are you from—the Zivver World?"

"No. I've never been there."

The echoes of his words captured her depressed expression.

"Then you've spent your whole life hiding the fact you're a Zivver—just like me," she said sympathetically.

There was no point in not encouraging her confidence. "It hasn't been easy."

"No, it hasn't. Knowing how much better you can do things, but having to listen to yourself carefully every step of the way so others won't find out what you are."

"I pushed it to a fine point—too fine, I suppose. Otherwise I wouldn't be down here now."

He heard her hand slide down along the side of the Pit, as though reaching out for him. "Oh, Jared! Does it mean as much to you—finding out you're *not* alone? I never guessed anybody else had to go through the same gestations of Radiation and fear that I did—always afraid of being found out at the next step."

He could appreciate the close relationship she must feel for him, the way her loneliness was crying out. And he sensed something within himself straining toward the girl, even though he was no Zivver in need of sympathetic response.

She went on effusively, "I don't understand why you didn't go hunting for the Zivver World long ago. I would have. But I was always afraid I wouldn't find it and would get lost in the passages."

"I wanted to go there too," he lied. And it was beginning to appear that he could play the role of a Zivver simply by following her lead. "But I have an obligation to the Lower Level."

"Yes, I know."

"I don't hear—that is, I don't ziv why you didn't join up with the Zivvers during one of their raids," he said.

"Oh, I couldn't do *that*. What if I tried and the Zivvers wouldn't take me? Then everybody would know what I am. I'd be driven into the passages as a Different One!"

She rose and stood zivving down into the Pit.

"You're leaving?" he asked.

"Only until I can figure out some way to help you."

"How long do they intend keeping me here?" He tried to change position but succeeded only in almost slipping off the ledge.

"Until the monsters come back. Then Uncle Noris is going to let them know we have you as a hostage."

Listening to her footfalls recede, he was fascinated with the whole range of things that might come out of his association with the girl. Even if Light and Darkness remained elusive, he at least might learn something about this intriguing ability the Zivvers had.

It was past midsleep when Jared, his muscles cramped and aching, finally managed to ease himself into a sitting position. He tapped the manna shell against rock and listened. It wasn't a very wide hole—about two body lengths across, he estimated. And he could hear that, except for the ledge on which he perched, the sides were barren of fissures and outcroppings that might have provided handholds toward the surface.

He brought a knee up against his chest and secured his foot on the shelf. Then, with arms outstretched against the slick wall, he rose bit by bit until he was standing. Slowly, he turned around, pressing his chest against the rock. Reaching overhead, he produced sharp tones by snapping his fingers. And the sudden drop-off in the sound pattern told him that the rim of the Pit was at least another arm's length beyond his extended hand.

He remained in that position for several hundred beats before he heard all Radiation breaking loose above. Until then there had been only the normal sounds of a world lying dormant in midslumber, with an occasional outburst of coughs ruffling the relative quiet.

Then everything seemed to boil over into a great excitement and confusion as one of the Protectors sounded the fearful warning, "Monsters! Monsters!"

Hoarse shouts, screams, and the audible agitation of people scurrying frenziedly about poured down the Pit.

Jared almost lost his balance as he tilted his head back and became aware that the entire opening above was whispering with silent sound. Unlike the sensation experienced during Effective Excitation, however, there was only one circle of the weird monster stuff. And it didn't seem to be actually touching his eyes. Rather, it corresponded in size and shape with his audible impression of the Pit's mouth.

He tottered on the ledge, flailing his arms to keep from falling, then stood with his face pressed firmly against stone as he listened to someone running in his direction.

In the next instant Jared recognized the Adviser's voice coming from halfway across the world, "You at the Pit yet, Sadler?"

There was another distant outburst of screams as Sadler drew to a halt overhead. "I'm here!" He thudded his spear against rock to sound out Jared's position on the ledge below.

This time it was the Wheel's voice that rose in challenge to the monsters: "We've got Fenton! We know he's working with you! Get back or we'll kill him!"

Another wave of screams suggested that the monsters were ignoring Anselm's threat.

"All right, Sadler," Lorenz roared. "Send him to the bottom!"

The spear tip grazed Jared's shoulder and he winced, sidling along the ledge. It came back again, slipped between his chest and the wall of the Pit and began prying him from his perch. Jared toppled over backward and his arms threshed air as he fought to keep from plunging into the unfathomable abyss.

His flailing hand touched and gripped the lance. He jerked himself desperately upright. He gave the spear a violent tug and the full weight of the man at the other end came along with it.

Abruptly the spear was free in his hand and he felt the rush of air as Sadler went plunging by, screaming all the way down.

The weapon was more than long enough to span the Pit. Jared used it as a prodding stick to locate a minor recess in the opposite side. Wedging its butt into the depression, he propped the point against the wall above him.

Panic subsided as quickly as it had broken out overhead. Apparently the invaders had accomplished their purpose and withdrawn.

Jared hoisted himself onto the wedged spear, reached up, gained a purchase on the lip of the Pit and pulled himself out.

"Jared! You're free!"

Echoes from her footfalls brought fragmentary impressions of Della racing toward him. And he could hear the soft *swish* of the coil of rope slung across her shoulder and brushing against her arm.

He tried to get his bearings. But the residual din of dismayed voices was too confusing to indicate which way the entrance lay.

Della caught his hand. "I couldn't find a rope until just now."

Impulsively, he started off in the direction he was facing.

"No." She spun him around. "The entrance is *this* way. Ziv it?"

"Yes. I ziv it now."

He hung back slightly, letting her remain a step or two ahead and following the tug of her hand.

"We'll circle wide, along by the river," she proposed. "Maybe we can reach the passage before they turn on the central caster."

And he had been hoping someone *would* do just that. Of course he hadn't realized that the *clacks* which would sound out the obstacles before him would also betray their presence to the others.

His foot contacted a minor outcropping and he stumbled. Eventually righting himself with the girl's help, he limped on. Then, constraining the anxiety of escape, he composed himself and called upon all the devices he had acquired through gestations of training when he had to learn to detect the subtle rhythm of a heartbeat, the swishing silence of a lazy stream agitated by the motion of a fish beneath its calm surface, the distant scent and slither of a salamander as it crossed moist stone.

More confident now, he listened for sound—*any* kind of sound, remembering that even the most insignificant noise is useful. There! That lurching catch in Della's breath as she drew in the next lungful of air. It meant she was stepping onto a slight elevation. He was prepared when he reached the rise.

He listened intently to the other things about her. Heartbeats were too indistinct to be useful except as direct sound. But there was something rattling faintly in her carrying case. He sniffed the imperceptible odors of a variety of edibles. She had packed a good deal of food and one morsel was striking the side of her pouch with each step. The slight *flops* meant echoes, if he listened attentively enough. There they were now—almost lost among the greater noises from the rest of the world. But they were sufficiently vivid to relay audible impressions of the things before him.

Now he was sure of himself again.

They left the bank of the river, cutting across behind the manna orchard, and had made it almost to the entrance when someone finally turned on the central echo caster.

Immediately, he caught the full composite of a few faint impressions that had worried him for the last few beats—a guard had just arrived to take his post at the entrance.

A moment later the man sounded the alarm. "Somebody's trying to get out! Two of them!"

Jared lowered his shoulder and charged. He crashed into the sentry, knocking him breathless and bowling him over.

Della caught up with him and they lunged into the passageway. He let her stay in the lead until they had rounded the first bend. Then he produced a pair of stones and pushed ahead of her.

"Clickstones?" she asked, puzzled.

"Of course. If we run into somebody from the Lower Level they might wonder why I'm *not* using them."

"Oh. Jared, why don't we—no. I suppose not."

"What were you going to say?" He felt perfectly at ease now, with the familiar tones of the pebbles faithfully bringing back true impressions of all the hazards ahead.

"I started to say let's go to the Zivver World where we belong."

He pulled up sharply. The Zivver World! Why not? If he was listening for a lessness of something that resulted from zivving, what better place to detect it than in a world where *plenty* of people were doing a *lot* of zivving? But could he get away with it? Could he successfully pose as a Zivver in a world full of Zivvers—and hostile ones at that?

"I can't leave the Lower Level just now," he decided finally.

"That's what I figured. Not with all the trouble they're having. But someperiod, Jared—*someperiod* we'll go there?"

"Someperiod."

She tightened her grip on his hand. "Jared! What if the Wheel sends a runner to the Lower Level to tell them you're a Zivver?"

"They wouldn't—" He paused. He'd started to say they wouldn't believe it. But with the Guardian dedicated to stirring up sentiment against him, he wondered.

When they reached his world, he found it odd that there were no longer any Protectors at the entrance. The clear, firm *clacks* of the central caster did reveal, however, the presence of *someone* standing there at the end of the passageway. And when he moved closer he received the reflected impression of feminine form, hair-over-face.

It was Zelda.

Hearing them she started. Then, nervously, she probed them with clickstones until they came into the full sound of the caster.

"You sure picked a Radiation of a time to bring a Unification partner back," she reproved after she had recognized Jared.

"Why?"

"There've been two more kidnappings by the monsters," she answered. "That's why we're not defending the entrance any longer. They took one of the Protectors. Meanwhile, the Guardian's managed to get the whole world worked up against you."

"Maybe I can do something about that," he returned irately.

"I don't think you can. You're not Prime Survivor any longer. Romel's taken over." Zelda coughed several times and it sent the hair flying from in front of her face.

He strode off toward the Official Grotto.

"Wait," the girl called. "There's something else. Everybody's boiling at you. Hear all that?"

He listened toward the residential section. The world was resounding with coughs.

"They blame you for this epidemic," she explained, "since they remember you were the first to have all the symptoms."

"Jared's back!" someone in the orchard shouted.

Another Survivor, farther along the way, took up the cry and passed it on to still a third.

Presently a score of persons could be heard filing out of the orchard where they had been working. Others spilled from the grottoes. And they were all converging on the entrance.

Jared studied the reflected *clacks* and picked up impressions of Romel and Guardian Philar in the forefront of the advance. They were flanked on either side by a number of Protectors.

Della seized his arm anxiously. "Maybe it would be safer if we just left."

"We can't let *Romel* get away with this."

Zelda added with a crisp laugh, "If you think this world's in a mess now, wait till you hear what Romel does to it."

Jared stood his ground before the approaching Survivors. If he was going to convince them Romel and Philar had merely taken advantage of them in the interest of personal ambition, it would have to be from a position of confidence and dignity.

His brother drew up before him and warned, "If you stay here you're going to hear things my way. I'm Prime Survivor now."

"How did the Elders vote on that?" Jared asked calmly.

"They haven't yet. But they will!" Romel seemed to be losing some of his self-assurance. He paused to listen and make certain he still had the support of the Survivors, who had drawn into a half circle about the entrance.

"No Prime Survivor can be removed," Jared recited the law, "without full hearing."

Guardian Philar stepped forward. "As far as we're concerned, *you've* had your hearing—before a Power more just than any of us, before the Great Light Almighty Himself!"

One of the Survivors shouted, "You've got Radiation sickness! That only comes from having truck with Cobalt or Strontium!"

"And you passed it on to everybody else!" another added, coughing spasmodically.

Jared started to protest, but was promptly shouted down.

And the Guardian said severely, "There are only two sources of Radiation sickness. Either you *did* have something to do with the Twin Devils, as Romel suggested, or the disease is a punishment from Light for your profanity, as I suspect."

It was Jared who was losing his composure now. "It's not true! Ask Cyrus whether I—"

"The monster got Cyrus yesterperiod."

"The Thinker—gone?"

Della tugged on his arm and whispered, "We'd better get out of here, Jared."

There were the sounds of clickstones and running feet in the passageway and he bent an ear to hear who was approaching.

By his pace, it was clear that the man was an official runner. And, when he broke his stride, it was further evident that he had sensed the congestion of persons at the entrance. He halted, then came forward more slowly, and without benefit of stones, to join them.

"Jared Fenton's a Zivver!" he disclosed. "He led the monsters to the Upper Level!"

The Protectors, most of them armed with spears, spread out and encircled Jared and the girl.

Then someone shouted, "Zivvers—in the passage!"

More than half the Survivors turned and fled noisily back toward their grottoes as Jared picked up the scent drifting in from the passageway. Someone redolent with the odors of the Zivver World was approaching—stumbling, falling, rising, and coming forward again.

The Protectors broke ranks as they jockeyed in confusion. The pair nearest the entrance drew back their spears.

Just then the Zivver staggered into the direct sound of the central caster and collapsed on the ground.

"Wait!" Jared shouted, casting himself at the two Protectors who were about to hurl their lances.

"It's only a child!" Della exclaimed.

Jared made his way to the girl, who was groaning with pain. It was Estel, whom he had returned to the Zivver party in the Main Passage.

He heard Della kneel on the other side of the child and run her hands over the girl's chest. "She's hurt! I can feel four or five broken ribs!"

Still, Estel recognized him and he caught the sound of her weak smile. He could sense, too, the animation in her eyes as he listened to them dart up and down in purposeful motion.

"You told me someperiod I'd start zivving—when I least expected it," she managed painfully.

Spear touched spear somewhere behind him and the echoes captured the grimace that twisted the child's smile.

"You were right," she continued feebly. "I was trying to find your world and I fell into a pit. When I climbed out again, I started zivving."

Her head slumped against his arm and he felt the life shudder out of her body.

"Zivver! Zivver!" The incriminating cry rose behind him.

"Jared's a Zivver!"

He seized Della's hand and lunged into the tunnel as two spears struck the wall beside him. He paused only long enough to snatch up the lances, then continued on into the passageway.

CHAPTER NINE

Half a period later, with long stretches of unfamiliar passages behind them, Jared paused and listened tensely.

There it was again! A distant flutter of wings—much too faint for Della's ears, though.

"Jared, what *is* it?" She pressed close against him.

Casually, he said, "I thought I heard something."

Actually, he had suspected for some time that the soubat was trailing them.

"Maybe it's one of the Zivvers!" she suggested eagerly.

"That's what I hoped at first. But I was mistaken. There's nothing there." No sense in alarming her—not just yet.

As long as he could keep the conversation going, he had little to worry about insofar as pitfalls were concerned. The words provided a steady source of sounding echoes. But subject matter was not inexhaustible and eventually there came lapses into silence. It was then that he had to resort to artifice to keep the girl from discovering he wasn't a Zivver. An ingeniously timed cough, an ostensibly awkward clatter of the lances, an unnecessary scuff that sent a loose stone rattling along the ground—all these improvisations helped.

He let a spear strike rock and was rewarded with the reflected composite of a bend in the corridor. As he negotiated it, Della warned. "Watch out for that hanging stone!"

Her alarmed words fetched him an impression of the sliver of rock in all its audible clarity. But too late.

Clop!

The impact of his head snapped the needle in two and sent fragments hurtling against the wall.

"Jared," she asked, puzzled, "aren't you zivving?"

He feigned a groan to avoid answering—not that the instant swelling on his forehead wasn't justification enough for the expression of pain.

"Are you hurt?"

"No." He pushed forward briskly.

"And you aren't zivving either."

He tensed. Had she guessed already? Was he about to lose his only means of entry into the Zivver World?

Even convinced that he wasn't zivving, however, she only laughed. "You're having the same trouble I did—until I said, 'To Radiation with what people think! I'm going to ziv all I want!'"

Using the reflections of her clearly enunciated syllables, he planted firmly in mind the details of the area immediately ahead. "You're right. I wasn't zivving."

"We don't have to deny our ability any longer, Jared." She held on to his arm. "That's all behind us now. We can be ourselves for the first time—really ourselves! Oh, isn't it wonderful?"

"Sure." He rubbed the lump on his forehead. "It's wonderful."

"That girl who was waiting for you at the Lower Level—"

"Zelda?"

"What an odd name—and a fuzzy-face too. Was she a—friend?"

At least the echo-generating conversation was under way again. And now he could readily hear all the obstacles.

"Yes, I suppose you'd call her a friend."

"A *good* friend?"

He led her confidently around a shallow pit, half-expecting a complimentary "*Now* you're zivving!" But it didn't come.

"Yes, a good friend," he said.

"I gathered as much—from the way she was waiting for you."

With his head turned away, he smiled. Zivvers, it appeared, were not lacking in normal human sensitivity. And he felt somewhat gratified over the pout-formed distortion of her words when she asked, "Are you going to—miss her much?"

Hiding his amusement, he offered bravely, "I think I'll manage to get over it."

He faked another cough and detected a vague hollowness lurking in the rebounding sound. Fortunately, he kicked a loose stone with his next step. Its crisp clatter betrayed the details of a chasm that stretched halfway across the corridor.

Della warned, "Ziv that—"

"I ziv it!" he shot back, leading her around the hazard.

After a while she said distantly, "You had lots of friends, didn't you?"

"I don't think I was ever lonesome." He regretted the statement immediately, suspecting that a Zivver in his position more logically *would* have been lonesome—dissatisfied with his lot.

"Not even knowing you were—different from all the others?"

"What I meant," he hastened to explain, "was that most of the people were so nice I could almost forget I wasn't like them."

"You even knew that poor Zivver child," she added thoughtfully.

"Estel. I only heard—zivved her once before." He told her about encountering the runaway girl in the corridor.

When he had finished she asked, "And you let Mogan and the others get away without even telling them you were a Zivver too?"

"I—that is—" He swallowed heavily.

"Oh," she said with belated comprehension, "I forgot—you had your friend Owen with you. And he would have heard your secret."

"That's right."

"Anyway, you couldn't desert the Lower Level, knowing how much they needed you."

He listened suspiciously at her. Why had she been so quick to provide the answers for which he had been only groping? It was as though she had whimsically put him on a hook, then deftly taken him off again. Did she *know* he was no Zivver? Somehow it seemed his entire plan to investigate the possible Zivver-Darkness-Eyes-Light relationship might be slipping into an obscure echo void.

Again he was jarred from his thoughts by the portentous sound of fanning wings—still too distant for Della to detect. Without slowing his pace, he concentrated on the ominous flapping. There were two of the beasts trailing them now!

The logical thing to do, he readily heard, would be to dig in and face the soubats promptly—before they attracted others to the pursuit. He held off with the hope that the passage would narrow sufficiently to let him and the girl through but not the soubats.

He slowed his pace and waited for Della to say something so there would be more sounding echoes.

Clop!

The impact of shoulder against hanging stone wasn't quite as jolting this time. It merely spun him half-around.

Angered, he snatched a pair of clickstones out of his pouch and rattled them furiously. To Radiation with what she thought! If the truth that he wasn't a Zivver was going to come out, let it come!

Della only laughed. "Go ahead and use your stones if it'll make you feel any more secure. I went through the same thing when I first started zivving steadily."

"You did?" He stepped off at a brisk pace now that what lay ahead was so sharply audible.

"You'll soon get used to it. It's the air currents that cause all the trouble. They're beautiful but tiring."

Currents? Did that mean there was some way she could be aware of slow, swirling air in the corridor—something *he* could *hear* only when it was further agitated by the passage of a spear or arrow?

It was Della who tripped this time. She fell against him, throwing them both off balance and sending them reeling against the wall.

She clung to him and he could feel the moist warmth of her breath on his chest, the cleaving softness of her body against his.

He held her for a moment and she whispered, "Oh, Jared—we're going to be *so* happy! No two people ever had more in common!"

Her cheek was smooth where it pressed against his shoulder and her banded tress of hair lay softly across his arm, dancing as it moved with the slight motions of her head.

Dropping his spears, he touched her face and felt the even flow of trim features, firm and fine from hairline to chin. Her waist, molded to the concavity of his other hand, was evenly curved and supple, flaring out to modestly rounded hips.

Not until then had he fully realized she might quite easily become more than just a means to an end. And he was certain he had been wrong in suspecting she was trying to deceive him—so certain that he found himself thinking of forgetting everything else and settling down with her in some remote, lesser world.

But sobering logic barged in on his reverie and he retrieved the lances abruptly, shoving off down the passage. Della was a Zivver; he wasn't. She would find happiness in her Zivver World and he would have to be content with his quest for Light—if he managed to survive his bold invasion of the Zivver domain.

"Are you zivving now, Della?" he asked cautiously.

"Oh, I ziv all the time. Soon you will too."

Experimentally, he listened sharply with the faint hope that he would notice some indiscernible change in the things about her. But he heard nothing. It must be as he had previously suspected: the lessness he sought was so minor that he would have to be in the presence of a number of Zivvers before its cumulative effect would be noticeable.

But, wait! There was a more direct approach.

"Della, tell me—what do you think about Darkness?"

And he could hear her echo-conveyed frown as she repeated the question and added uncertainly, "Darkness abounds in the worlds—"

"Sin and evil, no doubt."

"Of course. What else?"

It was evident she knew nothing of Darkness. Or, even if she could perceive it, she still didn't recognize it for what it was.

"Why are you so concerned over Darkness?" she asked.

"I was just thinking," he improvised, "that zivving must be something opposite to Darkness—something good."

"Of course it's good," she assured, following him around a lesser depression and along the shore of a suddenly emerged river. "How could anything so beautiful be bad?"

"It's—beautiful?" He tried to eliminate the questioning inflection at the last beat. But, still, the words came out more interrogation than statement.

Her voice was animate with expressiveness. "That rock up ahead—ziv how it stands out against the cool earth background, how warm and soft it is. Now it's not there, but just for a beat—until that breath of warm air goes by. Now it's back again."

His mouth hung open. How could the rock be there and not there in the next instant. It had continued to cast back *clicks* from his stones all the while, hadn't it? Why, it hadn't moved even a finger's width!

The passage, he could hear, was wide and straight, with few hazards. So he put his stones away.

"You're zivving now, aren't you, Jared? What do you ziv?"

He hesitated. Then, impulsively, "Out there in the stream—I ziv a fish. A big one, standing out against the cool river bed."

"How can *that* be?" she asked skeptically. "*I* can't ziv it."

But certainly it was there! He could hear the swishing of its fins as it stabilized itself. "It's there, all right."

"But a fish is no colder or warmer than the water around it. Besides, I've never been able to ziv rocks or anything else in water—not even when I've just thrown them in."

Covering over the blunder would call for boldness. "I can ziv fish. Maybe I ziv different from you."

She was audibly concerned. "I hadn't thought of that. Oh, Jared, suppose I'm not really a Zivver after all!"

"You're a Zivver, all right." Then he lapsed into a troubled silence. How could anyone expect to outsmart a Zivver?

The fearsome rustle of leathery wings overtook him and he marveled that anything that distinct could escape the girl's attention. The creatures had reached an enlarged stretch of the passage and, making the most of ample flying room, were streaking forward.

Then he pulled up and trained his ears acutely on the rearward sounds. No longer were there only two soubats stalking them. It was clearly audible that their number had at least doubled.

"What is it, Jared?" Della questioned his alert silence.

One of the creatures filled the air with its strident cry.

"Soubats!" she exclaimed.

"Just one." No point in alarming her when, with a little luck, they might lose the beasts entirely. "You take the lead. I'll bring up the rear—in case it gets in position to attack."

He prided himself on having worked a temporary advantage out of the situation. With her in front, he no longer had to prove occasionally that he was zivving. Now, with her hand in his, he had only to follow her lead. Still, vocal sounds were even more desirable for fetching obscure impressions, so he primed the conversation.

"Leading me by the hand like this," he offered facetiously, "you remind me of Kind Survivoress."

"Who's that?"

Trailing Della along a ridge that ran beside the stream, he told her of the woman who, in his childhood dreams, used to take him to visit the child who lived with her.

"Little Listener?" she repeated the name after he mentioned it. "That's what the boy was called?"

"In my dreams it was. He couldn't hear anything except the soundless noises some of the crickets made."

"If they were soundless, how did you know the crickets were making any noise at all?" She led him over a minor chasm.

"As I remember, the woman used to tell me such noises existed but only the boy could hear them. She heard them too whenever she listened into his mind, however."

"She could do *that*?"

"Without strain." His chuckle made it clear that he was merely poking fun at the absurdity of his imagination. "That's how she was able to reach me. I remember how she used to say she could listen in on almost anybody's mind anywhere—except a Zivver's."

Della paused beside a rock column. "*You're* a Zivver. She reached *your* mind. How do you account for that?"

There! He'd stumbled over his tongue again. And at a time when he was merely making conversation so he could hear the way. But he recovered instantly. "Oh, I was also the only *Zivver* whose mind she could hear. Don't take this too seriously. Dreams don't have to follow logical patterns."

She led the way into a broader stretch of passage. "Parts of yours did."

"What do you mean?"

"Suppose I told you I knew of a baby who never listened in the direction of a voice, but whenever his mother caught him listening at the wall, she always found a cricket clinging there."

Somehow that had a familiar ring. "Was there such a baby?"

"In the Upper Level—before I was born."

"What happened to him?"

"They decided he was a Different One. He was let out in the passages before he was even four gestations old."

Now he dimly remembered how his parents used to tell him the same story about the Different child of the Upper Level.

"What are you thinking about, Jared?"

He was silent a long while. Then he laughed. "About how I finally understand why I used to dream about a Little Listener. Don't you hear? I had actually been told about such a person. But the memory stayed below the surface."

"And your—Kind Survivoress?"

Another curtain parted on the sounds of forgotten memory. "Now I can even recall hearing the story of a Different One who had been banished from the Lower Level gestations before I was born—a girl who always seemed to know what other people were thinking!"

"There." Della continued on around a bend. "Now you have your odd dreams all explained."

Almost. Left now to be determined was only the psychological origin of the Forever Man in his imaginings.

He turned his attention ahead and listened to a distant, vast hollowness that enveloped the roar of a cataract. They were nearing the end of the passage and ahead, he was certain, lay a huge world—the Zivver World? He doubted it, for he had long ago lost the scent of Zivvers.

"It's horrible," Della said pensively, "the way people just banish Different Ones."

"The first Zivver was a Different One." He swung back into the lead, using his clickstones. "But when they banished him he was old enough to steal back for a Unification partner."

They broke out of the passage and Jared listened to the river flowing on across level ground, headed for the far wall. He shouted and the trailing echoes plunged back down from tremendous heights and across forbidding distances. The words rebounded from grotesque islands of tumbled rocks, setting up a clashing dissonance.

"Jared, it's beautiful!" the girl exclaimed, turning her head in all directions. "I've never zivved anything like *this* before!"

"We can't lose any time reaching the other side," he said calmly. "There should be another passage where the stream flows into the opposite wall."

"That soubat?" she asked, detecting the concern in his voice.

Without answering, he led her swiftly along a level course that had been eroded to smoothness during times past when the river had been fuller than it was now. Many breaths later they plunged through the passageway entrance in the opposite wall—just as the pursuing creatures emerged from the tunnel behind them and hurtled forward, filling the world with their malevolent stridency.

"We've got to hide!" he shouted. "They'll overtake us in a beat!"

They splashed through a bend in the river and echoes of the sound betrayed the presence of an opening in the left wall barely large enough to admit them. He followed Della through and found himself in a recess almost as small as a residential grotto. The girl dropped exhausted to the ground and Jared settled down beside her, listening to the enraged soubats congregating in the corridor outside.

Della rested her head on his shoulder. "Do you think we'll *ever* find the Zivver World?"

"Why are you so anxious to get there?"

"I—well, maybe for the same reason you are."

Of course, she *couldn't* know his real reason—or, could she? "It's where we belong, isn't it?"

"More than that, Jared. You sure you're not going there to—find some people too?"

"What people?"

She hesitated. "Your relatives."

His brow knitted. "I have no relatives there."

"Then I suppose you must be an *original* Zivver."

"Isn't that what you are?"

"Oh, no. You see, I'm a—spur." And she quickly added, "Does that make any difference—between us, I mean?"

"Why, no." But even that sounded too stuffy. "Radiation, no!"

"I'm glad, Jared." She brushed her cheek against his arm. "Of course, nobody knew I was a spur except my mother."

"She was a Zivver too?"

"No. My father was."

He listened outside the recess. Frustrated, the shrieking soubats were beginning to withdraw to the world they had just left.

"But I don't understand," he told the girl.

"It's simple." She shrugged. "After my mother found out I was going to be born, she Unified with an Upper Level Survivor. Everybody thought I just came early."

"You mean," he asked delicately, "your mother and—a Zivver—"

"Oh, it wasn't like that. They wanted to be Unified. They met accidentally in a passageway once—and many times after that. They finally decided to run off together, find a small world of their own. On the way, though, she fell part way down a pit and he got killed saving her. There was nothing else she could do except return to the Upper Level."

Jared felt a keen compassion for the girl. And he could understand how fervently she must have longed for the Zivver World. He had placed his arm around her and drawn her comfortably close. But now he released her, acutely aware of the distinction between them. It was more than the mere physical difference between a Zivver and a non-Zivver. It was a great chasm of divergent thought and philosophy that encompassed contrary values and standards. And he could almost grasp the disdain a Zivver would feel for anyone to whom zivving was only an incomprehensible function.

There were no more soubats in the corridor, so he said, "We'd better get on our way."

But she only sat there, rigid and not breathing. And, momentarily, he imagined he heard some faint, scurrying sounds that he hadn't noticed before. To make certain, he rattled his pebbles. Immediately he received the impression of many small, furry forms. Now he could hear the feather-soft touch of insect feet against stone.

Della screamed and sprang up. "Jared, this is a *spider* world! I've just been bitten on the arm!"

Even as they ran for the exit he heard her falter in stride. As she collapsed, he caught her in his arms and shoved her into the corridor, crawling through after her. But too late. One of the tiny, hairy things had already dropped onto his shoulder. And before he could brush it off he felt the sharp, boiling sting of lethal venom.

Clinging to his lances, he slung Della over his shoulder and stumbled on down the passage. The poison was coursing through his arm now and reaching torturously across his chest, into his head.

But he pushed on for more than one impelling reason: he couldn't lose consciousness here—the soubats would be back at any moment; nor could there be any stopping until he reached a hot spring where he might fashion steaming poultices and tend their wounds.

He struck a rock, bounced off, stood swaying for a while, then staggered on. Around the next bend he waded through an arm of the river and collapsed when he reached dry land again.

The stream flowed off through the wall and before them stretched a broad, dry passage. Pulling himself forward with the hand that still clutched the spears, he dragged Della along with him. Then he paused, listening to a *drip-drip* that came with a melodious monotony. His spear point touched rock and the *thunk* provided him with a composite of the passageway.

It was a strangely familiar corridor, with its slender hanging stone dripping cold water into the puddle below, not too far away from a single, well-defined pit. He felt sure he had been here many times before; had stood beside that moist needle of rock and run his hands over its cool, slick contours.

And, in his last impression before he lapsed into unconsciousness, he recognized all the details of the passageway outside the imaginary world of Kind Survivoress.

To be continued in Issue Three

A book on virtual reality, before virtual reality become real

Printed in Dunstable, United Kingdom